Also by Scott Turow

Personal Injuries
The Laws of Our Fathers
Pleading Guilty
The Burden of Proof
Presumed Innocent
One L

Reversible ERRORS

SCOTT

TUROW

Reversible
ERRORS

DOUBLEDAY LARGE PRINT HOME LIBRARY EDITION

FARRAR STRAUS GIROUX ▌ NEW YORK

This Large Print Edition, prepared especially for Doubleday Large Print Home Library, contains the complete, unabridged text of the original Publisher's Edition.

Farrar, Straus and Giroux
19 Union Square West, New York 10003

for Jonathan Galassi

reversible error

n. a legal mistake made by a trial court which is so significant that an appellate court reviewing the case must set aside the trial court's judgment. The trial court is then instructed either to dismiss the case, to retry the case, or to otherwise modify its decision.

CHARACTERS

ROMMY "SQUIRREL" GANDOLPH
Convicted of the 7/4/91 murders

ARTHUR RAVEN
Rommy's lawyer for his final appeal in 2001

PAMELA TOWNS
Arthur's associate on Rommy's case

SUSAN RAVEN
Arthur's sister

LARRY STARCZEK
The detective on Rommy's case in 1991 and 2001

MURIEL WYNN
The prosecutor on Rommy's case in 1991 and 2001

GILLIAN SULLIVAN
The judge who convicted and sentenced Rommy in 1992

AUGUSTUS "GOOD GUS" LEONIDIS
Murdered 7/4/91

JOHN
Gus's son

LUISA REMARDI
Murdered 7/4/91

GENEVIEVE CARRIERE
Luisa's friend

ERNO ERDAI
TN Air Security Supervisor for Luisa and Genevieve

COLLINS FARWELL
Erno's nephew

PAUL JUDSON
Murdered 7/4/91

PART ONE

INVESTIGATION

1

Attorney and Client

THE CLIENT, like most clients, said he was innocent. He was scheduled to die in thirty-three days.

Arthur Raven, his lawyer, was determined not to worry. After all, Arthur reasoned, he was not even a volunteer. Instead, he'd been drafted by the federal appellate court to ensure that after ten years of litigation, no sound arguments remained to save Rommy Gandolph's life. Worrying was not part of the job.

He was worried anyway.

"I'm sorry?" asked Pamela Towns, his young associate, from the passenger's seat. A gurgle of anguish had escaped Arthur as he had come, once again, face-to-face with himself.

"Nothing," said Arthur. "I just hate being the designated loser."

"Then we shouldn't lose." Pamela, with rosy good looks fit for TV news, flashed a bright coast-to-coast grin.

They were far from the city now, doing eighty on cruise control in Arthur's new German sedan. In these parts, the road was so flat and straight, he did not even have to touch the wheel. The prairie farmlands raced by, corn stubble and loam, silent and eternal in the wan light of morning. They had left Center City at seven to beat the traffic. Arthur hoped to hold a brief introductory meeting with their new client, Rommy Gandolph, at the state penitentiary at Rudyard and to be back at his desk by two o'clock—or three, if he decided to risk asking Pamela to lunch. He remained intensely conscious of the young woman nearby, of the tawny hair falling softly on her shoulders, and of the hand that crept to her thigh every several miles to retract the hiking of her tartan skirt.

Eager as he was to please her, Arthur could offer little hope for the case.

"At this stage," he said, "under the law, the only thing that could possibly amount to reversible error would be new evidence of actual innocence. And we're not going to find that."

"How do you know?" asked Pamela.

"How do I know? Because the man confessed to everybody but the *Daily Planet*." Ten years ago, Gandolph had copped to the police, then gave a handwritten statement to the prosecutor, Muriel Wynn, and finally repeated his admissions on videotape. On each occasion, he had acknowledged he was the person who'd shot two men and a woman and left them in a restaurant food locker in a case still referred to, in the tempered words of the press, as 'the Fourth of July Massacre.'

"Well, he kept saying on the phone he's innocent," said Pamela. "It's possible, isn't it?"

For Arthur, who had been a Deputy Prosecuting Attorney before coming to work seven years ago at O'Grady, Steinberg, Marconi and Horgan, there was no possibility of that at all. But Pamela, at twenty-five or twenty-six, had just started practice. Saving an innocent client was the sort of adventure she'd imagined in law school, riding like Joan of Arc toward radiant Justice. Instead, she'd settled for a big law firm and $120,000 a year. But why not have everything? Well, you couldn't blame people for their fantasies. God knows, Arthur Raven realized that.

"Listen to what I found in Rommy's probation records," said Pamela. "On July 5, 1991, he was sentenced to time served for a violation of probation. The murders were early on July 4th. So 'time served' would mean he was in jail, wouldn't it?"

"It would mean he was in jail at some point. Not necessarily on July 4th. Does his rap sheet show he was in jail on July 4th?"

"No. But it's something to investigate, isn't it?"

It would have been something to investigate a decade ago, when the records to prove it was nonsense still existed. Yet even at that, the federal appeals court was likely to grant Gandolph a brief stay of execution, during which Arthur and Pamela would be obliged to scramble in dogged—and futile—pursuit of this phantom theory.

Rankled by the prospect of more wasted time, Arthur nudged the cruise control wand a bit higher and felt some dim satisfaction in the big auto's response. He had purchased the car two months ago as a trophy of sorts after he became a full partner in his law firm. It was one of the few luxuries he'd ever permitted himself, but he had barely turned the key when he began to feel he was disrespecting the memory of his father, who had recently passed, a loving man, but one whose eccentricities had included a cramped frugality.

"And listen to this," Pamela was saying. She had withdrawn Rommy Gandolph's rap sheet from the thick folder on her lap and read out the entries. Gandolph was a thief and a fence. He'd had half a dozen convictions—burglary, theft, possession of stolen property several times. "But nothing with a gun," said Pamela. "No violence. No female victims. How does he suddenly become a rapist and a murderer?"

"Practice, practice, practice," answered Arthur.

From the corner of his eye, he saw Pamela's full mouth turn briefly downward. He was screwing this up. As always. Arthur did not know exactly what he had done wrong with women to leave him single at the age of thirty-eight. Appearance was one issue, he realized. He'd had the droop and pallor of middle age since his teens. In law school, he'd had a brief, hurtful marriage to Marjya, a Romanian immigrant. After that, for a period he'd seemed to have neither the inclination nor the time to start again. He had given so much to the law—so much fury and passion in every case, so many nights and weekends where he actually felt pleasure in having solitary time to concentrate. And his father's declining health, and the question of what would become of his sister, Susan, had also been draining preoccupations for years. But now, seeking even the faintest sign that Pamela had some interest in him, he felt humbled by his foolishness. His hopes with her were as unlikely as hers for Gandolph. He felt the need to chasten them both.

"Look," said Arthur, "our client, Gandolph. 'Rommy'? Not only did Rommy confess early and often, but when he went to trial, his defense was insanity. Which requires his lawyer to admit Rommy committed the crime. Then we have ten more years of appeals, and post-conviction petitions, and *habeas corpus* proceedings, with two different sets of new attorneys, and none of them happens to mention that Rommy is the wrong man. Let alone Rommy, who only remembered that he didn't do it when he was about forty-five days away from getting the needle. Really, Pamela. Do you think he told the lawyers before us he was innocent? Every con knows this game—new lawyers, new story."

Arthur smiled, attempting to appear worldly-wise, but the truth was he'd never really accommodated himself to criminal defendants' shenanigans. Since leaving the Prosecuting Attorney's Office, Arthur had played defense lawyer infrequently, only when one of the firm's corporate clients or its bosses was suspected of some financial manipulation. The law he lived most days as a civil litigator was a tidier, happier law, where both sides fudged and the issues raised were minuscule matters of economic policy. His years as a prosecutor seemed to be a time when he'd been assigned each day to clean out a flooded basement where coliform bacteria and sewer stink rotted almost everything. Someone had said that power corrupted. But the saying applied equally to evil. Evil corrupted. A single twisted act, some piece of gross psychopathology that went beyond the boundaries of what almost anybody else could envision—a father who tossed his infant out a tenth-floor window; a former student who forced lye down the throat of a teacher; or someone like Arthur's new client who not only killed but then sodomized one of the corpses—the backflow from such acts polluted everyone who came near. Cops. Prosecutors. Defense lawyers. Judges. No one in the face of these horrors reacted with the dispassion the law supposed. There was a single lesson: things fall apart. Arthur had harbored no desire to return to that realm where chaos was always imminent.

In another fifteen minutes they had arrived there. Rudyard was a small town like many others in the Middle West, its core a few dark buildings, still smudged with coal soot, and several tin hangars with corrugated plastic roofs that housed various farm services. At the outskirts, a kind of mini-suburbanization was under way, with strip malls and tract homes, the result of the economic security afforded by an unusual anchor industry—the prison.

When they turned a corner on a movie-set neighborhood of maple trees and small frame houses, the facility suddenly loomed at the end of the block, like a horror-flick monster jumping out of a closet, a half-mile continuum of randomly connected yellow-brick buildings, notable for the narrowness of the few windows. Those structures in turn surrounded an old stone edifice stout enough to have survived from the Middle Ages. Toward the perimeter lay not only a ten-foot brick wall, but a graveled moat of projecting stainless steel spikes, and beyond that a boundary of cyclone fencing supporting five-foot spirals of razor wire, brilliant in the sun.

In the prison guardhouse, they signed in, then were directed to a worn bench for the long wait while Rommy was brought down. In the interval, Arthur reviewed Rommy's letter, which had arrived via various intermediate hands at the Court of Appeals. It was composed in a hodgepodge scrawl, with multicolored markings and other features too irregular even to be called childish. Just looking at the letter, you knew that Rommy Gandolph was both desperate and crazy.

Dear Judge,
I am on DEATH ROW for a CRiMe I
never CoMmitted. They Say I hAve had
all my AppeeLs, and it's all com out

against me EVEN so I AM INNOCENT. the lawrs who had file my PC Over in the STate says they CaN't represnt me now, on account of Fed laWs. what can I do? the day that I get my execution is sposed to be May 23!!!!. i can't have a stay or nothin unless I have a habeus going, but I don't have a Lawr do I. What can I do? can't Somebody over there Help me? I'm going to be killed, and I never hurt no one, not in this case or any other time that I rember RighT noW. HELP ME. I DIDN'T KILL NO ONE ever!!!!!

The United States Court of Appeals had entered an order treating Rommy Gandolph's correspondence as a successive petition for relief under the federal *habeas corpus* statute and appointing a lawyer for him—Arthur. Judges often waved their magic wand at random to turn some unwilling toad—a fully occupied lawyer—into a *pro bono* prince, with a demanding new nonpaying client whom the rules of court required he accept. Some might read the appointment as a compliment, the court asking a respected former state prosecutor to apply the legal equivalent of last rites. But it was an onerous addition to an already overburdened life.

Eventually Rommy's name was called. Pamela and Arthur were patted down in the holding area, and then the first of many electronic bolts was shot and a door of bulletproof glass and iron crossbars clanked irrevocably behind them, as they followed a guard. It had been many years since Arthur had been inside the joint, but Rudyard in its own way was timeless. Not the procedures. The procedures, as he remembered them, seemed to change every few days. The authorities—the state legislature, the governor, the prison administration—were forever trying to improve discipline, to stop the in-flow of contraband, to control the gangs, to keep the inmates, veteran scammers, from scamming. There was always a new form to fill out, a new place to stow money, keys, cell phones—all the big-house forbiddens. Always another gate to get through, a new search procedure.

But the mood, the air, the people—they were eternal. The paint was fresh; the floors gleamed. No matter. They could scrub it as clean as they cared to. With so many people confined in such close quarters, with an open privy in every cell, the atmosphere was tainted with the smell of human waste and some larger effluvium, which on first breath vaguely sickened Arthur, much as it had years ago.

Down a low brick corridor they approached a door of green metal plating. On it was stenciled one word: 'Condemned.' Inside they were steered to the attorney's room, which was not really one room but two, a space no more than five feet wide divided by a wall, which yielded halfway up to an arrangement like a teller's drive-through window—a pane of glass, with a metal trough beneath to allow papers to pass. Although it violated every principle of attorney-client confidentiality, the correctional system had won the right to keep a guard posted in the corner on the prisoner's side.

Behind the window was Rommy Gandolph, a brown-skinned wraith with a head of wild hair, swallowed in the loose folds of the yellow jumpsuit worn solely by inmates who'd been sentenced to death. His arms were shackled and thus he was required to reach with both hands for the phone that would allow him to converse with his lawyers.

On their side, Arthur picked up the lone handset and held it between Pamela and himself while they introduced themselves.

"You-all the first real lawyers I had," Rommy said. "Rest was state defenders. Think maybe I got a chance now I got real lawyers." Rommy leaned close to the pane to explain his predicament. "I'm the next Yellow Man takin the walk, you know that? Everybody lookin at me already. Like somethin oughta be different cause I'm gone be dead so soon."

Pamela bent at once toward the document passage and spoke encouraging words. They were going to get a stay of execution today, she promised.

"Yeah," said Rommy, "cause I'm innocent, man. I ain kill't nobody. I want that DMA test, man, see if I got any." DNA, always the first thought these days, held no hope for Rommy because the state had never claimed he had left at the scene any identifiable genetic evidence—blood, semen, hair, tissue scrapings, even saliva.

Without warning, Gandolph sighted Pamela down the length of an extended finger.

"You pretty as you sounded on the

phone," he told her. "Think me and you oughta get married."

Briefly arising, Pamela's smile suddenly passed into eclipse, as it appeared to grow on her that Rommy was deadly earnest.

"Man gotta get married 'fore he die, right?" Rommy asked. "Ain that a good idea?"

Great, Arthur thought. Competition.

"You'n me get hitched up," Rommy told her, "I can get a conjugal."

Judging from her rigid posture, this was not part of Pamela's vision of valiant representation. Arthur, who'd had no idea how to commence this interview, quickly picked up Judge Gillian Sullivan's judgment and commitment order from 1992 that sentenced Rommy to death, and began reading it out loud.

"Auga-what? Who now?" asked Rommy Gandolph.

"Augustus Leonidis," said Arthur.

"Am I knowin him?" asked Rommy. The lids twitched over his closed eyes as he made an effort to place the name.

"He's one of the three," said Arthur quietly.

"What three?"

"The three the state says you killed." Confessed to killing, Arthur thought. But no need to put too fine a point on it at present.

"Mmm," said Rommy. "Don't think I knowed him." Rommy shook his head, as if he'd missed a social call. Gandolph was nearing forty. He had a yellowish tinge to his eyes, and, by all appearances, the blood of the Americas in his veins. In contemporary parlance, he was 'black,' but there looked to be white and Indian and Hispanic in him as well. His hair was gnarled and uncut, and he was missing several teeth, but he wasn't ugly. Craziness just seemed to have eaten the center out of him. Looking at Rommy's eyes zag about like frenzied bugs near a light, Arthur held little doubt why his prior lawyers had focused on a psychiatric defense. As people commonly used the word 'crazy,' Rommy Gandolph without question was. Yet not crazy enough. Sociopathic. Borderline personality disorder, maybe even flat-out schizoid. But not thoroughly lost in the wilderness, not so entirely without a compass that he did not know wrong from right, which was what the law required for a defense.

"I'm not the kind to kill no one," Rommy offered, as an afterthought.

"Well, you've been convicted of killing

three people—Augustus Leonidis, Paul Judson, and Luisa Remardi. They say you shot
them and left them in a food locker." The
state also said he'd sodomized Luisa after
her death, although Rommy, most likely
from shame, had refused to acknowledge
that part. Judge Sullivan, however, who'd
heard the case on her own, without a jury,
had found him guilty on that count as well.

"I don't know nothin 'bout that," said
Rommy. He looked askance then, as if that
remark would close the subject. Arthur,
whose sister, Susan, was even crazier than
Rommy, tapped the glass to make sure
Rommy's gaze came back to him. With people like Rommy, like Susan, you sometimes
had to hold their eye to get through.

"Whose handwriting is this?" Arthur asked
mildly and pushed Rommy's written confession under the glass. The guard jumped
from his chair and demanded to see each
page, front and back, to ensure nothing was
concealed. Rommy studied the document
for quite some time.

"What you think about stocks?" he asked
then. "You ever own stock? What's that like
anyway?"

After a considerable interval, Pamela

started to explain how the exchanges operated.

"No, I mean *sayin* you own stock. How's that feel and all? Man, I ever get outta here, I wanna buy me some stocks. Then I'm gone get all that stuff on the TV. 'Up a quarter.' 'Down Jones.' I'm gone know what they-all on about."

Pamela continued trying to outline the mechanisms of corporate ownership, and Rommy nodded diligently after every sentence, but was soon visibly astray. Arthur pointed again to the sheet Rommy held.

"The state says you wrote that."

Rommy's inky eyes briefly fell. "Tha's what I was thinkin," he said. "Lookin at it and all, I'd kind of said it was mine."

"Well, that paper says you killed these three people."

Rommy eventually leafed back to the first page.

"This here," he said, "this don't seem to make no sense to me."

"It's not true?"

"Man, that was so long ago. When was it this here happened?" Arthur told him and Rommy sat back. "I been in that long? What-all year has it got to anyway?"

"Did you write this confession for the police?" Arthur asked.

"Knowed I wrote somethin back there in that precinct. Ain nobody told me it was for court." There was, of course, a signed *Miranda* warning in the file, acknowledging that any statement Rommy made could be used against him in just that way. "And I ain heard nothin 'bout gettin the needle," he said. "Tha's for damn sure. They was a cop tellin me a lot of stuff I wrote down. But I don't recollect writin nothin like all of that. I ain kill't nobody."

"And why did you write down what the cop was saying?" Arthur asked.

"Cause I, like, dirtied myself." One of the more controversial pieces of proof in the case was that Rommy had literally shit in his pants when the detective in charge of the case, Larry Starczek, had started to question him. At trial, the prosecution had been allowed to introduce Rommy's soiled briefs as evidence of a consciousness of guilt. That, in turn, became one of the prominent issues in Rommy's many appeals, which no court had managed to address without a snickering undertone.

Arthur asked if Larry, the detective, had beaten Rommy, denied him food or drink, or an attorney. Though rarely directly responsive, Rommy seemed to be claiming none of that—only that he'd written an elaborate admission of guilt that was completely untrue.

"Do you happen to remember where you were on July 3rd, 1991?" Pamela asked. Rommy's eyes enlarged with hopeless incomprehension, and she explained they were wondering if he was in jail.

"I ain done no serious time 'fore this here," answered Rommy, who clearly thought his character was at issue.

"No," said Arthur. "Could you have been inside when these murders happened?"

"Somebody sayin that?" Rommy hunched forward confidentially, awaiting a cue. As the idea settled, he managed a laugh. "That'd be a good one." It was all news to him, although he claimed in those days he was regularly rousted by the police, providing some faint support for Pamela.

Rommy really had nothing to offer in his own behalf, yet as they conversed, he denied every element of the state's case. The officers who'd arrested him said they had found a necklace belonging to the female victim, Luisa Remardi, in Gandolph's pocket. That, too, he said, was a lie.

"Them po-lice had that thing already. Ain no way it was on me when I got brought down for this."

Eventually, Arthur handed the phone to Pamela for further questions. Rommy provided his own eccentric version of the sad social history revealed by his file. He was born out of wedlock; his mother, who was fourteen, drank throughout the pregnancy. She could not care for the boy and sent him to his paternal grandparents in DuSable, fundamentalists who somehow found punishment the meaningful part of religion. Rommy was not necessarily defiant, but strange. He was diagnosed as retarded, lagged in school. And began misbehaving. He had stolen from a young age. He had gotten into drugs. He had fallen in with other no-accounts. Rudyard was full of Rommys, white and black and brown.

When they'd been together more than an hour, Arthur rose, promising that Pamela and he would do their best.

"When you-all come back, you bring your wedding dress, okay?" Rommy said to

Pamela. "They's a priest here, he'll do a good job."

As Rommy also stood, the guard again snapped to his feet, taking hold of the chain that circled Rommy's waist and ran to both his manacles and leg irons. Through the glass, they could hear Rommy prattling. These was real lawyers. The girl was gone marry him. They was gone get him outta here cause he was innocent. The guard, who appeared to like Rommy, smiled indulgently and nodded when Rommy asked permission to turn back. Gandolph pressed his shackled hands and their pale palms to the glass, saying loudly enough to be heard through the partition, "I 'preciate you-all comin down here and everything you doin for me, I really do."

Arthur and Pamela were led out, unspeaking. Back in the free air, Pamela shook her slender shoulders in relief as they walked toward Arthur's car. Her mind predictably remained on Rommy's defense.

"Does he seem like a killer?" she asked. "He's weird. But is that what a killer is like?"

She was good, Arthur thought, a good lawyer. When Pamela had approached him to volunteer for the case, he had assumed she was too new to be of much help. He had accepted because of his reluctance to disappoint anyone, although it had not hurt that she was graceful and unattached. Discovering she was talented had only seemed to sharpen his attraction.

"I'll tell you one thing I can't see him as," said Arthur: "your husband."

"Wasn't that something?" Pamela asked, laughing. She was pretty enough to be untouched at some level. Men, Arthur recognized, were often silly around her.

They passed a couple of jokes, and still bantering, Pamela said, "I can't seem to meet anyone decent lately, but this"—she threw a hand in the direction of the highway, far off—"is a pretty long trip to make every Saturday night."

She was at the passenger door. The wind frothed her blondish hair, as she laughed lightly again, and Arthur felt his heart knock. Even at thirty-eight, he still believed that somewhere within him was a shadow Arthur, who was taller, leaner, better-looking, a person with a suave voice and a carefree manner who could have parlayed Pamela's remark about her present dry spell with men into a backhanded invitation to lunch or even a more meaningful social occasion. But brought to that petrifying brink where his fantasies adjoined the actual world, Arthur realized that, as usual, he would not step forward. He feared humiliation, of course, but if he were nonchalant enough she could decline, as she was nearly certain to do, in an equally innocuous fashion. What halted him, instead, was the cold thought that any overture would be, in a word, unfair. Pamela was a subordinate, inevitably anxious about her prospects, and he was a partner. There was no changing the unequal footing or his leverage, no way Arthur Raven could depart from the realm of settled decency where he felt his only comfort with himself. And yet even as he accepted his reasoning, he knew that with women some obstacle of one kind or another always emerged, leaving him confined with the pangs of fruitless longing.

He used the gizmo in his pocket to un-latch Pamela's door. While she sank into the sedan, he stood in the bitter dust that had been raised in the parking lot. The death of his hopes, no matter how implausible, was always wrenching. But the prairie wind gusted again, this time clearing the air and carrying the smell of freshly turned earth from the fields outside town, an aroma of spring. Love—the sweet amazing possibility of it—struck in his chest like a note of perfect music. Love! He was somehow exhilarated by the chance he had lost. *Love!* And at that moment he wondered for the first time about Rommy Gandolph. What if he *was* innocent? That too was an inspiration almost as sweet as love. What if Rommy was *innocent*!

And then he realized again that Rommy wasn't. The weight of Arthur's life fell over him, and the few categories that described him came back to mind. He was a partner. And without love. His father was dead. And Susan was still here. He considered the list, felt again that it added up to far less than he had long hoped for, or, even, was entitled to, then opened the car door to head back to it all.

2

JULY 5, 1991

The Detective

WHEN LARRY STARCZEK HEARD about the murder of Gus Leonidis, he was in bed with a prosecutor named Muriel Wynn, who had just told him she was getting serious with somebody else.

"Dan Quayle," she answered, when he demanded to know who. "He fell for my spelling."

Irked, Larry agitated one foot through the clothing on the hotel carpeting in search of his briefs. When his toe brushed his beeper, it was vibrating.

"Bad stuff," he said to Muriel after he got off the phone. "Good Gus just bought the farm. They found him and two customers dead of gunshot wounds in his freezer." He shook out his trousers and told her he had to go. The Commander wanted all hands on deck.

Tiny and dark, Muriel was sitting up straight on the stiff hotel linen, still without a stitch.

"Is there a prosecutor assigned yet?" she asked.

Larry hadn't a clue, but he knew how it went. If she showed up, they'd assume somebody sent her. That was another great thing about Muriel, Larry thought. She loved the street as much as he did.

He asked her again who the guy was.

"I mean I just want to move on," Muriel answered. "I think this other thing—I think it may go somewhere. I might even get married."

"Married!"

"Hell, Larry, it's not a disease. *You're* married."

"Eh," he answered. Five years ago he had married for the second time, because it made sense. Nancy Marini, a good-hearted nurse, was easy on the eyes, kind, and well disposed toward his boys. But as Nancy had pointed out several times recently, he'd never said goodbye to any of the stuff that had led his first marriage to ruin, the catting around or the fact that his principal adult relationship was with the dead bodies he scraped off the street. Marriage number two was just about past tense, but even with Muriel, Larry preferred to keep his problems to himself. "You've always said marriage was a disaster," he told her.

"My marriage to Rod was a disaster. But I was nineteen." At thirty-four, Muriel had the distinction of having been a widow for more than five years.

It was the Fourth of July weekend and the Hotel Gresham, in the early afternoon, was strangely silent. The manager here owed Larry for a few situations he'd handled—guests who wouldn't leave, a pro who was working the lounge. He made sure Larry got a room for a few hours whenever he asked. As Muriel drifted past him for the mirror, he grabbed her from behind and did a brief grind, his lips close to the short black curls by her ear.

"Is your new beau as much fun as I am?"

"Larry, this isn't the National Fuck-Offs where you just got eliminated. We've always had a good time."

Combat defined their relations. He enjoyed it maybe more than the sex. They had met in law school, seven years ago now, when both had started at night. Muriel became a star and transferred to the day division. Larry had decided to quit even before he won custody of his sons, because he didn't have the right reasons to be there. He was trying to bolster himself after his divorce, to stay out of the taverns, even to improve the opinions of his parents and brothers who saw police work as somewhat below him. In the end, Muriel and their occasional interludes were probably the best things to emerge from the experience. There were women in his life, too many, where you yearned but it was never really right. You both carried on afterwards about how terrific it had been, but there was a sad calculation to everything that had occurred. That had never been the case with Muriel. With her gapped teeth and pudgy nose, built narrowly enough to wash down a drain, Muriel wouldn't be on many magazine covers. Yet after marrying twice for looks, Larry sometimes felt like tightening a noose around his own throat when he was with her, just for knowing so little about himself.

While Muriel finished batting powder over her summer freckles, Larry flipped on the radio. The news stations all had the murders by now, but Greer, the Commander, had clamped down on the details.

"I'd really love to catch this case," she said. She was three and a half years on the job as a prosecutor and not even close to assignment to a capital prosecution, even as the second or third chair. But you never got very far telling Muriel to slow down. In the mirror over the dresser, her small dark eyes sought his. "I love history," she said. "You know. Big events. Things with consequence. When I was a little girl, my mother was always saying that to me: Be a part of history."

He nodded. The case would be big.

"Doin Gus," Larry said. "Somebody's gotta sizzle for that, don't you figure?"

The compact snapped closed and Muriel agreed with a sad smile. "Everybody dug Gus," she said.

AUGUSTUS LEONIDIS had owned the restaurant called Paradise for more than thirty years. The North End neighborhood had gone to ruin around him shortly after he opened, when its final bulwark against decline, Du-Sable Field, the small in-city airport, had been abandoned by the major airlines in the early 1960s because its runways were too short to land jets. Yet Gus, full of brash immigrant optimism, had refused to move. He was a patriot of a lost kind. What area was 'bad' if it was in America?

Despite the surroundings, Gus's business had prospered, due both to the eastbound exit from U.S. 843 directly across from his front door and his legendary breakfasts, in which the signature item was a baked omelette that arrived at the table the size of a balloon. Paradise was a renowned Kindle County crossroads, where everyone was enthusiastically welcomed by the garrulous proprietor. He'd been called Good Gus for so long that nobody remembered exactly why—whether it was the freebies for unfortunates, his civic activities, or his effusive, upbeat style. Over the years, he was steadily named in the *Tribune*'s annual poll as one of Kindle County's favorite citizens.

Out on the street, when Larry arrived, the cops from the patrol division had done their best to make themselves important, parking their black-and-whites across the avenue with the light bars atop the vehicles spinning. Various vagrants and solid citizens had been attracted. It was July and nobody was wearing much of anything, since the old apartment buildings nearby didn't have the wiring to support air-conditioning. The poor girls with their poor-girl dos of straightened hair shellacked with fixer were across the way, minding their babies. At the curb, several TV news vans preparing for broadcast had raised their antennas, which looked like enlarged kitchen tools.

Muriel had driven separately, but she was lurking near the broad windows of the restaurant, waiting for Larry to edge her into the case. Strolling up, Larry pointed to her in vague recognition and said, "Hey." Even dressed casually, Muriel wore her Minnie Mouse high heels. She always wanted more height and, Larry suspected, also a chance to emphasize a pretty nice derriere. Muriel used what she had. Watching her blue shorts wagging in the wind, he experienced a brief thrill at the recollection of the flesh now concealed to everyone else.

He flipped his tin at the two uniforms near the door. Inside, on the left, three civilians were seated together on one bench of a booth—a black man in an apron, a wrung-out woman in a beige housedress, and a younger guy with rounded shoulders and an earring big enough to twinkle at Larry from thirty feet. The three seemed to be their own universe, isolated from the whirl of police activity around them. Employees or family, Larry figured, waiting either to be questioned or to ask questions of their own. He signaled Muriel and she sat down near them on one of the revolving soda fountain stools that grew up like a row of toadstools in front of the counter.

The crime scene was being processed by dozens of people—at least six techs, in their khaki shirts, were dusting for prints—but the atmosphere was notably subdued. When there was a crowd like this, there could sometimes be a lot of commotion, gallows humor, and plenty of buzz. But today, everyone had been hauled in off holiday leave in the middle of a four-day weekend, meaning they were grumpy or sleepy. Besides, the Commander was here. He was solemn by nature. And the crime was bad.

The Detective Commander, Harold Greer, had set up in Gus's tiny office behind the kitchen, and the team of detectives he'd called in was assembling there. Gus, unexpectedly, was tidy. Above the desk was a Byzantine cross, a girlie calendar from a food wholesaler, and pictures of Gus's family taken, Larry surmised, on a return trip to Greece. The photos, showing a wife, two daughters, and a son, had to be fifteen years old, but that was the time Gus, like most guys in Larry's experience, wanted to remember, when he was really pulling the sleigh, building a business, raising a family. The wife, smiling and looking pretty fetching in a rumpled bathing suit, was the same poor wretch sitting by the door.

Greer was on the phone, holding one finger in his ear as he explained the status of things to somebody from the Mayor's Office, while the detectives around the room watched him. Larry went over to Dan Lipranzer for the lowdown. Lip, who had the slicked-back do of a 1950s-style juvenile delinquent, was, as usual, by himself in a corner. Lipranzer always appeared cold, even in July, drawn in on himself like a molting bird. He'd been the first dick on the scene and had interviewed the night manager, Rafael.

Paradise closed only twice each year—for Orthodox Christmas and the Fourth of July, the birthdays of God and America, the two things Gus swore by. Every other day, there were lines out the door from 5 a.m. until noon, with a slower trade in the remaining hours comprised of cops and cabbies and many air travelers coming or going from DuSable Field, which had revived when Trans-National Air initiated regional service there a few years ago.

According to what the night manager had told Lipranzer, Gus had come in to pick up the cash and send his employees home right before midnight on Wednesday, July 3. Each worker received $100 from the register. As they were about to hang the Closed sign, Luisa Remardi, who worked for Trans-National as an airport ticket agent, had walked in. She was a regular, and Gus, who had a thing for every female customer, sent Rafael, the fry cook, and the busboy on their way, and took over the kitchen himself. Sometime in the next hour or two, Gus, Luisa, and a third person had been murdered. The last victim was a white in his late thirties, tentatively i.d.'d as Paul Judson, based on both a run of the plates of one of the cars still absorbing the July sun in Gus's lot and yesterday's missing-person report from his wife. Mrs. Judson said Paul had been scheduled to arrive July 4 on a 12:10 a.m. flight at DuSable Field.

Rafael had returned to reopen at 4:30 a.m. today. He hadn't thought much of the disorder he found, assuming that once Gus got rid of his patrons, he'd walked out quickly rather than turn away new customers. Near five this morning, Mrs. Leonidis, Athena, phoned in distress because Gus hadn't shown up yesterday at their cabin near Skageon. Searching around, Rafael noticed Gus's Cadillac still in the lot, and began to worry that the trail of blood near the register wasn't from thawing meat Gus had dragged upstairs to the kitchen. When the fry cook arrived, they called the cops and, after some debate, finally pulled the handle on the freezer in the basement on the chance someone was still alive. Nobody was.

It was close to 3:30 p.m. when Greer put down the phone and announced to the twelve detectives he'd summoned that it was time to get started. Despite the heat, near ninety, Greer had worn a wool sport coat and tie, realizing he was destined for TV. He had a clipboard and began announcing assignments, so each cop would know his or her angle while examining the scene. Harold was going to run the case as a Task Force, receiving all reports himself. That would sound impressive to the reporters, but Larry knew the result would be six detective teams bumping into each other, covering the same leads and missing others. A week from now, Greer, for all his good intentions, would have to start dealing with everything else piling up on his desk, and the dicks, like cats, would wander away.

Larry tried to make his face plaster when Greer announced he was teamed with Wilma Amos. Wilma was your basic affirmative-action item whose highest and best use was probably as a hat rack. Worse, it meant Larry wasn't getting anywhere near the lead on this case. Instead, Wilma and he were delegated to background the female vic, Luisa Remardi.

"Guided tour," said Harold and walked out through the kitchen. Harold Greer was an impressive guy to most people, a good-sized, well-spoken black man, calm and orderly. Larry didn't mind Harold—he was less of a politician than most of the ranking officers on the Force, and he was able, one in the small cadre of officers Larry thought of as being as smart as he was.

The techs had taped off a path and Harold instructed the dicks to go single file and keep their hands in their pockets. Somebody with a degree in criminology would say Harold was a lunatic for taking a dozen extra people through a crime scene. It risked contamination, and even if everybody wore toe shoes, a defense lawyer would make the viewing sound like Hannibal's trip over the Alps with elephants. But Harold knew no investigator would feel like he owned a case unless he'd surveyed the scene. Even bloodhounds had to have the real scent.

"Working theories," said Harold. He was standing behind the cash register, which rested on a plateglass case whose angled shelves held stale cigars and candy bars. On the exterior, bright purple fingerprint lifts now stood out like decorations. "Theory number one, which is pretty solid: This is an armed robbery gone bad. The cash register is empty, the bag for the bank deposit is gone, and each victim has no watch, wallet, or jewelry.

"Second theory: Today I'm saying a single perpetrator. That's soft," said Harold, "but I'm liking it more and more. The bullets we've recovered all look like .38 rounds, same bunter marks. One shooter, almost for sure. Could be accomplices, but it doesn't seem to play that way.

"Gus was killed right here, behind the register, going for the phone from the looks of it. One shot to the left rear of the cranium. Based on a preliminary exam, Painless is saying three to six feet, which means the triggerman was right near the cash register. Armed robbery gone bad," Greer repeated. From his inside pocket, Harold removed a sleek silver pen and pointed out the blood, a large pool dried on the dirty linoleum and spatters on the green wall phone. Then he continued.

"Once our shooter takes down Gus, he has a serious problem because there are two customers in the restaurant. This is where we go from a felony-murder to brutal and heinous." The words were terms of art—'brutal and heinous' murders qualified, in this state, for capital punishment. "Instead of running for the door like your average punk, our guy decides to go after the witnesses. Ms. Remardi is killed right here, single shot through the abdomen."

Harold had stepped down twenty feet to a booth opposite the front door in the original section of the restaurant. When Gus bought the place, long before he expanded into the adjoining storefronts, it must have had a medieval theme. Two rows of booths, composed of heavy dark planks lumpy from the layers of urethane, were joined at the center panel. At each corner, a square coat stand arose like a turret.

"Looks a lot like Ms. Remardi decided her best chance was to go for the gun. We have bruises on her arms and hands, one finger is broken. But that didn't work out for her. The fabric on her uniform around the wound is burned and the tissue is stippled, so the shot is point-blank. Judging from the exit wound, Painless is saying prelim that the bullet passed through her liver and her aorta, so she's dead in a few minutes."

The slug had been removed by the techs from the center panel. An uneven ring of dried blood showed up where the wood had shattered, exposing the raw pine underneath. That meant that Luisa had died sitting up. A coffee cup, with a bright half-moon of her lipstick, still rested on the table as well as an ashtray full of butts.

"If she's looking at an accomplice, it doesn't make much sense that she's fighting. So that's another reason we're figuring this was a one-man show." Under the table, where Harold pointed, a dinner plate, streaked with steak sauce, had shattered in the struggle. An inch of beef fat lay amid the fragments of crockery, as well as half a pack of cigarettes and a disposable lighter.

"Mr. Judson was eating back in the corner by the window. Rafael cleaned up a plate, a glass, and a 7UP can from that table this morning. On the right side of Mr. Judson's suit there's a line of dust, suggesting he was probably under the table, maybe hiding from the gunfire. Maybe just hiding. But the shooter found him.

"Judging from the shoe prints in the blood and the drag pattern, and the distribution of the postmortem lividity on Gus's and Luisa's corpses, Mr. Judson was forced at gunpoint to haul both bodies into the freezer in the basement."

Harold led his detectives, like a grade-school class, past the counter, where Muriel still sat, and through a narrow door. The stairway was lit by a single bulb, beneath which the group clumped down the wooden steps. In the brick cellar, they found a significant encampment. Three wheeled stretchers were across the way awaiting the bodies, which had not yet been removed because they were frozen. The police pathologist, Painless

Kumagai, had several tests and measurements to perform prior to allowing the corpses to thaw. As the group approached, Larry could hear Painless's sharp, accented voice issuing commands to his staff. Harold warned the cops behind him about the electrical cords bunched across the floor to light several halogen beacons Painless's team had set up in the freezer for photos.

Using the pen, Harold opened the food locker wider. Judson's body was right there, one leg in the doorway. Harold pointed out his shoes, both soles brown with blood. The tread patterns matched the prints in the trails upstairs. In their rubber gloves, Painless and his team were working on the far side of the freezer.

"After Mr. Judson had pulled the bodies into the food locker, he was bound with an electrical cord, gagged with a dish towel, and shot, execution style, in the back of the head." Harold's silver pen glided through the air like a missile indicating each point of interest. The force of the shot had driven Judson over on his side.

"And then, I guess to celebrate, our hero sodomized Ms. Remardi's body." One of the pathologists moved aside, fully revealing

Luisa Remardi's remains. Following the preliminary exam, they'd repositioned her as she'd been found, bent face-down over a stack of fifty-pound bags of frozen French fries. Above the waist, she was clad in Trans-National's rust-colored uniform. The exit wound in her back had made a neat little tear in the fabric, almost as if she'd merely snagged the vest, and the halo of blood Larry had seen vaguely imprinted on the side of the booth upstairs was enlarged there, darkening the fabric like a tie-dye. Her matching skirt and her red panties had been jacked down to her ankles and, beneath the starched tails of her white blouse, the melonish rounds of her buttocks were hiked in the air, penetrated by the dark ellipsis of her anal sphincter, which had been distended at the time of death. Somebody had worked her over down there—there was redness, meaning, if Harold was correct, this had occurred right after her death, while a vital reaction was still possible.

"Rape kit is negative, but you find the top of a condom wrapper here in her drawers, and what appears to be a lubricant track around the anus." At Greer's instruction, a younger pathologist directed a flashlight to illustrate the last point. The gel had failed to evaporate in the cold. Rapists these days worried about AIDS—and had heard of DNA. There was no accomplice, Larry thought. Not if that was the story. Necrophiliacs and backdoor boys didn't perform for an audience. Even creeps had shame.

Harold covered a few procedural orders, then headed upstairs. Larry remained in the freezer and asked Painless if he could look around.

"Don't touch," Painless told him. Painless had worked on the Force for two decades and knew to a moral certainty that the next cop was dumber than the one before.

Larry was the first to say he was a little witchy about the entire process of investigation, but he wasn't alone. Half the murder dicks he knew confessed, after a couple of whiskeys, to occasionally feeling the guiding presence of ghosts. He couldn't claim to understand it, but evil on this scale seemed to set off some kind of cosmic discord. For whatever it was worth, he often started with an instant of solemn communion with the victims.

He stood over Gus for a minute. Not counting gangbangers, who were suspects one day and murdered the next, it was rare for Larry to be acquainted with a vic. He hadn't known Gus well, except for enjoying his wild immigrant routine and the omelettes, always on the house. But Gus had that gift, like a good teacher or priest—he could connect. You felt him.

I'm with you, compadre, Larry thought.

The gunshot had penetrated the occipital plane at the back of Gus's skull, blowing away tissue and bone. Positioned as he'd been found, Gus's face was laid out on a box of beef patties, his mouth open. Dead fish. They all looked like dead fish.

As always, at this moment, Larry was intensely aware of himself. This was his profession. Murder. Like everybody else, he thought about buying a new garden hose and the line on tomorrow's hockey match, and how he could get to both boys' soccer games. But at some point every day, he snuck into the mossy cave of murder, to the moist thrilling darkness of the idea.

He had nothing to apologize for. Murder was part of the human condition. And society existed to restrain it. To Larry, the only more important job than his was a mother's. Read some anthropology, he always told civilians who asked. All those skeletons unearthed with the stone ax still right in the hole? You think this just started? Everyone had murder in him. Larry had killed. In Nam. God knows who he'd shot blowing off his M16 in the darkness. The truth was he knew the dead on his own side far better. But one day, during his brief time on patrol, he'd tossed a grenade down a tunnel and watched the ground give way and the bodies come flying up in a fountain of dirt and blood. The first man was launched in pieces, a trunk with one arm, the legs airborne alone. But the other two men exploded from the earth intact. Larry still recalled them flying through the air, one screaming, the other who was probably out cold, with this expression that you could only call profound. So this is it, the guy was thinking—he might as well have held up a sign. Larry still saw that look all the time. He beheld it on Gus's face now, the largest thing in life—death—and it filled Larry on each occasion with the exacting, breathless emotion of one of those perfect realist paintings you'd see in a museum—Hopper or Wyeth. That thing: this is it.

That was the end for the victims, the instant of surrender. But few gave up willingly.

With death so imminent and unexpected, every human was reduced to terror and desire—the desire to continue and the inexpressible anguish that she or he would not. No one, Larry believed, could die with dignity in these circumstances. Paul Judson, heaped by the doorway, surely hadn't. He was your vanilla suburbanite, a mild-looking guy, just starting to lose his blond hair, which was fine as corn silk. Probably the kind never to show much emotion. But he had now. On his knees, Larry could see salt tracks in the corner of his eyes. Paul had died, as Larry would, crying for his life.

Finally, Larry went to Luisa Remardi, who, as his responsibility, required the greatest attention. Her blood had stained the huge bags on which her body was heaped, but she'd died upstairs. Ripped apart by the bullet like a building in a bomb blast, the devastated arteries and organs had spurted out the blood which the stupid heart kept pumping. Luisa became sleepy first, and then as less and less oxygen reached her brain, hallucinations had begun, fearful ones probably, until her dreams bleached into fathomless light.

When the pathologists okayed it, he

climbed over the levee of bags to see her face. Luisa was pretty, soft under the chin, but with lovely, high cheekbones. Bright highlights were streaked into her dark hair, and even though she worked the midnight shift, she'd applied lots of makeup, doing an elaborate job around her large brown eyes. At her throat, you could see the line where the blush and base stopped and her natural paleness took over. She was one of those Italian chicks—Larry had known plenty—spreading out as she reached her early thirties, but not ready to stop thinking of herself as hot stuff.

You're my girl now, Luisa. I'm gonna take care of you.

Upstairs, Larry went looking for Greer to see if he could pull Muriel into the case. On the way, he stopped at a table where an evidence tech, a kid named Brown, was inventorying the discarded contents from Luisa's purse, which had been spread on the floor near the door.

"Anything?" he asked.

"Address book." With his gloves, Brown turned the pages for Larry.

"Beautiful handwriting," Larry noted. The rest was the usual mess—house keys, receipts, mints. Under Luisa's checkbook cover, Brown pointed out two lubricated condoms in the same maroon wrapper as the one in her panties. What did that mean, Larry wondered, besides the fact that Luisa got around? Maybe the bad guy found these as he was looking in her handbag for her wallet and got turned on.

But they'd never reconstruct events exactly. Larry had learned that. The past was the past, always eluding the full grasp of memory or the best forensic techniques. And it didn't matter. The essential information had reached the present: Three people had died. Without dignity. In terror. And some cruel fuck had exulted in his power each time he pulled the trigger.

Standing by the spot where Luisa had been murdered, Larry closed his eyes to transmit one more time. He was certain that somewhere, probably not far away, a man had just experienced a painful twitch in his heart.

I'm coming for you, motherfucker, Larry told him.

3

MAY 4, 2001

The Former Judge

GILLIAN SULLIVAN, forty-seven, recently released from the Federal Prison Camp for Women at Alderson, West Virginia, sat with a cigarette in a small Center City coffee shop, awaiting Arthur Raven. On the phone, Raven, whom she had known for well more than a decade, had made a point to say he wished to see her for business. Like so many others, he apparently did not want her to think he would be offering consolation or support. She was reconsidering her decision to come, not for the first time, when she saw Arthur, charging through the glass doors of the restaurant vestibule with a briefcase bundled under his arm.

"Judge," he said, and offered his hand. It struck a false note instantly. Even before her disgrace, it had been unlikely he'd call her 'Judge' in private.

"'Gillian' will do, Arthur."

"I'm sorry."

"It's awkward." She crushed out the cigarette, thinking only now that the smoke might bother him. Inside, no one ever complained about smoke. It remained a privilege.

In her time, Gillian had gone from prosecutor to judge and then to convicted criminal defendant. It was an extreme example, but even her wayward career reflected the nature of the criminal bar, which was much like a repertory theater company in which every attorney was apt to have a turn at each part. The prosecutor against whom you tried a case was on the bench the next time you saw her, and in private practice hustling your clients a decade after that. Rivalries and friendships were fortified or forgotten in the parade of years, while every achievement or failure endured somewhere in the memory of the community.

Understanding all that, Gillian nonetheless found the fortunes that had brought her together again with sad, driven little Arthur Raven somehow indigestible. Thirteen years ago, after twenty months on the bench, Gillian had received her first assignment in the criminal courts, presiding over misdemeanor cases and probable cause hearings. Arthur Raven was the Deputy Prosecuting Attorney delegated to her courtroom. They were each new to their jobs, and at that point she was certain her prospects were far brighter than Arthur's. It was common in trial practice to find men and women skilled in making themselves appealing, people who had mastered the outward gestures of candor and humility, even when they masked a volcanic core of egocentricity and ambition. With Arthur, what you saw was what you got: relentless intensity and a desire to win that bordered on the desperate. Half the time he was before her, she wanted to tell him just to take a pill. She probably had, since, even by her own reckoning, she'd never been especially kindly or patient as a judge. But who could blame her? Beneath it all, Arthur seemed to cling to the unlikely belief that victory would at last impart the more triumphant character he so clearly yearned for.

As if it was not a ridiculously loaded question, Arthur now asked, "And how have you been?"

"So-so," she answered. The truth was that after several years of coming to grips, she was realizing she had not come to grips at all. There were periods—most of the time now, and always for several years—when the sheer shame of her situation left her mad, mad in the sense that she knew every thought was disrupted by it, like a vehicle bouncing down a cratered road.

"You still look terrific," he offered.

In Gillian's experience, a man's motives for complimenting a woman were always suspect, a stepping-stone to sex or some less grandiose manipulation. She asked abruptly what this was about.

"Well," he said, "let me use your word. It's awkward. I've been appointed by the U.S. Court of Appeals on a case. A second *habeas*. Rommy Gandolph. Do you recall the name?"

She did, naturally. Only two capital cases had reached sentencing in the years she had sat in Felony. In the other, the death penalty had been imposed by a jury. Rommy Gandolph had been her responsibility alone. Bench trial. Bench sentencing. She'd reconsidered the case again a couple of months ago when she'd received a letter from Rudyard with the typically crazed claims of a prisoner who, ten years after the murders, suddenly said he had critical knowledge to share with her. Probably someone she'd sent to the joint, now hoping to get her down there to spit in her eye. Searching her memory of the Gandolph trial, she could still summon the photos of the bodies in the restaurant food locker. During the trial, one of the cops had explained that the freezer was vast because of the wide menu Paradise offered. A strange undoing.

"Right," said Raven when she described the case. "Good Gus. But you know the game. I have to plow every row. There are even moments when I'm delusional and think he might be innocent. I have this associate," he said, "she's been tearing this case apart, coming up with amazing stuff. Here, look at this."

From out of his thick case, Raven handed over the first of several sheets of paper. Apparently, he was trying to work up a theory that Gandolph had been in jail on a probation violation at the time of the murders. Few records remained, and Gandolph's rap sheet offered no corroboration. But within the last

few days, Arthur had found a transfer manifest showing that his client had been
transported to court on the morning of July
5, 1991, from the House of Corrections.

"And what does Muriel say to that?"
Gillian asked. Muriel Wynn, who'd been the
junior prosecutor on the case a decade ago,
was now the Chief Deputy P.A. and the
short-odds favorite to succeed Ned Halsey
as the Prosecuting Attorney in next year's
election. Gillian had never cared much for
Muriel, the kind of hard-boiled woman the
felony courthouse produced often these
days. But, truth be told, Gillian's appreciation for prosecutors, even though she had
once been one, had all but disappeared
given her experiences of the last several
years.

"She thinks Rommy's probation officer
must have gone out and collared him that
morning so he didn't blow his court date,"
Arthur said. "I don't buy it on a Friday, right
after a holiday, when nobody wanted to be
working. Muriel also says it's ridiculous to
think that both the client and the defense
lawyer missed the fact that Rommy was in
jail when the murders went down. But he
wasn't arrested until four months after the

crime, and Rommy doesn't know today from tomorrow."

Gillian's wager would have been that Muriel was correct. But she was unwilling to jump into the argument. With Arthur, she felt recalled to a mode of decorum she thought she'd left behind: she was trying to be judicial. Notwithstanding her efforts to respond neutrally, he appeared to detect her skepticism.

"There was a lot of bad evidence," he said. "I know that. I mean, Rommy confessed about twenty times. And Christ could return to earth to testify in my client's behalf and I'd still lose at this stage. But the guy had no history of assaults or armed robberies. Which Molto and Muriel explained at trial by claiming my guy was dusted, and now all the research on PCP says it doesn't correlate to violence. So, you know, there's stuff."

"And how did the Court of Appeals appoint you, Arthur?"

"Beats me. They always figure big law firms have the resources. Besides, someone up there probably remembered I have death-penalty experience from prosecuting Francesco Fortunato."

"The fellow who poisoned his family?"

"Three generations, grandparents through children, and laughed out loud in court every time we mentioned one of their names. Even so, I nearly passed out as the jury read the death sentence. That's when I transferred to Financial Crimes. I'd probably die myself if I had to push the button in the execution chamber, but I still believe in capital punishment in principle."

Oddly, Gillian didn't—not now or before. Too much trouble, in a few words. A decade ago, after Rommy Gandolph's trial was over, his defense lawyer, Ed Murkowski, admitted to her that he'd taken a bench sentencing because he'd heard a rumor about her views. But she wasn't sitting there as a legislator. If any crime warranted execution, Gandolph's did.

"And what is it that you want to know from me, Arthur? If I have second thoughts?" At this point no one would care about her opinion. And she had no doubts anyway about Gandolph's guilt—she'd settled that again in her own mind months ago when the prisoner's letter had arrived from Rudyard. She could still recall another remark Murkowski, Gandolph's lawyer, had passed after sentencing, when all of them, including the prosecutors, had communed in her chambers for a moment now that the awful words had been spoken. Gillian had commented dryly about Gandolph's insanity defense and Ed had responded, 'It was better than the story he had to tell, Judge. That was nothing but a slow guilty plea.'

She had some thought to explain all of that to Arthur, but his black eyes had suddenly dropped to her ashtray, studying the gray remains there as if they were tea leaves. Arthur, she realized, was finally going to get to the point.

"The Court of Appeals is killing me with kindness," he said, "probably because they appointed me. I begged for a chance to do discovery and they sent the matter down to the District Court until June 29th, before they decide whether to permit Gandolph to actually file a new *habeas*. So I'm turning over every stone." He finally ended his studied efforts not to look at her. "Listen, I have to ask. While you sat in Felony, were you doing what got you in trouble later, when you were hearing personal-injury cases?"

She had not been enjoying this conversation much as it was, but now that she recognized the direction, a familiar freeze overcame her.

"Do people say that?"

"Gillian, please don't play games. Or get insulted. I'm doing what I have to do."

"No, Arthur, I wasn't taking money when I heard criminal matters. No one bribed me on Rommy Gandolph's case—or any other case at that time. It began in Common Pleas, where it seemed to be the order of the day." She shook her head once, both at the lunacy of it and because her remark sounded faintly like an excuse.

"All right," he said, but he was plainly applying a lawyer's judgment to her answer, weighing its verity. Watching him calculate, she decided that Arthur did not look particularly well. He was short, and had never appeared especially fit, but he was aging before his time. His dark eyes had retreated into bruised-looking flesh that suggested overwork and poor diet, and his hair was thinning. Worst, he still had an aspect of hound-dog eagerness, as if his tongue at any second might lop out of the corner of his mouth. She recalled then that he had a situation, family trouble, someone chronically sick. Perhaps it had worn him out.

"And what about the drink, Judge?"

"The drink?"

"Did you have an alcohol problem when you sat on Rommy Gandolph's case?"

"No."

"You weren't drinking?"

He was skeptical—justifiably, she knew.

"What do other people say, Arthur?"

"What other people say won't matter much, if you're going to testify that you weren't drinking hard at the time."

"I drank, Arthur. But not to excess."

"Not at that time?"

She flexed her tongue a bit in her mouth. Governed by common understanding, Raven had missed his mark. She could correct him, or say, 'Never,' and see if Arthur eventually wandered to the right place, but she remembered the instructions every skilled lawyer offered in preparing a witness: Answer the question you are asked. Briefly, if possible. Do not volunteer.

"No, not at that time." She tossed her cigarettes into her suede shoulder bag, and snapped it authoritatively. She was ready to go, and asked if Raven was finished. Instead, he took a second to run a thick finger around the rim of his coffee cup.

"I have a personal question," he said at last, "if you don't mind."

He was probably going to ask what everyone wondered. Why? Why had she allowed a life of limitless promise to subside into dependency and, in short order, crime? Raven was too socially awkward to hesitate where courtesy kept others from going, and she felt the familiar iron hand of resentment. Why didn't people understand that it was unfathomable to her? Could anyone who was not, even now, such a thoroughgoing mystery to herself ever have fallen so low? But Raven's concerns were more pedestrian.

"I keep wondering why you came back here. I mean, you're like me, right? Single? No kids?"

Were he uncaged, Raven apparently would have flown away. Yet she felt an impulsive reluctance to compare herself to Arthur. She had been alone, but by choice, and always took it as a temporary condition. She'd been thirty-nine years old the night the federal agents arrived at her door, but a marriage, a family, remained solid figures in the portrait she'd drawn of her future.

"My mother was dying. And the Bureau of Prisons was willing to give me credit for helping take care of her. It was the Bureau's choice, frankly." Like other answers she'd offered Raven, this one, too, was comfortably incomplete. She'd left prison broke—the government and her lawyers had taken everything. And Duffy Muldawer, her 'sponsor' in the parlance of twelve-step programs, had been willing to offer her a place to stay. Even at that, she sometimes shared Raven's puzzlement about why she'd returned to what was, in all senses, the scene of the crime. "Once my community release time is over, I'll probably ask to move."

"She's gone? Your mother?"

"Four months ago."

"I'm sorry."

Gillian shrugged. She had not yet sorted out how she felt about the death of either of her parents—although it had long seemed one of her few strengths that she did not dwell on this sort of thing. She had had a home and a childhood that were worse than many, better than some. There were six kids and two alcoholic parents and a continuing state of rivalry and warfare among all of them. To Gillian, the whole significance of her upbringing was that it had inspired her to go on. It was like coming from Pompeii—the smoldering ruins and poisoned atmosphere could only be fled. Civilization would have to be reinvented elsewhere. She had put her entire faith in two things: intelligence and beauty. She was beautiful and she was smart, and with such assets she had seen no reason to be dragged down by what was behind her. The Jill Sullivan born in that house emerged as the Gillian she had willed into existence. And then destroyed.

"My father died three months ago and I'm still a wreck," Arthur said. His short brow was briefly molded by pain. "He never stopped making me crazy. He was probably the most nervous human being ever to walk the earth. Anxiety should have killed him years ago. But, you know, all that hovering and clucking—I always felt how much he cared." Raven's eyes, stilled by recollection, rose to her, confessing in a darkly plaintive look how rare such persons were in his life. Arthur was like some puppy always sticking his wet nose in your hand. In an instant, even he appeared embarrassed, either by how much he'd revealed or by her evident discomfort. "Why am I telling you this?" he asked.

"Probably because you think someone like me has nothing better to do," she answered.

Her tone was purely conversational, and she thought at first the words must have meant something other than what they seemed to. But they didn't. For a moment the pure brutality of the remark seemed to stun them both. A quiver passed through Raven's doughy face, then he straightened and closed one button on his coat.

"I'm sorry to have bothered you. I made the mistake of thinking we had something in common."

Intent on collecting herself, Gillian found her cigarette pack in its leather case in her purse and lit up again. But her hand shook as she struck the match. Surrendering to shame was such a danger for her. Once it began, she could never climb out from under the mountainous debris. She watched the flame crawl ahead, rendering the gray fiber to cinder. Across the table, she could hear the zipper on Raven's briefcase.

"I may have to subpoena you for deposition," he said.

Touché, she thought. And tear her apart, of course, once he got the opportunity. Deservedly, too.

"Will you accept service by mail?" He asked how to reach her without going through the federal court probation office, and she told him she was living in the basement apartment in Duffy Muldawer's house. Duffy, a former Roman Catholic priest, had been the Chief State Defender in Gillian's courtroom years ago and, as a result, Raven's constant opponent. Yet Arthur did not so much as bother with polite inquiries about Duffy's well-being. Instead, without looking her way, Raven aridly took down Duffy's address in an electronic organizer, one of a million marvels, each smaller than the next, that had become indispensable to Americans in the four and a half years she'd been away. The blue threads of smoke languished between them and a server briefly intervened to ask if either cared for more coffee. Gillian waited for her to go.

"I had no reason to be rude to you, Arthur."

"That's all right, Gillian. I know you always thought I was boring."

She smiled bitterly. But she felt some admiration for Arthur. He'd grown up. He could dish it out now. And he was on the mark. Nonetheless, she tried again.

"I'm not very happy, Arthur. And I suppose it makes me unhappier to see the people I used to know. It's a painful reminder."

That was stupid, of course. Who, after all, was happy? Not Arthur Raven, ungainly, uncomely, alone but for his family trouble, which she now remembered was a sister with mental problems. And no one was concerned with Gillian's emotional state anyway. Not that they doubted she was suffering. But they believed she deserved it.

Without response, Raven rose, stating simply that he would be in touch, and proceeded toward the door. Watching him exit, she caught sight of her reflection in the cheap mirrors, veined in gold, which boxed the posts supporting the restaurant ceiling. She was often startled to see herself, because, generally speaking, she looked so much better than she felt. There was something telling, she realized, about the fact that, like stainless steel, she appeared unharmed by the battering. But she was tall with strong posture, and even time didn't take its toll on good cheekbones. She was losing color by now. Her strawberry-blond hair was a rodent shade, on its way to gray; and, as she'd long found true of fair-skinned persons, she was showing every line, like porcelain. But the fashionable details—a fitted twill suit, a strand of pearls, a hacked-down hairdo spiked with mousse—supported the composed bearing that seemed to radiate from her. It was a look she'd assumed in her teens, as false as the self-portrayal manufactured by most adolescents, but it had never been forsaken, neither the appearance of outward command nor the sense of wanton fraud that went with it.

Certainly, she'd deceived Arthur Raven. She had answered misleadingly, then lashed him, to ensure he didn't linger to learn the truth. Raven had been led astray by rumor, the vicious talk about her that had circulated years ago when her life collapsed. They said she was a lush—but that wasn't so. They said she drank herself silly at lunch and came on the bench half crocked in the afternoon. It was true she'd fallen asleep up there, not just a momentary drowse, but laid her face down on the bench and was so far gone that after the bailiff woke her, she could see the ribbing of her leather blotter impressed on her cheek, when she looked in a mirror. They made fun of her inebriate mumbling and the ugly name-calling that escaped from her. They lamented the squandered brilliance that had put her on the bench at the age of thirty-two, only to drink away the gifts that had led to a Harvard Law School degree. They clucked about her failure to heed the warnings she'd been given repeatedly to sober up. And all the time she kept her secret. Gillian Sullivan was not a drunk, as legend had it, or even a pill popper, which was the suspicion of the court staffers who insisted that they never smelled liquor on her breath. No, Gillian Sullivan, former Deputy Prosecuting Attorney and then Judge of the Superior Court, was a smackhead, a stone doper, a heroin addict.

She did not shoot—she never shot up. As someone who treasured her appearance, even in her most desperate state, she would not deface herself. Instead she smoked heroin—chased the dragon, in the lingo. Tooted. With a pipe, a tube of aluminum foil, she sucked up the fumes as the powder in the heat turned first to brown goo, then pungent delirium. It was slower, minutes rather than seconds until the fabulous flush of pleasure began to take over, but she had been deliberate in everything throughout her life, and this, a sort of executive addiction, fit her image of herself, neater and less detectable—no pox of track marks, none of the telltale nosebleeds from snorting.

It had started with a guy. Isn't that how it always starts? Toby Elias was a gallant, handsome, twisted creature, an assistant in the Attorney General's Office, whom Gillian had some thought of marrying. One night he'd returned home with a hit of heroin lifted from a case he tried. It was 'the taste' one doper had offered another as the prelude to a sale, introduced in evidence, and never returned after the verdict. 'Why not?' he asked. Toby always managed to make perversity stylish. His ironic unwillingness to follow the rules meant for everyone else had beguiled her. They chipped—snorted—the first night, and reduced the quantity each night thereafter. It was an unearthly peace, but nothing that required repetition.

A month later, Toby stepped in front of an 18-wheeler. She never knew if it was an accident. He was not killed. He was a body in a bed for months, and then a dripping wreck in a wheelchair. And she had deserted him. She wasn't married to the man. She couldn't give him her life when he hadn't promised his.

Yet it was a sad turning point, she knew that now. Toby had never recovered and neither had she. Three or four months after that, she'd pinched a taste on her own for the first time. During a trial in front of her, she allowed the defense chemist to open the sealed evidence bag to weigh how much heroin had been seized. The rush seemed more delicious now. She forged opportunities, ordered tests performed when none had been requested, encouraged the prosecutors to lock their exhibits in her chambers overnight rather than tote them back to the P.A.'s Office. Eventually, the tampering was discovered, but a courtroom deputy was suspected and banished to an outlying precinct. After that, she had to score on the street. And she needed money.

By then she was taken for a drunk. As a warning, she'd been transferred from the Felony Trial Division to Common Pleas, tort court, where she heard personal-injury cases. There somebody knew. One of those dopers she'd sentenced had recognized her, a pretty white lady lurking in the bombed-looking blocks less than a mile from the courthouse. He'd told the cop he snitched to. From there, word traveled to the Presiding Judge in Common Pleas, a villain named Brendan Tuohey, and his henchman, Rollo Kosic. Kosic visited her with the news, but offered no corrective. Just money. Take his advice from time to time about the outcome in a case. There would be money.

And she complied, always with regrets, but life by now was the misery between hits. One night there was a knock, a scene out of *1984* or *Darkness at Noon*. The U.S. Attorney and FBI agents were on her doorstep. She'd been nailed, for bribery, not narcotics. She cried and blabbed and tooted as soon as they were gone.

After that night, she'd turned to Duffy, her current landlord, a recovering alcoholic with long experience as a counselor from his days as a priest. She was sober when she was sentenced, her habit the only secret that survived a period in which she otherwise felt she'd been stripped naked and marched in chains down Marshall Avenue. She was not about to revive all of that now, surely not for Arthur Raven or for a murderer who had been beast enough to rape the dead.

Yet the sudden viciousness that had escaped her with Arthur had shaken her, like finding a fissure in the ground under your feet. Seeking to spare herself further shame, she had, instead, compounded it. For hours, she would be dwelling on Raven and the way his mouth had softened to an incredulous little 'o' in the wake of her remark. She would need Duffy tonight, his quiet counsel, to keep her from drowning.

With that much clear, she stood from the small table and caught sight again of herself. To the eye, there was a lean, elegant woman, appointed with care. But within was her truest enemy, a demon self, who, even after imprisonment and disgrace, remained unsatisfied and uncurbed, and, except for its will to see her suffer, unknown.

4

JULY 5, 1991

The Prosecutor

A WAIL, sudden enough to stop Muriel's heart, broke out from the booth across from her as she sat at the soda-fountain counter. A black man in a full-length apron, probably the cook, had slid to his feet and the prospect of his departure seemed to have freshened the anguish of the woman there. Dark and thin, she was melted against him. The younger man, with a glimmering stud in his ear, lingered behind the two haplessly.

"The widow," whispered one of the techs, dusting the front case under the register. "She won't go home."

The cook eased her over to the young fellow, who reluctantly raised an arm to her shoulder, while Mrs. Leonidis carried on fiercely. In one of those moments of cold-blooded clarity for which Muriel was already noted in the P.A.'s Office, she suddenly recognized that Gus's widow was going through the standard gestures of grief as she understood them. The crying, the shrieking was her duty. A more genuine reaction to her husband's death, true mourning, or even relief, would come long from now in private.

Since the day she'd started as a prosecutor, Muriel had had an instinct for the survivors of violence. She was not sure how connected she'd been to her parents, or whether any man, including her dead husband, had ever mattered to the quick. But she cared for these victims with the radiant nuclear fury of the sun. It had not taken her long to see that their suffering arose not merely from their loss but also from its imponderable nature. Their pain was not due to some fateful calamity like a typhoon, or an enemy as fickle and unreasoning as disease, but to a human failure, to the demented will of an assailant and the failure of the regime of reason and rules to contain him. The victims were especially entitled to think this should never have happened—because, according to the law, it shouldn't have.

When Mrs. Leonidis was again under some control, she marched past Muriel to the Ladies'. The young man, who had escorted her halfway, cast Muriel a sheepish look as the rest-room door closed.

"I can't talk to her," he explained. "My sisters are on the way from out of town. They'll get her out of here. Nobody listens to me." Soft-looking and skittish, the young man was balding early and his hair was cropped as closely as an army recruit's. Up close, Muriel could see that his eyes and nose were raw. She asked if he too was related to Gus.

"*The* son," he said, with gloomy emphasis. "The Greek son." He found some bitter humor in what he had said. He introduced himself as John Leonidis and offered a clammy hand. When Muriel had responded with her name and job title, John suddenly brightened.

"Thank God," he said. "That's what my ma is waiting for, to talk to the prosecutor." He slapped at his pockets until he realized he was already holding a pack of Kools. "Can I ask you something?" He took a seat on the stool beside her. "Am I a suspect?"

"A suspect?"

"I don't know, there's all kinds of stuff in

my head. The only person I can think of who'd want to kill Gus is me."

"Did you?" Muriel asked, conversationally.

John Leonidis fixed on the glowing end of his cigarette. His nails had been nibbled to ragged slivers.

"I'd never have had the balls," he said. "But you know, all this 'good' stuff. It was P.R. At home, he was a pig. Like he made my mother cut his toenails? Can you imagine? In the summer, he'd sit like a sultan on the back porch in the sun while she did it. I mean, it could make you vomit."

John gave his head a bitter toss, and then, with little warning, he began to cry. Muriel had been out of sorts with her own father before he died two years ago, and she had an instant appreciation of the tornado of confusion buffeting John. Tom Wynn had been President of the UAW local at the Ford plant outside Fort Hill, and a field rep, a man who spoke brotherhood in the plant and bile at home. Following his death, after too brief an interval, Muriel's mother had married the principal of the school where she taught, but she was happier in love now than Muriel had ever been. Like John, Muriel had been left to labor with the stillborn emotions that accompanied everything unfinished with her father. As John struggled for his composure, pinching the bridge of his nose, Muriel laid her hand over his on the marked Formica of the counter.

By the time John's mother emerged from the rest room, he had gathered himself. As he had predicted, when he introduced Muriel as "the prosecutor," Athena Leonidis, who only a moment before had been wilted by grief, stiffened to deliver her message.

"They should be dead, I want them dead," she said, "the filth who did this to my Gus. Dead. With my own eyes. I will not sleep till I see." She dissolved again and fell upon her son, who, over his mother's shoulder, cast Muriel another bleak look.

But she understood Mrs. Leonidis. Muriel, too, believed in punishment. Her mother, the teacher, was the touchy-feely type, turn the other cheek, but Muriel had always agreed with her father, who defended some of the bare-knuckles maneuvers of life in the union by saying that humans were not going to be good on their own, they needed some encouragement. In an ideal world, you'd give everybody who lived right a medal. Yet there was neither tin nor time enough to do that in this life. Thus, another kind of object lesson was required so that the good got something for their efforts. Pain had to be wrought upon the body of the bad. Not because there was any special delight in their suffering. But because there was pain in goodness—the pangs of denial, the blistering under the hand of restraint. The good deserved an even trade. Murder required death. It was part of the fundamental reciprocity that was the law.

The Detective Commander, Harold Greer, appeared. He encouraged Mrs. Leonidis to go home, but it was Muriel he wanted. Greer introduced himself back in Gus's small office.

"I've been waiting for somebody from the P.A.'s Office for two hours. Tommy Molto's nowhere to be found." Molto, the head of Homicide, had recently regained his job in a civil suit, after being fired for supposedly framing a defendant. No one yet knew quite what to make of Tommy. "Larry says you're smart."

Muriel hitched a shoulder. "Consider the source."

Sober by nature, Greer nonetheless managed a spirited laugh. Larry probably never had a boss he didn't turn into a rival.

"Well, if you're smart enough to get a search warrant on a holiday weekend, you're smart enough for me," said Greer.

She ended up making notes on the back of one of the green tablets of order tickets the waitstaff used. Harold needed warrants for the cars in the parking lot, and, as a double-check, the houses of Gus's staff. Before they parted, Muriel felt obliged to repeat John Leonidis's remarks about wanting to kill his father.

"Hell," said Harold and frowned. Nobody liked having to beat up on the bereaved.

"It's just the shock," said Muriel. "You know how it is. Families?"

"Right," said Greer. He had a family, too. "Get me those warrants, huh? And give me your phone numbers in case I need something else."

She had no clue where she'd find a judge to sign a warrant at 4 p.m. Friday on a holiday weekend. When Harold left, she remained in the tiny office, feeling saddened by the proximity of Gus's personal things, while she phoned felony judges at home. Gillian Sullivan, Muriel's last choice, sounded, as usual, well sauced and sleepy, but she was available. Muriel headed for the office in the County Building, where she'd have to type up the warrants herself.

She was excited. In the P.A.'s Office, there was a standing rule: once you touched a case it was yours. The maxim kept deputies from dumping their dogs, and political heavyweights from clouting their way onto plum assignments. Even so, she'd probably be stuck as third chair, because it would be a capital prosecution. Only if John and Athena were the kind to say no more killing would the P.A. hesitate to seek execution, and the Leonidis family clearly was not in that frame of mind. So it would be a trial— no one pled to capital murder—a big one. Muriel would see her name on the front page of the *Tribune* before this was over. The prospect sparked the nerves all over her body.

As a child, she'd had a prolonged fear of dying. She would lie in bed trembling, realizing that the whole long journey to grow up would only bring her closer to that point of terrifying blackness at the end. In time, though, she accepted her mother's counsel. There was only one way out—to make your mark, to leave some trace behind that would not be vaporized by eternity. A hundred years from now, she wanted somebody to look up and say, 'Muriel Wynn, she did good things, we're all better off now.' She never thought that would be easy. Hard work and risk were part of the picture. But obtaining justice for Gus, for all these people, was important, part of the never-ending task of setting her shoulder to the bulwark and holding back the grisly impulses that would otherwise engulf the world.

Leaving, she found Larry on the pavement in front of the restaurant, holding off Stanley Rosenberg, the rodent-faced investigative reporter from Channel 5. Stanley kept wheedling, no matter how many times Larry told him to talk to Greer, and finally Starczek, who generally had little use for journalists, simply turned away.

"Fucking vulture," he said to Muriel, who walked beside him. Their cars were in the same direction. She could feel the grimness they'd left back there lingering with her on the gray streets, like an odor that stayed in your clothing.

"So Harold hired you?"

"You do good work," she said. They'd reached her Honda. She thanked Larry circumspectly and said "See ya," but he reached for her arm.

He said, "So who is it?"

When she finally caught the drift, she told him to forget it.

"Hey, you think I'm not gonna hear?"

They went a few more rounds before she gave in.

"Talmadge," she finally said.

"Talmadge *Lor*-man?"

"Really, Larry. In your whole entire life, how many other people named Talmadge have you met?"

Talmadge, a former Congressman and now a renowned business lawyer and lobbyist, had been their Contracts professor when Larry and Muriel were in law school. Three years ago, Talmadge's wife had died at forty-one of breast cancer. Having shared a spouse's untimely death had drawn Muriel and him together. The relationship sparked, but it was off-and-on, which was how it always seemed to go with Muriel and men. Lately, though, they'd been gathering momentum. With both daughters in college now, Talmadge was tired of being alone. And she enjoyed the force field around him—epical events always seemed to be at hand when you were with Talmadge.

"You're really going to marry Talmadge Lorman?"

"We're not getting married. I told you I had a feeling this might, maybe, could, perhaps, probably-not lead to something. It's a million miles from that right now. I just wanted to give you the heads-up about why I won't come running when you whistle."

"Whistle?"

Perhaps it was the conversation, which seemed weird on both ends, but she felt a fugue state grip her, as if she were hovering over the scene, outside the person of Muriel. Often in the last few years she'd had moments like this, where the real and true Muriel seemed to be there but unde-tectable, a tiny kernel of something that existed but had no visible form. She'd been the usual pain-in-the-rear teenager, who thought the entire world was a fraud, and in some ways she'd never gotten over that. She knew that everybody was in it for themselves. That's what had drawn her to the law—she relished the aspect of the advocate's role that required her to rip through everyone's poses. Yet the same convictions made it hard to cross the breach with anybody else.

That was what seemed to bring Larry back time and again on the merry-go-round—she knew him. He was smart—smarter than nice—and she enjoyed his jaundiced humor, and his equally sure sense of her. He was a big man, Polish and German in terms of his background, with innocent blue eyes, a big, round face, and blondish hair he was starting to lose. Masculine, you'd say, rather than handsome, but full of primal appeal. Playing around with him was the kind of screwball whim that marked her earlier years, when she thought it was a riot to be the wild child. But he was married—and a cop to the core. Now she told herself again what she'd told him—she had to move on.

She looked down the street to be certain they were unobserved, and took hold of one button on his shirt, a loose acetate number he wore under a poplin sport coat. She gave it a final familiar tug, a request, at close quarters, for mercy. Then she started her car. The engine turned over, and her heart picked up when she remembered the case.

5

Running Leads

ON HIS WAY to DuSable Field to ask more questions about Luisa Remardi, Larry stopped off in the Point to see a house. About ten years ago, right after he'd worked the murder of a real estate broker, Larry got into rehabbing, turning over a property every eighteen months or so for a pretty good dollar. When he was younger, he'd regarded law enforcement as a way station. He loved the work, but until he dropped out of law school and accepted the Force as Kismet, he'd envisioned some higher destiny for himself among the power elite. These days, whatever visions of stature he retained rested on real estate.

On a mild fall afternoon, Larry pondered the house, which a broker had tipped him would be listed later this week. The Point, long a sanctuary for Kindle County's small African-American middle class, had begun attracting singles and young families of all races looking for better deals on houses close to Center City. This place, a big Victorian, was a Yuppie magnet if ever there was one. It had been split into apartments, but many of the original features remained intact, including the square widow's walks surrounding the belfries on each end, and the original spear-topped cast-iron fence in which yellow leaves were now trapped in soft heaps.

There was also a great sunny corner out front where he could bed zinnias, nasturtiums, dahlias, gladioli, marigolds, and mums, so there'd be blooms from May to October. Over time, he'd discovered that money invested in planting returned three-to-one in enhanced curb appeal. Oddly, the gardening had slowly become perhaps his favorite side of the endeavor. His father's father was a farmer in Poland. And now Larry was back there. What he loved was that it dialed him in on stuff that never mattered before. In the middle of the winter, he'd think about the frost in the soil, the microbes that were dying, and the nurturing snow. He kept track of the angle of the sun, and changed his mind each day about whether he wanted rain. The earth was beneath the street—that was how he always thought about it.

It was well past 4 p.m. when he approached the airport. The Task Force that Harold Greer had assembled at Paradise had stormed through the Tri-Cities for about five weeks, but as Larry had anticipated, Greer had no luck running an investigation out of police headquarters in the great, stone edifice of McGrath Hall. That was nothing but a medieval palace, full of rumors about who was humping who and which undeserving jerk the Chief and the commanders were favoring. No serious police work went on there, except the persistent cop pastimes of politicking and grousing. In August, the FBI thought they had grabbed the right guy in Iowa. It didn't prove out, but by then most of the detectives had headed back to their old stuff. So far as Larry could tell, he was the only dick on the Task Force still generating reports more often than every couple of weeks.

Luisa had proved enigmatic enough to maintain his interest. Even the autopsy had raised questions about the precise circumstances of her death. Around her anus, Painless had identified a number of superficial linear tears marked by faint streaks of blood. Dead people didn't bleed. Larry's current theory was that she'd succumbed to a first sexual violation, hoping to save her life. But what did Judson, the third victim who eventually dragged her body downstairs, do while Luisa was being assaulted? Had an accomplice held a gun on him?

By now, Larry had parked in front of the huge Administrative Center TN Air had recently completed. With the advent of shorter-stopping jets, Trans-National had reinitiated service at DuSable, serving a distinctive target market, namely businessmen and gamblers. The airline offered no-frills fares to other Midwestern cities, and to Las Vegas and Atlantic City, where planes flew twenty-four hours a day. The program had been an astonishing success. Three other national carriers had bought gates, and the county airport authority had authorized a huge expansion, hoping to relieve the round-the-clock mess at the massive Tri-Cities Airport. The major hotel and restaurant chains were breaking ground nearby and TN, to much fanfare, had recently opened this new Administrative Center, where, five years ago, a deserted housing project had stood. The concrete structure had a glass atrium attached to the front in the shape of a rolling pin. It was typical new construction—thin walls and bright lights. Larry didn't go much for modern.

He had asked TN Security to arrange another interview of Genevieve Carriere, a ticket agent whom everyone referred to as Luisa's best friend. Nancy Diaz, a former Kindle County copper, like most of the Security staff, had Genevieve in her office when Larry arrived, and Nancy left Larry alone with her while Nancy headed off to cover something else.

"Erno wants to talk to you when you're done," Nancy told him from the door. Erno Erdai was the Deputy Head of Security at the airline, and ran the show out here. Larry had known Erno for years—they had started in the Academy together—but Erno hadn't bothered to greet him the first couple of times Larry had come snooping around. Erno always wanted Larry to know how big he'd gotten.

Nancy's interior office had a desk with wood-grained laminate and intense fluorescent glow to make up for the lack of windows. In her persimmon uniform, Genevieve sat with her legs crossed at the ankles, demure as a schoolteacher, which she had formerly been. She was putting her husband through med school, and had found it easier, and better paying, to work the graveyard shift out here, so she could be home during the day with their one-year-old. A trifle plump, with a small silver cross at her throat, Genevieve had a round-cheeked look, accentuated by a bit of an overbite. She'd been raised to lift her chin and look folks in the eye when she spoke to them, and Larry thought he'd detected the quiver of something unspoken when he'd interviewed her two and a half months ago.

They talked about her baby for a second. Larry had questioned her last time at her station, where a leather threefold with photos had been propped on the counter. Today, Larry told her he wanted to ask about money.

"Money?" replied Genevieve. "We don't know much about money. I wish we knew a little bit more."

"No," said Larry, "Luisa's money."

Genevieve found that even more confusing. She said that Carmine, Luisa's ex,

shorted her most months and Luisa was always stretched. Luisa had lived with her
elderly mother and her two daughters.
About five years ago, she'd transferred out
to DuSable from the big airport and worked
alternating flex shifts with Genevieve, 8 p.m.
to 6 a.m. one day, 6 p.m. to midnight the
next, the only agent on duty when the
planes to and from Las Vegas turned
around. The schedule enabled Luisa to get
her girls off to school in the morning and see
them when they returned, even to be home
on odd nights for dinner. She slept during
the day.

As described in Larry's interviews, Luisa
came across as a spunky city girl, caught in
a familiar pinch. She'd had Carmine's babies
and then been ditched—maybe she'd put
on a few pounds, maybe she reminded
Carmine in the wrong way of his mother, or
hers. Once he was gone, Luisa was left with
a big-time mortgage on their four-bedroom
dream house on the West Bank, but she was
determined not to make her daughters suffer for their father's stupidity. The result was
debt. Lots. Larry counted a $30,000 dent in
her credit cards as of a year ago. Then she
began sending her entire paycheck to the

bank. So how was she paying for things like groceries and school supplies? Cash, it turned out. Luisa had cash in hand wherever she went.

If there was another Homicide detective who knew how to tear up somebody's finances, Larry hadn't met him yet, and he felt a certain amount of pride as he laid the documents he'd retrieved from the banks over a number of months on the desk in front of Genevieve. Luisa figured for Genevieve's wild friend—more bad words in Luisa's mouth, more nights in the clubs, more guys in her bed than Genevieve had ever dared. He suspected Genevieve had done a lot of listening, but now she shook her head in wonder.

"I never heard anything about this. I swear."

When you saw too much folding money, it figured to be something unholy and Larry had pounded the names of everybody in Luisa's address book into NCIC, the FBI's national criminal database, with no hits. But he tried out a less scandalous explanation on Genevieve. Was there, perhaps, an older gentleman in Luisa's life?

"If there was," Genevieve answered, "I

didn't hear about it. She didn't have much use for men. Not after Carmine. Not for relationships anyway. You know, she'd party on Saturday night, but she never mentioned any sugar daddy."

"Any other activities or associates that might explain the cash?"

"Like?"

"Drugs?" Larry awaited any tell, but Genevieve seemed sincerely taken aback. "There's this item in her personnel jacket," Larry explained. In the name of aircraft safety, all TN employees were required to pee in a cup every quarter. Two months before her death, Luisa had come up dirty. Then, while TN Security was investigating, they'd received an anonymous tip that she'd been selling on the premises. The union steward was called in and Security demanded a pat-down search to which Luisa had succumbed only over furious objection. The search came up dry and, on second submission, her dirty result proved to be a false-positive. Yet once Larry saw her cash, he'd begun thinking there might have been something to it after all. An airport employee was in a unique position to help import drugs.

Genevieve had a different theory.

"It was a setup," she said. "I heard all about it. Lu was outraged. She didn't have a bad drop in ten years with the airline. Then they search her? How fishy is that?"

"Well, who set her up, then?"

"Luisa had a mouth. You know how that goes. She probably irritated somebody."

"Any guess who?"

Genevieve looked to Larry as if she might have had a name or two in mind, but she wasn't about to make Luisa's mistake of speaking out of turn. He tried several ways to get her to spill, but she maintained that pleasant little smile and kept rolling her eyes. It was getting late. He didn't want to miss Erno, so he let Genevieve go, saying he might contact her again. She did not appear especially excited by the prospect. It was an unfortunate aspect of his job that he often antagonized people like Genevieve who he actually thought were all right. Did Genevieve know where Luisa's cash came from? Seventy-three percent of Americans in our poll said, Yes. But she was clearly convinced it had nothing to do with Luisa's murder. One way or the other, Genevieve was probably guarding her friend's memory, and Larry actually respected her for that. Maybe a mobbed-up uncle was helping out. Maybe Luisa's mom, an Old World type, was running numbers in her former neighborhood in Kewahnee, or, more likely, bailing out her daughter with cash Momma had long kept in her mattress.

He spent a few minutes circling a potted plant outside Erno's door before the secretary showed him in. TN's Head of Security was stationed out at the big airport, making Erno the honcho here, and he had one of those offices too big for the furniture they gave him. The light from the large windows glazed his desk on which nothing rested, not even dust.

"Can I ask?" Erno said, when they were settled. "The suits in Center City always like to hear it first, if they're gonna read about anybody around here being naughty."

Erno had been smuggled out of Hungary in 1956, after the Russkies hanged his father from the lamppost in front of the family house, and a trace accent still played through his speech like incongruous background music, elongating certain vowels and sticking other sounds far back in his throat. It was essential to Erno's character to act as if nobody would notice. He was one of those guys who always wanted to sound like he was on the inside, and given that, it figured he'd be scratching around to find out what Larry had come up with. But his curiosity gave Larry leverage. Instead of answering, Larry flipped open a small spiral-topped notepad and said he wasn't getting the skinny on the narcotics search referenced in Luisa's personnel file. Considering the price of admission, Erno wiggled his mouth around and finally scooted forward so he could place both elbows on his desktop.

"I wouldn't want you to write this down," he said, "but I think my boys got a little rambunctious. This young lady, Luisa, from what I hear, she was Excedrin headache number 265. You've seen her evaluations in the file. You know, 'Insubordinate.' It's misspelled several times. I think she got pretty ornery when she come up dirty, enough to make a suspicious guy more suspicious."

Erno offered the last with a wry look. He was suggesting his guys had made up the 'tip' as an excuse for the search. It happened on the street all the time. Genevieve had this one right: Luisa had talked her way into trouble.

"So that's a zero?"

"Dry hole," said Erno authoritatively. He reached into a desk drawer and placed a toothpick in the side of his mouth. Erno was nervous and slender. He had a narrow face, a long thin nose, and eyebrows so pale you could barely see them. To Larry, he'd always been a hard man to like. There was an edge to Erno and a frequent sour frown, like he'd smelled some stink, which might well have been you. He probably would have made an all-right cop, smart enough and serious about the job, but he never got that far. While he was still in the Academy, he got into a domestic situation where he shot and killed his mother-in-law. The coroner's inquest had included testimony from Erdai's wife, who confirmed that the old lady had come after Erno with a knife, but the brass on the Force would not bring on a guy who'd killed with his service revolver even before he had a star.

In the strange way things go, this had been an okay break for Erno. Some coppers from the Academy hooked him up with the security department at TN. He kept peace at the airport, helped Customs nab smuggled drugs, and tried to make sure nobody stole a free ride on an airplane. He went to work in a suit and tie. These days, he had a nice house in the suburbs and a pension plan and airline stock, and a large staff of ex-coppers under him. He'd done fine. But for years he'd remained a wanna-be, hanging around at Ike's, the Tri-Cities' best-known cop bar. He craved the weapon and the star and the stamp of a certified tough guy. He'd nibble at a beer, taking in the coppers' stories with the same look of middle-aged woe about things he'd missed out on that a lot of people showed at this stage, maybe, even, including Larry.

"What's your angle with the dope, any-way?" Erno asked. "I thought Greer was figuring she's popped by Stranger Danger. Wrong time, wrong place."

"Probably. But your girl Luisa, she had some big money coming in."

That seemed to pep up Erno. Erno, in Larry's experience, was one of those hunkies with a strong interest in money, especially his own. He didn't really boast; when he talked about his stock options, he was more like a guy telling you about his low cholesterol. Ain't I lucky? He reminded Larry of some of his elderly Polish relatives, who could give you the case history on every dollar they'd ever made or spent. It was an Old World thing, money equaling security. Being a Homicide dick taught you two things about that. First, people died for money; the only thing they died for more often was love. And second, there was never money enough when the bogeyman rang your doorbell.

"From where's she getting money?" Erno said.

"That's what I wanted to ask you guys. She stealing something?"

Erno turned sideways to consider the question. Across the street, on the north-south runway, a 737 was settling down like a duck onto a pond. The plane, a screaming marvel of rivets and aluminum, sank toward the tarmac a few degrees off center, but alighted uneventfully. Larry figured Erno's windows for triple-pane, because there was barely a sound.

"She wasn't ripping tickets, if that's what you're thinking," Erdai answered.

"I was wondering more whether she had her hand in the till."

"No chance. Accounting's way too tight when we get cash."

"And why not tickets?"

"Tickets? That's the best thing around here to steal. One piece of paper can be worth a thousand on the street. But people always get caught." Erno outlined procedures. Agents issued tickets, usually by computer or sometimes by hand. The ticket wasn't valid unless the issuing agent was identified, either by way of a personal computer code or, for the hand tickets, through the agent's own die, a metal plate which fit in a machine like a credit card imprinter that was used to validate blank ticket stock. "Anytime somebody travels, accounting matches up the flight coupon with the payment. No payment, my phone rings. And the issuing agent, that's the first door you knock on."

"So? Your phone ringing?"

"One, two tickets now and then. But you know, nothing that's gonna make thousands for somebody, if that's what we're talking. No missing die. That'd be a biggie. The airline's a bear on this stuff. Lock you up and sue you, they don't care if it's a buck ninety-five. Zero tolerance. It works, too. They got everybody scared shitless. How'd your talk go with Genevieve? She got any clue where Luisa was hiding her money tree?"

Larry grunted. "Three monkeys."

"Really?" Erno made a face.

"Really. Any chance she was into the same shit as Luisa?"

"Never say never—but I'll say it anyway. Too goody-goody. Follows every rule. Why not lay a grand jury subpoena on her? Somebody like that won't stiff you, once you make her swear an oath to God. I bet if you squeeze her, you'll find out what Luisa was up to."

It was an idea, and Larry wrote it down in his notebook, but Muriel and Tommy Molto wouldn't sign off. The grand jury meant defense lawyers who'd start howling about busting on nice white people for no better reason than a hunch.

Erno asked what else Larry was thinking.

"Well, there isn't that much left, right?" Larry said. "I don't see Luisa keeping a book—especially with half the people coming through here on their way to Las Vegas."

Erno acknowledged the logic of that.

"So what kind of problems do you have?" Larry asked him.

"Right now, this is still a small town. Our biggest issue is the bums in the winter. You know, these pooches who're on the street in the North End want a warm place to hide out. We got these guys everywhere—in the johns, hiding in back on the baggage claim carousels. They steal, they scare people, they puke on the floor."

"Any hookers?"

There were a lot of lonely travelers looking for company. A young lady like Luisa, in her airline attire, might pass for somebody's fantasy of a flight attendant—lunchtime, coffee break, after work, the dead of night when nothing was doing anyway. But as Erno pointed out, there was barely any hotel space around here for a young lady in that line of work to ply her trade.

"I wouldn't say you've been a fuck of a lot of help," said Larry.

Erno pushed his tongue into the side of his mouth, which in his case was what passed for a smile.

"Actually," he said, gesturing with the toothpick, "I may have one thing for you. I don't even know if I oughta be mentioning it. There's a kid—well, he's no kid—there's a guy I know. Well, not a guy, not just a guy. To be straight with you, Larry, he's my fucking nephew. You wouldn't necessarily know that when you see him."

"Not as good-looking?"

"No, he's good-looking. His dad was a big good-looking stud, and he's a big good-looking stud, too. But he's a different tint than you and me."

"Ah," said Larry.

"My sister, you know—when I was a kid in the South End, all the old guys were ever on about was running the Nubians outta town. You know, we had 'em on three sides, and it's like we don't want them brown bastards, with their drugs and whoring. *Fekete*. Dark. That's the word in Hungarian. All the time, *'Fekete!'* like it's cussing. So naturally, there are chicks, they get to the age when it's, Fuck you, Momma, Daddy, and all this Roman Catholic bullshit. Their idea of living dangerous is to give it up as fast as they can for the first black guy to say howdy-do. My kid sister, Ilona, she's one of these hunky broads, just couldn't stuff enough black meat into her cannoli.

"So this is how my nephew stumbles into the world. My parents, you know, they can't figure who to kill first, my sister or themselves, so right from the jump, it's the big brother, Yours Truly, who's giving them a helping hand. And that's a soap opera with about six hundred installments. You got time for the skinny version? It'll help make sense of the rest of it."

"I'll put in for overtime," said Larry.

"Well, the kid, you know, he's a brown-skinned fatherless bastard, just to put it in a nutshell. The old neighborhood don't have much use for him and he got even less use for the neighborhood. My sister, she means to do right and only makes things worse. She sends him to public school, instead of Saint Jerome's, so he's not the only black kid, and soon enough, that's what he is, a black kid, talking just like them and running with the gangs and the dope. And I'm all the time like a guy with his hand in a fire, trying to pull him out. First conviction is T's and Blues"—a prescription painkiller and cough syrup, the cheap high in the '80s before crack—"I go to the Favor Bank and get him the Honor Farm.

"But you know, I think it's in the genes with those people, I really do. He keeps going back down. With the drugs, of course. He's tried them all. And potential? Bright. But you know the race thing—it bugs him. He hates his ma, he despises me. We can't tell him what to do because we don't know what it's like, being a black man in white America. Oh, he can give you every asshole speech you ever heard. I had him working out here when we opened back up, but he needs to be a flipping executive, not some house darkie standing by the metal detectors, besides he wants to travel. Join the army, right? He's dishonorable out of the service in eight months—drugs, natch—so we send him to the old country. That ain't his roots, he says, and bugs out for Africa. But guess what? Nobody plays basketball, not old home week there either. So he comes back, and says he's ready to be a grown-up. Decided he wants to work in the industry after all."

"The industry?"

"Air travel. See the world and get paid for it. That's downright hilarious, because all the airlines do big-time dope screening, they'd sooner hire an orangutan than a kid with a drug felony. But I know a lot of the big travel agencies after all this time. So I just about wear out my knees, but he gets hired on at Time To Travel, and God strike me dead, he does okay. Collins—that's his name, Collins—Collins gets his associate's degree, and his agent's license. He likes wearing a coat and tie. He likes talking to people. He's good with the computers. He gets promoted to an actual agent, instead of a gofer. And for about five minutes I thought to myself, This might work, this kid might make it. And of course he gets fucked up on drugs again and cracked for selling. That's a three-fer. The first conviction gets reinstated. He does eighteen months. And in this state, he loses his travel agent license.

"The last part, I swear, when he got out, that irritated him more than his time inside. I tell him to move, get away from the influences. There are thirty-six states where he's still certified as an agent. But you know the end by now. I got the call last week. He's over in County."

"The jail or the hospital?"

"Crossbars Motel."

"For?"

"Buy-bust."

"How much?"

"Six zones, as they say." Six ounces. "Class X."

"That's tough."

"Terrible tough. This'll make him Triple X." Triple X, three felony convictions for narcotics, would mean life in prison, no parole, unless Erno's nephew offered something to prosecutors. Larry still couldn't see where this was going. Erno knew plenty of guys in Narcotics whose ring he could kiss.

"He'll have to find his tongue, I'd say," Larry told Erno.

"Yeah, well, those gangbangers he did business with—he'll look like punchboard, that's what he figures, if he snitches out any of them. But he might have something else. You know, he calls me whenever he gets it in the wringer. I tell myself not to pick up the phone anymore, but what can you do? Yesterday he's crying and carrying on, and in the middle of it he says he heard something or saw something on your case."

"This case?"

"That's what he says. He says he saw a guy with jewelry. And he thinks the jewelry belonged to one of your vics."

"Which one?"

"Didn't ask. I heard you were coming, I promised I'd mention it. Truth is, knowing Collins like I do, it's probably jailhouse bullshit—Rudy told Trudy who told Judy. But if it's actually something, Larry, if he hands it to you, you got to get him out from under."

"I don't have any problem with that," said Larry, "but he better hit the bull's-eye."

"It'd be a first," said Erno.

Larry took the name—Collins Farwell. The light was fading when he left the building, and across the street another jet with the zigzag TN logo on the tail drove itself up into the sky with shuddering force. For no reason he could think of at first, Larry was happy. Then it came to him: he had to call Muriel Wynn.

6

MAY 15, 2001

Gillian's Letter

COMING IN FROM THE RAIN, Gillian Sullivan looked as she always had to Arthur Raven, collected and serenely beautiful. She shook out her umbrella in the vast reception area of O'Grady, Steinberg, Marconi and Horgan and handed over her slick plastic raincoat. Her short, hedgehog hair had wilted a little in the damp air, but she was carefully dressed in a dark, tailored suit.

Arthur led her to a conference room dominated by a green granite table, veined in white. Through the steel-frame windows of the IBM Building, the River Kindle, three dozen floors below, was scaled in the dwindling light. Gillian had phoned yesterday, stating without elaboration that there was a matter to discuss, ending the conversation with one more apology for her rudeness the last time they'd met. Arthur had told her the incident was forgotten. It was his ingrained habit to shirk off the hurt arising from his dealings with women, and in this case, like many others, he might even have brought her reactions on himself. You couldn't really expect somebody to be polite, after you'd suggested they'd been too drunk or venal to care about another life.

He lifted a phone to summon Pamela. In the interval, he asked Gillian if she was working.

"I'm selling cosmetics at Morton's."

"How is that?"

"I spend the day delivering compliments of questionable sincerity. There's a check every two weeks, most of which, candidly, has gone to replenishing my wardrobe. But I feel competent. Makeup and clothing were probably the only other subjects I knew well besides law."

"You were always glamorous," said Arthur.

"I never felt glamorous."

"Oh, you were regal up there. You were. Really. I had a crush on you," Arthur offered. He felt like a schoolboy standing at the corner of the teacher's desk, but his embarrassment actually evoked a passing smile from her. Of course, 'crush' was not quite the right word. Arthur's attractions were seldom that innocuous. His fantasies were vivid, passionate, and utterly consuming. Every six months or so for most of his life since the age of twelve or thirteen he had fallen desperately for some glorious, unattainable female, who lingered in his mind like a mirage. Gillian Sullivan, the courthouse glamour girl, physically striking, intellectually formidable, had been a natural for this role, and he was smitten not long after he had been assigned to her courtroom. At sidebars or in an instruction conference, when he was close to the judge, always fastidiously assembled and powerfully scented, he had often been obliged to position his yellow pad strategically to hide an oncoming erection. He was hardly the only Deputy P.A. intensely aware of Gillian's carnal appeal. Mick Goya, in his cups at a tavern near the courthouse, had once watched Gillian pass by, cool and elegant as a palm. 'I would fuck a wall,' he'd said, 'if I thought she was behind it.'

Even after Gillian's long fall from her pinnacle, she continued to have an effect on Arthur. Her troubles had left her thin enough to be called skinny, but she looked far better than when he'd last seen her years ago, pale and addled by drink. Being himself, he had actually been excited by the notion of her visit.

Pamela arrived and shook hands quite formally without really managing a smile. Sentencing Rommy to death would have been enough to win Gillian a place on Pamela's enemies list, but the young woman had been appalled when Arthur had explained Gillian's circumstances. A judge taking bribes! Observing Pamela's frosty demeanor, Arthur realized that Gillian must have frequently encountered such reactions, especially when she wandered into the sanctuaries of the law. It was brave of her to come.

The three sat together at the end of the granite table where the coppery light fell. To Pamela, Arthur had speculated that his meeting with Judge Sullivan ten days ago had probably dislodged some detail from her memory. Instead Gillian opened the clasp on her handbag.

"I have something I think you should see." She held a white business envelope. Even before she slid it toward Arthur, he recognized its markings. In the upper left corner,

the return address of the Rudyard penitentiary was printed, with the inmate's pen
number handwritten below.

Inside was a letter dated in March of this
year, carefully printed by hand on two yellow
sheets. As Arthur read, Pamela stood over
his shoulder.

Dear Judge,
My name is Erno Erdai. I am an inmate
at the Maximum Security Facility at
Rudyard, doing ten on an agg battery,
for shooting a man in self-defense. My
out-date is in 4/02, but I don't expect to
see it, as I've had some cancer and am
not in the best of health. You probably
wouldn't remember, but I used to be
Associate Chief of Security at TN Air in
charge at DuSable Field and came into
your courtroom a couple of times when
we filed complaints about stuff at the
airport, mostly unruly passengers. Any-
way, I'm not trying to stroll down
memory lane, although I have plenty of
time for such things, if you ever care to.
(That's a joke.)
Why I am writing is because I have
some information concerning a case

that was before you where you sentenced a man to death. He is on the Condemned Unit down here, and is actually the next one scheduled to take The Walk, so this is kind of urgent because I expect what I have to say will make a big difference in whether that happens.

This is not the kind of thing I want to talk to just anybody about, and frankly I'm having a hell of a time getting the right people to pay any attention. A couple years back, I wrote to the Detective on the case, Larry Starczek, but he's not interested in me now that I can't do him any good. I also wrote the State Defender's Office, but those people don't answer their clients' letters, let alone from some con they never heard of. Maybe it's just because I spent all these years being half a cop, but I never met a defense lawyer I liked or trusted all that much. You might have had better experiences. But I'm off the subject.

If you hadn't of had your problem, I probably would have contacted you a while ago. I heard you were out and from my way of thinking I'm probably happier to talk to you now. Cons don't judge. I'm hoping you're willing to take the trouble to straighten out something where you didn't have all the right information. The mail I send from here gets screened—you probably know that yourself—so I'd rather not put any more in writing. You can never tell how people around here are going to react to stuff. It's a distance, but you should come down to hear this yourself. If you look me in the eye, you'll know I'm not fooling around.

Very Truly Yours,
Erno Erdai

Pamela had gripped Arthur's shoulder—probably when she reached the line about this prisoner having information that would make a big difference in whether the next execution occurred—and as a result he felt the need to preach caution to her again. This letter didn't even mention Rommy. And there was no end to the attention-seeking antics of inmates who were, literally, the worst people around.

Gillian was awaiting their reactions. Arthur

asked if she had any memory of this Erno Erdai, but she shook her head.

"And why are you sure he's talking about my client?" he added.

"I only issued two death sentences, Arthur, and Texas executed the other man, McKesson Wingo, a long time ago. Besides, Starczek wasn't the detective on that case."

He turned to Pamela, expecting jubilation, but she was examining the envelope Erdai's letter had come in, focused, it appeared, on the postmark.

"So you got this in March?" She was facing Gillian. "You just sat on it for two months?" Her confrontational tone surprised Arthur. Pamela generally maintained the outward manner familiar to her entire generation, a vague amiability suggesting that nothing in life was worth the strain of a disagreement.

"We're all here now," Arthur said mildly. Clearly, though, Pamela had this right. Gillian had taken her time, deliberating about what to do, or whether she wanted to do anything at all.

"I thought more about it after our meeting," Gillian told Arthur.

Pamela wasn't satisfied.

"But you still haven't gone down there to see this man?"

Gillian frowned. "That's not my job, miss."

"And watching them execute someone who shouldn't be—that is?"

"Oh, for God's sake!" Arthur shot his hand toward Pamela like a traffic cop. She went silent, but still cast a baleful glance Gillian's way. He asked Gillian if Pamela could copy the letter and Gillian, whose face was masked by a slender freckled hand, nodded. As Pamela snatched up the pages, Arthur had no doubt Gillian Sullivan was wondering why she had bothered to come.

DURING THE TIME Gillian had been in the law, both as a prosecutor and a judge, it had been an article of faith never to surrender her composure. No matter how rascally the defendant or lawyer, she would not provide them with the pleasure of an emotional response. As Arthur's young associate, in ankle boots and a leather skirt with onseam detailing, strode from the room, Gillian's first instinct was to offer advice. Contain yourself, Gillian wanted to tell her. But Pamela, of course, would have answered, justifiably, that she wanted to be nothing like her.

"What do you feed her, Arthur?" Gillian asked when the door slammed. "High octane?"

"She's going to be a great lawyer," he answered. His tone suggested he recognized that was not fully a compliment.

"I still get mail forwarded from inmates all the time, Arthur. I don't even know how they find me. And all of it's crazy." There were the predictable pornographic fantasies that the memory of an attractive woman in power inspired in bad men locked away, and several other messages, not all that different from Erdai's, sent in the implausible hope that she might rethink certain situations and repair them now that she knew what imprisonment was like. "I can't take any of it seriously," Gillian said. "You know what this is, Arthur, this letter. I know you do. The gangbangers are always up to something."

"'Erno Erdai'? Sounds white. Rommy's black. And too weird for any gang to hook up. There's nothing about gangs in his record."

"They have all kinds of alliances in there. It's like the Wars of the Roses."

Arthur shrugged and said the only way to find out was to go speak to Erdai.

"I think you should," she answered. "That's why I brought the letter."

"The letter says he wants to talk to you."

"Oh, please," Gillian said. She reached into her purse. "May I smoke in here?"

Smoke-free environment, said Raven. There was a lounge, but the air was so rank she might as well just breathe in ash. Gillian closed the purse again, resolved, as ever, to contain her cravings.

"It's not even appropriate for me to go down there," she said.

Arthur made a face, perhaps out of an effort not to smile. And she quickly understood. There was no authority left to punish her for an ethical lapse, no one to banish her from the bench or revoke her law license. They'd done all that already. Anything they couldn't jail her for was all right at this stage.

"Gillian, nobody's going to criticize me— or you, for that matter—for doing what we have to in order to hear his story. He didn't make any bones about what he thinks of defense lawyers."

"He may well speak to you anyway."

"Or hate me and refuse to talk to either one

of us after that. Gillian, I have six weeks left until the Court of Appeals decides whether to turn out the lights on this man. At this stage, I can't waste time or take chances."

"I cannot go to Rudyard, Arthur." The thought constricted her stomach. She did not want to feel that deadened air again, or deal with the perverted reality of convicts. She had spent most of her time in seg, separated from most inmates, because it was too hard for the Bureau of Prisons to figure out who was the sister or daughter of someone she'd prosecuted or sentenced and who, as a result, might be carrying a murderous grudge. And that was just as well. She was seldom at ease with the other prisoners with whom she was housed, women who were pregnant when they entered the facility, or who had been removed from general population for one infraction or another. They were all victims to the core, certainly in their own minds and often in fact. Most had had nothing to start and went down from there. Some were bright. Several were actually entertaining company. But when you got to know them, sooner or later you crashed against character defects the size of Gibraltar: lying, a temper like Vesuvius, a misperception of the world that resembled color-blindness in the sense that there was some aspect of normality they simply couldn't see. She kept to herself, helped out with legal problems, and was referred to, despite her efforts to discourage it, as 'Judge.' It seemed to please everyone there—prisoners and, even, staff—to know that one of the mighty had fallen.

Raven, however, was not about to give up.

"Look, I don't want to preach," he said, "but this Erdai, he has a point, doesn't he? You made the decisions. You found this man guilty, you sentenced him to death. Don't you have some responsibility, if my guy doesn't deserve that?"

"Arthur, to be blunt, I've done more than I had to already." She had wrestled it through for several days before deciding to bring him the letter. It was foolish, she knew, to risk any further contact with Raven, who might become more precise with his questions about her past. And she felt no allegiance to the law, whose stratagems and puzzles had once delighted her, but which, like a sovereign, had expelled her from its kingdom. But she smarted at the memory of that one cruel remark to Arthur. It was not the law but the rules she had set down for herself, with the avuncular assistance of Duffy, her sponsor and landlord, that required her to be here. No more messes, no more casual destruction of others or herself. When necessary, make amends.

Still yearning for nicotine, she stood and wandered to a corner of the room. She had not been in a law office in the months she had been out of the penitentiary, and the plummy atmosphere seemed somehow hilarious. Everyone had grown so much richer in the time she was away. It was unimaginable that normal people lived with this luxury—the rich woods, the granite, a silver coffee service of Swedish design, and rolling armchairs of buttery calfskin. She had never yearned for any of this. But it was still difficult to see Arthur Raven, able and driven, but perhaps not gifted, so comforted by fortune.

As he watched her, Raven was unconsciously stroking the fried-up hair that stood straight on his scalp at the few points where it still resided. Arthur, as always, appeared to have been working hard—his tie was dragged down, and there were ink spots on his hand, and on his shirt cuff. Intuitively, she sought some way to deflect him.

"How is your sister, Arthur? Is my memory right? Is that who was ill?"

"Schizophrenic. I got her into an assisted living arrangement, but I'm over there all the time. The last words my father said to me were, 'Take care of Susan.' Which wasn't very surprising. He'd been telling me that since I was twelve."

"Other sibs?"

"It's just Susan and me."

"And when did your mother die?"

"My mother's hale and hearty. She just washed her hands of all of us thirty years ago when Susan got sick. She went to Mexico for a long time, then wandered back here. She was kind of a free spirit. And she and my father were a strange match. She's got a little place here in Center City and supports herself as a model for life—drawing classes at the Museum Art School."

"A *nude* model?"

"Oh sure. 'The human body is a beautiful thing at all ages, Arthur.' I guess it's more of a challenge to draw wrinkles. I really don't know." Raven was smiling somewhat tentatively, a bit bewildered by what he was confessing.

"You see her?"

"Now and then. But it's like visiting a distant aunt. I mean in high school, I had a couple of friends, black guys actually, who'd been raised by their grandmothers. They knew their moms the way I did—like having a much older pal. It was how I grew up. What else do you know?"

He smiled the same way. Mrs. Raven, clearly, was the other pole from May Sullivan, who had demanded preeminence in the lives of all family members. She was brilliant and a savage wit, but the bottle of Triple Sec was open on the kitchen counter by the time Gillian came home every afternoon from St. Margaret's. The evening always proceeded in the same sick suspense. Who would Ma go after? Would she scream or, as was often the case in her fights with Gillian's father, resort to violence? Her rages could bring a house with ten occupants to a freighted silence that lasted hours.

Arthur, who had appeared to welcome Gillian's interest in him, nonetheless reverted to his effort to get her to visit Erdai. Discipline, she recalled, was always one of his professional strengths.

"I don't know how to talk you into this," he said. "I won't ask much. Just smooth the way with the guy." Arthur promised she would not even have to listen to Erdai's story, if she chose, and that he would drive her down himself to be certain she made it back and forth from the institution in one day. "Look, Gillian. I never wanted this case. The court just threw it on me, like a saddle. And now I haven't had a day off in four weeks. But I'm doing it, you know, my duty. And I have to ask you to help."

Openly plaintive and disarmingly humble, Arthur extended his short arms toward her. He smiled as he had when he spoke of his mother: this was all he knew, and there was no choice but to accept it. He was a nice man, Gillian realized. He'd grown up to be a nice man, someone who'd come to know more of himself than she would have predicted. He knew he was one of life's ardent eager beavers, a do-right afraid to do wrong, and he knew, as he'd said last time, there were persons, such as she, who judged the likes of him boring. Yet that, she suddenly saw, had been her mistake. Not her only mistake. But one of them. She had always owed Arthur and those like him a great deal more respect. Realizing that was a step in her rehabilitation. Because it came to her now that rehabilitation was in fact her plan. In some secret part, she had intended all along, when her strength returned, to reform and remake herself, to refill with stronger stuff the fathomless crater she'd blown through her life.

"I'll go," she said. As soon as the words were uttered, they seemed like precious china knocked from a shelf. She watched their fall and impact—the light that spread on Raven's face—suspecting at once that she'd made a dreadful mistake. All she desired was a safely anesthetized life. She had been living out a daily plan—take her Paxil and minimize significant contact with what had gone before. She felt an ex-addict's natural panic to think her resolve had broken down.

Showing her to the handsome reception area, Raven offered a variety of inept expressions of gratitude, then retrieved her wet umbrella and her coat. A giant rug, a bright design by a modern master who'd branched from paintings to textiles, covered the polished hardwood and Gillian, still deeply shaken, stared at the abstract figures. Twice with Arthur Raven in as many weeks, some spirit, like a woodland elf haunting a tree, had spoken for her.

She said goodbye abruptly and descended in the high-speed elevator, fully
baffled by herself and, especially, the brief
fluttery sensation in her chest, which
seemed like a small flame in the corner of a
cage. It would not last long and so she did
not have to decide if it might be hope.

7

OCTOBER 4, 1991

The Jail

IN THE HOUSE OF CORRECTIONS, most inmates had several names. If the Laws found out you had a record, there was less chance to walk a beef, or get bail. So when perps were arrested, they tended to forget what Momma had called them. Usually guys had been cooling for weeks before the Identification Division in McGrath Hall compared ten-card fingerprint records from booking with what was on file and figured out who was who.

Unfortunately for Collins Farwell, he had matched early. Although he'd checked in as Congo Fanon, by the time Muriel got Larry's call, the jail had Collins's given name. She was trying a bank robbery case, but she agreed to meet Larry at the jail after court, and when she arrived, he was waiting for her on one of the granite blocks that served as a bench in the lobby. His large blue eyes lingered as she approached.

"Lookin pretty spiffy," Larry told her.

She was dressed for trial in a red suit, wearing a little more makeup than when she was in the office pushing files. Always a little too familiar, Larry reached up to touch one of her large loop earrings.

"African?"

"As a matter of fact."

"Nice," he said.

She asked what was up and Larry offered a more elaborate version than he had on the telephone of what Erno had told him yesterday. It was 5 p.m. and the prisoners were locked down for the count, which meant Larry and she would have to wait to interview Collins.

"Wanna take a look at him in the meantime?" Larry asked.

He badged them in and they climbed up on the catwalks, the grated piers outside the cages. Muriel lagged a bit. She had not had time to change shoes and it was easy to put a high heel through the grating. A stumble could lead to more than embarrassment. Civilians, male and female, learned to keep their distance from the cells. Men had been nearly garroted with their neckties, and women, naturally, endured worse. The Sheriff's deputies who served as guards maintained a live-and-let-live truce with the inmates, and were not always quick to intervene.

Walking along, it was the usual jailhouse scene—dark faces, bad smells, the insults and sexual taunts hurled toward their backs. In some cells, the men had strung clotheslines, further dividing the minimal space. Often photos were taped to the bars—family, or girlie shots sliced from magazines. During the lockdown, the men lounged, or slept, played radios, called out to one another, frequently in gang codes. An officer in drab, a big black man, had come to escort them when they moved through the last gate to the tiers and was plainly irritated to have been bothered. He rapped his stick twice on the bars to indicate they had reached Collins's cell, and sauntered off, running his baton against the bars just to let the boys know he was around.

"Which one of you is Collins?" Larry asked the two men in there. One was on the pot and the other was playing cards, through the bars, with the inmate next door.

"Yo, man, can't I get no privacy or nothin." Seated on the stainless steel fixture, Collins pointed at Muriel, but went about his business in defiance of the intrusion.

They strolled away briefly. When they returned, Collins was just pulling up the zipper on his orange jumpsuit.

"You narco or what?" Collins asked when Larry flipped his shield. Collins Farwell was medium color, with light eyes and a perfectly cropped sponge of African hair. As advertised, he was large and handsome. His eyes were nearly orange and as luminescent as a cat's, and he was clearly aware of his good looks. Peering at Muriel, Collins adjusted the jumpsuit on his shoulders to make sure the fit was just so.

"Homicide," Larry said.

"I ain fuckin kill't nobody. That's not my act, man. Must be some other nigger you come for. Ain no killer. I'm a lover." Collins sang a few bars from Otis Redding to prove the point, providing considerable amusement in several of the cages stacked on the floors above and below him. With that, Collins turned and dropped the zipper on his jumpsuit, and strolled back toward the potty. He looked directly at Muriel, expecting her to scurry, and she held her ground for a minute.

"Whatta you think?" Larry asked, when they were on the way back down.

"Damn good-looking," Muriel answered. He resembled her mother's favorite, Harry Belafonte.

"I'll see if we can get his mug shot in a frame for you. Are we wasting our time?"

She asked what Larry thought.

"I think he's the average jailhouse piece of shit," Larry said. "But I got an hour if you do."

After feed time, when Collins was back in general population, they could bring him down to an interview room without fanfare. In the administrative office, Larry asked the officer on duty to arrange that, saying only that they had to question Farwell concerning a murder. Half the staff in here was jumped-in to a gang, or otherwise affiliated, and word would trail back quickly if they thought Collins was cooperating. The duty officer took Larry and Muriel to a small interview room, a trapezoid of cheap plasterboard, scuffed with heel marks several inches up the wall. They sat in plastic swivel chairs, which, like the small table between them, was fixed to the floor with heavy hex bolts.

"So how's Talmadge?" Larry's eyes angled away promptly, as if he regretted the remark once it was out. Lots of people were mentioning Talmadge to her now. A photo, taken at a fund-raiser, had appeared in the paper last week. Still, this wasn't a discussion she was having with Larry.

"You know, Larry, I never figured you as jealous."

"That's informational," he protested. "You know. Like the weather report. Like how's your health and your family?"

"Uh-huh."

"And?"

"Come on, Larry. I'm seeing the man. We have a nice time."

"And you're not seeing me."

"Larry, I don't recall ever 'seeing' you very often. As far as I can tell, you never thought about me when you weren't horny."

"So what's wrong with that?" Larry asked. She nearly went for it, before she realized he was having her. "I'll send flowers every day now and billets-doux."

'Billets-doux.' Larry could always surprise you. She just looked at him.

"I'm giving you space," Larry said. "I thought you wanted space."

"I want space, Larry." When she closed her eyes, her lashes seemed to catch in her makeup. Somehow Larry, who lived on his instincts, knew something was up. Two nights ago, as Talmadge was leaving her place, he had pressed her head to his chest and said, 'Maybe we should start thinking about making this permanent.' She had recognized all along this was where they were headed, but a palsy had shaken her anyhow. In her own way she had been working hard since then not to think of what he had said, meaning at bottom she'd thought of nothing else.

It felt as if she were looking down into the Grand Canyon. Somehow her first marriage, which was rarely even a topic of reflection, was in the dangerous distance below. She had married at nineteen, when the dumb things people did were legion, and when she believed she was getting a prize. Rod had been her high-school English teacher, caustic and bright and still unmarried at the age of forty-two—it had not even occurred to her to

wonder why. The summer after she graduated, she ran into him on a corner and flirted
boldly, having discovered in those years that
sexual forwardness did wonders for a girl
whose looks didn't stop traffic. She'd pursued him, begged him to join her for lunch, to
go to movies, always on the sly. Her parents
were horrified when she announced their
wedding. But she worked and finished college in five years, taught in the public
schools, and went to law school at night.

In time, of course, Rod's charm had worn
thin. Well, that was not really true. He remained one of the most devastatingly funny
humans she'd known—the wise-guy drunk
at the end of the bar who got off the best
lines in English comedies. But he was, in a
phrase, a human being who'd never become. He was a brilliant boy, bound hand
and foot by his own unhappiness, and he
knew it, often claiming that his fundamental
problem in life was that you couldn't hold a
Stoli, a cigarette, and the TV remote with
only two hands. He was probably gay, but
too cowardly to face it. Certainly his interest
in sex with her had not seemed to last much
beyond their engagement. By the third year
of their marriage, his sexual disinterest had

led her to other men. Rod knew and did not seem to care. In fact, he went to pieces whenever she mentioned divorce. He could not face his mother with that. She was a severe, bloodless, upper-class type, whom he should have told to fuck off ages ago. Instead, he allowed her to judge. Until the day he died. The cause was a coronary, which the early deaths of his father and grandfather had long presaged. Despite all the warnings, Rod never exercised and went to the doctor only to mock him, but for Muriel, the loss had been unexpectedly monumental, not only of Rod himself but of the glory he was to her when she was nineteen.

Having married a man old enough to be your father, you look back and say, I had issues. Yet in retrospect, her core motive still felt identifiable and familiar: she had just wanted to get somewhere with her life. Rod, feckless and drunk, and Talmadge, a force for the eons, had less in common than a rock and a plant. And the fifteen years since she'd first married was a literal lifetime. But the omen of how mistaken, how invisible she could be to herself in these things continued to haunt her. With Larry, however, she was determined to appear resolute.

"I can't believe Talmadge is such a big deal to you," she said.

"I don't know," he answered. "It looks like I'm on the loose." He was getting divorced, he said, and seemed to mean it this time. Nancy and he had gone to a lawyer together, a woman who'd first tried to talk them into sticking it out. There were no problems with property. The only issue was his boys. Nancy was too attached to leave them and had actually proposed getting custody, but Larry had eighty-sixed that. For the time being, they were stalemated, but figured to settle eventually. They both wanted out.

"It's sad," said Larry. He seemed to mean that, too. He didn't bother looking at her. To his credit, Larry had no appetite for cheap sympathy.

Outside they heard the jailhouse music of jangling chains. A guard knocked once and steered Collins Farwell into the room, shackled from the waist, and bound hand and foot. The officer placed Collins at an adjoining table and padlocked his ankle chain to a black hasp bolted on the floor.

"Wanna time-cut, man," said Collins, as soon as the officer was out the door.

"Whoa," said Larry. "Take a few steps back there, bud. Maybe we ought to say howdy."

"I said I want a time-cut," answered Collins. Off the tiers, his accent was noticeably whiter. He addressed Muriel, apparently realizing that it was the P.A. who'd make the decisions.

"How much dope did you have when they busted you?" she asked.

Collins rubbed his face, where the kinky stubble of several days had gone unshaved, probably a fashion statement. Within the jail, Collins couldn't be questioned without fresh *Miranda* warnings, which had not been administered. In the tortured logic of the law, therefore, nothing he said here could be used against him. Muriel explained, but Collins had been around the block often enough to understand that on his own. He was just taking a moment to ponder tactics.

"Had half a pound, man," he said, finally, "till the narcos took their pinch. Six zones now. Left just enough so it's still an X." Collins laughed as he contemplated the depravity of the police. They'd sell two ounces on the street or blow it themselves. He was still headed for life without parole.

"How about you tell us what you've got?" Muriel asked.

"How 'bout you tell me what my time-cut is, and stop acting like I'm some dumb jail-house nigger just gone fall out for the po-lice."

Larry rose. He stretched briefly, but as things developed, that was a ruse so he could circle behind Collins. Once there, he grabbed the chain locked to the floor and jerked the links until they tightened in the young man's groin, snapping him back. Muriel cast Larry a warning look, but he knew how far to go. He placed a hand on Collins's shoulder from behind.

"You have way too much attitude, my friend," Larry told him. "Now, you don't have to talk to us. You really don't. We can go away and you can do life. But if you want out from under, then you better start behaving yourself. Because I don't see a line of prosecutors outside the door waiting to cut you a better deal."

When Larry released the chain, Collins peered back at him with an insolent look, then turned his stare on Muriel. Almost against his will, he was appealing to her. Even Collins wasn't certain how big a badass he actually was. She waved to Larry and they went out the door, waiting to speak until the deputy had stepped back in to watch his prisoner.

"I hate haggling with dope peddlers," said Larry. "They're always so much better at it than me."

Muriel laughed out loud. Larry could put in on himself. That was one thing Talmadge would never learn. Larry was still wearing his coat, a mid-length black leather jacket, and whispering with him in the close confines of the jail, she felt the animal heat that always radiated from his sheer bulk.

"I don't know if this afterbirth's trying to get something for nothing," he said, "or if he has the keys to the kingdom."

"Well, there's only one way to find out," she said. "This isn't window-shopping. He has to put what he's got on the table. Once he spills, we see if it proves. If he hands us a killer and testifies, then maybe Narcotics will reduce it to less than six ounces and let him go for ten to twelve years. But I can't promise him anything on my own."

Larry nodded. It was a plan. Muriel grabbed his thick arm before he could turn back.

"But maybe you should let me do the talking. I think you already nailed down the bad-cop part."

When they re-entered, Muriel explained the ground rules. With time to himself, Collins's tone had grown slightly more agreeable, but he still shook his head.

"Didn't tell nobody I'd testify, man. I'm gonna be inside some time, now. Isn't that so? No matter what I say, I'm inside, right?"

Muriel nodded.

"That's hard time if I testify. G.O.'s," he said, referring to the Gangster Outlaws, "they don't wait to see you go state twice."

"Look," said Muriel, "you're not our dream date either. A Triple X who's talking to get out from under life doesn't sell to a jury like a nun. But if you won't get behind what you're gonna tell us, it's worth nothing."

"Can't testify," said Collins. "Put me on the lie box, man, okay," he said, "but no way I can get up there. I'm strictly a c.i." Confidential informant.

They went at it a few more minutes, but Muriel was willing to pass on his testimony. She still had the feeling that Collins would clean up okay, but a case that required a Triple X as a witness wasn't worth bringing in the first place. Ultimately, she offered to try to sell a timecut in the office, but only if Collins's information led to a conviction. And they'd have to hear what he had to offer right now.

"And what if you-all trick on me, man? Arrest this dude and fade me? Where am I then?" Collins's eyes, a light umber shade, fell on Larry, as he inquired about getting swindled.

"I thought your uncle told you I was okay," Larry said.

"My uncle, man," said Collins and laughed at the idea of Erno. "What is it he knows? Put lipstick on a pig, man, it's still a pig."

In spite of herself, Muriel smiled, but Larry had stiffened. 'Pig,' even these days, pushed a button with most cops, and Muriel touched Larry's arm while she told Collins this was the best she could do, take it or leave it.

Collins stretched his neck, rotating it as if to ease some small discomfort.

"I was in this tavern," he said then. "Lamplight."

"When?" she asked.

"Last week. Right before I got cracked.

Tuesday. And there's this hook who comes round there. Just some raggedy street thing, you know."

"Name?"

"Folks there call him Squirrel. I don't know why. Probably cause he's, like, nuts." Collins took a second to enjoy that. "Anyway, I was kickin with some dudes and this Squirrel, he's kind of sneakin round, selling shit."

"What shit was he selling?" asked Larry.

"He had gold last week. Chains. And he's pulling them outta his pockets, and he's got something—what the hell do they call that lady's necklace with a face on it?"

"Cameo?" asked Muriel.

He snapped his long fingers. "One of these brothers at the bar wanted to see it, and Squirrel shows him, but he's like, 'No way, man, that's not for sale.' Turns out, it opens up, you know, under the face, it's a locket, and it's got two little pictures inside, two babies. 'Kin gonna give good money for that,' he says. Kin, I'm thinking. Damn if I knew what that was about. So later I was back to, you know, the lavatory, and I saw him again, and we just fell to rappin, and I say to him, 'What you mean "kin"?' 'Hell,' he says, 'lady I got that offa, she six under now. Busted a cap in her.' And this brother, man, you know, he don't look like he'd take off anybody. I'm like, 'Man, you sky-up?' 'Word,' he says, 'smoked her and two more back there on the Fourth of Ju-ly. You seen it, too, man, TV and all, I was famous and everything. I got me a whole lotta shit offa all them, but I done unloaded it, 'cept that piece, cause ain nobody gonna give what her kin will pay. Gone do like ransom or somethin, once't it get cold and all, and I need me money for a place to stay.'" Collins shrugged. He wasn't sure what to think of it himself.

Larry asked for a description of the locket. Many of the items lifted from the victims had been mentioned in the papers, and Larry was clearly looking for undisclosed details.

"Any more?" Muriel asked Collins, once he'd answered Larry.

"Mmm-mmm," said Collins.

"Not even a full name on this character?" asked Larry.

"I don't know, man. Could be somebody called him Ronny, something like that."

"You think he was woofin about killing those three people?"

Collins looked at both of them. He was finally without poses.

"Could be," he said. "Right now, I'm hoping like hell he wasn't, but you know, a man gets buzzed, who knows what he's gonna say? He was struttin, that's for sure."

Collins was doing this the right way, Muriel thought, telling it straight. At the end of the day if Squirrel was not the man, she would still be able to put a word in for him.

Larry asked several more questions to which Collins had no answers, then they sent him back to the tiers. They said nothing about him until they reached the street, outside the vast fortress that was the House of Corrections.

"Straight?" she asked him then.

"Probably so. If he was gonna dress it up, he could have done a lot better than that."

Muriel agreed. "Any chance Collins was in it?"

"If he was, and Squirrel gives him up, then Collins is meat. Collins can figure that. So I'd bet no."

That one, too, Muriel saw the same way. She asked how much of what Collins had said about the cameo had been in the papers. "We never let out it was a locket," Larry said. "Those are Luisa's daughters' baptism pictures in there. And I'll tell you what blows my mind is he's right, the thing is big stuff to the family. Some kind of heirloom from Italy. The mom got it from her mom, who got it from hers. This puke, Squirrel, one way or the other, he has to know something."

"You calling Harold?"

"I wanna eyeball Squirrel first." That meant Larry was afraid the Commander would assign other detectives to find Squirrel. Police officers kept track of their arrest statistics, as if there was a scoreboard in lights down at McGrath Hall. Larry, like everyone else, wanted the big ones.

"I won't say anything to Molto," Muriel answered.

They stood in the encroaching cold, drawn together, as was so often the case, by the speed of their compact. Their breaths clouded and trailed away and the air held the bracing somber scent of autumn. Along one side of the jail, the line was forming for evening visits, composed principally of young women, most of them with a child or two. Several of the kids were crying.

Larry looked at her at length in the dim light.

"Time for a soda pop?" he asked.

She squinted through one eye. "That sounds a little dangerous."

"You love danger," he said.

That was true. She had always loved danger. And Larry was part of it. But she was determined to grow up.

"The defendant in my case is gonna jump on tomorrow. I should work on the cross." She provided a little sealed grin meant to reflect just a vapor of regret, then turned toward the P.A.'s Office across the street.

"Muriel," Larry said to her. When she revolved, he had his hands jammed in the pockets of his long jacket and he flapped them against his side. His mouth moved, but he clearly had no idea what to say next. Instead, they stood in the night, facing each other, and let her name, spoken with the faintest woeful echo, remain the last word.

8

OCTOBER 8, 1991

Squirrel

"SQUIRREL?" asked Carney Lenahan. "We're always chasin after that birdbrain."

"What is he?" Larry asked. "A doper?"

Lenahan's partner, Christine Woznicki, answered. "He's the ring around the bowl." She gave Larry Squirrel's proper name, Romeo Gandolph, and he wrote it down. They were in the squad room at Area Six, a little after 8 a.m. The watch commander had just finished briefing the new shift and the two officers were ready to go out on patrol. Woznicki was awfully nice-looking, but with a tough set to her jaw and a lanky dryness that reminded Larry of a leather strop. Probably that kind, not that he cared either way. Her father had been on the job when Larry started his career here in Six more than fifteen years ago. Stan Woznicki had also ridden with Carney. The longer you live, Larry thought, it's just a big wheel.

"A thief is what he is," said Lenahan. "And a fence. Steal it or sell it, preferably both. Worse than a gypsy. We run his screwy little ass in here once a month, at least. Ed Norris had him on the ring yesterday."

"For?"

"S.O.S." Same old shit. "Lady Carroll got a wig store on 61st. That's what she calls herself, Lady Carroll. So Lady Carroll gets a little wrecked and don't lock her back door. This birdcage, Squirrel, that's his thing, back doors, hiding in a cabinet till after closing time. Yesterday a.m., half her stock has taken a walk. And most of the trade on 61st is wearing a new mop. So Ed let Squirrel lounge here for the evening but he wouldn't cop. It was him. Believe me. Fenced it for sure."

Carney had to be right at the end of the trail, sixty if he was a day. Everything about the guy was gray, even his face under the wan interior light. Larry loved cops like this. They'd seen it all and done it all and still had something good left. When Larry came on the job in 1975, Carney was still complaining that the Force had bought air-conditioned cruisers. That was just looking for trouble, he said, encouraging the element that didn't want to get out of the car in the first place.

"Any property?" Larry asked. "When Norris grabbed him?"

Lenahan flicked a look at Woznicki, who shrugged.

"What he gets he unloads fast," she answered.

Larry said he'd like to see Norris's report. When he asked if Squirrel had any connection to Gus, Carney laughed deeply.

"Mongoose and cobra, those two," he said. "Gus figured Squirrel had a hard-on for his cash register. I guess he tried to get his hand in there once. Gus caught Squirrel so much as sittin at his counter for a coffee, he'd run him out." At Paradise, anybody who paid his tab was equal. Gang lords sat next to pols and $20 hookers. When there was trouble, local kids getting noisy, vagrants who took up residence, or morons like Squirrel, Gus preferred to deal with it himself, even if a copper was in one of his booths. "One time I saw Gus go at him with a butcher knife," Lenahan said. "Don't think those two were writing love letters."

Larry felt a sensation travel through him. He was the doer. Squirrel.

"What about drugs?" he asked. "He use?"

Woznicki answered. "He don't have any kind of jones. He gets high like the rest of them. For a long time, he was sniffing paint," she said, referring to toluene, "which may be part of his problem. He's a few sandwiches short of a picnic, that one. Squirrel, you know, he's just livin the life. He wants to steal enough to get completely noodled come nightfall, so he can forget how strange he is. You ain't gonna have to consult the Buddha to figure him out."

"Does he carry?" Larry asked, meaning a gun.

"Not so I seen. Kind of a weak puppy, actually," Christine said. "He'll run his mouth, but I don't know if he'd actually go to war. You figure him for the guy who capped Gus?"

"I'm starting to."

"I didn't think the little fuck had it in him." Marveling, Woznicki tossed her narrow, long-jawed face about for a second. That was one of the sad lessons of police life. People were a lot more likely to be worse than you expected, before they were better.

Lenahan and Woznicki left for patrol. In the front, Larry asked the records clerk to pull documents. Rommy's criminal history arrived by fax from downtown in half an hour, but the clerk said Norris's report from last night must still have been in filing. While the clerk was looking, Larry called Harold Greer.

Harold was in a meeting, which was just as well. Larry talked to Aparicio, Harold's right hand, who was too amiable to ask many questions. There was one other call Larry needed to make.

"You want a warrant?" Muriel asked. She was in her office waiting on her jury.

"Not yet. Just stay close."

"Always," she told him.

Always, he thought. What the hell did that mean? The other night, outside the jail, he had looked at Muriel in her go-to-court out-fit, her red high heels elevating her scampish height, and suddenly felt the world was only empty space. The fiber of feeling that connected him to her was the most certain thing in it. The strength of that sensation, which was not only the welling of desire but some larger yearning, had left him speechless after uttering her name. "Always," he muttered, cradling the phone.

After another hour, he asked dispatch to

round up Lenahan and Woznicki. They were only a few blocks away and he met them behind the station. It was past noon now and the lot was as crowded as a shopping center.

"T's up?" asked Woznicki through the driver's window of the cruiser. "You still looking for that report?"

"As a matter of fact."

"I called Norris a while ago."

"Okay, but right now I could use some help scooping up Squirrel. Where do I find him?"

"Usually the street," said Lenahan. "It's not cold enough yet for him to take the hike to the airport. Whenever he's run one of his little jobs, we find him at the same pizza parlor on Duhaney."

"What's he do there?"

"Eat. I don't know if he gets high from the thrill or he's just hungry."

"Probably hungry," said Woznicki. "Hop in and we'll take a ride."

Today, Squirrel had skipped the pizza. After a couple of hours, they ended up at the joint where Collins said he'd encountered Gandolph. It was called Lamplight and it was strange it had any name at all. It was a shithole. You knew you were in trouble when a place kept cyclone fencing across the window while it was open. Near the door, there was a small liquor counter, the merchandise locked behind heavy gratings, and a dim barroom in back. Larry had made this scene a thousand times before: only a few lights that worked, including the reflecting beer signs, and what they revealed was aged, filthy, and broken. The paneling in the room was so old it had started to fray, like worn cloth, and the toilet in the one john was stained, with a seat that had been cracked in half and a cistern that leaked and was always running. Even from the front door, the whole place smelled of rot and a vague gas leak. There were customers back there all day, little groups of young men standing around, talking stuff nobody believed, now and then dealing dope in little coveys in the corner. It was that activity, in all likelihood, that had brought Collins around.

Outside, on the sidewalk near the door, there was more of the same: smacked-out hookers trying to score a john or a fix, guys with disability checks or habits of their own. The paper-bag crowd. When the three officers strolled up, they all scattered. Carney and Christine went in the front and Larry ambled around to the alley, in case Squirrel opted for the stage door.

He heard Lenahan whistle for him a minute later.

"Detective Starczek, make the acquaintance of Romeo Gandolph."

The man Carney was pushing along was a scrawny, crazed-looking little thing, with eyes flashing around like Mars lights. You weren't going to have to convene a grand jury to figure out how he got the name Squirrel. Larry pushed him against the patrol car and patted him down. Rommy whined, asking several times what he had done.

"Shit," Larry said. "Where's the locket, Romeo?"

Romeo, as expected, said he didn't know nothing about that.

"Shit," said Larry again. Gandolph wouldn't have held the cameo for months, only to sell it now. Larry described the piece, but Squirrel kept saying he hadn't seen nothing like it.

Larry thought of Erno's warnings about Collins. This wasn't the first time a jailhouse snitch had run changes on Larry. He was ready to let Squirrel stroll, but Lenahan unexpectedly grabbed Gandolph by the scattered hairdo and pushed him into the back of the cruiser. Squirrel was moaning that his arm still hurt from last night, when he'd been cuffed for most of the evening to an iron ring above his head on the wall.

At Six, Lenahan pointed Rommy to a bench—he knew the way himself—then took Larry's biceps. He could tell there was a problem from the way Carney kept looking up and down the hall.

"You ain gonna find any reports or nothing from last night."

"Because?"

"Cause you ain gonna find that cameo in Property."

Larry groaned. He was just too old for this shit.

"Carney, I know it's not on you, but this meatball's gonna tell me he had that locket last night when they pinched him. You know that. So what am I supposed to tell Harold?"

"I understand," said Carney. "I'm doin what I can. We been looking for Norris all day now. He's off. Girlfriend swears he's on the way in."

They were interrupted by a communications clerk. Larry had a call. His first thought was Muriel, but it was Greer instead. Larry tried to strike a cheerful note.

"I think we're about to clear this case, Commander." He gave Harold some of the details.

"Who's with you, Larry?"

He knew Harold meant Task Force detectives, but Larry played dumb and mentioned Lenahan and Woznicki.

"The Lone Ranger rides again," said Greer to himself. He told Larry he would get a Homicide detective there on the double.

When Larry lowered the phone, there was a big black guy waiting. He had on a snappy, short leather jacket and a knit shirt that didn't quite cover his full belly. He was smiling as if he had something to sell. Which he did, in a way. This was Norris.

"Hear you need this," he said. He took the cameo out of his coat pocket. He hadn't even bothered to put it in a plastic sleeve.

Larry had made it for a long time on this Force by saying live and let live. Best he knew, the Pope wasn't drawing up papers to nominate him for sainthood either. But he did the job. Maybe that was his greatest source of pride. He came on every day to do the job—not to catch a nap or shake down dopers or hide in the station house while he schemed about a long-term disability leave. He did the job, like every other good cop he knew. This was too much. He grabbed the locket roughly from Norris's hand. The christening pictures were inside, two babes both still bloated from the savage trip down the birth canal.

"You're just Dick Fuckin Tracy, aren't you?" Larry said to Norris. "You pinch a guy who's got jewelry in his pocket that was on TV every day for a week because it belonged to a murder vic. And the guy you snatch happens to have had a known thing with another of the victims. And what are you thinking about? How much you can get when you sell the fucking evidence. I hope there aren't any more at home like you."

"Ease up. This ain your man. This is just some little local wackhead booster. He wouldn't cop on the wigs, so I's teaching him a lesson. What's the harm?"

"Harm? I got a great chain of evidence, don't I? Booking sheet, evidence log? How do we prove to Bernie the Attorney this is what you took off his client?"

"Don't bust my chops, man. Everybody here knows how to testify."

Larry turned away, but Norris called after him.

"You know, if he's wrong on the murders," he said, "I oughta get a piece of the bust."

Larry didn't bother to answer. You couldn't talk to a guy like that.

9

MAY 22, 2001

Inside

OUTSIDE the Men's Maximum Security Penitentiary at Rudyard, Gillian had a final cigarette. She kept her back to the prison and instead surveyed the pretty Midwestern street of small frame houses, where the lawns had recently greened and the maple trees in the parkway were all in new leaf. Arthur was still in his fancy automobile, speaking on the car phone to his office. 'My robber baron against your robber baron,' was how he'd described his practice on the drive down, but, like all lawyers *in medias res*, he seemed given over to it, soothing clients and plotting strategy in the fierce war of words that was civil litigation.

For Gillian's sake, Arthur had left his carnivorous young associate back in the IBM Building. Rocketing along the highway, beside the corn plants which were bursting through the earth with their green leaves drooping like welcoming hands, Arthur and she had conversed pleasantly. He had told her what he'd learned about Erno Erdai, the prisoner they were going to see, and they had also talked at length about Duffy Muldawer, her landlord, with whom Arthur had happily renewed acquaintance this morning, reminiscing over their courtroom battles years before, when Arthur was a Deputy P.A. in Gillian's courtroom.

In truth, Duffy had never been much of a lawyer—he'd gone to law school as an adjunct to his priestly duties, and ended up as a State Defender when love, which sadly did not last, had led him to abandon his vows. His true gift was in his original calling. Gillian had discovered that in 1993, when she had entered one of the fabled twelve-step programs. With a sentencing in her future, it was imperative to clean up, but she could not abide the cant, the formulae, the circles of lost souls baring their troubles and still lost. In desperation, she'd called Duffy, who'd offered to help when the first articles about her appeared in the papers. He was her one true confessor.

Without him, she might have remained at the bottom forever.

As Arthur's call wore on now, Gillian ground her cigarette into the gravel of the lot and checked herself over in the reflection of the car's smoked windows. She'd worn a black David Dart pantsuit, with a cardigan-style jacket, pearls, and gold button earrings. The effect was intended to be demure, to attract as little attention as possible inside the institution. But Arthur, who'd apparently been watching her through the windshield while he finished on the phone, seemed to have missed the point.

"You look great, as usual," Arthur said, standing up from the car. He spoke with the same enthusiasm he had in his office. She sensed in Raven, as with so many males, a hint of tireless sexual appetite. But she was largely inured to men. She had even begun wearing a plastic wedding band to work. Saleswomen apparently had the same reputation as nurses and the gals lingering in a watering hole at closing time. Men actually seemed to cruise the counters. Now and then, some appeared to recognize her from her former life, and within that cohort were a few males who, for whatever demented reason, seemed to regard her as either easy pickings or an unfulfilled yen. She rebuffed them all. Sex had never been especially easy for her, anyway. Too much Catholic school or something like that. She had loved being attractive, the power it bestowed. But the mechanics of love, much like love itself, had never really been very satisfying for Gillian.

She thanked Raven for his kindness and turned to face the institution, summoning resolve. For decades, at moments like this, Gillian had conjured the image of a ball bearing, gleaming, smooth, and impenetrable, and that was what was in her mind as they reached the front gates of Rudyard.

Inside the guardhouse, Arthur did the talking. The plan was for her to visit alone with Erdai, who was expecting her, in the hope he would agree to see Raven next. She was not sure exactly what faced her, but the police reports and other documents Arthur had shown her made Erdai's story sound uncomfortably like hers. He'd worked his way up from police cadet to a significant executive position at TN, and then, in an inexplicable instant, had lost hold of everything. In February of 1997, Erdai had been at

Ike's, a well-known hangout for police officers, when he'd had a run-in with a man named Faro Cole. According to Erdai's statements afterwards, he had once investigated Cole for a ticket fraud against the airline. Described as a black male about thirty, Cole had entered the tavern and displayed a gun, shouting that it was Erdai's fault he was broke. Several cops in the place had come at Cole with weapons drawn, and the man had thrown his arms in the air, still holding the revolver, but by the barrel, not the trigger. Finally, after brief negotiations, he'd handed the gun to Erdai and agreed to go outside with him to talk. No more than five minutes later, Cole had burst back through the door of the bar. By all accounts, Erdai, who was about five feet behind him, dropped the young man with a single shot through the back.

Erdai claimed, improbably, that the shooting was self-defense, but he found little support, especially in light of the ballistics and path reports. Erno was charged with attempted murder. Cole, who recovered, conceded, through an attorney, that he had been stoned and provocative and even made no objection to Erno's lawyer's plea for leniency. But because Erdai had shot and killed his mother-in-law several decades before, the P.A.'s Office was adamant that he'd already had his second chance. Erdai pled to Agg Battery, Firearm, and received a sentence of ten years, which would have gotten him out in five, had he not developed a stage-four cancer of the lung. The Warden's Office had confirmed to Arthur that Erdai's prognosis was poor. Notwithstanding that, the Prisoner Review Board had denied his request for commutation or compassionate furlough, much as they turned down everyone else. Erdai was going to die in here, a thought that seemed fully appalling to Gillian as she waited on a bench beside Arthur.

"Is he still lucid?" Gillian asked Raven.

"According to the medical staff." Her name was called then. "I guess you're going to see for yourself."

"I guess so," she answered and stood. So far as Gillian could tell, Erdai was Rommy Gandolph's last hope, and Arthur had become visibly nervous as the moment of truth neared. Coming to his feet to wish her good luck, he offered a damp hand, then Gillian headed off in the company of a female correctional officer. When the main gate to the cellblock finally smashed closed behind them, Gillian's heart squeezed. She must have made a sound as well because the c.o. turned to ask how she was.

"Fine," Gillian answered, but she could feel her face was pinched.

The officer, who was stationed in the infirmary to which they were heading, had introduced herself as Ruthie, a stout chatterbox with straightened hair. Even a prison could not dim her cheerfulness, and her tireless commentary about varied subjects, including Erdai, recent construction, and the weather, made a welcome distraction.

When they arrived, the infirmary proved to be a separate two-story structure connected to the main block by a dark hall. Gillian followed Ruthie down the corridor to another double set of barred doors. A guard sat in a small control room on this side, monitoring ingress and egress through bulletproof windows. Ruthie lifted the visitor's pass hanging from Gillian's neck and the buzzer sounded.

Within the prison hospital, there was an odd liberty. It was like entering an asylum. The worst offenders were chained to their beds, but only if they caused trouble. As in the yard, even the murderers wandered about freely. In the ward to which Ruthie led Gillian, two unarmed correctional officers sat in the corners on folding chairs, moseying around now and then to limber up, but appearing otherwise aimless. Halfway into the room, Ruthie pulled back a curtain and there in a bed was Erno Erdai.

At the moment, he was recovering from a second surgery to remove a lobe from his lung. He had been reading a book, his hospital bed raised to support him, and wore a washed-out hospital gown, while an IV dripped into his left arm. Erdai was thin and pale, with an arrow tip of a long nose. When his light eyes came up, they lingered on Gillian before he coughed harshly. After he recovered, he extended his hand.

"I'll just leave you to talking," Ruthie said. She did not actually depart. She found a plastic bucket chair for Gillian, then crossed to the other side of the ward, where she made some show of looking in the other direction.

"I knew your old man, you know," Erdai said. His speech had a faint foreign lilt, as if he'd come of age in a home where English was a second language. "In the Academy. He was my instructor. He taught Street Tactics. He was good at it, too. They say he was hell out there." Erno laughed. He had a tongue depressor on one side of his mouth and chewed on it periodically. Gillian had often heard as much of her father, but it was hard to reconcile with the man whom she saw her mother wallop time and again. Gillian was always desperate for him to fight back. He was six foot three and could have toppled his wife with one swat. But he was scared of May like the rest of them. Gillian had hated him for it.

"I don't suppose you remember me from being in your court," Erdai asked, "now that you see me?" It seemed important to him to think he had made an impression, but she saw no need for gallantry.

"No, I'm sorry."

"Well, I remember you. And you look a damn sight better off. Do you mind me saying that? Doesn't seem like you're drinking now."

"No."

"I don't mean anything by asking," said Erdai. "I drank too much, too. Only I'm not like you. I'd start right in again. The stuff in here the inmates make? You take your life in your hands and it tastes like it, too. I drink it anyway when I get the chance." Erno shook his head briefly, then glanced at the book that remained open in his hands, a history of World War II. She asked if he liked it.

"It's all right. It's something to do. Did you read a lot when you were inside?"

"Some," she said. "Not as much as I thought I would. Now and then, I try to remember what I did, and most of it's blank. I really think I spent a lot of time just staring."

There were entire chains of association she'd had to abandon. Thinking of herself as a judge. As a respectable citizen. The law, which had been her life in many senses, was all but erased. As far as she could tell now, she had gone through the first year or so in prison with the equivalent of screen fuzz in her brain. The set was on; no signal was receiving. Rarely, very late at night, she cried, usually when she had been aroused by a dream and endured that moment when she realized that she was not in bed, alone, awaiting the trials of another day, but was instead here—in prison, a felon, a junkie. She had gone down and down like something tossed into a channel that ran to the center of the earth. The feeling of those moments, which she'd have been glad to leave behind her forever, returned for an instant and she straightened up to subdue it.

"So you want to hear my story?" Erdai asked.

Gillian explained about Arthur. She'd come because it seemed important to Erno, but it was the defense lawyer who was better suited to listen to whatever he had to say.

"So that's what the lawyer's about," said Erno. "I thought he was coming to give you advice. Well, he'll just twist it around to suit what's best for him. That's how they do it, isn't it? Whatever to get his name in the papers?"

"Well, he certainly won't be looking out for you. You know that. If you're worried—"

"I'm not worried about anything," he said. "What's he gonna do? Get me the death penalty?" Erdai looked toward his feet, shrouded by the bedcovers, as if they were somehow the emblem of his mortality, which he might comprehend in a few vacant instants. "You know, it always bothered me that he was here—Gandolph? We never see the Yellow Men, but I knew he was across the way. It was on my conscience. But I thought I was getting out, so why screw with it? Now, it'll be the other way. He's done the time for everything they didn't catch him on anyway." He used his tongue to move the stick to the other side of his mouth and smiled at the notion. Gillian, confused by this soliloquy, considered asking a question, but thought better of it.

"Well, that's how we used to look at it, right?" Erno asked. "They all did something."

She doubted she had been that cold. She didn't believe many defendants were innocent, but she drew the line at locking them up because they were probably guilty of something else. She did not, however, want to quarrel with Erdai. The man was brusque. Undoubtedly, that had always been the case, but Gillian sensed there was now something settled in his anger. It was deep inside, either coped with or controlling him, she couldn't tell which.

"I have to admit," he said, "I never figured on seeing your face. I just wanted to find out if anybody else had the gumption to do it— you know, to go out of their way on this to set it straight. I've always hated being the only fool. I give you a lot of credit for coming."

She told him she wasn't sure she had much to lose, except the day.

"Oh, sure you do," said Erno. "Once they start trying to figure out what went wrong in that case, the papers'll drag all of it up again. About you? You know they will."

She had not thought of that, not once, mostly because she had no clear idea what Erdai might be saying. Nonetheless, with his warning, she felt an icy constriction at her center. Obscurity was the only refuge she had now. But in a second, her anxiousness eased. If somehow she again became a *cause célèbre*, she would go. She had returned to the Tri-Cities, knowing that if she did not look all of it over again through sober eyes, she'd never come to terms with what had happened. And she was not prepared to leave yet. But she would be someday. Departure remained part of her plan.

Erdai was studying her without apology.

"You think I should talk to this lawyer?"

"He's a nice man. I think he'd be fair."

Erno asked Arthur's name, hoping he might know him. He remembered hearing of Raven in the P.A.'s Office, but they never had any business.

"Obviously," said Gillian, "if you have

information that would tend to show Gandolph shouldn't be executed, Arthur should hear it."

"Yeah, I got information." Erno laughed. "He didn't do it."

"Gandolph?"

"He's innocent," Erdai said flatly, and watched her at length. "You don't believe that, do you?"

This was, she knew, the most consequential question he'd asked her, but she did not wait long to respond.

"No," Gillian said. When she was inside, at least half the inmates claimed they were innocent, and over time, she'd given credence to a few. In a state facility like this, where the justice that brought the cons here was sometimes done on a wholesale basis, the numbers were probably higher. But she had paid close attention many years ago when Rommy Gandolph was in her courtroom. Heroin was still a pastime then, and she had understood the gravity of a capital case. Even in Erno's presence, she could not accept that she, that all of them—Molto and Muriel and the detective, Starczek, even Ed Murkowski, the defense lawyer, who'd privately acknowledged believing Gandolph was guilty—could be so thoroughly misled.

"No," said Erno, and his light eyes, trapped in their weathered sockets, again stayed on her quite some time. "I wouldn't either." He descended into another spasm of coughing. Gillian watched him rock back and forth, waiting to ask what he meant. But when he was finished, he took a couple of good breaths, then addressed her peremptorily. "All right," he said, "go tell the lawyer I'll see him. They're coming to take me down for a test. Bring him back up here in an hour or so." With that Erno again raised his book. The conversation was done. He never bothered looking at her again as she said goodbye.

10

OCTOBER 8, 1991

The Confession

ON TV, murderers were usually evil geniuses with a lust for death. A couple of times in his career, Larry had run across a lawyer or executive who'd hatched a brainy plan to get rid of his wife or his partner. But gang members aside, most of the guys Larry cracked fell into two groups: bad seeds who'd started torturing cats by the age of six, or, more often, mutts who'd been kicked around long enough to learn to do it to somebody else, the type who pulled the trigger just to prove for once they didn't have to take everybody's shit. That was Squirrel.

In a small locker room within Area Six, which doubled for interviews, they sat at adjoining corners of a square steel table, almost as if Gandolph were a dinner guest.

Larry knew better than to talk to Squirrel without a witness, but Woznicki and Lenahan had a call, break-in in progress. Larry figured he'd clear away the brush with this guy, then bring in a prover when he started to get something good.

"You ever seen that?" Larry asked. The locket sat on the gray table between the two men. The profile of a woman in a lace collar was finely etched against the brown backing. Beautiful as it was, even Squirrel was smart enough not to touch it. The sound of an answer or two strangled somewhere in his throat.

"I don't recall directly, man," he said finally. "Tha's a nice piece. I might 'member if I seen that piece."

"Are you fucking with me, Squirrel?"

"I ain fuckin with you, man. I don't hardly wanna fuck with no police."

"Well, you're fucking with me. I just got that from the officer who took it off you. Are you calling him a liar?"

"I ain sayin liar. You the one sayin liar."

"Well, is he a liar?"

"Don't know 'bout that." Squirrel slid his brown thumbs along the lines of a gang graffito engraved in the table by some youth unimpressed with his surroundings. "Crook more like," said Squirrel. "Some crooks is liars, too. Ain that right?"

"Is this philosophy class, Squirrel? I missed the sign on the door. Lemme ask you again. Is this yours?"

"Nnn-uhh, I wasn't supposed to be havin that."

Larry smiled. The guy was so simple you had to like him.

"I know you weren't supposed to have it. But you had it, right?"

A wild flash of uncertainty lit up again behind Squirrel's eyes. This kid had been raised way too close to the power lines.

"Hey, you know," he said. "I'd kinda like to go. You know."

"Go?"

"Yeah, the Boys." Gandolph smiled as if he'd said something clever. On the left side of his mouth, he was missing several teeth. Larry also noticed Squirrel had begun tapping his foot.

"Well, sit here and keep me company for a minute. I want to hear a little more about that cameo."

"Po-lice stole it off me."

"No, they didn't. I'm a police officer. Here. I'm giving it back. Right? Here."

Squirrel still resisted any temptation to reach out.

"How'd you get your hands on that in the first place?" Larry asked.

"Mmm," said Rommy, and spent a long time rubbing his mouth.

"I think you better say something, Squirrel. That piece is about to get you in a peck of trouble. It's stolen, Squirrel. You been down that road before. PSP?" Possession of stolen property. "And I think you're the one who stole it."

"Nnn-uhh," said Squirrel.

"You know a woman named Luisa Remardi?"

"Who?" He leaned forward, but did not do a good job of faking it. At Luisa's name, his eyes had grown tight as coffee beans.

"Well, help me, Squirrel. That cameo is Luisa's. And if you don't know Luisa, where'd this cameo come from?"

Gandolph's narrow face worked around as he pondered his problem.

"Got it off another lady," he said at last.

"Really?"

"Yeah, she kind of give it me to hold, you know, cause she owed me for somethin."

"And what might that be? That she owed you for?"

"Just some little thing I done give her. Can't even recollect too clear."

"And what was this lady's name?"

"Man, I knowed you was gone aks that. What was her name?" said Squirrel.

"Yeah, right. Her name was What. 'What' was her name." Larry grinned, but there was no point being mean to Squirrel. He wouldn't get it. "How about this, Squirrel? I'll make a call and we can ride over to the Hall and you can take the box and tell the examiner all about Ms. What. Think you'll pass, Squirrel? I don't. But let's find out, okay?"

"Don't know 'bout any lie box," said Squirrel. He simpered in the hope he might be amusing. "Hey, man, lemme up for just a shake. I'm like to bust somethin if I keep waitin."

"You know how that cameo was stolen, Squirrel?"

"Come on, man. Lemme go. I'm 'bout to shit my pants."

Larry grabbed Squirrel's wrist and looked him square in the eye.

"You shit your pants on me, Squirrel, I'll make you eat it." He gave Gandolph a second to take that in. "Now tell me, Squirrel. You ever meet Gus Leonidis? Good Gus? Did you know him at all?"

Gandolph's gooey eyes jitterbugged around again.

"I don't think I 'member no one by that name. Leo what?"

Larry mentioned Paul Judson. Squirrel denied knowing him, too.

"From the way I hear this, Squirrel, if I peel off your trousers, I'm gonna see the dent Gus's boots left in your butt, cause he kicked it so often."

Squirrel couldn't keep himself from laughing. "Yeah, tha's good. Dent there." But his amusement faded quickly, and he began muling around again. "Man, I laugh one more time, I'm gonna have a doody right on your floor."

"You know who Good Gus is now?"

"Yeah, okay, I know."

"And this cameo was stolen from a lady at Gus's restaurant."

Squirrel took way too long.

"How you like that," said Squirrel. "Stole at Gus's. How you like that?"

Larry squeezed Squirrel's wrist again, harder this time.

"I told you, don't fuck with me, Squirrel." Squirrel turned his head away and tapped his foot madly. "Squirrel, where did you get the cameo?"

"Lady," said Squirrel.

Off his belt, Larry unsnapped his handcuffs and threw one bracelet around the wrist of Squirrel's he was still holding. "Oh, man, don't run me in. Man, those guys in the jail, man, they bad to me. They really are. I'm a neutron, man. They bad to me." He meant he was neutral, not hooked up with any gang, and as a result, meat for anyone. "Come on, man. At least lemme go first. Okay?"

Larry fastened the other cuff through the bolthole in one of the lockers behind Gandolph.

"I gotta go to the head," Larry said.

He took his time, returning in about twenty minutes. Squirrel was writhing, bucking back and forth in the chair.

"Whose cameo?"

"Whoever you say, man."

"And how'd you end up with a dead woman's jewelry, Squirrel?"

"Lemme go, man. Please lemme go. This ain right a-tall, man."

"You killed Gus, Squirrel."

Squirrel began to whine and moan, much as he had in the cruiser, pretending to be on the verge of tears.

"Okay, I kill't him. Lemme go. I'm beggin here, man."

"Who else?"

"Huh?"

"Who else did you kill?"

"I didn't kill no one. Come on, man."

Larry left him alone for another hour. When he came back, the stink was phenomenal.

"God almighty," he said. "Jesus." He threw open a window. The weather had turned in the last few days and winter was more than an idea. The air was dry and cool, about forty-five degrees. Squirrel had begun crying again as soon as Larry was through the door.

Larry returned with a garbage bag and a newpaper. He had Gandolph, who wore no underwear, peel off his trousers and toss them in the bag.

"Don't I get a lawyer or nothin?"

"I'll get whoever you want, Squirrel. But what do you need a lawyer for? How do you think that looks?"

"Looks like he gone sue your ass, man. Makin me shit my pants. That ain right. That ain legal or nothin."

"What kind of stuff is that, every creep can crap all over himself and call the cops bad guys? I don't think that works."

Squirrel cried harder. "Man, that wasn't how it was a-tall."

There was a little smear of shit on one of his shoes and Larry told him to throw it in the bag, too. Squirrel sobbed as he dropped it inside.

"You cold, man. You the coldest po-lice I ever met. Where'm I gone get shoes, man? These here, they the onlyest shoes I got."

Larry replied that it might be a little while before Squirrel left. He covered Gandolph's chair with newspaper and told the man, who remained naked below the waist, to sit again. Mumbling to himself, Squirrel appeared too distraught to listen. Larry slammed his hand on the table to shut him up.

"Squirrel, what happened to Gus? Good Gus? What happened to him?"

"Dunno, man." He lied like a child, his face cast down.

"You don't know? He's dead, Squirrel."

"Oh, yeah," he said. "I think I done heard that."

"Bet that broke your heart. Guy who wumped you the way he did."

Dumb as he was, Squirrel saw where that would go. He used his fingers to wipe his nose.

"I dunno, man. All kinda folk wump me. Seem like. Po-lice wump me."

"I haven't wumped you, Squirrel. Not yet."

"Man, why you doin me like this? Shittin my pants and makin me sit in it like I'm some baby, man. Strippin me naked."

"Now listen, Squirrel. You're runnin around with the jewelry of a dead woman. Who was killed at the same time as a man who beat down on you whenever he saw your spotty little face. Now are you telling me that's just a funny fucking coincidence? Is that what you're saying?"

"Man, it's cold in here. I ain got no clothes on. Look here. I got goof bumps and everythin."

Larry slammed the desk again. "You killed them, Squirrel! You shot Gus. You shot him and you shot Luisa and you shot Paul. You rifled that register you were so hot to get your mitts on. That's what happened. Then you dragged those poor people into the freezer, and you cornholed Luisa Remardi. That's what happened."

Squirrel shook his head no. Larry figured it was time for something else.

"We have your fingerprints, Squirrel. At the scene. Did you know that? All over the register."

Gandolph stilled. If he hadn't been inside, or near the register, then he'd have known Larry was lying. But there was no chance Squirrel was going to cash him in on this.

"I ain said I wasn't never there. I been in there. Lots of folk tell you that. Kinda liked to play with Gus and all."

"Play? Is that what you call killing him?"

"Man, bein in there, sayin howdy and all, that ain the same as killin."

"Keep saying no, Squirrel. We have plenty of time. I got nothing better to do than have you lie to me."

Larry turned off the radiator before leaving the room. Forty minutes later, he re-entered with Wilma Amos, his Task Force partner, who had finally arrived. Squirrel was hunched down by the lockers, perhaps hoping to work the cuff off, or just to withstand the cold, and he screamed out.

"Don't you bring no lady in here when I don't got no pants on."

Larry introduced Wilma, who straightened her stout form to cast an appraising look in Squirrel's direction. Squirrel had turned as far from her as he could, covering himself with his one free hand.

"Just wanted to ask in Detective Amos's presence, Squirrel. You want food? You want a cold drink?"

He told Larry he was a mean po-lice, no question about that.

"I guess the answer's no," Larry told Wilma. They'd agreed in advance that she'd leave, but stand outside the door to make notes.

"I want some pants, man. Tha's what I want. I'm gone die or somethin from the cold."

"You have pants, Squirrel. You can put them back on any time you like."

Squirrel began crying again. With gusto. He was beat now.

"Man, what'd I do, you gotta do me like this?"

"You murdered three people. You shot Gus and Luisa and Paul. You robbed them all. And you screwed that lady up the poop chute."

"You keep sayin that, man."

"Because it's true."

"Is it?" Squirrel asked.

Larry nodded.

"If I done somethin like that, kill three people and all, how come I don't 'member nothin about it."

"Well, I'm helping you remember. I want you to think, Squirrel."

They always said they couldn't remember. Like a drunken husband coming home. Larry frequently said he couldn't remember. And he couldn't. If he didn't want to. But sooner or later as you talked to the perps, it came back. There was always something critical, details the cops themselves hadn't tumbled to yet, which emerged.

"When all this happen?" Gandolph asked listlessly.

"July Fourth weekend."

"July Fourth," Squirrel repeated. "Seem like I wasn't even around July Fourth."

"What do you mean not around? Were you on a cruise?"

Squirrel wiped his nose again against the

back of his hand. Larry took his wrist once more.

"Rommy, look at me. Look at me." Awestruck and overcome, Gandolph raised his soupy brown eyes. And Larry felt some of the thrill—he couldn't resist. He had Squirrel now. He owned him. "You killed these people. I know you killed these people. Now tell me. You tell me if I'm wrong. I say you did. I say you killed them and had a good time with that lady."

"I never done nothin like that to no lady."

"Well if you didn't, who did? Was there somebody with you?"

"Nnn-uhh," Rommy said. Then he seemed to recollect himself. "Shit, man, I don't even 'member none of this. How I gone know if somebody with me? All I'm sayin is I wudn't do nothin like that to no lady, no matter how bad I hate her."

Larry scratched his ear, a gesture of studied casualness. But he'd heard something new.

"Did you hate Luisa?" he asked.

"Well, hate, you know, man. 'Hate no man.' Ain that what Jesus said?"

"Well," said Larry, flicking his ear the same way, "what did you have against Luisa?"

Squirrel moved his hands around ineptly. "She just one of them bitchy-type bitches. You know? Promise you one thing and doin the next. You know how that go."

"Sure," said Larry. "And I forget now. How did you know her?"

For the first time, Gandolph seemed to be grappling with memory.

"You know, she just some cutie pie I'd be rappin to at the airport."

The airport, Larry thought. Some flipping detective he was. Maybe somebody should have just beat him over the head with a brick a couple of times. So Squirrel knew Luisa from the airport. It was falling in place now.

"You and she ever get together?"

"Naw." Rommy laughed bashfully, both shamed and flattered by the idea. "Wasn't never nothin like that. I don't aks out many them ladies."

"Well then, why'd you say she was a bitchy bitch? She play you? She do you wrong?"

"Man, you got some funny ideas about this."

"Do I? I don't think so. I'll tell you what's funny, Squirrel. You said you didn't know any of these people. But you did. You knew Gus. You knew Luisa."

"No way, man. I didn't say that a-tall. All I'm sayin is I didn't murder none of them."

"Just like you didn't know any of them, either."

False in one thing, false in all: the logic of the law. Squirrel understood that, judging from his sudden motionlessness.

"Look, Rommy. Honestly, I'm trying to help you here. I want to understand the way it looked to you. I mean, you pass Gus's window, you notice this bim who's been trickin on you. You come in. You're a little hot with her. And Gus is trying to run you out. I can see how maybe this got out of control. I mean, you don't look like a killer to me. You're not a killer, are you?"

In the end, that was how you got them all to cop, by saying you understood, by nodding when they said, What choice did I have?

"Not how I ever thought I was," Gandolph answered now.

"So how'd this happen?"

Squirrel didn't reply.

"Rommy, what kind of stuff you use? Wack? You use wack?"

"Man, you know. I don't do much of nothin. Sometimes I sniff some paint is all.

Only the last time I was in Manteko, the doc there, he said it wasn't so good for me, said I didn't have enough cells to spare."

"But you've dusted yourself now and then, right?"

Squirrel agreed.

"You think maybe you were dusted on July Fourth? Guys don't remember much. And it makes them pretty ornery, Squirrel. Lot of nice dudes do a lot of bad stuff on PCP."

"Yeah," said Squirrel. He liked that part.

"Come on, Squirrel. Tell me the story."

Squirrel very briefly dared to look at him squarely.

"Don't bring no more ladies in here."

"No," said Larry.

"And can you shut that damn window there?"

"Well, let's talk some," said Larry.

In another fifteen minutes, he shut the window. By then, Wilma had brought in an army blanket. Squirrel hunkered within the folds, while Wilma sat in the corner, scratching out notes as Gandolph confirmed the basics: he saw Luisa through the glass as he was passing by Paradise. On reflection, his best memory was he'd taken a hit of PCP.

"Okay, so you walk in there one in the a.m. What happened then?" Larry asked.

"Man, I can't hardly 'member none of this. Cause I was dusted and all."

"Come on, Squirrel. What happened?"

"Man, old Good Gus. He say, like he always done, to get out."

"And did you get?"

"Well, if I shot them all, how could it be I done git?"

"And where'd the gat come from?"

Rommy shook his head, truly puzzled by the question.

"Man, I ain never had me any gun. Like to shoot myself soon as anyone else, how I always figure."

He probably had that right.

"Well, you had a gun that night, right?"

Gandolph stared at the gray enamel on the steel leg of the desk.

"Seem like Gus have him a gun."

Larry glanced at Wilma. No one had said that. But it made sense. In Gus's neighborhood, you wouldn't want to just wait for the cavalry.

"Yeah," said Rommy. "Gus had him a pistol. Pointed it at me one time when he throwed me out. Winter, man, snowin and ice comin right down, and I's standin shiverin and he tole me to git."

"So you knew where the gun was?"

"Back under the cash register. Under them cigarettes and the Hershey bars in that glass thing."

"And that's where you got it?"

Squirrel looked around. "Man, can't you turn the heat on in here or nothin?"

Larry stood by the radiator. "Is that where you got the gun?"

Squirrel nodded. Larry opened the valve and brought Squirrel over. Typical Task Force bungle, Larry thought. No one ever asked the family if Gus owned a gun, because each detective assumed somebody else had covered it.

He left Wilma with Squirrel while he phoned Gus's son, John. Somewhat warily, John confirmed that his father kept a revolver behind the counter. He didn't remember much, except that Athena had insisted on it, but he put Larry on hold and in a few minutes had found the bill of sale in his dad's files. Four years ago, Gus had purchased a .38 Smith & Wesson Chief's Special, a five-shot revolver—the murder weapon Ballistics had identified from the land grooves on the slugs at the scene. Nor had the techs, for all their searching, found any casings. With a revolver, the cartridge casings remained in the chambers.

They always knew, Larry thought. The killer always knew something obvious that had eluded everybody else. He told Wilma to phone Greer and then called Muriel himself.

11

MAY 22, 2001

Kind

FOR ARTHUR, the thought of several hours alone with Gillian Sullivan had been enough to wake him for the day at 4 a.m., and on the road with her this morning, he had alternated between periods when he was hopelessly wordstruck or given over to garrulous babbling. Now his heart leapt at the sight of her through the mesh security window between the barred doors at the rear of the guardhouse. But his response was not to any of his private longings. It was the consequence for his client that fired every nerve. Arthur was hovering by the interior door, even before she'd been buzzed through.

"He'll talk to you," she said.

"Great!" Arthur dashed back to his briefcase and swept up the pages of a draft motion to dismiss in another matter, which he'd been revising. Returning, he found her smiling at his eagerness.

"Not yet, Arthur. He needs an hour or so." Gillian explained Erdai's circumstances.

Somewhat chagrined, Arthur went to the front desk to make arrangements. When he had called the Warden's Office to set up the visit, he'd expected problems due to the fact that Gillian was a convicted felon, a category of persons not always warmly welcomed as prison visitors. Instead, all the questions had focused on Arthur himself, because Erdai didn't recognize his name. Erno had been cryptic with the prison authorities about his business with Gillian—they seemed to think it concerned his estate—and in the end, Arthur had been permitted to accompany Gillian on the supposition, which he never discouraged, that he was her lawyer. As a result, the lieutenant at the front desk now informed Arthur that in order to see Erdai, Gillian had to go back in with him. She frowned when Arthur explained. Apparently, she was counting on having endured the last of the cellblock.

"Can I buy you lunch at least?" Arthur asked. He was starving anyway. Gillian agreed without any visible enthusiasm and lit a cigarette the second they left the guard-house.

"Did he tell you what he had? Erdai?" Arthur asked.

"He said your client was innocent."

"*In*-nocent?" Arthur stopped in his tracks. His mouth, he realized, was hanging. "Did he explain that?"

Gillian shook her head as she blew smoke into the wind.

"Except, he believes your guy will get out and has done enough time. I assume he's going to tell you somebody else killed those people. But he didn't say who. Or how he knows that."

"And did you believe him?"

"He asked the same thing, Arthur, and I told him no. Not that he makes a bad im-pression. He's bright. That's for certain. You can judge for yourself. My opinions are pre-formed, I suppose."

Being himself, Arthur tried several more questions, even after it was clear Gillian couldn't answer them, but he finally fell silent as they walked to his car. *Innocent.* He was not certain exactly what he had been expecting to hear from Erdai. After rereading his letter to Gillian a dozen times, Arthur's main speculation had been that Erdai, who worked at DuSable Field, which was not far from Paradise, had witnessed the crime or talked to someone who'd been there, and had new information. Yet, as always, Arthur had refused to listen when Pamela tried to engage him in hopes that Rommy was not guilty at all. Innocent. His heart was skipping around and to calm himself, he focused on the locale. He was at Rudyard, where people arrived because they did not know how to behave—they were thugs and liars and outlaws. Hopes notwithstanding, Arthur's reasoning part told him that at the end of the day he was likely to share Gillian's conclusion about Erdai's veracity.

Looking for a restaurant, they found thin pickings in the small town. Prison visitors were overwhelmingly poor and far more apt to brown-bag it than to eat much besides drive-in fare. The restaurant they settled on was dark and very large, a family place with linoleum tables grained to resemble wood. From the looks of it, Arthur suspected it had once been a bowling alley.

Gillian ordered a salad. Arthur took the special, which was meat loaf.

"It probably won't be very good," Arthur said as the waitress receded. "A place like this? It's been cooked and overcooked. It'll be like eating a cannonball."

When Arthur's lunch was set down before him, he took his knife, as he always did, and separated everything on the plate—he gave the peas a space apart from the potatoes, and scraped the blade in a circle so that the brown gravy formed a precise pool around the meat loaf. Gillian, who was stubbing out her second cigarette with the arrival of the food, observed him with plain interest.

"Force of habit," he told her.

"So I take it. And how is the meat loaf? As you feared?"

He chewed a moment. "Worse."

"May I ask why you ordered it?"

"My father always made us order the special. He thought it was the best deal. It made him frantic if we did anything else. I mean, you asked about my mother the other day? Stuff like that, ordering the special—I'm sure that's why she left." He swallowed hard on the meat loaf, which had formed like a cud. "I can see her point."

Gillian smiled broadly. His intent was to amuse her, but he knew he'd touched on one of the long-term difficulties he'd had as the child of such ill-matched human beings—he saw each parent's point of view. He shared his father's bitterness at his mother's desertion, but he understood her indignity at being tethered to a person who often inflicted his anxieties on everyone else. His mother, however, was rarely as generous with Arthur. She found her son too much like his father, conventional and dismally unadventurous. By reminding himself that his mother was an eccentric, he had managed, with effort, to disregard her judgments, which went largely unspoken in any event. But now, nearing forty, he was increasingly haunted by her example—someone who had broken free of all traditional restraints to pursue the life she wanted. What did he want? The mystery of it seemed large enough to swallow him at times.

"You gave me to think you were quite fond of your father, Arthur. When I met you at Duke's?" She added the last words with noticeable care.

"'Fond'? In my life, my father was like gravity. I mean, without him the world would have just fallen apart." These days, his father was Arthur's favorite subject. Talk kept him alive for Arthur, the images near at hand. He understood what he was doing and how futile it was. But he couldn't stop himself. That was what had gotten him into trouble in that first meeting with Gillian. Yet now, clearly as recompense, she sat against the leatherette backing of the booth, a cigarette between two manicured fingers, granting him unwavering attention.

Harvey Raven had spent his entire working life as a second-line employee in a relative's scrapyard, salvaging used auto parts. Somehow, it was a necessary element of all that frightened and concerned Mr. Raven to believe that if only a few things were different, his life would have been if not right, at least calm. If only he had gone to college. If only he had money. If only he were an owner of the scrapyard and not a working stiff. If only, if only—it was the slogan of his life. And who was to say he was wrong? All the time Arthur had spent in the law firm mixing with the well-to-do, the cultivated, the well-heeled, he had known they were clueless about people like him. They didn't understand that desert thirst for money or the security it bought. They didn't understand what it was to be at the world's mercy. Arthur's heart still reveled when he recalled his father's exultant look at Arthur's law-school graduation or at the news seven years later that Arthur was leaving the Prosecuting Attorney's Office to join the law firm at the astonishing salary of $100,000 a year.

"People don't think much about the valor of ordinary lives," Arthur said to Gillian, "you know, of folks who are supposed to be just normal. But the older he got and I got, the more I saw how heroic my father was. I mean, it was basically a miracle that a man so scared for himself had managed to look out for other people and to care so much about them." Arthur had now reached the point in the cycle where he felt his throat thicken and the pressure of tears, but he was, as ever, powerless to end this celebration.

"And my father died with courage, too. He had liver cancer. It just ate him up. He went to the doctor and got the whole grim prognosis—six months left, most of it in terrible pain. And he was philosophical. To the end. I felt like grabbing him by the hospital gown. Jesus Christ, I wanted to say, you were scared of everything your whole life, you worried about stuff you never needed to worry about, you let it make you crazy, and now this? Now he was calm and accepting. And we had a great time, really, as a result. When he had good moments, we would laugh. It turned out we'd had a wonderful life together, when you added it up. He loved me. I loved him. He'd stuck with us, when maybe not every guy would have. I'd done the stuff he wanted me to do. He knew I'd take care of Susan. I mean, there was just so much gratitude from both of us."

Arthur, by now, had lost the battle. He averted his face to spare Gillian, but the tears poured from his eyes. He groped behind him for his handkerchief. When he had recovered, he saw that Gillian was now rigid, probably with horror.

"Oh, God," he said, "what an ass I'm making of myself. I cry all the time since my father died. I cry about TV shows. I cry when I watch the news. I keep trying to understand the logic. We need to love other people so badly and it only makes life unbearable when they're lost. Is there any sense to that?"

"No," she answered in a small, hoarse voice. She had flushed. The faint freckles on her neck now stood out, and her eyes, with the clear line of makeup and the cloud of blush on the lids, were closed. "No," she said again, and took a breath. "You have a strange effect on me, Arthur."

"A good one?"

"I can't say that."

"Yeah," he said, resigned to the facts.

"No, no. It's nothing about you. It's me, Arthur." She struggled with something, looking down at her long hands. There was still color all the way to her collar. "The gratitude you described, the admiration—I've never had that. Never." She mustered a smile but not the courage to look at him. In a moment she asked if they could go.

Driving back, Arthur did not say a word. After a few hours with her, he was beginning to gain a sense of Gillian Sullivan's complications. Lord knows, they should have been apparent, given the mess she'd made of her life. But her demeanor, even now, seemed so serene and commanding that he was surprised to discover an unpredictable element to her personality. Her responses to him ran hot and cold. Accustomed to attempting to please women, he felt a little like a tetherball. Overall, though, she seemed to like him far more than he'd expected. Despite cautioning himself, he'd found that recognition exciting.

When they arrived at the institution, Gillian

still seemed unsettled. This time it was the prospect of going back in that appeared to bother her. She leaned forward in her seat, taking in the facility's vast sprawl and shaking her head. Arthur apologized for forcing her to go through this twice.

"It's not your fault, Arthur. I knew what I was doing in coming here. It's just been rather much to face. The memories."

"Kind of the ultimate bad time?" he said.

Gillian, who was already fumbling again in her purse for a last cigarette, took a second to think.

"People have their standard imagery about prison, don't they? We all do. Everybody imagines certain parts will be especially dreadful."

"Like what? Sex?"

"Certainly, sex. Yes. That's standard-issue. The fear of living without it. The fear of homosexual encroachments. Most of the lesbian activity when I was inside took place among the staff. That's the truth.

"Sex ends up as just one more thing you're cut off from. That's the main form of punishment—separation. From people. From habits. From food. From life as you know it. That's precisely what prison is supposed to

be. There's the irony, of course. After everything is said and done, after all the anxiety
about incidental horrors, like getting mauled
by bull dykes, the real punishment is exactly
what's intended. It's like suffering an ampu-
tation. You stop wanting. You just quit. I did.
Desire is replaced by boredom. They bore
you to death in there. You think, Well, I can
get interested in anything, I'm bright. But because everybody is just marking time,
nothing seems to matter. You know you've
been sentenced to feel the weight of time
passing, and you do. I had moments when I
could literally hear the watch ticking on my
wrist. Every second being lost."

Watching her, the harrowed look as she
stared at the prison, Arthur, unwillingly,
found himself crying again, silently now, a
runnel descending each cheek. He wiped
his jaw first with his hand and apologized
once more, although by now she seemed
unconcerned by his lack of composure.

"Once I start," he said.

"Not at all. You're very kind, Arthur." She
seemed somewhat struck by what she had
said, and faced him fully. "Very kind," she
repeated, then looked down at her unlit cigarette and left the car.

12

OCTOBER 9, 1991

Breaking the News

MY NAME IS ROMEO GANDOLPH. I am 27 years old. I read and write English. I am making this statement freely and voluntarily. No one has promised me anything to make this statement. I understand that this statement is being videotaped while I read it.

After midnight on July 4, 1991, I stopped in by Paradise which was a restaurant. The owner Gus was getting ready to close. Gus and I had been knowing each other for a long time. I had tried to steal money once from out of his cash register. He had chased me down the street and caught me and beat me bad. After that, whenever he saw me, he would tell me to get away from his restaurant. Sometimes he was like joking, but sometimes he was straight serious. Once when I walked into the restaurant, he took out a pistol from under the cash register and told me to leave.

On July 4, 1991, I happened to see a lady I knew through the window and I went inside. Her name was Luisa Remardi and I used to say hello to her and stuff when I was hanging at the airport.

When I come in on July 4, Gus said I was figuring to mope around the place and hide till he closed so I could steal something. I had taken a dose of PCP and Gus made me angry. We started in shouting with each other. Gus headed under the register to get that revolver, but I got there first. Gus kept yelling and stuff at me and went for the phone to call the police and I just shot him. I wasn't thinking.

Luisa was screaming out that I was crazy and all and wouldn't shut up. When I went over to tell her to keep quiet, she jumped at the gun and I ended up shooting her, too. There was one other guy in the restaurant, a white guy. He was hid under the table, but I seen him. I pointed the gun and told him to *pull Gus and Luisa down to the cold place in the cellar. Once he done it, I didn't wait but another second to shoot him. I stole what I could off of everybody and then left out of the place. I got rid of the gun. I'm not completely sure where.*

I had taken a lot of PCP and I don't remember all of this too clear. This is the most I can remember right now. I am very sorry for what I done.

Muriel sat across from Squirrel in the interview room. Nearby, an evidence tech focused a video camera on a tripod, the unit's small floodlight casting an intense beam over Squirrel, who was now clad in an optic-orange jail jumpsuit. Batting his eyes in the brightness, Squirrel had stumbled at several points as he'd read, asking Muriel to remind him of certain words. The first time, about halfway through they'd rewound and started again. His hands had been shaking as he held the paper, but otherwise he appeared all right.

"Is that all there is to your statement, Mr. Gandolph?"

"Yes, ma'am."

"And is that statement in your words?"

"The Detective over there, he helped me."

"But does this statement reflect your best memory of what happened on July 4, 1991?"

"Yes, ma'am."

"This is how you described to the Detective what happened?"

"Yeah, after we talked it over some, yeah."

"And did anybody hit you or threaten any violence against you to get you to make this statement?"

"No, not how I 'member."

"Well, would you remember if somebody hit you?"

"Ain nobody hit me."

"Did you have food and water?"

"I had some now. Didn't feel much like eatin 'fore now."

"And do you have any other complaint with your treatment?"

"Well, you know, I messed in my trousers. That wasn't so nice. I was like a kid or somethin sittin here in it." Squirrel gave his disorganized hairdo a solitary shake. "Best not to talk 'bout it now." Then he added, "And they mostly freezed me to death, too."

Muriel looked to Larry.

"I had to open the window because of the stink."

There was still a reek when she'd arrived. 'Sure-shit case,' Larry had joked. She'd responded with the line her father had always uttered as he entered the one bathroom her family shared, 'Smells like somebody died in here.' Later, she reminded Larry to inventory Gandolph's pants for evidence—talk about proof of a consciousness of guilt.

She asked Rommy if there was anything he wanted to add.

"Still and all," he said, "I just can't believe I done nothin like this. I'm not the kind to hurt even a fly. I never done nothin like this before." He put his head into his hands.

"We're going to discontinue taping now. The time is now 12:32 a.m. on October 9th." When Muriel nodded, the tech killed the light.

A copper from the watch desk came to put Rommy back in the holding area until 6 a.m., when they'd take him down to the House of Corrections. His hands cuffed behind him, Rommy remained dazed and subdued.

"See you, Rommy," Larry said.

Rommy briefly looked back and nodded.

"What'd you do to him?" Muriel asked, when he was gone.

"Nothing. I did my job."

"You're pretty amazing," she said.

Larry smiled like a kid.

Greer had arrived outside during the taping. At one in the morning, Harold was clean-shaven with nary a wrinkle in his starched shirt. Greer was an acquaintance of Talmadge's, and Muriel had sat beside him only a week ago at the City of Hope Dinner, where he'd struck her as one of those black men who'd always accepted that he had to be better, the type never to let down his guard, especially if somebody white was around. He'd done it so long he didn't even know it. Hands on his hips as he addressed Larry, the Commander did not seem completely pleased with his Detective. He asked first how Larry had found Gandolph.

"I got a tip. Doper in the jail said he saw him with this cameo."

"And Gandolph had it on him when you grabbed him?"

"Yep." Larry nodded several times. "I'll make sure Lenahan and Woznicki are on paper on that, too."

"What about the sex?" Greer asked. "He won't wear it?"

"Not yet."

"So what's our theory?" Greer asked both of them.

"My theory," said Larry, "is he had the hots for Luisa, he assaulted her at gunpoint and did it again after she was dead. But I say don't push it in court. We're missing something and we'll just stumble around."

When Greer turned to Muriel, she explained why Larry was wrong, trying to be nonchalant in order to not show him up. But the assault had to be charged.

"You won't get the evidence in, unless you do," she said. "And with a capital case, you want to make sure the jury hears that stuff. The evidence is light on that count, but my guess is you'll get a conviction. It wasn't the bogeyman who did that to her. Rommy's either the doer or an accomplice. He's legally responsible either way."

Greer's eyes didn't move as he listened, clearly impressed. When Muriel rolled out of bed in the morning, there was an endless list of things she did not know for sure about herself, whether she wanted to be single or married, what her favorite color was, whether she could ever stand to vote for a Republican, or even if she'd made a mistake by never having a fling with a girl. But when you put a case file in her hand, her judgment was as perfect as the sun. Problems were like buds, which in her mental hothouse blossomed into solutions. In the law-enforcement community, her legend was already growing—she was leaving a vapor trail, they said.

"*Is* there an accomplice?" Greer asked.

"He says no," said Larry. "When he realizes we're talking about the needle, you're gonna find out. He's not taking the long walk, if he's got another name."

Greer contemplated, then finally offered Larry his hand. While he was at it, he shook with Muriel, too.

"Very good work," he said. There were reporters outside. He asked Larry and Muriel to stand with him while he faced the cameras to make a brief statement. The lights flared on as soon as they entered the old brick lobby in Six, which was as far as the reporters were allowed to go. Even at this hour, each of the stations had a crew on hand, and there were two print journalists as well. The media crowded around while Greer announced the arrest, providing Gandolph's name and age and criminal record. They already knew about Luisa's cameo; there weren't many secrets in a police station. Greer confirmed that Squirrel had the piece in his pocket last night. With that, Harold called it quits. The cameras had plenty for the newscasts all day.

Greer pointed at Muriel when they separated. "Regards to Talmadge," he said. Neutral enough, but she could feel Larry react. She walked toward the parking lot with him. Larry seemed on the verge of saying something dumb again, but Stew Dubinsky from the *Trib*, round as a cherub, came dashing up. He wanted to do a feature on Larry—intrepid investigator scores again. Larry declined, but was uncharacteristically polite to a reporter. He seemed to know that Stew, who covered the courthouse, was important to Muriel.

Once Dubinsky gave up, Larry and she stood between their cars. The parking lot was as bright as a night game. Nobody cared to read about muggings behind the police station.

"Your jury do the right thing?" Larry asked.

"They came back this afternoon. Guilty, all counts."

He smiled for her sake. Larry clearly was tired and, in his weariness, starting to look old. His thinning hair stood up when the wind blew, and he had that fragile northern European skin, the same as Scandinavian blonds, already growing ruddy and dry. She still thought of Larry as a fixed piece of her youth, and it was almost incomprehensible that time was starting to work him over.

When they'd met, she was supposed to be helping him with Torts, and she ended up sleeping with him instead, the first time while her husband was in the hospital with the heart troubles that killed him two years later. It was stupid, of course, but it was stupid in an adolescent way—she had merely been seeking the borders, engaging in a little bit of outrage as she sank into the bland world of law and adult responsibility. But the relationship had gone on. In a strange, fitful way. After Larry remarried. After Rod died. They would say it was done, and then she'd see Larry in the courthouse and one thing would lead to another. The quest, such as it was, continued, full of the yearning and willingness that belonged to the time when you knew nothing for sure about who you wanted. For her, that time was finally passing. She felt strangely sorry for them both.

"I'm starving to death," Larry said. "You wanna eat something?"

She was reluctant to abandon him again. He'd looked like she'd stabbed him the other night, outside the jail. Then she thought of something perfect.

"What about Paradise?"

"Great." Larry hadn't been able to share much with John on the phone and had promised to connect when he could. John was supposed to be at the restaurant all night.

When they got there, John was nowhere to be seen. It turned out he was working the kitchen. Through the narrow stainless steel opening where the waitresses hung their orders and the cooks passed the food, John noticed them and emerged holding a spatula, an apron wound twice around him. Its sheer size made it obvious it had belonged to Gus.

"It's true?" He pointed to a radio which was next to the register. When they said yes, he took a seat on one of the stools. He fixed for a moment on a darkened patch in the paneling, then dropped his face into his hands and broke down completely. Glossy with tears, John began thanking both of them obsessively.

"It's our job, John," Muriel kept saying as she patted him on the shoulder, but she nearly wept herself. The nerves lit up across her body in a starburst of feeling, a sense of living connection to what was right.

"You don't know how hard it is," John said, "thinking the person who did it is still walking around. I felt every minute like I had to do something, that I was letting my old man down if I didn't."

Muriel had spoken often with John since July, and over the months it had become clear that in death Gus had grown far dearer to John than he had ever been alive. Muriel had seen this happen before, but she did not fully understand the transformation. Necessity had forced John to take over the restaurant, and a few months of standing in Gus's shoes had undoubtedly enhanced a son's appreciation for his father's viewpoint, not to mention the rigors of Gus's life. But she was often startled when she received John's calls to hear the ferocity with which he talked about his father's murderer. At moments, she suspected he hated the killer for inspiring that shameful instant in which John had welcomed his father's death. However it had happened, she sensed that the pain and shock of the killing—and the fact that it had ended any chance of healing between father and son—had wrapped themselves around the prior misery between the Leonidis men, so that John could no longer tell one from the other.

John launched himself into more abject thank-yous, and Larry finally saved them all by cuffing John's neck and saying he'd really come around for a free meal. Eager with gratitude, John rushed back to the kitchen.

They moved toward the tables. Being Muriel and Larry Together, a sort of Outward Bound experience in which taboo was the wilderness, they lingered near the booth where Luisa Remardi had been murdered. Muriel found them sharing another telegraphic glance and they sat simultaneously on either side. She had to look down for a minute to be sure she didn't laugh. She smoked when she was on trial, and had a pack in her purse. Larry held out his fingers and took one puff before passing it back.

"I hope you noticed I haven't mentioned Talmadge."

"Until now."

Larry tipped his chin down so he took on an inquisitorial look.

"You're going to marry this guy, aren't you?"

It was two o'clock in the morning. And Larry, whatever he was, deserved nothing less than the truth. Functionally, she had been dating for nineteen years, trying on men as if they were dresses, hoping all the while that she would look in the mirror one day and recognize herself. She was sick of it. She wanted the other side of life now—kids, stability, the sense that she was good enough to matter to somebody worthwhile. Talmadge excited her. He had a life she craved to be a part of. She shared his need to act eventfully, to have consequence. He was funny. He was rich. He was nice-looking. And he counted in the world—enormously.

She peered across the table. It was always a shock to her to find she cared so much about Larry, that there was not only a sensual buzz but sympathy and connection. And knowledge. More than anything else, they shared the same intuitions, as if they had both been wired the same way in the factory. Years from now, she realized, she'd identify this as the moment she'd made up her mind.

"That's my best guess."

Larry sat straight back against the blackish planks of the booth. He'd just told her what she was going to do, but he looked astonished.

"Yeah, well," said Larry at last, "the rich guys always get the girls."

"You think that's the attraction, Larry?"

"I think it's the whole scene—rich, famous, powerful. Talmadge can do a lot for you."

This conversation was a wrong turn from the beginning. Muriel looked away rather than answer.

"Don't tell me no."

"No," she replied.

Larry's wide face ground through a series of self-containing expressions. Despite his efforts, he was about to say something else, but John arrived with a plate of steak and eggs for each of them. After asking if anybody minded, John stole one of Muriel's cigarettes from the pack on the table and smoked while they ate. He remained unsettled, pulled at his earring, bit at his fingernails, and couldn't stop asking questions or adjust to the idea that the killer was finally caught. What seemed to bother him most was that it wasn't some ghoul who crawled out of a sewer, but a guy John had frequently seen in here.

"I mean, what's blowing my mind is, I mean, Gus thought the guy was funny. He was a pain. But for my dad, chasing this screwball away was kind of entertaining. If I'm remembering, there was one time my old man went after him with a butcher knife and a sandwich. He gave him a hamburger and then told him he'd kill him if he ever came back. It was a contest. For both of them. This guy—Gandolph?—he'd look through the window to see if my dad was around, and come sauntering in like he owned the place, then run like hell if Gus came out of the back. That went on in here once a week."

John kept going over it, and Muriel and Larry slowly tried to explain the pure accidental nature of these calamities.

"Look, it doesn't make it any better," Larry said, "but you know, your dad probably did like this guy. And if Squirrel hadn't taken a big dose of wack and didn't see this lady he had a yen for sitting right here, it would have been the usual dance steps. But it wasn't.

Not that night. That night there was all this shit Squirrel wanted that he couldn't have, a lifetime of it, and he went off. It's the same thing as if the gas main blew up under this restaurant. I mean, this is dumb, but it's true, John: it's life. It doesn't always work out right." She noticed that Larry stole a glance her way when he said that.

IT WAS NEARLY FOUR when they left Paradise. Larry was so damn beat that he felt he was unraveling from the edges, the slouching demons and unseen locales of dreams already sneaking at him from the periphery. Across the street the great highway roared. Urgency put you on the road at four in the a.m.—truckers who wanted to make a quick pass through the city, futures traders with an eye on the overseas markets, lovers who'd left somebody's bed in the middle of the night in order to stop home before morning. That universe of special needs went zipping by overhead.

Inside the restaurant, Larry had tried hard to console Gus's kid in order to comfort himself. It hadn't worked. John was still talking about all the tough guys his old man had faced down—mobsters who wanted to force him to take kitchen linens, and gang-bangers who tried to stick him up—and standing here with Muriel, Larry still felt like his heart had exploded.

"Muriel," he said in the same plaintive tone he'd heard from himself outside the jail, "I need to talk to you."

"About?"

"About Talmadge—" He threw a hand through the air in frustration. "About every-thing."

"I don't want to talk about Talmadge."

"No, listen to me."

He was weary enough to feel dizzy and a little sick to his stomach—but he was ill mostly with himself. For several days, he'd known why he'd been pouring energy into this case like a medic trying to revive a dead body, until he finally had. For Muriel, for Chrissake. Yet even seeing that much, he hadn't seen it all. He didn't just want to hang with her and trade snappy lines. Or get an-other shot at her in the rack. No, in his mushy, teenaged brain, until a little while ago some horse opera had been playing. He'd lasso the bad guy, and with that, Muriel would come to her senses and recognize he was the best fella around. She'd shuck Talmadge and her march to glory. Recognizing his own devices, too late and so clearly, he was crushed. Some great detective, he thought.

"I want you to listen," he said again.

Their cars were in the parking lot, near the spot where Gus's Cadillac and Luisa's and Paul's vehicles had grilled in the July sun for a day while their bodies had frozen. Muriel's Honda Civic was closer and they ended up sitting together on the front seat. Muriel wasn't neat. She used the floor in back like a trash bag—food wrappers, plastic packaging from things she'd opened, and personal mail from the office were slopped all over.

"You know how people always tell you when you're young to grow up?" Larry asked. "And you hear them, and it even seems like a pretty good idea, but it's like, what the fuck? What the fuck am I supposed to do? People tell you to get serious and you can't even figure out what you want."

As he spoke, Larry looked toward the unfaced brick wall in front of him. Years ago, an advertisement for a soft drink had been painted there and the spectral remains of some bountiful young woman with a glass in her hand were still apparent under the shell lights.

"I always wondered how in the hell I was going to figure it out. I mean, some people, like you, I think you've always known what you want and have been going for it since I met you. You know, to see your name in the sky. But I'm the other kind. I mean, I don't even know it's what I want until maybe I don't have it. Like when Nancy says, 'How about if I take the boys?' I mean, Jesus Christ, get real."

He found himself caught in a great swell of emotion as an image of his sons over- came him. He saw them following him around like puppies while he was cutting drywall, laying tile, working away at these houses. They loved to be with him. Darrell had a saw that he dragged across the dusty floors and Michael, with two hands on a hammer, was always driving nails at all an- gles into a two-by-four. Larry had to keep one eye on them every second, and even so, afterwards, in the middle of the night he'd wake, split by fear like a tree by light- ning, sure he had not been careful enough and that one of them could somehow come to serious harm.

He pinched his nose, dwelling with the pain in the hope he would not break down. He had great suspicion of a certain type you often found on the Force these days, men—and some women—who gave in to every lame sentiment because they were so hard on the street, who'd weep buckets when their parakeet bought the farm, but, hours before, couldn't so much as shake their heads over a seven-year-old killed in a hit-and-run. The idea he had of himself was to have some handle on all of it, to be able to say, as he'd tried to tell John, it hurts like hell, that's life.

"So that's how I am, dumb enough to not know what something is till it's gone. There are people like that," Larry said. "I'm not the only one."

In the dark, he could not really see Muriel's face, just the keenest light on her eyes and her profile in silhouette. She was leaning against the driver's door, with her head of short, stiff curls held erect in a posture clearly suggesting alarm.

"Where is this going?" She couldn't stop being Muriel. She had to be at the end of the curve when everybody else was still at the beginning. As near as he could tell, Muriel had come from a normal whitebread family.

But she must have been calculating in the womb. Like cows who always knew the shortest path to their destination, Muriel had a positioning system of her own that never failed to highlight the route to her best interests. Even when she was kind, as she often was, it felt a trifle remote, as if she'd also taken a second to figure out whether it was the right thing for her.

Summoning himself to answer, he glanced down and was surprised to see soil ground under his nails. Yesterday he'd been at another small house in the Point, his current project, getting some evergreens in while it was still time for fall planting. His mom had always hammered on clean hands, and it amazed him that he hadn't noticed the dirt until now, a sign of how focused he'd been on Squirrel since he woke nearly twenty-four hours ago.

"What if I told you I was sick of my own shit," he said to her. "Sick of looking for the life better than life. What if I told you I've actually started figuring stuff out." He showed her his fingernails. "I garden."

"Garden?"

"I mean, liking it. Growing things. Would that matter to you?"

"Larry," she said.

"I think I know what I need in my life. And what we have going—neither one of us has ever been very honest about it. There's a lot there—"

"There is," she said. She reached for his arm. "But, Larry." She was the one having difficulty now. She'd moved into the light and he could see her eyes close and flutter with the strain. "I don't think we can take this any further. *I* can't. I'm not there now."

He was hit hard again, worse perhaps than in the restaurant, and felt his breath burn in his lungs. Jesus, he thought. What a fucked-up creature I am. Making a play when the woman just told you she was marrying somebody else.

"I'm gonna feel like such a dip," he said, "if I actually cry."

She leaned across and touched the back of his neck.

"Come on, Larry. Jesus. This has never been for keeps. Come on."

"That's what I mean," he said. "It should have been."

"It's been good, Larry. It's been good in a zillion ways. But it's been a thrill ride, Lar. That's how we wanted it. Sneaking around.

Screwing our brains out. You can't try to pretend it's a regular life. I mean, I love it for what it was. That was great." She laughed, an unconstrained sound in the dim car, full of earnest amusement in memory. She squeezed him around the shoulders and brought her face close to his. "We had great times," she said and laid her other hand on his thigh as a reminder. He batted it away, and she returned it. They went that round a few times, laughing all the while, both of them enjoying the moment of physical combat, and the relief it provided. He finally grabbed her hand and she took the other one from his shoulder and used it to lower his zipper before he pushed her away.

"I don't need one last trip on the roller coaster, Muriel."

"I do," she answered, in her usual fearless way and placed her hand where it had been. He thought he was beyond being stimulated, but he was wrong. She lowered her face to him right there, and he enjoyed it for one second before easing her away.

"We're in a parking lot for Chrissake," he said.

She threw her keys in the ignition and pulled around the corner, her free hand on his hard-on, pumping it now and then while she drove. When she stopped again, she went at him full time. Larry looked down the alley, realizing they were in the correct neighborhood for this kind of thing—behind these buildings, under these phone lines, amid the spilled garbage and rusted Dumpsters pleasure had often been purchased on the cheap and practiced on the run. Muriel was making a feast of it, taking her time, nuzzling the knob of him, running her tongue under the ridge and then bringing her lips over the top, again and again, watching attentively and understanding exactly the reaction each move inspired. That was Muriel, too. Bold. Looking at the thing and savoring the power a woman derived from being willing. He kept thinking, God, this is fucked up, I'm fucked up. When he came, it felt as if he cried out forever.

13

MAY 22, 2001

Normal

"SO YOU JUST COULDN'T STAY AWAY FROM ME," said Ruthie, the correctional officer who'd escorted Gillian initially. With her stout form, she kept the heavy door into the guardhouse half open and beckoned to Gillian like an old friend, nodding to Arthur as well. "Thought you said you and Ernie were done talking," Ruthie said as they followed her into the dim corridor of stone and brick.

Arthur explained that the Lieutenant had demanded Gillian's presence and Ruthie laughed.

"There's some here," said Ruthie, "all the rules we got and they just have to make more." That surely was Gillian's experience. Prison officials were often in a class by themselves when it came to rigidity. And among them there were, inevitably, a few outright sadists, who were gratified to see people in cages. But at Alderson, Gillian also found many guards like Ruthie, good-natured souls who were there because it was the best job they could find, or because they were happiest with people who had no right to look down on them.

By the time they'd reached the infirmary, Ruthie had offered to walk Gillian back out as soon as Arthur was situated with Erdai, assuring them that the Lieutenant would never know the difference. Gillian was admittedly curious about what Erdai would say, but her days of evaluating witnesses, matching their stories against her memory of other evidence, had been brought to a forced end. For her, the safest thing was to leave.

Arthur had grown agitated again about what was before him and disappeared without much in the way of farewell through the infirmary entrance. Ruthie returned in several minutes to lead Gillian back through the warren of corridors and bars toward the front.

In the main building, a trusty wheeling a stainless steel cart turned full around as Gillian passed. She felt his gaze, but assumed he was ogling. Instead she heard her name.

"Ain't you Judge Sullivan?"

Ruthie came to alert beside her, but Gillian answered, "I used to be."

"This here is Jones," Ruthie said. "He's all right. Most of the time."

Ruthie was playing and Jones smiled, but his attention remained on Gillian.

"You gimme sixty," he said. "Agg Battery." It had occurred to her there would still be plenty of inmates in here whom she had sentenced, but her concerns had rested so much on her own reactions that she'd largely forgotten the risk of being around these men. And she sensed no danger now. Jones was tall, with a beard, but he was getting past the age where he was likely to be a problem to anyone.

"Shot someone?" she asked.

"Dude what was with me. We were doin a job in a liquor store. Clerk went for a gun and I shot my partner instead. Ain't that a bitch? And the state charged me for that, that and the armed robbery. I don't mind the armed robbery rap, but how come I'm doin time for shootin someone I didn't have any mind to shoot?"

"Because you meant to shoot the clerk," said Gillian.

"Naw, I didn't. I was jest jumpy."

"You could have killed somebody."

"Yeah, but I didn't. See that's the part I still don't un'erstand."

He understood. He just wanted to talk about it. It still kept him up nights to realize that so much of his life had been determined in an instant.

"That's nothing but old times now, Jones," Ruthie told him.

"Yeah," said Jones, "I'm gone get old doing that time." But he was laughing as he said it.

"How's your partner?" Gillian asked.

"Okay. His stomach ain't been right since, is the only thing. You give him just thirty. He gettin out in oh-three."

"He didn't have the gun."

Beaten back, Jones returned to his cart. He appeared reconciled, but in a day or two he'd be convinced once again that the whole deal was wrong.

Ruthie kept talking about him all the way to the guardhouse, informing Gillian about Jones's troubles with his family. Ruthie's idea of a secret must have been something she told only a quarter of the people on earth. But she was sweet. She helped Gillian pull her bag out of the locker where she'd been ordered to deposit it and, like a good host, walked Gillian right to the front gate on the other side of the guardhouse, and waved her hand to another Lieutenant behind the main desk to buzz Gillian out.

Gillian pulled open the heavy grating and looked out of the prison gloom into a spectacular late-spring day. It was yard time and even as she remained on the threshold, she could hear the tumult of the men, whooping and gabbing some distance away. At Alderson, railroad tracks abutted the facility. Most of the trains were a hundred cars long, bearing a shiny cargo of coal, but the D.C.-to-Chicago Amtrak also clattered by, close enough to see all the passengers clearly. Gillian could never look away. Instead, with unbearable envy, she studied the travelers, who were free to move on to places they wanted to go. The Normals, she called them in her own mind.

She turned back to Ruthie.

"I forgot something. I didn't put the time on the sign-out sheet."

"We'll get that," said Ruthie.

"I want to do it myself." She didn't. She simply wanted to re-enter and wave and have the door open again. When the lock shot back this time, it felt as if the mechanism had been wired into her heart. A Normal.

On a bench beneath a tree, halfway to the parking lot, Gillian rested. She watched the people come and go, Normals all of them. Like her. Eventually, she pulled from her bag the book she'd been reading. It was Thucydides. Duffy, who loved the classics, had pressed it on her, and to her surprise she had been finding great reprieve in history, in learning again the lessons of the distant past and the account of forgotten human folly. Her comfort, she suspected, arose from knowing she would someday be forgotten as well, that her sins would wash away in the great tide of time in which all but one or two people who'd trod the world beside her—a scientist, an artist—would be pulverized with her into nothing more memorable than sand. And today she was free to begin moving there. It was over, she told herself in that moment. If she could let it be, it was over.

It was more than an hour and a half before

Arthur returned. Gillian had actually been considering walking a few blocks into town for a cool drink, when he finally emerged from the guardhouse.

"Sorry it was so long. I wanted to see Rommy before I left."

She told him she didn't mind. It had been a much better day than she'd expected. "How did it go with Erdai?"

"Great," he said. "Couldn't have gone better." Something was wrong with Arthur, however. He seemed strangely unfocused. He looked into the air for a second, almost like an animal, trying to make out a scent on the breeze. He said no more and she finally asked how he felt about what Erdai had told him.

"Oh, I believed him. Absolutely. That's why I had to see Rommy. I wanted to tell him about this myself. I had to argue with the Captain, but they finally brought him down for a few minutes." Arthur smiled suddenly. "Basically, he couldn't understand why I was surprised. Like it was completely normal. 'Tole you I didn't have nothin to do with it.' He's excited about getting out of here. But it wasn't news to him that he's innocent. The one who'll never let me hear the end of this is Pamela. Rommy's innocent," Arthur said and stared down at the gravel around the base of the tree, then he said it again. "Rommy's innocent."

"May I ask? Did Erno alibi Gandolph? Or does he say he knows who the killer was?"

"Oh, he knows," said Arthur. "It was him. Erdai. It's a hell of a story. But it all fits. Every detail. And it has to be true anyway. Why would a dying man bother lying? I mean, he killed all those people himself. Erdai did." Driven down by the weight of what he had just said, Arthur fell on the bench beside her.

Gillian waited. She was not sure she wanted to know more. No matter how isolated from the past or anesthetized she wanted to make her faculties of judgment, the story instantly struck her as implausible. It was too much to put down to coincidence that a dying inmate in the same institution with Gandolph was stepping forward to take credit for the crime.

Judging from his strange manner, she'd thought at first that Arthur, despite his statement to the contrary, actually shared her doubts. But she suspected now that his reaction was the reverse of skepticism. Years ago, her first boss in the P.A.'s Office, Raymond Horgan, who was now Arthur's senior partner, had told her that before his election, when Ray had been in private practice, he used to keep a slip of paper in his desk drawer. It was calligraphied with what he referred to as the defense lawyer's prayer: 'God save me from an innocent client.'

Convinced by Erdai, Arthur, she saw, suddenly stood on the highest cliff of his career. Rommy Gandolph's life, his innocent life, was in Arthur's hands. Justice, indeed, the whole principle of law—that it would make fairer the few elements of existence within human control—now depended on him. He was the main variable: his work, his wits, his ability to wage and win civil society's most momentous battle. The lost look swimming in Arthur's coffee-dark eyes was terror.

PART TWO

PROCEEDINGS

14

JUNE 12, 2001

The Chief Deputy

MURIEL WYNN, Chief Deputy Prosecuting Attorney for Kindle County, sat at her desk moving papers. In this job, she had discovered an orderly side to her character, which had eluded her in her earlier years. Her bedroom closet and her shopping lists were still governed by chaos, but she had always been her best at work. Her desk, nearly eight feet long, was arranged with the precision of a military base. The ramparts of papers—prosecution packages, internal memos, legal mail—sat with evened edges, equidistant from one another. Correspondence relating to next year's campaign for P.A., which would soon begin in earnest, was safely segregated on the upper quadrant, to be gathered at the end of the day and considered at home, on her own time.

A pop-up message appeared with a ding on Muriel's computer screen: "12:02 p.m.: Det. Lieut. Starczek here for hearing." She greeted Larry in the large open area outside her office, where six assistants jumped between desks, and visitors waited on the other side of an old mahogany rail. Across the way, sharing the same secretarial pool, was the P.A.'s Office, which her boss for the last decade, Ned Halsey, was ready to surrender to her as soon as the voters said yes next year.

For court, Larry had worn a tie and a linen sport coat, both rather stylish. He'd always liked clothes, although they no longer fit him as well. He was big and soft now, and his remaining hair, silky and whitening, had been carefully piled in place. But he had maintained the compelling bearing that comes from knowing who you are. At the sight of her, he smiled broadly and she felt his amusement—it was funny, pleasantly ticklish, that life moves on so unfathomably, that you go your ways and survive.

"Hey," she said.

"Hey," Larry answered.

She asked if he minded stopping for lunch. "I thought we could get something on the way to the Federal Building and talk about this stupid hearing."

"Cool," answered Larry.

Hearing him infected by his sons' vocabulary, she grinned and asked how the boys were.

"Are they mine? I thought they were the spawn of Satan." He had pictures in his wallet. Michael was twenty, a junior at Michigan. His younger boy, Darrell, was a high-school hero like his father and brother, although he played soccer rather than football. He looked to be a sure thing for a Division One scholarship, Larry said. "Only I may kill him before then. Talk about attitude. My folks, of course, they're still kicking, and they watch him and me and it's like old family movies. They think it's a laugh a minute."

Muriel took him into her office for a second to show off the photos of Theo, Talmadge's first grandson. Even at three, you could see he would take after Talmadge, large and broad. He was such a sweet guy, this little boy, the dearest soul in her life.

"None of your own, right, you and Talmadge?" asked Larry. It was probably the single question she most hated answering, but Larry clearly meant no more by it than confirming his memory.

"Never worked out," she answered and pointed him to the door.

In the elevator down, Larry asked her to explain today's hearing.

"Raven moved to depose a guy named Erno Erdai, who you supposedly knew," she said.

"I did."

"Well, Arthur wants to do the dep in the presence of a judge, so the judge can make credibility findings now, because Erno won't be around later, if the case proceeds. He's dying of cancer."

"Dying? Jesus, things went to hell for Erno in the last few years, I'd say. You know the story?"

As head of Violent Crimes, she'd reviewed Erdai's case at the time of the shooting four years ago. Ex-cadet, TN executive, and solid citizen goes nutzo at a cop bar. Mel Tooley had represented Erno and had tried like hell for probation, even getting the victim's lawyer, Jackson Aires, to say he had no objection. But she couldn't pass a guy on pen time because he lived in the suburbs. They locked up twenty black men a week in this town for shooting somebody. Erno had to go.

"How is old Arthur, by the way?" Larry asked.

"Still litigates like a man trying to save himself from drowning. He's okay."

"I always liked bringing cases to Arthur. You know, he was a plowhorse, not a race-horse, but he followed through."

"Well, that's what he's doing. Following through. He was pretty creased when the Court of Appeals dragooned him for this case, but he keeps pushing new buttons. This week he says Erdai's a critical witness."

"Yeah, 'critical,'" said Larry. "Critical of who?"

"You got it." She smiled. "You got some splainin' to do, Lucy. The motion claims Erdai tried to alert you to exculpatory evidence which you concealed."

"I hate when I do that," said Larry, then promptly denounced the whole notion as bullshit. "Erno wrote me a couple of letters from the joint, same as he did half the Force, looking for help once he got in there. What the hell was I supposed to do, send him a sympathy card? I guess Erno joined the other team inside. He's got an angle, right?"

"He must. I asked to talk to him a week ago, and he refused. The staff at Rudyard has no clue what he's up to."

A few doors down from the courthouse, Muriel stopped by Bao Din.

"You still eat Chinese?" she asked.

"Sure. But nothing real spicy."

The restaurant was old style with a bamboo curtain in the front entry and Formica tables, and the larded smells of fried peanut oil and yeasty foreign spices. Muriel harbored permanent suspicions about what passed for meat in the kitchen and stuck to vegetable plates. As a regular, and a person of influence, she was greeted warmly by Lloyd Wu, the proprietor, to whom she introduced Larry.

Given the allegations in the motion, she'd had no choice about asking Larry to attend the hearing, although they hadn't spent more than ten minutes together on any occasion in close to a decade. When he was around the office on a case, he would stop in sometimes. They'd take each other's pulse in a few moments, talk about his kids, the Force, and the office. They laughed a lot. After he left, she usually felt she had made an error horsing around with him. Not because of Larry himself—Larry the Elder was less of a hard case than the man she'd met seventeen years ago in law school. But he was a past she had self-consciously set aside, an attachment of the young, lost Muriel, a woman who was meaner, flightier, and unhappier than the current model.

But she needed Larry today. Dicks never forgot the evidence in a case. Carol Keeney, an appellate supervisor who'd been handling the matter for the last few years as it plodded toward execution, had found no mention of Erdai in the file, but Larry quickly reminded Muriel of the begats. Erno led to Collins. Collins led to Squirrel. She hadn't realized Erdai was the original source. Eyes closed, she waited for the digits to fall, but nothing came up. She leaned over the table.

"Old times' sake, Larry. Just us girls. Is there anything we have to worry about? I mean, just a fantasy of what they're aiming at?"

"You mean something Erno knows?"

"As opposed to what?"

"You're not a virgin, Muriel," said Larry, treading close to a line that was seldom acknowledged. There was street truth and court truth, and a good officer, like Larry, knew how to make one conform to the other without playing fast and loose. She let his remark go. "What kind of exculpatory evidence was this I supposedly hid?" Larry asked.

"Arthur never said and we never found out. I sent Carol over when the motion was up and she irritated the judge somehow and he granted it."

Larry groaned.

"You know how this goes, Larry. Harlow's the kind who thinks appointed counsel deserves every break, especially in a capital case. And he probably likes Arthur. His firm does a lot of federal work."

"Oh, great," said Larry. "I love federal court. It's like the Union League Club. Everybody talking very quietly and smiling at one another because they're not the poor peasants."

Muriel laughed again. She'd forgotten how amusing and accurate Larry could be. As Chief Deputy P.A. and heir apparent, she was well treated on the rare occasions when she entered the state's courtrooms these days. The Superior Court judges were elected, which meant sooner or later most of them would be on the same ticket with her. Federal court, however, was another universe, where the judges were appointed for life. Muriel had been over here only a handful of times in her career and felt about the federal system largely as Larry did.

"I think Harlow is just letting Raven take his best shot, Lar. It'll be okay in the end."

Larry nodded, looking soothed. Back in law school, he'd been the first human being ever to place faith in her legal abilities. To him, her word on the law was always gospel.

"You mean, I'm not gonna be bunking with Erno?" he asked. "I've been hoping for a way to get outta this racket."

"You'll never quit the job."

"Hell you say. I put in my papers, Muriel. I'm double five's in November and I'm out Jan One, Two-O-O-Two. People are always going to kill each other. And I know everything about that I need to. Besides, they'll name a new Detective Commander next year, who'll be either me, which is ridiculous, or somebody else, which is even stupider. Time's up. And you know, this thing I did rehabbing? I got six guys working for me now. Fifty-four is old for two jobs."

"Six guys?"

"We turned over eight houses last year."

"Yikes, Larry. You're rich."

"Not like you and Talmadge, but it's been pretty good. I'm a lot better off than anybody in my family ever expected. And the stock market, too. The net worth is a big number but everything's leveraged. Still." He smiled, as if he were somewhat amazed to be slinging the lingo, then asked how her life was.

"Good," she answered and left it at that. She ran the uniquely female race that began at daylight with the persistent anxiety that there would never be time to attend to everything, a fear, unlike many others, which was firmly rooted in fact. Nothing ever felt as if it were done perfectly—not her work or her marriage, even her stepmothering. But she had plenty in her life—great work, money, that wonderful little boy. She concentrated on those things and had moved past the disappointments.

"What about your marriage?" he asked.

She laughed out loud. "Grown-ups don't ask each other about their marriages, Larry."

"Why not?"

"Okay, how's your marriage? You never got out the door, huh? Did you and Nancy sign a peace treaty?"

"You know how that goes," said Larry.

"You wouldn't have me, so anybody else would be second best." That line didn't sound good, but he was smiling. "No, I mean, it's okay. She's a good person, Nancy. Really good. What can you say about a woman who adopts your children? Nothing bad. Life's not perfect, right?"

"Apparently."

"I tell you, I think more and more about my grandparents. My mom's folks? When he was sixteen, Grandpa's parents apprenticed him as a wheelwright—talk about a job with a future—and arranged for a wife. He saw my grandmother for the first time two years later, three days before he married her. And when you page ahead sixty-five years they were still clopping along. Never a cross word between them either. So go figure."

He was fiddling with the knob on the cheap little aluminum teapot as he spoke. Listening, Muriel found herself surprisingly at ease. It turned out there were bonds in life that couldn't be broken. And having slept with somebody was one of them. At least for her. And probably most people. She'd be carrying a piece of Larry around with her for the rest of her life.

"Okay, so it's your turn," he said. "Is it

hard? I look at Talmadge, when I see him on TV sometimes, and frankly, I think to myself, putting up with that act must be hard."

"Being married to Talmadge doesn't require much but a sense of humor and a black dress." She laughed at herself, but she was disturbed by the undercurrent. She had spent all those years thinking she would never succumb to lesser things the way everyone else did. Normal. Middle. Average. Those words were still enough to make her weak at the knees. "Talmadge is Talmadge, Larry. It's like riding in the chariot with the Sun God. You always feel the glow."

Her husband led the life of Millennium America, on an airplane somewhere three or four times a week. He had clients throughout the world, including several governments. Home to Talmadge was generally just a place he could safely retreat from his glimmering public persona to a surprisingly dark core. He sat up late, sipping whiskey, brooding, and salving the wounds he'd been too adrenalized to feel when they were inflicted on the battlefield. Although he was more often purely giddy at the size of his success, in his dark moods he seemed to believe the world had showered favor on him in order to demean him, to prove he wasn't truly worthy of all of it. She was required to comfort him at length.

"I have his respect," she said, "and that means a lot to me. We listen to each other. Give a lot of advice. Spend a lot of time talking. It's good."

"Marriage of the titans," he said. "The Super Lawyer and the Prosecuting Attorney."

For Muriel, it remained irritating that an ambitious woman was so much more acceptable when she was wed to an ambitious man. In truth, though, she'd probably figured that out when she married Talmadge.

"Nobody's elected me yet, Larry."

"You can't miss. Who the hell will even run against you? Everybody in law enforcement is lined up behind you. You got the woman thing going, not to mention all of Talmadge's pals with open checkbooks. The papers say you're gonna be Senator before you're done."

Senator. Mayor. She'd actually read both. Recognizing the sheer serendipity that led to such pinnacles, she refused to treat the speculation as anything other than rank amusement.

"This is the job I want, Larry. Frankly, I'm

running because it's so easy. Ned's laid his hands on. Talmadge will manage the campaign from Airfones. Even so, I still spend time wondering what I'm getting into."

"Bull. This has always been your dream."

"I don't know, Larry." She hesitated, trying to figure out where momentum was taking her, then gave up, which was the same old story of being with Larry. "Even a year ago, I was still hoping I'd have to think twice about running. But I've faced the fact that I'm never going to get pregnant. That was really the priority. I know so much about fertility—" She stopped. Never once in her life had she felt sorry for herself, but contemplating the years of examinations, medications, irrigations, of clock-watching, day-counting, temperature-taking, of hoping and hoping—the memory sometimes seemed enough to defeat her. As a younger person, it had never occurred to her where her desire to be of consequence in the world would lead. But that potent childhood vow to leave behind some trace of herself for eternity led, in the hands of nature, to a fierce passion to repeat herself, to raise, to nurture, to teach, to love. No yearning she had experienced in life, not the tide of libido, not hunger, not even ambition, could equal the force with which that need had arisen in Muriel after she was married. It was as if her heart were driven forward by a great turning wheel—beneath which, over time, it was crushed. She lived with the absence, a form of mourning, that would continue to her last day.

Larry was listening with concern, his blue eyes still. He finally said, "Well, you have my vote, Muriel. I want you to be P.A. It's important to me, you know, that you get what you want." There was purpose in his expression. It was a sweet discovery that he remained so committedly her friend.

They fought over the check, but Larry insisted on paying. He reminded her that he was, in her word, rich. Then they hiked through lunchtime foot traffic to the old Federal Courthouse. Kenton Harlow, the Chief Judge of the District Court, had assigned the deposition to himself, rather than push the matter off on a Magistrate Judge. The procedural posture of the case was bizarre anyway, a by-product of Congress's recent efforts to truncate the endless parade of appeals and collateral attacks that was death-penalty litigation. The Court of Appeals, which never heard live testimony, had

nonetheless reserved the right to evaluate
the evidence turned up during the limited
period for discovery and to decide for itself
whether the case should continue, a function that had traditionally been reserved to
the trial-level judges in the District Court. No
one Muriel had talked to had ever been
through a proceeding like this one.

The Chief Judge presided in the so-called
Ceremonial Courtroom. Given the amount of
brown marble behind the bench, the vast
room could have been mistaken for a
chapel. But Muriel's attention was soon
drawn by something else. In the first row of
walnut pews, on the scarlet cushions, several members of the press were assembled,
not just the beleaguered courthouse regu-
lars, but also several television reporters.
Stanley Rosenberg from Channel 5, Jill
Jones, a few others—as well as two sketch
artists. The only reason a gallery like this
would be present was if Arthur had tipped
them, promising big doings.

She grabbed Larry's arm as she gathered
the portent and whispered a term from his
days in Nam, so he'd understand the gravity of the situation.

"Incoming," she said.

15

JUNE 12, 2001

Erno's Testimony

"STATE YOUR NAME, please, and spell your last name for the record."

"Erno Erdai," he said and recited each letter.

From the bench above the witness stand, Judge Harlow repeated Erno's surname to be sure he had it. "Air-die?" asked the judge. That was like Harlow, Arthur thought. He'd grant anyone the courtesy of calling him by the right name, even after he found out Erno had shot five people in his lifetime and left four of them dead.

Judge Kenton Harlow was most often described as 'Lincolnesque.' The judge was lean and nearly six four, with a narrow beard and large, imposing features. He had a direct style and a rousing commitment to constitutional ideals. But the comparisons to Lincoln hardly came unbidden. He had been the model of Harlow's adult life. The judge's chambers were decorated with a variety of Lincoln memorabilia, everything from first editions of the Carl Sandburg biography, to numerous busts and masks and bronze figures of Honest Abe at all ages.

As a lawyer, a teacher, a renowned constitutional scholar, and as an Assistant Attorney General of the United States in charge of the Civil Rights 'Division in the Carter Administration, Harlow had fulfilled the credo he attributed to Lincoln, a faith in the law as the flower of humanism.

Arthur proceeded through the preliminary questioning of Erno. Erdai was already thinner than when Arthur had seen him in prison three weeks ago, and his lungs had begun to fail. The marshals had hiked a canister of pure oxygen on wheels onto the witness stand at Erno's feet, and the protrusions on a clear tube connected to the cylinder were holstered in his nose. Despite that, Erno seemed of good cheer. Although Arthur had told him it was unnecessary, Erno had insisted on wearing a suit.

"Your Honor, for the record." At the prosecution table, Muriel Wynn had arisen to renew her objections to the proceedings. Arthur had phoned Muriel a dozen times about Rommy's case, but he hadn't seen her in person for several years. She had aged agreeably. Slender people always seemed to, Arthur thought. There was gray in her tight black hair, but she wore more makeup now, a concession not so much to age, he surmised, as to the fact that as a prominent figure she was often photographed.

Muriel and he had been peers in the Prosecuting Attorney's Office and Arthur valued his relationship with her, as with most of his former colleagues. It chagrined him to recognize that after today, she would regard him the way prosecutors viewed most defense lawyers: another decent mortal whose soul had been sucked out of him by the vampires he represented. Yet his duties to Rommy had left Arthur with little choice. He could not have told Muriel what was coming without risking that she would have demanded delays in order to investigate Erdai's claims, hoping all the while that Erno would become too sick to testify, or even that he could be pressured in the institution to recant.

With a brio that had always seemed to

Arthur partly inspired by her size, Muriel argued to Harlow that Gandolph had exhausted the chances the law allowed him to avoid being put to death.

"So you think, Ms. Wynn," asked the judge, "that even if the police knew facts establishing Mr. Gandolph's innocence, the Constitution—our Constitution, the federal Constitution," said Harlow, archly implying that the state lived by the legal equivalent of jungle rules—"you think the time's up for me to consider them?"

"I believe that's the law," said Muriel.

"Well, if you're right," said the judge, "then you have very little to lose by hearing what Mr. Erdai has to say." Always the best lawyer in the courtroom, Harlow smiled benignly. He told Muriel to take her seat and instructed Arthur to put his next question.

He asked where Erno presently resided.

"I'm housed at the Medical Wing of the Rudyard State Penitentiary," Erno said.

"And for what reason are you housed there?"

"I have stage-four squamous-cell carcinoma of the lung." Erno turned to the judge. "I got about three months."

"I'm sorry to hear that, Mr. Erdai," said

Harlow. By habit, the judge seldom looked up from his notes and even in this moment of solicitude he did not vary from that practice. Arthur had tried several major cases in front of Harlow, and the judge had expressed continuing approval for Arthur's unassuming style and his diligence. For his part, Arthur revered Harlow, whose casebook he'd studied in law school. The judge was a great man. He was also often a handful. Harlow could be cranky, even volcanic. He was an old-fashioned liberal, reared during the Depression, and he regarded anyone who did not share his brand of democratic communalism as an ingrate or a greedy child. For years now, Harlow had conducted a running battle with the far more conservative Court of Appeals, ruing their frequent reversals and regularly attempting to outflank them. Arthur had taken advantage of that ongoing contest for Gandolph's benefit. Harlow made no secret of his resentment of the new legislation that gave the Court of Appeals, rather than judges at Harlow's level, the right to cut off successive *habeas corpus* proceedings in death-penalty cases. As a result, the judge had been immediately taken with Arthur's suggestion that Harlow evaluate Erno's credibility, because, by tradition, the Court of Appeals could not ignore his findings. In effect, this returned to Harlow a large measure of the power to decide whether the case proceeded.

"Have you ever been convicted of a crime, sir?" Arthur asked Erdai.

"I have. Four years ago I got into an argument at a bar with a guy I once investigated and ended up shooting him in the back. He'd come at me with a gun to start, but I shouldn't have shot him. He recovered, fortunately, but I pled guilty to Aggravated Battery and got ten years." Erno had drawn the microphone, which resembled a blackened seedpod on a stalk, right next to his lips. His voice was husky, and he tended to exhaust his breath, requiring occasional lapses. But he appeared calm. Speaking slowly, more formally, Erno's vague, gargling accent, a little bit of Dracula, was slightly more distinct than when he was talking in his preferred mode of Kewahnee tough guy.

Arthur continued exploring Erno's background, starting with his birth in Hungary and proceeding through his employment at TN. Harlow took careful notes. Ready to launch into the big stuff, Arthur faced

Pamela at counsel table to be certain he hadn't missed any preliminaries. Radiant with anticipation, Pamela shook her head minutely. Perversely, Arthur felt a bit sorry for her. In her first year of practice, Pamela was about to enjoy a triumph she might never equal. After this, it was possible that Pamela would never be content with what satisfied other lawyers. Then again, Arthur realized, the same could well be true for him. He found himself pleased by the prospect that the next question might change his life. And so he asked it.

"Calling your attention to July Fourth of 1991, Mr. Erdai, can you tell us what you did in the early-morning hours of that day?"

Erno adjusted the piece in his nose. "I killed Luisa Remardi, Augustus Leonidis, and Paul Judson," he said.

Arthur had envisioned a hubbub in the courtroom, but instead there was prolonged silence. Harlow, who had a computer screen on the bench where the court reporter's transcription appeared, actually looked up to watch the words fly by. Then he put down his pen and pulled on his jaw. From beneath the bird's nests of his untamed whitish brows, his gaze settled on Arthur. The judge allowed himself nothing else in his expression, but the intensity of his look seemed to reflect admiration. To bring this kind of evidence forward on the eve of execution—that, in Harlow's view, was the epitome of what the legal profession stood for.

"You may ask another question," the judge said to Arthur.

Only one was possible.

"Did Romeo Gandolph have a role of any kind in those murders?"

"No," said Erdai evenly.

"Was he present?"

"No."

"Did he plan or assist in these murders?"

"No."

"Did he help you after the fact in any way to conceal the crime?"

"No."

Arthur stopped then, for effect. There was motion, finally, in the back of the courtroom, as two of the reporters fled for the corridor where it was okay to use their cell phones. Arthur gave some thought to checking Muriel's reactions, then decided it might be taken as gloating and avoided looking her way.

"Mr. Erdai," Arthur said, "I would like to

ask you to tell the story in your own words of what happened on July Fourth of 1991, what led up to it, and what occurred in the Paradise restaurant. Take your time. Just tell the judge as you remember it."

Weakened, Erno placed one hand on the rail to face slightly in Harlow's direction. His gray suit, too heavy for the weather, bagged noticeably.

"There was a gal," he began, "who worked out at the airport. Luisa Remardi. A ticket agent. Not to speak ill of the dead, but she was a little bit of a tart. And I made the mistake of getting involved with her. You know, I thought it was just for kicks, Judge, but I sort of fell into it. As soon as I did, I began seeing signs she was stepping out. And this made me into a complete head case. I admit it." Erno touched the knot of his tie to loosen it slightly, while Harlow, in his tall leather chair, tossed his glasses down on his blotter so he could watch Erdai without distraction. Erno breathed deeply, preparing to go on.

"So I started keeping an eye on her. And naturally one night, I see what I figured. This would be July third. Luisa meets up with some guy in the airport parking lot, some deep dark corner, and she, you know, she hops him right there in his car. This'll tell you how crazy I was. I watched the whole thing. Every jiggle. Forty minutes or so."

Erno had his momentum now and Arthur was reluctant to interrupt, but evidentiary formalities required it.

"Could you identify the man with Ms. Remardi?"

"No clue. I didn't care much who it was. Just that she was jumping around on somebody else's pogo stick." There was a titter and Erno's eyes flashed up to the bench. "Sorry, Judge."

Harlow, who could be salty in private, waved it off.

"So finally she's had her fill and drives away and I follow. And she ends up at Gus's. At the restaurant there. Paradise. And I run in after her. It turns into a scene, I can tell you that. I'm calling her a tramp, and she's yelling back at me, I don't own her, I'm a married man for Chrissake, I can't make different rules for her than me. You can imagine." Erno shook his sallow face and looked down at the walnut rail of the witness stand as he absorbed the sad memory.

"Naturally, this caught Gus's attention. He

gave his employees July Fourth off, I guess, so he was there by himself. He comes over and tells me to scat and I tell him to eff himself. At that point I grabbed Luisa to haul her out. She's screaming, whaling on me, and all the sudden now here's Gus again, this time with a gun. You know, in my time, I had some stones. And I've been in there, I've seen Gus. He's not gonna shoot nobody. I tell him that. At which point Luisa reaches up and grabs the pistol. 'Yeah, but I will,' she says.

"And she would have. So I go after the revolver. I'm trying to jerk it away from her and kaboom. Just like in the freakin movies. I swear, when Gus had the pistol in his hand, I looked and the safety was on, but I guess wrestling around—Well, anyway, there's a hole right through the center of her. Smoke coming out of it, too. She looks down there, you know, like, What the heck is this, and the smoke is still rising. Then the blood starts to spread.

"Gus starts off to call an ambulance and I tell him, 'Wait.'

"'Wait? What for I wait? She be dead?' What it was, was I needed a minute to think it through, Judge. To come to grips. Because I can see just how this is going down.

Twenty years I worked for that airline and as soon as he lifts that phone, I can read all the headlines. Executive poking employee. Security head involved in shooting. Adios job. Just me and my missus having many happy-type content evenings together. And that isn't the worst of it yet. I already have another accidental shooting way back when. The wrong prosecutor looks at this, I could damn well end up doing time.

"So I just needed a minute, a *minute*, you know, to come to grips, to stop being so freakin scared, frankly. Just if he give me thirty seconds, maybe. But Gus, he was scorched. A shooting in his place. With his gun. When I say 'Wait' a second time, he walks away and goes to the phone. And I'm pretty wigged out and upset. All I want is to get a little control here. I tell him to stop. I tell him I'll kill him. He don't stop. He goes right there. And I shot him. Good shot. Good shot," said Erno again, in plain lamentation. "Right through the head.

"So I go back to the booth now. Luisa is not doing too well. Gonna bleed out and die. But there isn't a whole lot to do about it. Now at least I have a minute to think. And the only choice I got is to try to get away with this. I can't change it. The worst that happens is I get caught. At least I've gotta try.

"So I figure, make it look like a robbery. I go back and take everything out of the register. I pull off Gus's watch, his rings. I wipe down the table where Luisa was sitting so there aren't fingerprints. And I don't know, in a mirror I think I see something on the other side of the restaurant. I'm not real sure, but could be somebody else was in one of the booths when I ran in. I realize I better look, and lo and behold in the far corner, I see this guy hiding under the table. Just a guy. A guy like me. Suit and tie. He couldn't have made a run for it because I was between him and the door and so he's smart enough to hide, only it didn't work. That's all. It didn't work. I found him.

"I got him out from under there. He was blubberin and carryin on by then, sayin the same as I'd say, 'Don't kill me, I'm never gonna tell.' He started in showin me the pictures of his family in his wallet. He musta seen that on TV. And I told him the truth. 'I don't wanna kill you, fella. No way I want to kill you.' I had him drag Gus downstairs to that freezer. By then, Luisa was gone, so I had him do the same with her. Then I tied him up there, this guy, Paul, I think I read was his name. The whole time I'm wondering how I could not kill him. I'm thinking, maybe if he just ends up blind, you know, but Christ, putting a fork in his eyes or something, that's harder than pulling the trigger.

"I never was sure I could kill a man like that. I mean, I have a temper. I know that. I go off. Like I did with Gus. But kill somebody, cool as you please, just because it worked out as him or me?

"When I was a kid, in Hungary, they killed my father because the neighbors gave him up to the secret police, and I always kind of took my lessons from that. I never expected much from anyone but my family. You do what you have to, I figured. But I didn't know I actually believed that. Not till then. Cause I killed him. I shot him right through the back of the head, and you could see that the life was gone from him just that very second by the way he fell straight over on the floor. Then I took Luisa's jewelry off of her, and rearranged her clothes too, cause of her visit with that guy in the parking lot. I wasn't sure what would show in the autopsy."

Again, he awaited his breath. There was

no sound in the huge old courtroom but the hissing from his oxygen tank. Arthur was the only person on his feet, and it seemed to him no one else could have found the wherewithal to stand anyway. On the faces in the gallery there was awe—perhaps at the momentousness of evil, or the incongruity that Erno was sitting here and using the same words we all spoke to describe actions so far beyond our capacities. Or were they? From that region of uncertainty, everyone awaited what Erno would report next.

"All the time I was in that freezer, while the whole thing was happening, I was like a zombie. But afterwards, afterwards I didn't know what to think. Sometimes, I'd see people on the street—tramps and gang-bangers, guys with half a brain, everybody you look down on—and I'd think that none of them did anything like I'd done. They all had something on me. I was waiting to get caught. I was sort of preparing myself mentally for the day the coppers knocked on my door. But I'd done a good job. The police were running in every direction and bumping into themselves."

While Erno permitted himself another interval, Arthur surveyed the courtroom to see how he was doing. Pamela had her lips rolled into her mouth, appearing as if she didn't dare breathe for fear of disturbing the perfect rhythms of the moment. He winked at her, then finally dared to look at the prosecution table, first to Larry Starczek, whom he hadn't seen for years. Arthur had considered trying to exclude Larry from the courtroom because Erno was going to be testifying about him, but Arthur had ultimately decided that Erdai would make a better impression if he took on Larry face-to-face. And that judgment was correct. Larry was not behaving in a fashion likely to impress Kenton Harlow. He appeared on the verge of laughter. To him, the whole thing was so ridiculous, it qualified as humor.

Beside Larry, Muriel was far more pensive. She finished writing a note and her line of sight crossed Arthur's. He expected her to be furious. She would recognize at once that Arthur was exploiting her vulnerability as a prospective candidate. Convicting an innocent man and executing him was not the kind of on-the-job experience the voters typically had in mind for their elected prosecutor, and Arthur's aim was to set off a public clamor that would force Muriel to dismiss the case quickly to get it out of the headlines. But she had always loved the game, and Muriel actually tipped her head to him very slightly. Not bad, she was saying. Not that she believed it. Not for a second. But lawyer to lawyer, she had to give Arthur credit for pulling this off. Arthur nodded back in what he hoped was a respectful manner, then faced Erno once more.

"Mr. Erdai, I didn't ask you earlier. Were you acquainted with Romeo Gandolph at this time in July of 1991?"

"Acquainted? You could say I knew him."

"In what capacity?"

"As a complete and total pain."

Laughter of unexpected volume rang through the courtroom. Everyone had apparently craved the relief. Even Harlow chuckled on the bench.

"Squirrel, Rommy, whatever—he was kind of a street person. He used to hang out at DuSable Field in the winter to get out of the cold, and stuff had a habit of disappearing when he was around. So my guys and I kind of encouraged him to depart, you might say, on a regular basis. That's how I knew him."

"Do you have any knowledge how Romeo

Gandolph came to be charged for this crime?"

"That I do."

"Please tell the Court in your own words what happened."

"What happened?" asked Erno. He inhaled for a time on his oxygen. "Well, it's like the priest at Rudyard says. It's not as if I don't have a conscience. And I have this nephew. Collins is his name. Collins Farwell. I've tried to help him. I always have. All his life I worried about him. And he gave me a lot to worry about, I'll tell you that.

"Anyhow, he got himself cracked a few months after I killed those people. Narcotics. Triple X. Life in the can. And it worked on me quite a bit. Because here I am, a murdering bastard running free, and there's Collins who didn't do anything besides sell people what they wanted, and he's going to spend his natural life behind bars. I don't know. It bothered me.

"And then there's a part of me that figured I would never have any peace with this unless somebody else got nailed for it. Looking back, that was stupid. It was always gonna bother me. But at that point I thought, Well, if I can put this on somebody, then I'll be better off, and Collins'll be better off, too, because he had to give the prosecutors something to get out from under that life sentence."

Arthur asked the obvious—why Rommy?

"Well, Mr. Raven, the real answer is because I knew I could stick it on him. See, basically, it came down to this cameo, this locket, they found him with. That was Luisa's. And I knew Squirrel had it."

"Squirrel is Rommy?"

"That's what they called him."

"Can you explain how you happened to know he had that cameo?"

"Can, but it's a long story. A week or two before Luisa died"—Erno straightened up to correct himself—"before I killed her, I was checking on her all the time, spying on her is what it really came down to. But I come in early one morning as she's leaving, and she chews me up one side and down the other about all the thieves I let roam around this airfield. Bottom line, she'd taken this locket off, when it got wound up in her telephone cord, and she'd laid it on her counter. She goes away for a second and when she comes back, there's Squirrel slipping off like a shadow and the cameo is gone. She's cussing me out about this, and crying because it's been in the family for a couple centuries.

"Well, what are you gonna do? So I go hunt up Squirrel. Took a day, but I found him in some hellhole in the North End. Course, he said he didn't know nothin about it, but I said, 'Listen, knucklehead, that piece is worth a hell of a lot more to that lady than anybody you can peddle it to. Get it back and we'll make it worth your while, no questions asked.'

"Naturally, once I killed her, I didn't think much about that, except I noticed the papers were featuring the cameo as taken off her when she died, which I knew was a crock. I figured Luisa didn't want to confess to Mamma Mia that she'd lost the family treasure. You know, there's always a lot the cops think is true that isn't, but that's another subject." Erno cast a fast glance at Larry, then reached over to adjust his oxygen. He was starting to look tired.

"Anyway, must have been late September, I run into Squirrel out at the airport. I don't think he could have told you my name but he knew I'd promised him money. 'I still got this here,' he says and takes the cameo out of his pocket. Right there in the terminal. I thought my heart was going to fall out of my chest and roll down my trouser leg, just from shock, you know, because that thing was in the media and I didn't want to be within a mile of it. I told him I'd work on the money, and ran off, fast as if he was leprosy.

"Afterwards, I started in thinking, takin off like that might have been a dead giveaway. Maybe I should have had him arrested and carried on like he was the bad guy. I kind of liked that idea and began researching, you might say, talking to copper friends, pretending I was interested in Squirrel because he was a problem at the airport. Once I found out he had a thing with Gus, too, I started considering it seriously, you know, unloading this on him. Even so, I might not have done it, but then Collins got into that jackpot, and there was Rommy, sort of made to order.

"So far as Collins knew, Rommy was the right guy. I put it that I'd been developing information about Rommy, and I was just letting Collins dress it up a little and pass it on to get out of this jam. I told Collins I'd send some cops around, and he should make the best deal he could—squirm real hard about having to testify, because I wasn't sure how good Collins would do on the stand. Then, I just waited for a chance to lay all this on some officer, which turned out to be Larry Starczek, when he showed up at the airport a day or two later."

Erno lifted his hand to point across the courtroom to Larry, who, in the face of this dissection of how he'd been had, seemed finally to be reflecting on the possibility.

"The rest is history," Erno said.

There was a lull again as Arthur considered his notes. He was going on to Erno's letters to Larry and Gillian, but Erno held up his hand, which, for some reason—his health or the strain—trembled slightly.

"Can I say something here, Judge?" He coughed again, a harsh sound in the silent courtroom. "It probably won't mean much, but I'd like you to know this, because it's something I always consider. My nephew? He got out in five. Cause he ratted out Squirrel. But he's all grown up. He's come to Jesus, which is a bit much, but he's got a wife, he's got two kids, he's got a little business. I gave him a chance—well, more than one—but he took it. Finally. So in the middle of this horrible mess I made, there's that. I always think about it. I think about it a lot."

Harlow took this in, like the rest, neutrally, in a mood of somber contemplation. Arthur knew it would be hours before even the judge could puzzle through all the details. But he had a question now. Harlow turned first to Muriel to ask if she minded inquiry from the Court. She answered that she had several questions of her own, but would be happy to let the judge go first. That was the kind of courtroom posturing the judge revered as an art form. He granted her a small smile, before he returned to Erno.

"Before you leave this area, Mr. Raven, I want to be certain I'm following Mr. Erdai's testimony. As I understand what you're saying, sir, you expected to frame Mr. Gandolph, is that correct?"

"That's the best word for it, I'm afraid," Erno answered. "I mean, it was a flier, Judge. I was trying to do what I could for the kid, but I couldn't guarantee anything. I knew enough about how this all goes to realize Collins wouldn't get a real big break unless Rommy went down."

"Well, that's what I'm wondering about. Your calculation was that you'd accomplish that by having your nephew lead the police to the cameo in Mr. Gandolph's pocket.

Correct? That's not much of a case, is it? What happens if Gandolph has an alibi? Or explains how he got the locket?"

"That could've happened, I suppose. Course, I'd never have backed him up on the cameo. And you're forgetting that he had a bad history with Gus, too. But I had a pretty good guess what would, you know, transpire."

"And what was your guess?"

"My best guess? My guess was that sooner or later I'd hear that Rommy had fessed up."

"To a crime he didn't commit?"

"I mean, look, Judge." Erno stopped again, his chest and shoulders heaving. He was smiling faintly. "I mean, Judge, I've been around. You got a heater case and a sewer rat with one victim's jewelry in his pocket and a motive to kill another. I mean, Judge," said Erno, raising his worn, sallow face to the bench, "this ain't Shangri-la."

16

JUNE 12, 2001

Back to Court

THE OLD FEDERAL COURTHOUSE, a three-sided structure fronted by an arcade of fluted Corinthian columns, had been part of the original design of Center City in DuSable, the focal point of a broad plaza called Federal Square. As Gillian rushed along the granite walkways, pigeons with their shining heads barely rose into the air, giving ground to her, and a puff of underground exhaust ruffled her skirt. Like most Kindle County public transportation, her bus had been late.

Two days ago Arthur Raven had phoned, characteristically apologetic. He and his young associate had decided that if at all possible, Gillian should be at court. They wanted her present in case it was necessary to authenticate the letter Erno Erdai had sent her, or to confirm that she had received it in late March before any news broke about Arthur's appointment, an event which arguably might have inspired Erdai to fictionalize. It was a trifle compulsive on Arthur's part, but she had agreed to accept his subpoena with less reluctance than she might have expected.

Now she hurried up the courthouse's lovely central staircase, a gentle spiral of alabaster, unsuccessfully attempting to force from her mind the last time she had been here. That was March 6, 1995. All of the trials against other corrupted attorneys and judges against whom Gillian had been a potential witness were concluded without the need of her testimony. Her service to the government was complete. At her sentencing, several young Assistant United States Attorneys vouched for Gillian's sobriety and cooperation, and her lawyer begged for leniency. Moira Winchell, the Chief Judge here before Kenton Harlow, an icy paragon often compared to Gillian herself, remained horrified by the crime, and sentenced Gillian to seventy months in custody. It was at least one, probably two years longer than she had expected under the federal sentencing guidelines, particularly in light of her assistance to the prosecutors. Yet Gillian had pronounced thousands of sentences herself, rarely with any feeling of absolute certainty that she had weighed all factors perfectly, and to her enduring astonishment, she had found the need to speak two words to the judge when Winchell had finished with her. Gillian had said, "I understand."

On the top floor, she peered briefly through the small windows in the leather-clad swinging doors to the Chief Judge's vast courtroom. Within, Erno Erdai, with a plastic oxygen apparatus in his nose, gripped the rail of the witness box. On a bench that looked, amid pillars of marble, very much like a baptismal font, Kenton Harlow was studying Erno with a finger laid beside his long nose. Her impulse, which she quickly suppressed, was to open the doors and take a seat. A potential witness did not belong in the courtroom. Nor did she personally. Yet her trip to Rudyard with Arthur had led to nights of turbulent dreams. In their wake, as she'd admitted to Duffy when she left the house today, she'd found herself increasingly intrigued by what Erno would say, and the likely impact his testimony would have around the Tri-Cities and, in consequence, on her.

For nearly an hour, she waited across the marble hall in the narrow room reserved for witnesses, still reading about the Peloponnesian War, until the sudden commotion in the corridor made it evident that court had broken. Out of habit, she stood to use the small wall mirror, adjusting the shoulders on her dark suit and centering the largest pearl on her choker. Ten minutes after that, Arthur Raven arrived. He appeared earnest as ever, but there was a light about him which Gillian could not keep from envying. Arthur was triumphant.

He began with apologies. Muriel had just made a great show of telling Judge Harlow that she'd been bushwhacked, demanding twenty-four hours to prepare for cross-examination of Erdai.

"Are you saying I need to come back tomorrow?" Gillian asked.

"I'm afraid so. I'd ask Muriel if she even wants you, but frankly I don't think she'll talk to me at the moment about her plans. Tit for tat."

The wounds of war. Gillian remembered.

"I can give you another subpoena if you need an excuse at work," Arthur said.

"No, I have an understanding boss."

Ralph Podolsky, the manager who hired her, was the younger brother of Lowell Podolsky, a former p.i. lawyer, who'd crashed and burned in the same scandal that led to Gillian's downfall. Ralph had not mentioned his relationship to Lowell until her first day on the job, and never returned to the subject after that.

Gillian retrieved her purse. Arthur offered to show her how to escape downstairs, unnoticed by the reporters who, he said, were busy flagellating Muriel. In the elevator, she asked how it had gone with Erno Erdai.

"Amazing," said Arthur.

"Erno did well?"

"I thought so."

"You look exultant."

"Me?" The notion appeared to shock him. "All I've been feeling is the burden. It isn't just losing when they kill the client for your mistakes. I wake up three times a night. This case is the only thing I think about. You know, I've been in the trenches, digging for dollars, for years now—commercial stuff, big companies blaming each other for deals that hit the rocks. I like most of my clients, I want them to win, but there's not much at stake beyond that. If something goes wrong here, I'll feel like somebody sucked the light out of the universe."

The elevator sprang open. Behind it, Arthur showed her a passageway she'd never have found on her own, then followed her out onto the street, eager to exit before any of the print reporters saw him. He said he'd agreed to give his first interviews back at his office to the two leading TV stations. Morton's was three blocks from the court-house, on the way to Arthur's office in the IBM Building, and he walked beside her.

"What did the judge make of Erno?" she asked. "Any idea?"

"I think he believed him. It almost felt like he had to."

"Had to?"

"There was just something that came into the room." Arthur reflected. "The sorrow," he said. "Erno didn't wallow—he wasn't going to ask anybody to be sorry for him because he did horrible things. But there was a sad-ness to every word."

"Yes, sorrow," said Gillian. Perhaps that was why she had wanted to hear Erno. The foot traffic was light in the lull before evening rush hour. They strolled on a mild day, strik-ingly bright, as they weaved in and out of the shadows cast by the tall buildings on Grand Avenue. Gillian had pulled her sunglasses from her purse, but found Arthur eyeing her.

"You didn't do what he did, you know," he said. "It wasn't murder."

"Well, that's something to say for myself."

"And you've paid the price."

"I'll tell you the terrible truth," she said. She was aware that yet again she was on her way down a path with Arthur she steadily refused to tread with others, but you could not deflect Arthur Raven with subtlety or indirection. He cried when he was sad and in other moods laughed like a child. He was plain, his kindness was plain, and interacting with him required the same kind of unguarded responses. That was never an easy task for Gillian, and down at Rudyard she'd been surprised by how near at hand certain emotions—a canyon-deep sense of loss, especially—had been in his company. Yet by now he was well established as trustworthy.

"It's not what I did I feel worst about, Arthur. You'll take this the wrong way, and I don't blame you a bit, but I don't think the money changed the outcome of any of those cases. No one can say for sure, least of all me, and that's what makes what I did so insidious. But it was a system, Arthur, almost like a tax. The lawyers got rich, so the judges were entitled to a share. I was never conscious of taking a fall on a case, not because I was so honorable but because no one would ask me to. None of us wanted to risk arousing suspicions. I'm ashamed of the condition I was in during those years. And the massive violation of trust. But you're correct, the years away seem a reasonable penance for that. It's the waste that consumes me."

"The waste?"

"Having the kinds of chances in life I had and wasting them."

"Look, you have plenty of time for a new life. If you'll let yourself have one. You were always in your own time zone anyway."

She laughed out loud, only because the description was so apt. She inhabited a universe parallel to but not quite the same as others. Gillian-time, as Arthur suggested, moved slightly faster. She was out of college at nineteen, worked for a year to fund law school, and had graduated from Harvard at twenty-three, then returned to Kindle

County. In a sense, she'd never left, since she'd lived all three years with her father's cousins in Cambridge. She could have gone to Wall Street, to D.C., even to Hollywood. But for a policeman's daughter, the Kindle County Prosecuting Attorney's Office was the premier destination.

In all of that, however, the determining element was her will. In the current of the times, she had thought of herself as an existentialist: decide on a project and pursue it. It was shocking how far out of fashion will had fallen by now. Americans today viewed themselves as powerless as soft pavement, relentlessly steamrollered by their early childhoods. But perhaps that was better. In her case, once she'd started using, she'd exalted her celebration of will to the point of regarding herself as a Nietzschean figure, a Napoleonic Superwoman with the courage to set herself outside convention. She realized only years later in a prison cell that it was fear that had fueled her revulsion with middle-class morality, a sense of how crushingly she might otherwise have imposed its strict judgments on herself.

"People live through all kinds of shit, Gillian. In my family, there are people who survived years at Dachau. And they went on. They came here and sold window treatments and went bowling and watched their grandchildren grow up. I mean, you go on."

"I did this to myself, Arthur. I didn't live through some natural calamity or some exercise in human perfidy."

"You got caught. I mean, for Chrissake, what are you doing back here anyway? You're suffering or punishing yourself or reliving whatever weird psychological shit you were going through in the first place. I mean, it's over. You're different."

"Am I?" That, she realized, was one thing to be resolved.

"You stopped drinking. I was terrified to go see you that first time because I figured I'd find you half in the bag. But no, you're sober. So take heart. Move on. Move up. I open the paper three times a week and see the name of somebody I prosecuted when I was in Financial Crimes, and usually they're in the middle of making a big deal."

"And you think they're jerks."

"No, I think they're doing what they're entitled to. To go on. I hope they're wiser now. Some are. Some aren't. If they do it again, then I'll think they're jerks."

She was not fully persuaded, but the valor of his efforts was touching.

"Have I mentioned that you're very kind to me, Arthur?"

He was squinting at her in the late-afternoon sun. "Is that against the rules?"

"It's unfamiliar."

"Maybe I think we have things in common."

Whenever she saw Arthur, they somehow harked back to that first moment when she'd devastated him in the coffee shop. It had opened up something, even though it had seemed intended to close all doors. He continued to insist they were kindred spirits, while she remained dubious of any resemblance. She enjoyed Arthur. Save for Duffy, who had never fully qualified, she'd cut herself off from attorneys. Real conversation in the lawyerly fashion, real contact, earnest talk about motives and meanings, with someone able to cut to the core—it was a hunger. But that still seemed to her the limit of what they shared.

They stood now before the doors of Morton's. The building, by a famous architect who had taught Frank Lloyd Wright, was the example that had driven his pupil in the other direction. The exterior was ornate, with heavy impressions in the iron façade and twenty-foot glass doors framed in decorated brass. Vines formed the handles, which had been polished by the grasp of the thousands who entered each day, and were brilliant in the potent afternoon light. The cosmetics counter was just inside.

"My post." She pointed. She had long avoided working in the Center City store, where she was frequently recognized, but with summer vacations beginning, Ralph needed her here two days a week.

"Are you enjoying this job?"

"Well, I'm happy to be working. It's regarded as a privilege in prison. And it turns out it is. I saw an ad and thought it might be a good place to start."

The job had actually seemed like fun, although her interest in fashion had never been completely lighthearted. Over the years, she'd heard a thousand sayings about the world of style that struck her to the core, like pieces of perfect wisdom plucked from the Gospels or Shakespeare. 'Fashion is close to the quick of the soul.' 'Fashion is as much a part of life as sex.' For her it was this simple: at least *look* good. It was part masquerade, part child's play, part vulnerability to the judgment of others, and, more than anything else, the delight that came from molding those opinions. It made no sense—any more than the ridiculous and repetitive little-boy behavior with balls and sticks in which men obsessively engaged—but so many women, whether tethered by culture or instinct, craved beauty and assessed one another in terms of their efforts. These days, she had retired from competition. In comparison with the splendid young women who came from their health clubs to her counter, Gillian was now a 'former beauty,' words carrying the same sad undertone as 'former athlete.' But dealing with her customers, she was relieved every day to be so much less dominated by vanity, which she had taken to be an element of her demise.

"I take it this strikes you as superficial, Arthur."

"Well—"

"You can say it. That's the word. It's cosmetic, by definition."

"I suppose you could say I don't relate. I mean even unattractive people have instincts, but you have to come to terms with yourself."

"Oh, come on, Arthur!" She often found Arthur's abased view of himself wrenching. "Attractiveness for a man after a certain age has nothing to do with what it meant as a teenager. Big success, big salary, nice car. We all know how that goes. There's no such thing as a bad-looking man with a fat wallet."

"That doesn't seem to work for me."

"I doubt that."

"Probably because I'm immature," he said.

She laughed.

"I am," he said. "I still want my fantasies."

"Which are?"

"Somebody sleek and smart—I mean it's stupid, right? I want somebody who's everything I'm not."

"A young girl out of a magazine?"

"I'm not that immature. A grown-up would be nice." Arthur half averted his face. For a second he seemed dazzled by the sun, then added in a muted tone, "Someone like you."

"Me?" In panic, she faced about, hoping the conversation had not taken the turn she feared. "But someone more your age?" At forty-seven she had, by her best calculation, a decade on Arthur.

Arthur laughed once. "Oh, you'd do fine."

"I'm old enough to be your mother."

"Please."

"Your aunt."

"'No' will do, Gillian," he said mildly. "I'm used to it."

"*Ar*-thur," she said. "Arthur, I am a mess that no one can or should want to clean up. That's the truth. In candor, I don't say yes to anyone. That's not part of my life."

Jest had still not entirely left him, but he frowned and briefly lowered his head, allowing the open spaces in his scalp to reflect the strong light. Then he summoned himself to grin again.

"Forget it, Gillian. I was just kind of illustrating the point."

Some sisterly kiss on the cheek might have been in order, but that had never been her style. Instead she smiled in a way she hoped was a trifle less remote and promised to see him tomorrow. Raven smiled as well, but he went off at a plodding pace, his brief-case dragging by his side. In her midsection, the rot of guilt set in once again. The man in triumph, who perhaps had dared an unfamiliar boldness, was gone now. With a few words, she had vanquished him, returning Arthur to himself.

17

JUNE 13, 2001

History

ERNO ERDAI was being held in a locked ward at Kindle County General Hospital. As the marshals pushed him into the courtroom in a wheelchair, which Erno did not appear pleased to be using, Larry came over to see if he could help. With the deliberation of the elderly, Erno stood, and Larry and the deputy marshals eased Erno and his oxygen tank up to the witness stand, where his cross-examination would shortly commence. Although Erno had pointedly refused to gran t Muriel an interview in advance of his testimony, now that he'd finished blindsiding them Larry suspected Erdai would be happy to chat with him, copper to copper, as Erno was still likely to think of it. While the marshals retreated and Erno adjusted his nosepiece, Larry lingered with his arm on the dark walnut rail, admiring the Ceremonial Courtroom, where judicial inductions and citizenship proceedings were held. He loved all the bygone craft that was preserved in the old courthouse, even though he remained hostile to almost everything else about the federal system.

"So lung cancer? You smoke, Erno?"

"As a kid. In service in Nam."

"And how long is it that you've known you had this?"

"Cut the crap, Larry. I know you've been all over my file by now."

The file had been bootlegged out of Rudyard last night and driven up here. But half the personnel in the Warden's and P.A.'s Offices could be sued if Larry admitted that. Besides, it had been Muriel's responsibility to review the medical information. They all had been dashing around until nearly three, digging up whatever they could about Erdai.

Larry asked Erno how his family was doing.

"The wife's had better days, what with the paper this morning."

"And your kids?"

"No kids, Larry. Never could make 'em. Just my nephew. How're your kids, Larry? Two boys, right?"

"Right," said Larry. He described Michael's and Darrell's exploits, but he'd taken Erno's point about who'd paid better attention years ago. Larry remembered some things, though. He reached into his pocket and offered Erno a toothpick. Erdai made no effort to contain his pleasure and placed it at once in the side of his mouth.

"Don't see many of these inside. Bet you didn't think of a toothpick as a deadly weapon, Larry."

"Inside, it probably is."

"Inside, somebody'd pick out your eyeball with one, probably."

"How's a white former cop make do down there, with all the fun and games?"

"You make it, Larry. You got no other choice. I don't get in anybody's way. The one advantage I had is I knew you can live through unbelievable shit—I did as a kid. People in this country, Larry, they feel entirely too safe. You're never safe. Not how folks here want."

Larry filed that one away. He already had a few tidbits from this conversation that he'd share with Muriel once she got here. Erdai asked him how he was doing.

"Well, Erno, I didn't sleep much last night. You know why?"

"I can imagine."

"What I can't figure is what kick you're getting from making all this shit up."

Erdai gapped his mouth for a second around the toothpick.

"I understand you'd think that, Larry, but if you'd come down to Rudyard when I wrote you, I'd have told you, just like I told them. This is on the level, Larry. I'm sorry it makes you and your girlfriend look bad, but I'm not the first fella who wanted to tidy things up before he kicked."

You and your girlfriend. Larry took note of that, too. Erno had heard a lot hanging with the coppers at Ike's over the years. Mildly provoked, Larry let the pretense of congeniality pass and settled a dark look on Erdai, which he seemed to be expecting. Inscrutable and unflinching, Erno refused to turn away. Larry had never figured Erdai right. He'd missed how deep the iceberg went. He hadn't recognized Erno as a guy who could go off in a barroom, or lie for sport. But he was onto him now. The world was full of angry guys like Erno, who'd want to get even with anybody they could until their coffin was hammered shut.

When Larry turned back, Muriel had just bustled into the courtroom. Tommy Molto, who'd tried the case with her years ago—her boss at that time and now her lieutenant—was in tow, and so was Carol Keeney, an appellate lawyer, who'd been on the file for years, as the case meandered along. Tommy was fat and harried-looking, the same as he'd always been. He was starting to develop the droopy-jowled mug of a bulldog, but Larry had always liked Molto, who never stopped doing his best. Carol, on the other hand, appeared absolutely terrified, her thin lips grimly sealed. She was a slim blonde, a third- or fourth-year lawyer who should have ferreted out what this was about when Arthur filed his motion, instead of simply dumping it on Muriel's desk and telling her that she'd probably have better luck with Judge Harlow. Everyone would tell Carol to forget about it, but Larry knew her future in the P.A.'s Office was basically a black hole.

Raven, who'd entered with his pretty blond associate, reached Muriel at counsel table, a step or two before Larry. Muriel was unpacking her heavy latched transfer case, while Arthur yammered about a witness he had outside. Muriel had probably slept no more than an hour or two, but she appeared invigorated by the challenge ahead, despite the fact that she'd been incinerated in the morning papers and on TV. The Reverend Dr. Carnelian Blythe from the South End, who seemed to regard every indignity suffered by an American black as equivalent to slavery, had already laid claim to Squirrel and was leading marches and giving press interviews on the courthouse steps this morning, using Gandolph to reinforce his never-ending lament about the brutal character of the Kindle County Unified Police Force. Blythe probably hadn't even known Rommy's name before yesterday.

"I don't care, Arthur," Muriel said now. "I'll stipulate that she received the stupid letter. You don't have to call her."

When Arthur turned, Larry offered his hand, which Arthur accepted happily. The old prosecutors always regarded their time as P.A.'s as their glory days, because it was before they started whoring for money.

"The offers pouring in from Hollywood after last night?" Larry asked. Arthur had been all over the tube, pretending in every interview that he more or less expected Muriel to arrive in court this morning and beg Rommy Gandolph to forgive her. Arthur appeared to enjoy the joshing, but headed off in a moment to find his witness.

"What's Arthur on about?" Larry asked Muriel.

"Gillian Sullivan. He subpoenaed her to authenticate Erno's letter, in case he needs it on redirect."

"So that's who it was!" Larry had actually seen Gillian in the corridor, but she was so far gone from memory that he'd blanked on everything except that he knew her. She hadn't looked bad, especially considering where she'd been, still thin and pale and coolly attractive. In the P.A.'s Office, people always compared Gillian and Muriel, the office stars in succeeding generations, but in Larry's mind it was never a contest. Gillian was cerebral and disconnected; she lorded it over people, even if they'd known her or her old man since she was in parish school. Muriel had a common touch, a sense of humor, and time for people. The end of the story, with Muriel up and Gillian down, conveyed what Larry regarded as a fitting moral.

And he was confident Muriel would once more reward his faith. He watched as she set her files out on the table precisely, even details that trifling already worked out in her head. She was in court far less often these days, but Muriel remained the best stand-up lawyer Larry knew. Best in court. Best in the office. Maybe the best lay of his life, and probably the only woman he'd met who seemed to hear and feel all the same rhythms he did in the rumbling world of courts and cops and crimes where they lived most of the time. The end of his thing with her might have been the very low point of his adult existence. He couldn't imagine she'd been real happy to have to call him, and he'd been twice as bummed to hear her voice. What he hadn't understood when he was younger was the beauty in a settled life.

ARTHUR HAD FEW ILLUSIONS about his talents in court. He was organized and sincere, occasionally forceful but seldom electrifying. Yet he could not imagine living any other way. He never tired of the rush of big cases, when anticipation tightened through him like an instrument string and raced in the voices of the spectators filling the courtroom benches. Nowhere else were the events that shaped the life of a community determined as swiftly, as openly, as in court. Everyone— the lawyers, the parties, the onlookers— entered understanding that history was about to happen.

Much as he enjoyed this, there was a relief in leaving his anxiousness behind momentarily, crossing the quiet corridor to the small witness room. With a knock, he pushed inside. Gillian sat by the window, looking abstracted, as usual, as she peered out. Her purse was in her lap, and her legs, in white hose, were neatly crossed at the ankles. Her attention might have been drawn by Reverend Blythe on his bullhorn in the square below. Arthur was scheduled to meet Blythe this evening, when the Reverend, bald-headed and brilliant, a man of massive achievements and even larger ego, would undoubtedly attempt to manipulate Gandolph's case to Blythe's own advantage. Arthur dreaded the appointment, but it was far from his mind now.

At the sight of Gillian, he felt a distinct surge within. It had excited him for several days after their trip to Rudyard to settle in the BMW and detect her scent. Despite the shameful hash of things he'd made in front of the doors of Morton's yesterday, the sense that he had actually entered into some kind of relationship with this woman, even if it existed only in the currents of the law, remained a thrill. Gillian Sullivan!

"Arthur." She smiled pleasantly as she came to her feet. He explained that Muriel had agreed to stipulate that Gillian had received Erno's letter. Her testimony would not be required. "You're done," he told her. "I can't thank you enough for everything. You've been very courageous."

"Hardly, Arthur."

"I'm really sorry about the way you got knocked around this morning in the papers." Both the *Trib* and the *Bugle*, the leading suburban daily, had seized on Gillian's conviction and her known drunkenness to further question the outcome in Rommy's case. Although Arthur had held the same thoughts himself last month, he'd let them fall from mind in the process of sharing her company and had actually felt offended today for Gillian's sake.

"It was a few lines, Arthur. I was prepared for worse."

"I feel like I set you up," he said, "and it never crossed my mind."

"It would be entirely unlike you to try to take advantage, Arthur. I would never think that."

"Thank you." They both smiled somewhat timidly. Then he offered his hand. For an instant it actually pained him to release her from his life again, but there was hardly a choice. Rather than shake, Gillian studied her ivory-toned handbag as if it contained not merely the odds and ends of female existence but the solution to something Delphic.

"Arthur, may I say a word to you about what came up last night?"

"No," he answered at once. In the lunacy of triumph, he'd cracked open the dank toy chest of his fantasies. By now, he could barely stand to remember that. The utter privacy of his wild hopes was all that allowed him to maintain them. "Forget it. I was out of line. It was unprofessional, frankly. I mean, I'm inept. At that kind of thing. That's the truth. There are reasons somebody's alone at thirty-eight, Gillian."

"Arthur, I was alone when I was thirty-eight. And will be at forty-eight. You needn't be so hard on yourself."

"You're alone because you choose to be."

"Not completely. I'm inept in my own way, Arthur."

"Stop, Gillian. I'm doomed. I know I'm doomed. The world is full of people like me, who can't connect. It won't change. So don't try." He offered his hand again, but she frowned deeply.

He explained that the judge was due on the bench any second, and they left the witness room. In the corridor, Gillian asked him if Erno was ready.

"We've prepared the hell out of him," Arthur said, "but you never can tell until they're under the spotlight. You know that."

For a second, she peered through the small windows in the courtroom doors.

"It will be very dramatic," she said.

"You're welcome to watch," he said. "If you have the time."

She drew back at the thought.

"I'm quite curious, Arthur. I've often regretted not listening to Erno down at Rudyard. Perhaps it's the papers, but more and more, I feel as if I have a stake in this. But won't it be too unorthodox, if I'm in there?"

"I'll ask if anybody cares." He opened the

heavy, leather-clad door and motioned to the bailiff to indicate Gillian was with him, so the officer would find her a seat.

As Arthur expected, Muriel had no concerns about Gillian. It was part of her courtroom macho, in any event, to pretend that she would be unaffected if God and His angels were here to watch her cross. When Judge Harlow sprang onto the bench, Arthur asked to be heard at the sidebar. Harlow was tall enough to simply scoot his chair over and lean across the side rail, while Arthur asked if there were any issues raised for the Court by the presence of Ms. Sullivan, the original sentencing judge, as a spectator. He explained how she'd come to be here.

"Gillian Sullivan, is it?" asked Harlow. He looked out at her, squinting through his heavy glasses. "One and the same?"

Arthur nodded. The judge asked Muriel if she had any objections.

"I object to the fact that we weren't informed when she got the letter, but I don't care that she's here. She has no role in these proceedings."

"Guess she wants to see for herself," said Harlow. "Can't say I blame her. All right, let's get moving."

The judge shooed the ring of lawyers away, but as they returned to their places, Arthur was aware that for the moment, all of them—Muriel, Tommy Molto, Carol Keeney, Larry, who'd tagged along, even the judge, and surely Arthur himself—were staring at Gillian, who sat, perfectly groomed and largely expressionless, along the aisle in the very last row. It struck Arthur that she had been correct. She did have a stake here, a more genuine one than most of them. For she, in some senses, was the accused. The question at hand was whether a decade ago she had, for whatever reason, rendered judgments afflicted by reversible—and fatal—errors. Gillian endured their scrutiny without shirking, while they all awaited the answer.

18

JUNE 13, 2001

Erno's Cross

"SO THE QUESTION, MR. ERDAI," said Muriel, "the real question is, were you lying then or are you lying now?" Even before Harlow had told her to proceed, Muriel had taken her place in front of Erno, reminding Larry of a boxer off his stool prior to the start of a round. She had lingered one more second, a small, lithe figure absorbing the entire attention of the courtroom, before putting her first question.

"Then," said Erno.

"Is that a lie?"

"No."

"But you do lie, Mr. Erdai, don't you?"

"Just like everybody else."

"You lied to Detective Starczek in 1991, didn't you?"

"Yes, ma'am."

"You lied and put the noose around another man's neck. Is that what you're telling us?"

The toothpick scuttled from one side of Erno's mouth to the other before he said yes.

"Despicable behavior, wasn't it?"

"Nothing to be proud of."

"But even though you're a despicable liar, you're asking us to believe you now. Correct?"

"Why not?"

"We'll get to that, Mr. Erdai. By the way, did I introduce myself?"

"I know who you are."

"But you've refused to meet with me, correct?"

"Because that will only help you make it look like I'm lying, when I'm telling the truth."

On the bench, Harlow smiled faintly. As far as Larry could see, the judge was often amused by the jab and counter of the courtroom.

"Well, let me make sure I understand what you're telling us, Mr. Erdai. You're telling us that you killed three people in July of 1991. And three months later, the police hadn't caught you, right?"

"True."

"Did you want to get caught?"

"What would you think?"

"I think you would have done anything not to be apprehended—is that fair?"

"That's about the size of it."

"You had many friends on the Force, didn't you?"

"Many."

"So you knew the investigation was still-born, correct?"

"Does that mean dead?"

"Let's say dying."

"Dying's about right."

"So if you'd actually killed those people, you had every reason to believe you were going to get away with it, correct?"

"Realistically, yeah. But I was still worried."

"Right. You were worried. And despite that, and even though you knew the investigation was dying, you decided to provide information that would revive it. Is that what you're saying?"

"Because of my nephew."

"And you didn't provide an anonymous tip—you went right to Detective Starczek."

"He came to me, but it's the same difference."

"Same difference," said Muriel. She was prowling now, moving back and forth. The fingers were spread on both hands, as if she'd catch Erno if he tried to escape. She'd worn what Larry regarded as a girlish dress, a print with a tie at the waist and a big bow at the throat, a gesture intended as much for the television viewers as the judge. If she could have put on a PTA button for the cameras, she might have. But anyone who'd seen Muriel in court would know she was as lethal as a panther.

"Is he a good detective?"

"One of the best."

"And would you agree that good detectives usually know when they're being spun?"

"If they know to look out, sure. But nobody's got the radar on twenty-four seven."

"But not only did you wake up this sleeping investigation, you did it, you say, by lying to somebody who you knew was good at seeing through lies, right?"

"You can put it your way," said Erno.

"And then you had your nephew lead the police to a cameo, knowing that if Gandolph told the truth, he could very well mention your name. Is that right?"

"I'da said he was full of it, and just throwing my name around cause he'd found out somehow that I was the one who put the cops onto him. I'd thought about that."

"And you thought that lie would be convincing?"

"Sure."

"Because you know how to lie convincingly, don't you?"

Harlow sustained Arthur's objection before Erno had to answer, but the judge appeared to smile at the art of the question.

"Now, you told us yesterday that you understood that your nephew would get nothing from the police or the prosecutors unless Gandolph was convicted, right? Yet you had no way of predicting, for example, whether Gandolph had an alibi, did you?"

"I knew he'd been around the airport to steal Luisa's cameo."

"In the summer? I thought Gandolph was at the airport only when the winter weather forced him out there."

Erno made a face. He'd tried to squeeze past Muriel and she'd stopped him cold. After a little more squirming, he agreed he had told the judge yesterday that Gandolph was at the airport in the winter, and that he couldn't have been sure whether Squirrel had an alibi. Erno ate his own words sourly.

"So this is how it adds up, Mr. Erdai," said Muriel, and counted off each of her points on her fingers. "Although you didn't want to get caught, you breathed new life into a dead investigation. You did that by lying to an investigator who you knew was good at catching liars. And you pointed him toward someone who, in fact, could connect you to one of the murder victims. And you did all of that not even knowing if the man you say you were framing had a locked alibi. Do you understand now why we shouldn't believe you?"

Arthur objected at volume for the first time and the judge said, "Sustained." Piqued, Erno was unwise enough to continue on his own.

"It may not make sense to you, but that's what happened. I had to do something for my nephew. People don't always make sense."

"And this doesn't make sense, does it, Mr. Erdai? What you're telling us? It's one of those things that doesn't make sense."

Arthur objected again. Without looking up from his scribbling, the judge suggested that

Muriel move on. She turned for a second and her small dark eyes sought out Larry, to see how it was going. He covered his mouth and held his thumb up on his cheek. Muriel nodded minutely. She thought so herself.

"Does it surprise you, Mr. Erdai, to know that an automated check of fingerprints from the crime scene showed that none of them are yours?"

"I wiped everything off. I was careful. Like I said."

"No DNA. No blood. No saliva. Semen. Nothing like that from you will be found at the scene, will it?"

"No. But you didn't have any of that from Gandolph neither."

"You know our evidence against Mr. Gandolph very well, don't you, Mr. Erdai?"

"I followed this case real close. Obvious reasons."

"And the gun, sir? What became of that?"

"In the river. With everything else."

Muriel grinned briefly, the expression of a veteran who'd met lots of guys with all the answers. She strolled back to the podium to glance at her notes, then stared for a full beat at Erdai.

"Are you dying?" she asked then.

"That's what the doctors say."

"You believe them?"

"Most times. Sometimes, I kinda start thinkin maybe they're wrong, docs have been wrong before, but mostly I know better."

"So, as far as you're concerned, you have nothing to lose with what you're telling us today. Right?"

"I don't follow."

"Really? Can you name anything you care about losing."

"My soul," said Erno. "If I got one."

"If you got one," repeated Muriel. "Let's stay here on earth. Anything here you care about losing?"

"My family," said Erno. "I care a lot about them."

"Well, they're standing by you, Mr. Erdai, aren't they? What else?"

"I'd hate to lose my pension from the airline. I worked a long time and I want to make sure my wife has something."

"Well, you don't lose your pension, do you, for murder?"

"If it's a crime against the company."

"Was this?"

"Only if Luisa was management."

Loud laughter volleyed from the gallery.

The courtroom was full today. The press reports had had their predictable effect of filling every available seat.

"So you won't lose your pension. And you're not going to live long enough to get prosecuted again for perjury, right?"

"There's nothing to get prosecuted for."

"Either way, there's no chance you'll have to do more time, is there?"

"I suppose."

"And what about your nephew, Collins Farwell? He lied to Detective Starczek about having certain conversations with Rommy Gandolph, didn't he?"

"Yeah, but he thought Gandolph was the right guy."

"And where is Collins now?"

"He's got a lawyer named Jackson Aires. You can give him a call."

"A lawyer? So he could get advice about this situation?"

"Basically. I'm paying the bill, since I'm the one who put him in this spot to start with."

"And do you know if the lawyer has assured Collins that he can't be prosecuted for the lies he told in 1991, because the statute of limitations has run?"

"Isn't that supposed to be confidential?"

"Put it this way, Mr. Erdai. You understand nothing is going to happen to Collins as result of your testimony, don't you?"

"I hope nothing happens to him."

"And where is he?"

Erno looked at the judge who nodded firmly to him.

"Atlanta. Doing good down there, too, like I said."

"Congratulations," said Muriel. "Now, what about on the other side, Mr. Erdai. Are you going to gain anything by coming forward now?"

"A clean conscience."

"A clean conscience," said Muriel. "You say, Mr. Erdai, you've shot five people in your lifetime—murdered three, killed your mother-in-law, and tried to murder a fifth person who bothered you in a bar. And this will make you feel better, is that right?"

There was a riffle of laughter behind Larry. It sounded as if Carol, who should have known better, had been the first. Harlow's eyes rose and the courtroom instantly fell silent.

"I can't change any of the rest of it, Muriel. This is the best I can do."

Calling Muriel by her first name was pure

Erno. As far as Larry knew, they didn't have even a nodding acquaintance, but Erdai always figured he was a blood brother with everybody in law enforcement.

"Well, hadn't you applied for a compassionate furlough several months ago? And then, when that was denied, a compassionate transfer? In order to be closer to your wife?"

"True."

"Also denied?"

"Yes."

"Your wife has a hard time making it down to Rudyard?"

"It'd be a lot easier if I was here."

"Where did you sleep last night?"

"County General."

"Did your wife see you there today?"

"Before court."

Muriel ran it down. He'd seen his wife yesterday, too. And the day before. And Arthur had filed a petition with the court suggesting that Erno not be returned to Rudyard while Gandolph's case was pending.

"Does it mean a lot to you to see your wife every day? At this stage?"

"Right now? Especially now, yeah, it means quite a bit. She doesn't deserve the last few years. Not a day of it." His voice weakened and Erno, with little warning, flushed. He dragged down his nosepiece and covered his face with his hand. Harlow had Kleenex on the bench and handed the box down with clinical efficiency. Muriel waited this out with no sign of impatience, because Erno could hardly have done much more to prove her point. She changed subjects once his breath had returned.

"Let's talk about the crime for which you're imprisoned, Mr. Erdai."

"What's that got to do with the price of beans?" asked Erno. Arthur, on cue, rose to object. The conviction was relevant, Arthur pointed out, only for whatever it said about Erno's credibility. The circumstances were beside the point.

"I'll tie it up," said Muriel. That was the trial lawyer's version of 'the check's in the mail,' but Harlow, sitting without a jury, said he'd give Muriel some leeway, particularly since this proceeding was a deposition, not a trial.

"I don't let lawyers break their word to me twice," the judge added.

"I wouldn't expect you to," said Muriel, before turning back to Erno, who, Larry

thought, recoiled just a bit as she reap-
proached. Erdai's go-round with Muriel thus
far had already left him looking less peppy.

"As a matter of fact, Mr. Erdai, you're in
prison only because your friends on the Police Force didn't back you up—isn't that
right?"

"I'm in prison because I shot a man."

"But you told the officers who were at this
tavern, Ike's, where the shooting took
place—you told them you'd pulled the trigger in self-defense, didn't you?"

"To my way of thinking, it was."

"And many of the officers who'd witnessed that shooting and heard you claim
you were merely defending yourself were
friends of yours, weren't they? Officers you
were there drinking with?"

"Sure."

"Was it disappointing to you, Mr. Erdai,
that none of them supported you in saying
this was self-defense?"

"Not when I had a chance to think about
it."

"But initially?"

"I don't know what I expected."

"But it wouldn't have bothered you, would
it, if they'd backed your version?"

"I guess not."

"Have you ever known officers to protect their own?"

"I think it's happened before."

"But it didn't happen with you, did it?"

The mean part of Erno showed through for the first time, a sulfurous ignition behind the eyes. He was adept enough, however, to calm himself before he said no.

"And so you had to plead guilty, correct?"

"That's what happened."

"Now, what about Detective Starczek?" Larry sat up on reflex at his name. "Was he another of your friends on the Force?"

"Larry? I've known him going on thirty years. We were cadets together."

"And these letters you wrote to Detective Starczek—"

Unexpectedly, Muriel returned to Larry at the counsel table. She whispered with her lips barely moving: "Reach in my briefcase and take out the mail in the first compartment." A flutter of uncertainty zipped through him, but he'd caught up with her by the time he'd extracted the three letter-sized envelopes. According to the return addresses, they were her statement from the state retirement fund and two credit card bills. With the letters in hand, she faced the witness.

"You never wrote Detective Starczek telling him you killed anyone, did you?"

"Told him I needed to talk to him."

"Didn't you tell him straight out you wanted his help?"

"I might have. You know, as I remember, I called him once or twice, only he wasn't there, and they won't accept collect calls from the joint anyway, so I wrote him two, three letters and he didn't answer."

Arthur stood, waving at what Muriel held in her hand.

"Your Honor, I haven't seen those letters."

"Judge, I didn't receive any preview of Mr. Erdai's testimony. And besides, I haven't displayed them to the witness. Mr. Raven may inspect whatever I show the witness."

Arthur continued objecting and Harlow finally called them to the sidebar on the far side of the bench, away from Erno. Larry joined the procession.

"What's the story with the letters?" whispered Harlow.

"I don't have any," Muriel told him.

Larry figured the judge would go off, but instead Harlow smiled broadly.

"Bluffing?" asked Harlow.

"I'm entitled," she said.

"So you are," said the judge and motioned everyone away. Muriel had the court reporter read back the last two questions and answers.

Larry turned to watch Arthur, fearing he might try to cue Erno that Muriel was faking. You could never tell what kind of dog poo a guy would turn into as a defense lawyer, but Arthur remained poker-faced as he explained to his associate what was happening from behind his hand.

"Now, at the time you wrote Detective Starczek, you wanted to get into a medium-security facility, didn't you?"

"Well, my lawyer tried to arrange that. And when he couldn't, I asked some guys could they help."

"And are you telling us, Mr. Erdai, that you thought you'd get to a medium-security facility by informing Detective Starczek that you'd committed a brutal triple murder?"

Notwithstanding Harlow's prior look, there were again a few giggles from the spectators' pews.

"When I wrote Larry, I'd basically given up on medium. Corrections says you're in maximum if you committed an offense with a firearm. Period."

"And can you give us the name of anyone on the Force who tried to get the Corrections Department to make an exception on your behalf?"

Erno took the toothpick from his mouth. He was cooked on this one, because he knew no one would come to court to back him up. In answer to Muriel, he said he didn't recall.

"And no matter why you wrote to Detective Starczek, we agree you never mentioned these killings, correct?"

"True. I told him I had to talk to him about something important."

"Detective Starczek didn't respond?"

"Right."

"He didn't want to deal with you now that you couldn't do him any good. Is that how you felt?"

"Naw, I wouldn't say that."

Muriel returned to Larry for a copy of the letter Erno had written to Gillian, then started toward the witness. Ten feet to Larry's left, Raven immediately clambered to his feet.

"Judge, I haven't seen that," Arthur said. With an innocent look, Muriel displayed

Erno's letter first to Raven, then Harlow. Larry read over another copy Muriel had left on the table. The words were right there, even though Arthur's dashed look made it apparent that he'd missed their significance. As Muriel returned to the podium, Larry saw her pass Arthur a collegial smile, a pleasant 'gotcha' as if they were playing Scrabble or tennis. Then she turned back to Erno and used the letter like a knife to the liver.

"Did you write to Judge Sullivan that the detective on the case had no interest in you 'now that you can't do him any good'?"

Erno read it over several times. "That's what it says here."

"Would you say you were resentful?" asked Muriel.

"Call it what you want."

"I'll call it resentful," said Muriel. Harlow sustained the objection, but he smiled again. Larry by now had gotten a line on the judge. Kenton Harlow liked lawyers, admired what they did. He believed that the truth would emerge from the hard-fought courtroom contest, and he was clearly taken with Muriel's style.

"Well, let's put it this way," said Muriel. "You provided information to Detective

Starczek on what you knew was a major case, right?"

"Okay," said Erno.

"And your friend Detective Starczek made the case? He got credit for it."

"Him and you," said Erno.

"He and I. And the Police Force got credit for it, correct?"

"Right."

"That Force where no one would help you get to medium security."

"Okay."

"That same Force where nobody backed your story that the shooting four years ago at Ike's was self-defense."

"Yeah, I suppose."

"And by saying what you're saying now, you're essentially taking back what you gave Detective Starczek and the Police Force before. Yes?"

"I'm saying the truth."

"True or not, you're trying to correct or withdraw the effect of the information you provided previously. Aren't you?"

"Cause that was a lie."

Muriel moved to strike and Harlow forced Erno to answer. He had no choice but to say yes. It was all too obvious by now, but a little ruffle passed through the rows of press when he spoke the word. They had the lead for their stories.

Muriel then began to question Erno about his relationship with the Gangster Outlaws, one of the street gangs that dominated the prison at Rudyard. This was information that Larry had worked most of the night developing, and Muriel laid it out nicely. Erno had gotten on with a G.O. cellmate and had eventually fallen under the protection of the gang, for whom Erno was thought to occasionally obtain information from old pals in law enforcement. Erno would not acknowledge the last part.

"Well, do you know, Mr. Erdai, that there have been several cases where members of the Gangster Outlaws who were incarcerated have provided false confessions to crimes other G.O.'s were accused of?"

"Objection," said Arthur. "There's no evidence that Mr. Gandolph is a member of any gang."

"The question," said Muriel, "is whether Mr. Erdai knows that."

"It's irrelevant," said Arthur.

"I'll hear it," said the judge.

"I've heard that," said Erno.

"And have you also heard, Mr. Erdai, that the G.O.'s control death row at Rudyard?"

"I know there's a lot of them there."

"Including Mr. Gandolph?"

"I wouldn't know about that. You have to understand, those death rows, the Yellow Men, are off by themselves. They don't see anybody else. I haven't had a word with Gandolph in all the time I've been in the facility."

"Well, Mr. Erdai, are you telling us that given your experience in the institution, if somebody from the G.O.'s, who've protected you, wanted you to tell a story, especially a story that wouldn't hurt you but that would hurt Detective Starczek and the Police Force who'd let you down, a story that would even help you spend time with your wife before you died—are you really telling us you have too much integrity to do that?"

Arthur had come to his feet long before Muriel finished. He quietly said, "Objection," and Harlow quickly responded, "Sustained." But Muriel had essentially given her closing argument for the press. With her job more than done, she moved back toward counsel table, then stopped abruptly.

"Oh," she said, as if what was coming

was merely an afterthought. "After you hauled these bodies down to the freezer, Mr. Erdai, what is it you say you did to the corpse of Luisa Remardi?"

"I pulled her skirt and her underwear down to her ankles."

"And then?"

"Then, nothing."

"So you just disrobed her for, what, curiosity?"

"I disrobed her, because I knew she'd been having sex an hour before and I figured it would show in the autopsy. I wanted it to look like she'd been assaulted. It was the same idea as taking everybody's stuff to make it look like a robbery. I was just trying to cover up."

"And you didn't, in fact, perform anal intercourse with the corpse."

"Nope."

"You know, don't you, that the police pathologist, Dr. Kumagai, testified at trial that the corpse had been sodomized."

"I know that Painless Kumagai has made a lot of mistakes over the years."

"But you don't know why a common condom lubricant was detected in her anus?"

"I think you ought to ask the gentleman

she was passing time with in the parking lot."

"And do you think that accounts for why her anal sphincter was distended after the time of death?"

"I'm not a pathologist."

"But you'll agree, Mr. Erdai, that your testimony doesn't explain that piece of evidence, does it?"

"I haven't explained that, no."

"Thank you," said Muriel.

She settled beside Larry. Below the table, quite unexpectedly, he felt her fist knock against his.

MURIEL'S CROSS had gone almost entirely as Arthur had acted it out in his conferences with Erno at the jail. The only exception was the line in Erno's letter about Larry having no use for him now; Arthur hadn't recognized the implications. But that aside, Erno had been well prepared. The difference was Muriel. She won any competition on style points.

By the time she had finished, Judge Harlow was sitting up straight in his chair on the other side of the bench, literally keeping his distance from Erdai. As Arthur rose for redirect examination, he was aware he had work to do. He buttoned his coat, and double-checked on Pamela's notes, before he started what was called, in the parlance, rehabilitating the witness.

"Mr. Erdai, Ms. Wynn questioned why you would take such risks to yourself for your nephew's sake. Can you explain that to His Honor, Judge Harlow?"

Erno studied the rail on the witness box for quite some time.

"This family—my family—we survived a lot. I mean, they had a hell of a time in the Second World War and then in 1956, my father took part in the revolt—" Erno screwed up his face. "He was killed—he was shot and then hung from his feet on the lamppost in front of our house, to tell it like it was. Our neighbors sold him out to the AVH, the secret police. And my mother and my sister and me, it was quite a story getting out of there and getting here. And then Collins, my nephew—he was the only child either of us had, my sister and me. And I knew if he went to prison for the rest of his life, then that was it. I mean, I thought a lot about my father hanging from that lamppost—they left him out there for days, they wouldn't let us cut him down, it was a warning." Erno reached to cover his mouth, as if he was going to be ill, and instead broke down completely. After a minute, he mopped his entire face with the judge's tissues and, as before, took a while to get his breathing back on track.

"I felt he could be something, Collins. He was smart, just stuck in a tough spot. But I thought I owed it to my father, to my mother, too—to the whole family—to try to get him one more chance. I had to do what I could."

Arthur waited to see if Erno would offer more, but he'd said his piece. By now, Arthur and Pamela had spent hours with Erno, and one of the hard truths of the case was that Arthur did not particularly like him. It was not because Erno was a criminal, nor even because of the exceptional gravity of what he had done. Over the years, Arthur, like everyone else who worked in the system, had encountered absolute miscreants who were bright as a new penny, and even beguiling. But there was an inalterable coldness to Erno. He was blunt, and not merely indifferent to feelings but somewhat proud of the fact. He did not ask to be liked. And yet his hardness left Arthur with an unshakable conviction that Erno was telling the truth, and also with considerable admiration for Erno's willingness to proceed without demanding to be regarded as either a saint or a martyr. He knew he wasn't.

"All right, then. One more area. Ms. Wynn raised questions about the motives for your testimony. Can you tell us why you agreed to speak to Judge Sullivan and me—why you decided to tell the truth about what happened on July Fourth, 1991."

Predictably, Muriel stood up to object to the assumption that Erno was telling the truth. The judge brushed her aside, the way he'd done to Arthur a couple of times.

"Let's just try our lawsuit, folks. Let's not worry about who's in the peanut gallery," Harlow said, clearly adverting to the press. "Okay, Mr. Erdai. Explain yourself. Why are we hearing about this now?"

Erno steadied his breathing before he began.

"I would say at first, when I set up Gandolph, I didn't really worry much about him. I figured, if you laid end to end everything he got away with, he probably deserved quite a bit of time anyway.

"Now, like I said, if Larry had come down when I asked, I'd have told him. I hadn't worked out in my head exactly how I'd do that, but I'd have done it, because I'd owe him to be straight. But now, I realize I owe it to Gandolph.

"There's nothing like dying, I'll tell you. You may think you understand that you're only here temporary, but when the doctors tell you—I don't know, maybe old folks feel different about it. My ma was happy to go at eighty-six. But when it's before your time— for me—I spend a lot of the day being scared. It's coming. You know it's coming. And there's nothing you can do. It's coming. It's cruel, actually. You live your whole life, you survive all this stuff and still the end's got to be so cruel.

"Now, you know, guys on their deathbed, they rediscover their faith, and I've rediscovered mine. I listen to the priest. And I think a lot. I've done a lot of terrible things. I don't know if God gave me this disease as punishment, or if it just happened because stuff happens—He won't be sending any telegrams to explain it. But it comes in your mind, eventually, that you have it in your power to make things better. And that's what got me thinking about Gandolph. He's been over there, every day for nine-plus years now, and he knows every day, just like me, it's coming. It's coming, and he can't do nothing about it. Like me. Only he doesn't deserve it. If I just tell the truth, he gets out from under. He's going through what I'm going through, every day, but he doesn't have to. That's what I kept thinking. I can't change it for me. But I can change it for him. All I have to do is what's right."

Erno hadn't been looking at anyone as he gave this oration. His eyes were cast low and he was speaking in the same bare voice, raspy and a bit disembodied, in which he'd answered throughout. But when he finished he looked up and nodded decisively to the judge.

With a long finger laid beside his nose, Harlow was manifestly weighing what to make of Erno. Arthur and Pamela had spent a considerable amount of time asking the same question of one another. Despite Erno's plainspokenness, there remained an elusive quality to him, which Arthur had eventually decided arose from Erno's uncertainty about himself. Arthur had no doubt Erdai meant every word he'd just said, yet there was a sense in which the man found such reflections alien. Sometimes Erno reminded Arthur of his schizophrenic sister, Susan, who often claimed to be under the command of voices from elsewhere in the cosmos. Erno had testified that when he shot Paul Judson, he learned something grisly about his own nature. But that was nowhere near as unaccountable to him as the forces that had impelled him at the end of his life to reverse what little he could of the damage done by his savage side. Erno accepted that he was doing right. But he still seemed utterly confounded about what was in it for him.

Eventually, the judge asked Muriel if she had any redirect. After conferring with Larry, she said no.

"Mr. Erdai," said the judge, "you are excused." Harlow studied Erno a moment longer, then added in a flat voice, "Good luck to you, sir," and without looking back, left the bench.

19

JUNE 13, 2001

Still Victims

AS THE SESSION CONCLUDED, Muriel, still flying on adrenaline, faced the gallery, where the onlookers, shoulder to shoulder, were struggling to their feet. There were at least a dozen reporters here on special assignment, and scores of civilians drawn in by the headlines of the last twenty-four hours.

This morning Ned Halsey had gallantly suggested Muriel leave the case—and the controversy—to him. But the reporters knew Gandolph's prosecution had been pivotal in her career; if Arthur actually proved Squirrel was the wrong man, the press would hang her whether she was in the courtroom or not. And she would not have deprived herself of the challenge anyway. She craved these moments of premium demand, no matter how dire, when the world pressed at her like a clamoring sea. Raven was approaching with a bundle of new motions. Molto and Carol needed to be consulted on the next legal move. Larry was awaiting direction on where his investigation of Erdai should head. And the journalists were already lurching forward to see if they could squeeze some pre-emptive comment from her. But this was the destiny she'd wanted since childhood. 'The arena' was Talmadge's term, but she did not care for the gladiatorial overtone. To her it was more a matter of using herself completely, feeling that every cell had to contribute to managing her place in her times.

With the instinctive clarity with which these matters always made themselves manifest to her, she abruptly saw what she had to do. John Leonidis was present, seated in the rear, as he had faithfully been for more than nine years now, whenever there were court sessions of consequence. She ignored everyone else, and with the reporters gathered round, placed an arm on John's shoulder and led him across the hall to the witness room. The press, she knew, wouldn't go away until she'd commented.

John had not come down alone. He intro-

duced a smooth-skinned man, Pan, a Fil-
ipino perhaps, who was a good deal
younger than John. Even after Muriel closed
the door to the small room, the din of the
milling outside the courtroom reached them
vaguely. John had been enraged by the proceedings. He bit off a piece of his thumbnail
while he fulminated, explaining to Muriel, as
if it were news to her, that Erdai was lying to
get even with the Kindle County police and
had been fed all details.

"I want to tell those idiot reporters out
there what's going on," said John.

For Muriel, it was ideal to be defended by
the victims. Nonetheless, she told John he
should speak only if he wanted to.

"Believe me, I want to," said John. "I
think about this piece of dirt every day.
Gandolph? Every day, Muriel, I realize I lost
something else to this guy. Lately, the last
few months, I keep wondering if my old
man would have been proud of me." John
had good reason to believe Gus would have
taken great satisfaction in him. Not only had
John continued to operate Paradise, where
business was better than ever in the resur-
gent neighborhood, but he had also
franchised mid-priced Greek restaurants

across the country in partnership with a local hotel owner. Muriel had lunch at the Center City place, GG's Taverna—GG for Good Gus—at John's invitation a few times every year. He would sit at her table, smoke, and go over the case, which remained as fresh in his mind as if it had been tried yesterday.

"I think, you know, Gus would have had some problems with some things in my life," said John, "same as my mom, but I think it would have turned out okay, with him, too. I really believe that. But I'm entitled to know. Right? Everybody is. This shitbag, Gandolph—he's not God. But he was God in my life."

For John, like most survivors, his father's murder, and the killer's punishment, would always resound with personal meanings. Yet the principal reason John could not let the case end was simply because it hadn't. For John Leonidis it had been almost a decade of holding his breath, hoping against hope that the injustice of Gus's death would not be compounded by seeing Rommy Gandolph escape what the clanking legal machinery had said he deserved.

Years ago, John had been the most

adamant of the victims about the death penalty for Gandolph. By the time of the trial, Paul Judson's wife, Dina, had moved to Boulder and was doing everything she could to start fresh; no one had heard from her for years. Luisa's mom, who'd been ruffled by Larry during the investigation, appeared in court to ask for death, but seemed cowed. John, on the other hand, would have been happy to go to law school and try the case himself. Muriel had assumed originally this was for his mother's sake. But what he had testified to, during the victims' allocution before sentence was imposed, was that he believed his father would have wanted capital punishment, too.

'He'd give a person a chance,' John had said about Gus. 'He'd give you six chances, if he really thought you were trying. But at the end of the day, he was old school. He was tough. Sooner or later, he would have said enough is enough. My father was good to Gandolph. And got nothing for it but a bullet in the head. He would have wanted this guy dead. So that's what I want.' Even at the time, Muriel was uncertain that John's vision of his father was completely accurate, but who was she to say? She could still recall, though, the mood in the courtroom when John spoke, the gravity that had come over Gillian Sullivan as she listened from the bench. Idealists could posture about the indignity of the state killing—it was a lot better than having citizens take matters into their own hands, which is what could occur with people like John, people with griefs and debts to the dead that required action. For him, Rommy Gandolph's death had become a priority, part of the role as his father's stand-in that he had assumed from the moment Gus died.

Muriel opened the door, waving to Carol so she would accompany John and his friend downstairs to the courthouse lobby, where the TV cameras waited. Several reporters shouted Muriel's name and she promised to be along in a moment. Larry, however, immediately shepherded four females over the threshold—two adolescent girls, an agreeable-looking woman near forty, and at the rear, an older lady whose hair was dyed a lifeless black. She was the only one of the four whom Muriel recognized.

"Mrs. Salvino, of course," said Muriel, welcoming Luisa Remardi's mother. The old woman was tough and to the point, and

Muriel had always taken it that Luisa was a chip off the old block. The young girls with her had faces almost identical to one another, but the two years between them resulted in a significant contrast in their overall appearance. The second to enter wore makeup and was almost a foot taller than her sister. But both were lean and dark, long-jawed, with stray lanks of jet hair and large dark eyes. Each was very pretty. Muriel realized at once they were Luisa's daughters.

In her usual abrupt way, Mrs. Salvino dismissed Muriel's greeting.

"This here," she said, "don't you people ever come to an end with this?"

"Nuccia," scolded the fourth female.

"Muriel," said Larry, with an uncharacteristic ceremonial air, "you may remember Genevieve Carriere. She was a close friend of Luisa's." Genevieve had been called upon as a driver and escort. Mrs. Salvino was one of those Kewahnee Italians who went to Center City only two or three times a year, and always with apprehension.

"I got no need to come down here," Mrs. Salvino said. "Darla heard the television. So she decided she's coming, which is mostly an excuse, if you want to know, to skip school."

"Like I need an excuse," answered her older granddaughter. The little one was shy and wore braces and hung back by the door. But Darla was clearly a handful. Sixteen now, she wore the skimpy clothing and heavy makeup that Muriel saw all the time on the street. Her figure was far too full for the narrow camisole that stopped short of her navel. Muriel was often bemused at how taken aback she was by the sexual brashness of these girls, because she knew that she'd have taken full advantage of such license, had it been permitted in her day.

"You got no need to hear all of this," said her grandmother.

"*Hel*-lo, Grandma! It's on television. And it's my own mother and you don't tell us nothing. I mean, that's totally bogus."

Larry intervened. "I don't think you learned anything about what happened, Darla. That was just a bitter, dying man entertaining himself."

"I sorta believed him sometimes," she answered in the usual contrary fashion of people her age. "This other guy, the one they say done it. It all sounds so sketchy with him.

I don't think somebody as sick as this dude even has the energy to make stuff up."

"You should know about making up," said her grandmother.

Darla briefly offered Mrs. Salvino a sick simpering look.

"The only thing with this one," said Darla, "is that he's like such a total gross-out to look at."

Muriel and Larry, still caught in the warring mood of the courtroom, laughed at the same time, greatly amused by the cruelty to Erno.

"No, truly," insisted Darla, "I mean, I know he's sick and all, but he couldn't ever have been, like, good-looking. That's just so not Mom. All the pictures I seen of her with guys—even my father—they were always, like, hotties." The girl spoke with some urgency, and Muriel was struck by the pathos of Darla's adoring reconstruction of her mother. The older Muriel became, the more aware she grew of the freight of pain carried inside every courthouse. As a younger person, what she sensed was the anger—of both the victims and the defendants, who frequently felt ill used—and, even more grippingly, her own righteous need to smite evil.

But now what stayed with her was the legacy of hurt—for Darla, even for the criminals, who often had the sense to regret what they had done, and certainly for their families, who were usually as innocent as the other bystanders, their sole mistake loving someone who'd come to no good.

To Darla, it was obviously important that her estimate of her mother be correct. She turned to Genevieve, who had watched Darla's byplay with her grandmother with the whisper of a smile.

"Isn't that right, Aunt Genevieve? Mom totally wouldn't have been with somebody like that."

"Never," said Genevieve. "Your mother always hated that man." Genevieve touched the girl's bare shoulder and thus missed the look Muriel exchanged with Larry.

"Why did she hate him?" Muriel asked.

Six was a crowd in here, amid an old tweed sofa and a government-issue table and chairs. Immediately conscious of an error, Genevieve looked off to one of the corny woodland scenes on the wall rather than confront the attention suddenly on her.

"There was just bad blood," she said and turned a manicured hand in the air, as if it were all too vague. Her hair was prematurely white, which was actually quite striking, since she had retained a flush, round-cheeked youthfulness right down to her overbite. Overall, Genevieve gave an impression of substance. It was a decade later and she was still looking out for her friend's children and mother. Muriel had spent years now envisioning herself on the sidelines of soccer and baseball fields in the company of women like this, mothers who nurtured by reflex and who were probably the best people on the planet.

"Maybe the girls could wait outside," Muriel suggested, thinking they might have motivated Genevieve's reluctance.

"Like hell," answered Darla. "We're not babies. She was *our* mother."

In spite of herself, Muriel smiled, probably because she'd been every bit as abrasive and opinionated herself at sixteen. The thrill of going too far, of treading forbidden ground to find out who she was, had never fully left her. Andrea, Darla's younger sister, looked less certain about staying, but ultimately chose to keep her place, too. In the meantime, Larry continued to press Genevieve.

"So you don't know anything about Erno and Luisa being an item?"

Genevieve looked at her watch and lifted a beckoning arm to the girls, but was willing to offer a parting thought.

"I'd sooner believe he killed her than that," she said.

Muriel held up a hand to detain Mrs. Salvino. "Did Luisa ever say anything to *you* about Erno?"

"Who knows?" answered the old woman. "Who paid attention?"

"Did she talk about men?"

"For God sake," said Mrs. Salvino, "I was her mother for God sake. You think I asked those things?"

"I think you'd ask," said Darla.

Mrs. Salvino raised the back of her hand and made a spitting sound between her teeth and Darla answered with another gesture, an openhand challenge, which, in all likelihood, she'd adopted from her grandmother. But Darla was smiling. She had more appreciation for Nuccia Salvino than she was likely to admit.

As Genevieve continued to edge the group toward the door, Muriel told Mrs. Salvino the reporters might try to question her.

"I got nothing to say."

"They'll want to know what you think,"

said Muriel. "Whether you believe Erdai killed her."

"Maybe," said Mrs. Salvino. "Maybe this one and the other one done it together. I don't know. She's dead. That's what I know."

"We have no comment," said Genevieve.

Muriel bade goodbye to all of them. Genevieve left last and Larry laid his fingertips on her sleeve.

"We'd really like to talk to you some more."

Genevieve was quick to shake her head. She had an excuse ready. Family vacation. Every year, as soon as their kids were out of school, they headed for Skageon for a month.

"When do you leave?" Muriel asked.

"Tomorrow," said Genevieve, "early."

"Well, maybe we'll make the trip up there," said Larry, and Genevieve's dark eyes shot his way.

Remembering the press downstairs, and recognizing the futility of Larry's hectoring, Muriel opened the door and let Genevieve go. She and Larry were alone now, an odd reprieve with the churning sounds continuing outside.

"We should go up there and depose her," said Larry. "She'd twist and turn, but I don't make her for the kind to lie under oath. I don't see us getting anything out of her without a subpoena, though."

"I wouldn't mind having that stuff about Luisa always hating Erno on the record. We have to make him a liar however we can."

"You did a pretty good job of that."

She accepted the compliment with a smile, but she'd learned that winning lawsuits was more than courtroom pyrotechnics. Most cases were determined before they started by the character of the judge or the jury, and Kenton Harlow worried her.

"If he makes findings that Erno is credible," she told Larry, "I'm going to be stuck with this case for a long while. Talmadge thinks if it drags on, Reverend Blythe may talk somebody into running in the primary."

"Somebody black," said Larry.

"Naturally," she answered, but shook her head at the prospect. She had no relish for that kind of fight, especially one where she'd be painted as the race-baiting prosecutor.

"So what's the alternative?" Larry asked.

"You know the alternative, Larry. Figure it out fast. Either incinerate Erno or say we fucked up and stop the bleeding as soon as we can."

"We didn't fuck up anything. The death-penalty crazies always strum the same tunes. This guy was wrong on this, Muriel, you know it. I didn't bounce him around to get a confession. Erno can go whistle with that Shangri-la shit."

"I'm just saying."

"Besides, all due respect to Talmadge, if we screwed the pooch, Blythe would add another hole to your anatomy. You might have to stop that check for campaign posters."

"If that's how it goes," she answered immediately. Her tone was too defiant, even superior, and she could see him shrink back. It struck an old note somehow, something that had been there years ago. She felt guilty about that. And she probably hadn't spoken the truth. The other day, she'd told Larry that she might have surrendered her shot at the P.A.'s Office in exchange for the joy of being a mother, and she meant every word. But to have neither of the things she'd yearned for? She knew herself well enough to realize she wouldn't have given up on the job easily.

"He's the right guy, Larry. But let's punch

some holes in Erno's canoe. I'm going to get hold of Jackson Aires to try to get a word with Erno's nephew. And keep working on the gang angle. The G.O.'s may have promised Erno something we haven't figured out yet. And see if you can dig up the guy Erno shot at Ike's. Something tells me he won't stand up and salute for that self-defense crap Erno was peddling."

Larry liked all those ideas. The peace between them felt good.

"Press time," said Muriel. "Do I look tough but fair?"

He joined his thumbs and raised his forefingers as if they were a lens.

"Something like that."

She smiled at him for a moment. "I forgot how much fun it is to work with you, Larry."

When Muriel opened the door, she found Darla, Luisa's older daughter, leaning against the threshold. The girl sprang up at the sight of Muriel.

"I forgot to ask," she said. "I was just wondering if there's any chance we can get it back?"

"It?"

Darla gave Muriel one of those intolerant

adolescent glances, as if Muriel were as thick as a stone.

"The cameo. My mom's cameo. It's in evidence, right? Mr. Molto said we can't have it until this whole thing is over and done with. But, you know, we've been waiting, like, so long, and I was just wondering, because—" For all her toughness, Darla suddenly looked stricken and could find no more words.

But Muriel required no explanation. Darla wanted the cameo because as the older daughter it was her birthright; because it marked her tie to her mother and held an image of Darla, taken at the moment of her first existence, which Luisa had literally worn over her heart. For the girl's sake, Muriel felt sudden fury and frustration. A decade now, and the law for all its noble intentions and its screw-loose workings, had not even allowed a motherless child the comfort of touching her most precious inheritance.

Muriel briefly hugged Darla, swearing to work this out quickly, then strode toward the elevators, trying to regain her calm. Furious would not play well on camera. But she was glad for her moment with Darla, the opportunity to re-experience the intensity of her concern and resolve. Enough of the games of the Redcoats and Indians. Enough of defense attorneys bounding out of the woods on Squirrel's behalf screaming 'Surprise!' Enough withholding justice, and peace, from the people who deserved it. The end was overdue—for the case, for the lawyering, and for Rommy Gandolph himself.

20

JUNE 13, 2001

Susan

FROM HER SEAT in the last row, Gillian Sullivan slipped toward the door as soon as court broke. She was already on her way down the corridor, her low heels as distinct as taps on the marble, when she heard her name from behind. Stew Dubinsky, who was the *Trib*'s longtime felony court reporter, jogged a few steps and arrived beside her, winded by the effort. There were few persons on earth she wanted to see less.

By entering the courtroom, she had risked this confrontation, and knowing that, she had told herself more than once to leave. But there might as well have been a padlock on her seat, until Erno's last word had been spoken. What impelled her to stay rather than turn her back, as she'd so often sworn she wanted to do? She had so many mistakes to rue. Thousands of them. How could she be focused so singlemindedly on this one? But she had scoured the paper this morning, even sat in front of Duffy's TV last night, while the late news played over his horsey snores. She was hooked, as she had been at some level since the day she'd gone with Arthur to Rudyard. Were these the excesses again of a conscience always starving for shame? Yet there was no further fooling herself. Whatever the truth was here, it was, somehow, a truth about her.

Dubinsky had passed from overweight to porcine. The face she had known him by years ago was still there, but had sunk like a relief into a puddle of blubbery abundance. Stew had never been her favorite. He was unreliable in virtually every regard, habitually late, sometimes cavalier with facts, and often underhanded in gathering them. Several years ago he'd lost his courthouse press card for a while, when he'd been found with his ear pressed to a jury-room door.

In a few words, she explained to Dubinsky why she'd been present. It was plain, however, that he saw her as an angle his competitors wouldn't have. He found his recorder in his jacket pocket. Instinct told her that if she remained the object of reports like this morning's, her job would soon be in jeopardy, but she was afraid that putting Dubinsky off would make him more determined. She said several times that she had to go, but Stew kept promising he had just one more question. By now he'd ventured past Rommy Gandolph's case to inquiries she had no interest in answering about her present life.

"Here you are," someone said and took firm hold of her elbow. It was Arthur. "We have to go right now, Judge, if I'm going to drive you back. I just got a page. I have a client who's been arrested and I need to bail her out." He was pushing Gillian down the hall.

Dubinsky stayed on their heels, but with Arthur here, Stew shifted his focus. He wanted Raven's reactions to virtually every point Muriel had raised. Arthur stopped walking at one juncture to see if Dubinsky could be shaken, but he ended up following them to the roof of the small parking structure across from the courthouse where Arthur's new automobile waited.

"Hey, private practice looks all right," said Stew, touching a fender.

"It's not from this case," Arthur assured him. He helped Gillian inside and quickly drove down the ramp.

"You're my hero." Eyes closed, Gillian put a hand to her chest. "Has Stew gotten worse or am I just out of practice? You don't really have a client in lockup, do you?"

"Unfortunately. My sister."

"Your sister!"

"It happens all the time, Gillian. But I need to get over there."

"By all means. Just drop me on a corner."

"Where are you going?"

"Please, Arthur. Attend to your sister. I work in the store in Nearing this evening. I'll take the bus."

"Well, I'm going to West Bank Two. You may as well ride along. You can take a bus from there, if you want."

She couldn't see what problem she would cause him by riding as far as the police station, and she had unfinished business with Arthur. She still held some hope of smoothing over the awkwardness of yesterday's parting, and she also was curious about his reactions to today's proceedings. As it turned out, he asked her first what she'd made of Erno.

"I think Muriel's a very good lawyer," said Gillian. "She raised a lot of dust."

"Did you believe him?"

She had not really pondered that. To believe or not had somehow seemed secondary. It was not her decision, for one thing. Moreover, she could feel now how much the spectacle itself had drawn her in. She had not been inside a courtroom since she'd been sentenced. But it had enlivened her today in a way she had refused to imagine. The lawyers, the judges; the way the sound carried; the flash of emotion that exceeded even what took place in a theater because it was so resoundingly real. When Erno had spoken about his oncoming death, it was like a sustained lightning strike. She half expected to smell ozone in the large room.

Gillian was not all that surprised to experience a measure of envy. She'd always cherished the courtroom. Yet what had shocked her was how near at hand it remained—the calculation and reflection that went into each question, the effort to read through the judge's inscrutable responses. She realized only now that she had dreamed of it all every night.

"Very frankly, I'm not sure I want to believe

him, Arthur. But I thought your redirect was quite brilliant, as effective in its own way as Muriel's cross."

"Hardly," said Arthur, although he could not contain a smile. Nor was Gillian being polite. Arthur had been first-rate. Cross-examination required flourish, as the interrogator became the visible embodiment of disbelief. Redirect had an artistry of its own, far more subtle, in which the lawyer, a bit like a parent asserting a gentle influence over an unruly child, indiscernibly steered the witness back into a flattering light.

"I suppose, at this stage, I have an open mind about Erno," she said. "Can you corroborate him somehow?"

"I can't figure out how. Not with the physical evidence. If he said he'd assaulted her, maybe there would be a pubic hair, DNA, but there's nothing."

"Why do you think he denies that? The sexual assault?"

"From the day I went down there with you, he's insisted Painless got it wrong. I actually think it counts in his favor. If he were really trying to tailor his testimony to the evidence, he'd have admitted that, too."

They were advancing slowly in the dense

afternoon traffic. Gillian mulled. At this stage, merely raising doubts about the conviction would not be enough to get Gandolph off death row. Ten years along, it was far too late for that. But there was a chance Muriel would want to get the litigation out of the spotlight.

"Muriel might talk to you about a deal, you know," she told Arthur.

"You mean a deal for life? Even if he's innocent?"

"What would your client say?"

"That's the equivalent of trial by ordeal. Offer him life. If he's guilty, he'll jump at it. If he's innocent, he might say yes, too, just to live."

"His choice, isn't it?" Gillian asked, but Arthur shook his head.

"I want him to be innocent. I'm as bad as Pamela now." He glanced at her with a trace of little-boy bashfulness. "This is better than being a prosecutor. You do right as a prosecutor. But not like this. I have to take on the entire world. This is the first time in years I haven't felt beaten down when my feet hit the ground in the morning." Arthur, never one to hide his feelings, briefly bore the pure light of exhilaration.

Gillian smiled, but she again felt herself wandering where she no longer had the right to go. Instead, she asked Arthur about his sister, and he briefly recounted Susan's history in one of those deadened tones that suggested not true detachment but rather that all hope had finally been run over by pain. It was a common story: periods of stability, then crashing relapses and hospitalization. Susan had disappeared several times, awful stretches when Arthur and his father had hunted for her on the streets, and in which, the last time, she'd turned up in Phoenix, strung out on speed—the worst thing imaginable for a schizophrenic—and three months pregnant. For Arthur's father in particular, who had remained ever hopeful that the beautiful girl of glimmering promise would somehow be returned to him, the cycles of her illness had been crushing.

"Do drugs help?" Gillian asked.

"They help a lot. But sooner or later she refuses to take them."

"Because?"

"Because the side effects of some of them are awful. She gets the shakes. Tachycardia. Her neck gets sort of paralyzed with her head tilted to one side. One reason for the group home is so we can watch her get a shot of Prolixin once a week. She did better on the Risperdal, but that's every day, which never works out. This stuff just sort of tames her. And she hates it. With all of them, I think the worst thing for her is that life is drab, compared to what's in her head when she's not taking anything. You're talking about somebody with an IQ of 165. I can't even imagine what's going on in there. But I know it's vivid, wild—electrifying. She's still a genius. To her the outside world is about as relevant as the Middle Ages, but she reads three papers every morning and never forgets anything."

Arthur said that for several years now, a childhood friend of Susan's, now Senior V.P. at Faulkes Warren, the mutual-fund house, had arranged jobs for her—keypunching, collating, sorting industry reports. She'd actually shown skill as an analyst. If she didn't have to sit in a room by herself, or be hospitalized twice a year, Arthur said, Susan might be making a quarter of a million dollars. Instead, her behavior always left her on the verge of dismissal. As a result, he had struck a deal with Susan's employers. When his sister went into a paranoid spin, they would simply call the police to remove her. Arthur had an old friend at West Bank Two, Yogi Marvin, a sergeant, who dispatched a squad car. Susan usually welcomed the police, certain they'd arrived to quell whoever she was sure had done her wrong.

"Shit," said Arthur as they came down the street toward the station now. "There she is." West Bank Two was a functional contemporary structure, the shape of a shoe box made out of brick. In front of its glass doors, two women appeared to be arguing, while a uniformed officer stood to the side. Arthur parked in a space only a few feet from them and dashed forward. Gillian left the car and waited by its radiant fender, uncertain if it was more impolite to stay or to slip away.

"I need my cigarettes," Susan was saying. "You know I need my cigarettes, Valerie."

"I do know you need your cigarettes," said Valerie, "and Rolf knows that, too. That's why we wouldn't take them." Valerie, Gillian took it, was a social worker in the assisted living home where Susan resided. Arthur had said one of them was on the way over. If a lifetime's experience was any guide, Gillian would guess Valerie was a nun. Her patience, as she attempted to talk Susan down, was otherworldly, and her attire was only slightly more chic than a habit—a shapeless jumper and thick shoes. Valerie's face was round and pleasant and appeared not to have been touched for years by any chemical agent, even cold cream.

"You told me not to smoke at work," said Susan, "and you thought I was ignoring you and so you took them."

"Susan, I think you know that I wasn't at work with you. What I told you was that Rolf is asthmatic and that because he's in the next space, you should follow their rules and smoke in the lounge. That doesn't mean that I would take your cigarettes. Or that Rolf would."

"I know Rolf took my cigarettes."

Arthur asked if it would help if he went to the store and bought another pack for Susan.

"But why won't they make Rolf give back the cigarettes he took? I want to smoke a cigarette now."

Catching sight of Gillian at the curb, Arthur gave her a desperate look. She had left Alderson hoping never to witness another screaming battle about cigarettes, a daily event in prison, and largely on impulse she reached into her purse.

"I have one," she said.

Susan recoiled and her hands shot up protectively. Although Gillian had been no more than a few steps away, Susan had plainly missed her. Arthur introduced Gillian, calling her a friend. Gillian's hope to end the dispute over cigarettes was quickly fulfilled. Susan's suspicions now focused on her.

"You don't have any friends who smoke," Susan said. She was addressing her brother, but looking toward Valerie rather than having to turn in Gillian's direction again.

"You can see Gillian has cigarettes," Arthur said.

"You don't like me to meet your friends."

"I don't like it when my friends aren't nice to you."

"You think I don't know I'm schitzy."

"I know you know that, Susan."

She took the cigarette without ever quite facing Gillian's way, but muttered a meek thank you. On the bench, Gillian had seen her share of acute-phase schizophrenics. There were also at least half a dozen women in Alderson who clearly suffered the same illness and should have been hospitalized

rather than imprisoned. Given that experience, Susan's appearance was something
of a surprise. She could have been a suburban housewife on her way for groceries,
dressed in jeans and a T-shirt. She was
pudgy and pale and surprisingly neat, hair
trimmed short and showing quite a bit of
gray. She was older than Arthur, early forties,
Gillian supposed, and strikingly pretty, with
even features. But she was entirely de-
tached from her external self. Accepting the
cigarette, her hand shot at full length from
her, as if she were a tin man. Her eyes were
dull and her face was rigid, seemingly acknowledging that regular emotion of any
kind presented an untenable risk.

"Is she a shrink?" Susan asked her brother.

"No."

Susan blinked spasmodically, wincing
whenever she began to speak, and for the
minutest time, her light eyes flashed toward
Gillian.

"You're a Compliant, aren't you?"

"I'm sorry?" Gillian turned to Arthur, who
looked pained. The word, he said, was
Susan's coinage. Schizophrenics who refused drug therapy were commonly referred
to as noncompliant. It took Gillian an instant

to register what Susan was suggesting about her.

"You and Valerie are always trying to get me to meet people who've recovered," Susan said.

"We think it would help you. But Gillian is not one of them."

Susan, who had simply held the cigarette until now, lit it with matches from her pocket and closed one eye in her own smoke. Despite her fairly assertive declarations, in the intervals between them, Susan was quick-eyed and frightened.

"I know you're not Gillian Sullivan."

"I'm not?" Gillian asked, before she could think better of it.

"Gillian Sullivan was a judge who's in prison."

She saw what Arthur had meant about Susan retaining the content of the newspapers.

"I was released from prison several months ago."

In response, Susan took a step too close, revolving her face like a searchlight as she suddenly scrutinized Gillian.

"What drugs are you on?"

Arthur reached for Susan's arm, but she shook his hand away.

"Paxil," said Gillian.

"Me, too," said Susan. "But what about neuraleptics? Antihallucinogens?" When Gillian hesitated, Susan shook her head emphatically. "You've been there, I can see it."

Those who pretended they did not understand the insane were doing just that—pretending. Susan was right: Gillian had been crazy. Not in Susan's fashion. Susan had been unable to cross the valley that most of us traversed in childhood, surrendering our own mythology in favor of a shared one. But Gillian had been in retreat from reality. She knew that. She addressed a world of bad acts and hard consequences from the bench, and then, in the stupor of heroin, reclaimed her fantasy of valiance and invulnerability. In the instant before she nodded out, she always felt regal and dominant in the same way she had when she'd played with dolls as a child. No, she had nothing on Susan and would never assume she did.

"I've been there," said Gillian.

"I can always tell," said Susan, and shot a plume of smoke in the air, with the exasperated imperial air of Bette Davis. "But I don't understand why you say you're Gillian Sullivan."

Still trying to win the point, Arthur reminded his sister that he had been assigned years ago to Judge Sullivan's courtroom.

"I remember," said Susan. "I remember. You were in love with her. You're in love with someone else every three weeks."

"Thank you, Susan."

"You are. And none of them love you."

Arthur who had looked immeasurably fatigued as soon as he arrived, for an instant appeared too flattened to bother with anything else.

"That isn't my fault, Arthur."

"I don't think it is."

"You think if you didn't have this crazy sister to look after, then everything would be hunky-dory."

"Susan, I like it more when you don't try to confront me. I love you and I want to help you and you know that. I have to get back to my office. I'm on trial. I told you about the case. The man on death row?"

"Are you going to get him out of prison?"

"I hope so."

"Did you get her out of prison?"

"She finished her sentence, Susan."

"You got her out of prison so you could show her to me, didn't you? What is she taking?"

"Actually," said Gillian, "in my case, it was what I stopped taking that made me better."

Encouraged by her success so far, Gillian had thought her remark would be helpful, but it proved a serious mistake. Susan for the first time became volatile, throwing her stubby hands through the air.

"I keep telling them that! If they'd just let me stop, I'd be back, I know I'd be back! She's back and she doesn't take anything."

"Susan, Gillian was in prison, not a hospital. She served her sentence. Now she's putting her life back together."

"Like you want me to do."

Arthur was stymied here. It did not seem much to concede, but apparently he'd learned over the years that granting any point would reinforce Susan.

"I would like that, Susan, but you have to do what makes sense to you."

"I want to get better, you know, Arthur."

"I know you do."

"Then you can bring her back."

"Gillian?"

"Whoever she is. Bring her on Tuesday. Three is better anyway."

Arthur, for the first time, appeared alarmed.

"I don't think she's available Tuesday night. You work then, don't you?"

Gillian watched Arthur for cues, but it seemed his question was genuine. She shook her head circumspectly.

"Now you don't want me to be around her," Susan said.

"Susan, ask yourself if you're making an effort to cooperate."

"Why won't you let her come on Tuesday? You don't really want to help me. You want me to keep getting this shit and she doesn't want me to, and so you don't want me to talk to her."

"Susan, I really like it when you're not so provocative. Why don't you go home now with Valerie?"

Susan remained agitated, insisting that he was trying to keep her away from Gillian. And he was, of course—Gillian could see that, albeit for her sake, rather than to hurt Susan. She felt inclined to volunteer for whatever 'Tuesday' was, but hesitated because of the unpredictable results so far of her attempts to be helpful.

Instead, Arthur temporized, telling his sister that they would see. Susan quieted briefly, then refused, almost visibly, to move toward equilibrium.

"I know she won't come."

"Enough, Susan," said Arthur. "This is enough. You've had a cigarette. I've said we'll see about Gillian. Now go with Valerie."

It was several more minutes, but eventually Susan and Valerie were both in the white van from the Franz Center, as the group home was known. Susan departed, vowing to discover who Gillian really was. As soon as the vehicle pulled out of sight, Arthur fell over himself apologizing, first to the cop who'd stood by throughout, then to Gillian. He explained that whenever one thing went wrong with Susan—the cigarettes, today—the whole scaffolding was likely to collapse.

"Arthur, there is nothing to apologize for. But may I ask the significance of Tuesday?"

"Oh. She gets her shot. And then we go to the apartment. It was my father's apartment, but I'm there now, mostly for her sake. We make dinner. It's become a big deal, especially since my father died. I think that's what she meant when she said three is better."

"Ah. It would be no great difficulty for me to come, if it's really important to her."

"I won't ask that. And frankly, Susan wouldn't pay any attention to you, once you got there. I can tell you that from experience. There's no continuity. Except the paranoia."

Arthur insisted on driving Gillian the short distance to the mall. She briefly demurred, but it was close to five already. As they sped from the police station lot, Gillian asked if it was hopeful that Susan spoke of recovery.

"Every conversation with Susan is about recovery. That's been going on for nearly thirty years."

Thirty years. Contemplating the energy that Arthur's sister required, she felt another surge in her admiration for him. She would have been exhausted long ago.

"I know you won't believe it," he said, "but I think she really liked you. She usually acts as if strangers aren't even there. That business about getting out of prison—I don't have to explain. It's bound to interest her. But I'm sorry she was so insulting."

"She was far too accurate to be insulting."

Arthur did not seem to know what to make of that remark, and for an instant the car was full only of the radio's babble. With a moment to think about it, Gillian found herself vaguely amused. Despite Arthur's frequent declarations of common cause with Gillian, it was his sister, not he, who was the kindred soul, a woman blessed with uncommon looks and intelligence, torn down by mysterious inner impulses.

"Susan is every bit as smart as you said she is," Gillian told him. "She's quite penetrating."

"She certainly nailed me," said Arthur. He exhaled and actually touched the spot on his suit coat over his heart. There was no need to ask which comment had caught him. 'And none of them love you.' She felt yet again the vastly thwarted nature of Arthur Raven's life.

They had reached the mall. Arthur circled his sleek car around the drive in front of Morton's, but she hesitated to leave. It seemed more important than ever that she not cause him further distress, and that she utter some of the consolations she'd considered after their encounter in front of the Center City store yesterday.

"Arthur, not to prolong a sore subject, but I have to say one more word. What made me unhappy when we parted yesterday was that you seemed to feel refused. And I assure you, it isn't personal."

Arthur winced. "Of course it's personal. It's the most personal thing of all. What else could you possibly call it?"

"Arthur, you're not considering the realities."

"Look," he said to her. "You're entitled to say no. So don't feel bad about it. The world is full of women who've preferred not to be seen with me."

"Arthur! That is surely not the issue." She said this with more conviction that she might have predicted. No, Arthur was not Prince Charming, but she held to old-fashioned convictions that beauty was a female prerogative. Truth be told, his looks did not bother her so much as his height, four to five inches below hers, even in low heels. Yet she enjoyed his company. As she always recognized, he was entirely in the grasp of his own compulsions. He could no more cease steering his peas into a pile on his plate than breathing. But he knew it. It was his vision, even acceptance, of himself that rang the chimes of something appealing—that and his ability to soldier on doing what was right. In fact, his steadiness and his refusal to be rebuffed by his sister's lunacy had added significantly to her impression of him. It was not Arthur but she who was the problem.

"Arthur, frankly, *you* shouldn't want to be seen with *me*."

"Because of your role in this case?"

"Because it will taint you in an entire community whose respect is essential in your professional life." She stared at him. "What would you envision, Arthur? Dinner and dancing? Why not a law firm cocktail party? I'm sure your partners will be impressed that you're keeping company with an aging ex-convict who disgraced your profession."

"A movie?" he asked. "It's dark. Nobody will see." He was smiling, of course, but it was soon clear he had tired of the conversation. "Gillian, you've told me ten times that I've been kind to you, and you're returning the favor. But look, we both know this is mostly a matter of instinct. And I can see very well what instinct is telling you."

"No, Arthur, for the last time, that is not the point. You *are* kind. And kindness is in rather short supply in my world. But I would be taking advantage of you, Arthur. You wouldn't get what you deserve. No one ever has."

"I'll take that as no. Without hard feelings. The subject never even came up. We're friends." He used a button beside him to unlock the car door and did his utmost to smile brightly. Once again, he offered his hand. She felt entirely infuriated and refused to take hold. He wouldn't see this in any light but the most hurtful to him.

"So dinner on Tuesday?" she asked. "What time? Where do we meet?"

His soft mouth parted a bit.

"That's not necessary, Gillian. Susan will get by. Anyway, it's bad to let her tantrums prevail. And I can't impose that way."

"Nonsense," she told him as she stepped to the curb. She leaned down into the darkness of the car, where Arthur looked out, befuddled. "We're friends," she said and took some pleasure in slamming the door.

21

JUNE 15–19, 2001

Collins

JACKSON AIRES, the lawyer Erno had hired for his nephew, Collins, was difficult. Privately, he was apt to refer to his clients as 'thugs,' but he thought even less of cops and prosecutors. The only thing he liked about them was the competition. For Aires, there really was a single issue in the law anyway—race. Everything in his world came down to white versus black. A few years ago, during a trial, he had referred to Muriel, in front of a jury, as 'the slavemaster.' She could not say the outburst had worsened their relationship. It had always been terrible.

Jackson sat in Muriel's office listening to her pitch, with his slender fingers steepled. Jackson was well past seventy now, but spry and lean and still at the top of his game. He had a sponge of white hair like

Mandela's, a resemblance that was probably not inadvertent. Like all defense lawyers,
he was unaccustomed to holding an advantage, and when he had one, as he did now,
he was completely insufferable. Tommy
Molto, dark and disheveled, sat beside
Jackson on the other side of Muriel's huge
desk, making no effort to hide his dyspeptic
reactions as Aires carried on.

"Im-munity," Aires answered, when Muriel
told him they wanted a word with Collins.

"Immunity?" Muriel asked. "Why does he
need immunity? The statute of limitations
ran out a long time ago, even if he did lie to
us in 1991."

"'Why' is between him and me, Muriel. No
immunity, and he'll assert his constitutional
rights under the Fifth Amendment."

"How about a proffer?" Muriel asked,
meaning a prediction from Aires of what
Collins would say.

"Now why would I want to do that? That
man is down there in Atlanta, Georgia, having a completely wonderful life. He has no
need to talk to you, Muriel."

"Jackson, why do I have the feeling you've
been chatting with Arthur? I just answered
his motion, asking Judge Harlow to force me

to give your guy immunity." Both Arthur and Jackson knew that the power to bestow immunity was strictly the prosecutor's, and that she would never do it without the assurance that it was required to make her case.

"That's what Arthur wants, Muriel. For my sake, you can just forget you ever heard Collins's name. But my man's not talking to Arthur or you without full protection under the law."

"He can take the nickel, Jackson," Muriel said, "but I want it on the record, so the judge knows we made the effort to find out what he had to say. Will you accept service of the deposition subpoena?"

"And what good would that be doing my client?"

"Free trip home?"

"Lady, he's a travel agent. He gets a free trip home whenever he wants. Besides, *habeas* proceeding is civil discovery. You want to depose him, you gotta go to him. And I don't think Mr. John Q. Public is gonna think much of you making two trips to Georgia at his expense, just so you can listen to this man say he's not answering any of your damn questions."

"Two trips?" asked Molto. Muriel wouldn't

have given Jackson the satisfaction of asking, although she hadn't understood, either. There was a rulebook at play here—the Federal Rules of Civil Procedure—that literally was not on her shelf.

With the chance to gloat, Jackson did, smiling hugely. His teeth were smoke-stained and snaggled and seldom seen in court, where his only expression was a mask of indignation. In order to subpoena Collins, Aires said, they would have to go first to federal court in Atlanta to get a subpoena that could be enforced there.

"Maybe we'll do that," said Muriel. "Maybe we can ride the same plane down for the deposition. I'll send you a notice."

"You think I don't know a damn bluff when I see one? Muriel, that license on my wall is so old that the sheep they made it from rode on the Ark with Noah. Did you know that? I'm too old to bluff, Muriel."

Molto walked Jackson out. She talked a moment with Tommy when he returned, then left a message for Larry. A little after five, he arrived on her threshold, rapping politely on the open door. She was impressed as always by Larry's size as he stood there, the way he imposed himself on space. Big people had it all.

"Busy?"

"Never for you, Lar."

In the large reception area outside her door, the assistants were all gone for the day, and the phones, routed to voice mail, had fallen silent. Larry's fingers still rested on the door frame. She'd stopped him cold with that little trick in her voice. She'd heard it herself. Someone listening in now, or in the witness room the other day, might say she was flirting. Force of habit, she supposed. Old self over the new. He was a paunchy middle-aged guy but the linings of the cells still recollected his appeal. It was fun, of course, to feel younger and more vital—the sap of youth rising. But it was stupid, too.

She recounted her meeting with Jackson. Larry couldn't understand why Collins would demand immunity.

"Probably," said Muriel, "because he knows I won't give it to him. My guess is that Collins and his uncle aren't on the same page. By taking five, he stays out of the middle. Which is why we're making a trip to Atlanta."

"We are?"

"Yes, we are. I'm going to get a subpoena and you're going to serve Collins as soon as it's issued."

"Can I talk to Collins if his lawyer says not to?"

"*I* can't speak to a represented party. But Jackson won't accept service. So some law-enforcement officer has to pay Collins a visit, explain the subpoena and the nature of the case. If he chooses to speak to you against his attorney's advice, that's not our fault." Muriel enjoyed the thought of Jackson's reaction. He always screamed loudest over his own blunders.

On Tuesday morning, Larry was at the gate at the Tri-Cities Airport, looking distraught when she dashed up. For Muriel, making planes, like so many other things in her life, was a contest. If the gate agent wasn't swinging the door closed when she arrived, she felt she'd wasted irretrievable minutes.

"How the hell can you stand that?" Larry wanted to know as they struggled to their seats. "Flying's bad enough as it is." They each had brought an overnight bag, but the baggage compartments were full. The Georgia Department of Law, which was assisting them, said it would take no more than an hour for the subpoena to be issued, but it would be late in the day by the time Larry caught up with Collins. With rush hour traffic, there was the prospect of having to stay over. Larry jammed his bag under the seat in front of him, complaining that he'd ride the entire way to Atlanta feeling as if he'd taken a chair in a dollhouse.

"Sorry, Lar. I still hadn't connected with Claire—Talmadge's daughter? I was supposed to have our grandson tonight."

"Hope you take it as a compliment, but when I hear 'Over the River and Through the Woods,' it's not your face in the picture."

"I'm good, Larry. This is the best chance I'll get, and I'm taking it." Even talking about that little boy, she felt some of the delirium and longing that often accompanied his presence and his absence. Her face apparently betrayed that.

"Adopt?" asked Larry.

"Huh?"

"Did you think of that?"

"Oh." She paused to girdle her heart. "We nearly adopted a boy about three years ago. African-American. Crack mom. The whole deal. And it fell apart. It just about killed me. But you know the saying—maybe it's for the best. Neither of Talmadge's daughters give him better than a C as a father. Even so, every now and then I think about one more try."

"Talmadge is reluctant?"

"There's not a lot of enthusiasm. The way he travels—I'd pretty much be flying solo. It's complicated."

"And does he do better with his daughters now that they're grown?"

"They accept him. Besides, they like *me*." She pressed a finger into her own belly and they both laughed. Talmadge's unavailability was, in fact, part of Muriel's bond with the young women. They all understood that Talmadge belonged to the world, not merely to them. For her part, Muriel tolerated this, even respected it, not only out of admiration but because, at the end of the day, the terms of her own life were not all that different. That was where she and Talmadge were at their best, rocketing along on each other's jet stream, but the mundane intimacies other couples looked forward to—walks in the park, picking wallpaper, or even sex—were rarer for them. Nor did Muriel have a companion in those moments when her striving took her inward, instead of out into the world.

These thoughts, not happy ones, were unwelcome, much like the entire conversation. The rush of the airplane gave them only minimal privacy. And she felt recalled to an ancient reaction that there was something fundamentally wrong in speaking with Larry about Talmadge. She went back to work.

"Okay," he said. "I'll give it a rest."

Without looking up from her tray table, where she'd laid several draft indictments, she said, "I wish you would."

"It's only—"

"Yes?"

"None of my business, I know," he said.

"Don't let that stop you, Larry. It hasn't so far."

She heard him let go of his breath. "Fine."

"Finish it, Larry. And then we're done. Last shot. Fire away."

"Well, it's just sometimes when you chat about old Talmadge, it reminds me of the way you used to talk about what's-his-name."

"What's-his-name?"

"Your husband of blessed memory."

"Rod?" She actually laughed, loud enough that in spite of the engine's thrum, she could see a passenger stir across the row. There was no comparison. Talmadge was a behemoth, a local institution. Rod was a sot.

"Thank you for sharing, Larry," she said, and opened another file. But the conversation wasn't done for her, because she suddenly remembered how she'd seen Rod when she'd chased him—luminous and engaging, surely not a wreck crushed against the rocks in his cocktail glass. So, for a second, she followed Larry's thought and colored in the numbers. Both older. Distracted. Both her teachers. Both stars in her firmament. And both with a grandness about themselves that instinct might have told her camouflaged cavernous self-doubts. A freezing draft blew over her heart. What did all that mean? Everything? Nothing? She was forty-four years old and had made her deal, made her life. The philosopher beside her had told her the fundamental truth weeks ago: life wasn't perfect. She stretched against the confines of the airplane seat and, by habit, stashed these thoughts to again return to work.

* * *

NOW AND THEN, Larry had to get on a plane to question a witness, and on big cases, he was willing to go grab a murderer for an extradition. But the truth was that after Nam, he didn't much like leaving home. Before athletic schedules started to interfere, he took Nancy and the boys to Florida each summer, and every March he still traveled with a group of detectives to Vegas, where they behaved for four days as if they were twenty. They drank and gambled and called every escort service in town for prices, then went back to their lives, feeling a little like dogs that had escaped the backyard fence and were now only too happy to see that bowl of chow. But all in all, he'd rather not have come to Atlanta. The air was so thick you could swim in it. And he wasn't comfortable at close quarters with Muriel.

By 2:30, they were done at the tall, white federal courthouse. Afterwards, Muriel and Larry stood outside, planning the remainder of the afternoon with an Assistant Attorney General named Thane and an investigator from the Fulton County Solicitor's Office who'd been delegated to assist them. The

CNN Center and the Georgia Dome were visible across a canyon of roadway underpasses. Larry would be able to tell the boys he'd seen the sights.

The four of them agreed that Larry and the investigator, Wilton Morley, would serve Collins, while Muriel waited at the office of the Department of Law with her cell phone. If Collins was suddenly moved to give an interview without his lawyer, Muriel wanted to be on hand to document it properly. In the event she didn't hear from Larry, they'd meet at their gate at the airport for the flight home.

Morley had an address for Collins in a suburb north of the city. On the phone, with the damn Southern accent, Larry had no clue about Morley's race, and here he was, black as coal and easy to deal with. Black and white were different here than in the North. Larry had noticed that in the service decades ago and it still felt true. Blacks had won down here more concretely. They'd beaten back slavery first, then Jim Crow. It made everybody happier to have actual bodies to declare dead.

In the car, Morley showed Larry records he had gathered. A credit report listed

Collins as the owner of Collins Travel, his own agency. As Erno had insisted, Collins's rap sheets, both local and national, revealed no further arrests since his release from prison five years ago. Seventy-eight percent of the guys who did time went back. But now and then, Larry actually took heart from the other portion. With the worst cancers, oncologists would be ecstatic with a 22 percent cure rate. True, a lot of guys who went straight didn't really reform—they just got more skilled at not getting caught, and Larry had no way to know if Collins was one of them. It was a little suspicious that a man only a few years out of the joint would have the wherewithal to open his own business, and a travel agency would be a perfect shell if you were laundering drug money. But Morley had heard good things about Collins.

"One of my guys, he goes to church with this Collins," Morley said, "and buys his airline tickets from him. Says he does a great job. Whatever that means."

Atlanta to Larry was like L.A. South, an appealing terrain—here hills and trees—surrendered to highways and shopping malls. Collins lived and worked thirty minutes northeast of downtown off Jimmy Carter

Boulevard, in an old town, now engrossed by sprawl. In the mile or two from U.S. 85, they passed every chain restaurant Larry had ever heard of and several churches that looked like Kmarts.

Morley circled by the agency once. It was on the end of a flat-roofed commercial strip with a stressed concrete façade, next door to a dry cleaner and a pet shop. On reflection, Larry had decided it was better to approach Collins alone.

"You're in the South now, man," said Morley when Larry suggested the investigator stay in the car. "Things may not be the same as where you come from."

Larry didn't know exactly what Morley was referring to. He probably thought a Northern copper would just walk in and punch Collins in the face.

"I hear you," said Larry. "Don't lose eyeshot of me. I just think I'll have a better chance to get something from this guy if it feels like old home week, instead of a pinch."

Morley parked on the other side of the busy avenue. While they were watching the agency, two people emerged, a man, big enough to be Collins, in a stylish shirt and tie, and an older woman whose hand he was shaking. After parting with her, the man walked down the block to a transmission shop adjacent to the strip mall. The overhead doors on the bays had been lifted, and even from a distance, Larry could hear on the wind the high-pitched whine of the power tools and the smell of the bad chemicals they used to keep the gears from grinding. The man was conversing with someone at the front end of an old Acura that was elevated on the greased shaft of the hydraulic lift. Larry looked both ways, then jogged across the street.

When the man stepped around the car again, Larry recognized Collins for certain. He walked up smiling. Collins took Larry's eye briefly, and then turned away and strolled back to his agency. When Larry saw Collins next, he was out the side door of the building, moving at full speed. For just a second, Larry watched him run.

This case, he thought. Jesus Christ, this fucking case.

Then he took off after Collins, who had disappeared up an intersecting residential street. Larry knew this was not especially smart, a white guy chasing a black guy through a neighborhood where somebody could just pull out his peashooter and send a bullet through a window. As an unruly teenager, he'd loved the rush of danger, but Nam had finished that for him. Danger, he'd learned, made you dead, not better, and he ran hard in the hopes of chasing Collins down quickly. Gaining on him, Larry was yelling the usual stupid stuff, "I just need to talk to you."

Collins was headed straight uphill and after another couple of hundred feet, he gave up. Either he'd heard Larry, or more likely he was on the verge of collapse. There were fifty pounds more to him than a decade ago and he stood heaving desperately with his hands on his knees.

"What the fuck are you doing?" Larry asked several times. Over his shoulder, he saw Morley flying up the block, his gun drawn. Larry motioned with both hands to stop. Morley did, but kept watch from where he was.

When Farwell could speak, he said, "Heck, man, I just don't wanna talk to you." In the intense heat, Collins had sweated completely through his clothes. You could see the outline of the sleeveless T underneath his white-on-white dress shirt.

"Bolting's the best way to get run in."

Collins got ornery for the first time. Up until now it had been a business discussion.

"I haven't done any kind of thing for you to run me in, man. I live a clean life. You check that out. I'm clean." Collins's face was a little rounder and he'd started to bald, but he remained uncommonly good-looking, with those striking eyes, the color of raw leather. In the summer, the white in him had tanned and lent a glow to his complexion.

"Listen," said Larry, "I came down here with a subpoena cause your smart-ass lawyer wouldn't take it off of us. That's all. But I'm glad you're clean. Really, I love to see this. You've done a good job."

"Darn right," said Collins. "I got God's help, man, and I said no more. All of that when I known you, that's long gone. Lord said He could make me a new man, and I took Him up on the offer. You know. Made me an offer I couldn't refuse. I been baptized and cleansed of my sins."

"Good," said Larry, "great." He wished he had one of those junior badges that Community Relations handed out to kids. That's what Collins wanted.

The day was growing more pleasant, its

dense heat on the wane. They were on a block of smaller houses, most of them white clapboard with green shingle roofs and front verandas, a number of which had been screened. Stands of Georgia pines threw down deep shade along the block. Collins, too, looked upward momentarily with some sign of appreciation, then without a word, Larry and he began walking back down the hill. Larry waved to Morley that he was okay. Morley walked backward for about twenty feet, still with an eye on them.

"That your backup?" Collins asked.

"Right."

Collins shook his head. "Man comes with backup and all I'm doin is leading a peaceful life."

"That's why he stayed in the car, Collins. I'm just serving a subpoena."

"Man, you can gimme all the subpoenas you want. I don't have to talk. That's what the attorney said. Fifth Amendment, man."

"Well, sooner or later, you're gonna have to come up to the Tri-Cities and tell that to the judge eye to eye. Unless you want to answer some questions now."

Collins laughed. He'd heard similar gambits before.

"I'll talk when the attorney says. That Fifth Amendment, only way it works is for a man to just shut up. He says once you start goin on, you can't just up and stop when you want. And you know darn well I did a lot of stuff back in the day that I don't need anybody to be hearin about. Don't want to get pulled back down to where I been. Took me a long time to climb up, man."

"Look, I'm not writing anything down. This is just us mice. I only have one real question anyway. Your uncle is saying you lied to me back in that jail ten years ago when you put it on Rommy. He's saying you tricked on me."

Collins considered the pavement as they walked.

"My uncle's a good man."

"We'll put that on a plaque, Collins. What I want to know is if he's telling the truth. Straight stuff. Did you have my lunch?"

"Look—" Collins stopped. "Man, I can't hardly remember your name to save my life."

"Starczek."

"Right, Starczek. Starczek, it's like they say—you ain only gonna believe one answer, man. You know that. If I tell you, 'Yeah,

I lied back then,' you're gonna say, 'Aw, he's just got his uncle's back.' All you want to hear is that my uncle's some kind of lying fool. And he's not. Most definitely not."

They had reached the agency and entered the same side door, still wide open, through which Farwell had departed. It led to a small back room, where stationery and ticket forms were stored. Out front, there were two desks, one for Collins and another, behind a freestanding divider, that probably belonged to a receptionist or secretary. There was nobody there now. Collins took a seat and motioned Larry to an armchair on the other side of his desk. On the paneled wall behind Collins, a large calendar with a religious scene hung beside a simple cross, carved of wood, probably mahogany, almost the same color as the paneling.

"How's business?"

"Not bad. Darn airlines don't want you makin any money. I'm more in the tour business, these days. Lot of church groups goin to different sites."

"And this is your place, Collins?"

"Yep."

"Very nice." Larry looked around appreciatively, as if he meant it.

"My uncle lent me the money to get started. Paid him off last year."

"Uncle Erno?"

"Only uncle I got. That man has been a blessing to me. It took me way too long to know it, but he has been the hand of Jesus Christ in my life. Truly. I would never talk against Erno. He's a good man. And come to Christ himself now."

"Spare me," said Larry before he could think better of it. He was always suspicious of true believers, the people who thought they were clued in to a higher truth—whether it was religion or yoga or vegan food—that the rest of us were too blind to see.

"Don't you laugh, Starczek, when I'm talkin 'bout my Lord and Savior. That's the most serious thing in my life."

"No, Collins, I'm getting my chuckles from your uncle. He's lying and you know it."

"See, now. There you go. Just like I told you. You think a man who'll stand in judgment before the throne of God any day now is just gonna lie? Not me. That's not what I think. I think he's going to tell the Lord's truth."

"Well, if he's telling the truth, why won't you come up there and back him up?"

"He doesn't want me to. He's done all that needs be done. I go up there naked, no immunity or nothin, you know darn well you folks are gonna call me a liar and go after me. That'd just be putting myself in harm's way. No point in that."

Without question, that was how Aires had explained it to Collins. Not that he was wrong.

"Yeah, well, if Erno's straight up, don't you think you owe something to Gandolph?"

At the mention of Squirrel, Collins grew decidedly more somber. He slunk down somewhat in the broad desk chair.

"Only one thing I'll say to you about Gandolph, and I won't say no more. When I pray each night and ask Jesus' forgiveness, first thing I mention is Gandolph. First thing. I ask God to forgive me every day for what we did to that poor hook." Collins looked across the desk fearlessly, his light eyes held wide, and applied a mighty nod.

Whatever these guys were up to, it was all too deep to Larry. He reached into his pocket and took out two copies of the subpoena. He filled out the return on one, describing where and on whom the subpoena had been served, and handed over the other copy. Collins studied it, while Larry surveyed several pictures on the desk. A big sweet-looking blond woman appeared in most of them, often with two towheaded twin girls.

"They're mine," said Collins, "if that's what you're wondering."

"The kids?"

"Yep. Look white as you do. When I went to leave the hospital with those babies in my arms, security guard wouldn't let me out with them. And she was black herself. Anne-Marie, my wife, she really started hollerin, too. She's touchier than I am when folks go racial. But those babies're mine. Time was, I didn't even wanna know anyone white. But a man can't escape the truth. Truth is, every relative I claim as mine is white. And I'm a black man. You try and figure that out. Only thing that makes any sense is that Jesus had something special in mind."

Once rebuked, Larry tried to contain himself this time at the mention of the Lord's plan, but Collins still detected a tremor of doubt.

"You think I'm, like, some nut. But this is the truth of my life, man. They let me outta Rudyard, I wasn't on the street more than a month, and I was back to all my stupid ways. There isn't a sin I hadn't committed. And you know what happened? Same as you'd know was gonna happen. I got myself shot, man. And I came out of it like it was nothing. Here I am. Two arms, two legs. Doctors, man, at County, they couldn't believe it. That bullet was like a cruise missile. Like it was taking directions. Here's this boy's spine, I ain gonna hit that, then I'm gonna take a little turn so I miss his kidney, then I'm gonna go a little right so I don't tear up any of those major veins or arteries. It was a miracle. You know why?"

"Not exactly."

"Cause Jesus was sayin something to me, man. He was sayin, I have given you signs and given you signs and you still wanna be a fool. So I'm gonna work an actual miracle. If you can't recognize that I am here and looking down on you and wantin better for you, if you don't know it now, then there just isn't any more I can do for you. You wanna be a fool, then be a fool. But no man is gonna come to heaven without Me. You can sit in one more cell and say, Never again, but until you take Me in your life, you won't come out from under all that. But if you do, if you take Me in, then there's no need for any more. Not one more moment. And there hasn't been.

"So if it's time for me to talk, Starczek, then Jesus will let me know. And once I swear my oath to Him, you gonna know every word is true. But right now, this is where Jesus wants me. And where I'm gonna stay. Fifth Amendment, man."

Collins walked Larry around to the door, shook his hand, and wished him well. He even added a little salute to Morley across the street.

22

The Raven Family

EARLY TUESDAY, Judge Harlow issued a brief written order, ruling on several discovery motions Arthur had filed. Virtually all were denied, but Harlow's reasoning was welcome. The motions could be ventured later, the judge said, "inasmuch as the testimony of Erno Erdai appears to the Court to be of sufficient credibility to allow this matter to proceed." The Court of Appeals retained the actual authority to determine whether Gandolph would be permitted to go forward with his new *habeas corpus* petition, but Harlow's ruling gave Rommy an enormous leg up. If the appellate court ruled as expected, Rommy Gandolph would live several more years, while Arthur and Pamela pursued his exoneration. They celebrated and called their client. Afterwards, the reality settled on Arthur that he was headed for an indefinite period of scrapping and scuffling on Rommy's behalf. Rommy was now his cause—and his albatross.

This news served as a welcome distraction from the prospect of this evening, when Gillian Sullivan was scheduled to join Susan and him. Arthur had convinced himself that Gillian would find an excuse, but late in the afternoon his secretary placed a message slip in front of him, while he was on the phone with a reporter. It said, "Ms. Sullivan will be in the lobby at five."

Gillian Sullivan in his terrible little apartment. For a second, he was seized by terror and shame.

She was there as promised. On the way to the Franz Center to pick up Susan, Arthur did what little he could to prepare Gillian for his sister. The problem, however, was that even after nearly thirty years, he found little predictable about Susan's behavior. Schizophrenia was all too often a disease of the gifted, and there was no end to the inspired contrivances with which Susan could fortify her anxiety and suspicions. Whatever came his way, Arthur was hardened in his patience—threatening or critical responses just made her worse. Only in private did Arthur allow himself to react. Susan e-mailed him several times a day, and without anything to distract her, her brief messages were occasionally fully lucid. At times, she sounded as witty and perceptive as a columnist.

"Sometimes when I get those e-mails," said Arthur, as they neared the Center, "it breaks my heart. I'll sit in the office and cry. But you know, my father made himself crazy thinking about what might have been. And there's even a way it's disloyal to Susan not to accept the illness as part of her."

The North End neighborhood surrounding the Franz Center was comprised principally of worn shingle-sided homes, mingling with a few stouter structures. Arthur pulled up in front of the large, banged-up-looking brick house and spent an instant surveying the block. A group of roving boys, most wearing silky gang jackets despite the heat, were on the corner.

"You better come in," he told her. "It might not be so smart to be a white lady just sitting around." As Gillian stepped out, the chirp of Arthur's remote attracted attention from down the block. "You can watch my car from the window," he said, "and inventory the pieces as they're removed."

Susan's accommodations were referred to as supervised living. Each of the eight residents had a separate studio apartment, and Valerie or one of the other M.S.W.'s was on duty twenty-four hours a day to assist. When Susan was stable and working, she was able to cover much of the expense on her own, but that was because of a large state subsidy and a grant from the Franz Foundation that supported the Center. The state funding was under constant threat, and Arthur was always writing letters or contacting his assemblyman to prevent the Center from perishing. His father's estate— which, due to Harvey Raven's scrimping, was larger than a man of his means should have left—remained in trust as a backstop.

Susan's apartment was small and well kept these days. There were periods when her hygiene deteriorated, and she seldom thought on her own of appearances, but she complied with the social workers' suggestions about cleaning up. There was not a picture on the wall, or any electronic appliances, since sooner or later they would foster a delusion of attack. Generally, it was their mother's voice Susan heard, warning her about some invisible menace.

The Nurse Practitioner who administered the Prolixin was already there, and the shot had been dispensed by the time Arthur was through the door. Susan was ready to go. Arthur reminded her again about Gillian, as he knew Valerie had several times during the week, but Susan gave no sign of recognizing what he was talking about until she was settled in the front seat of the automobile and they were under way.

She then asked her brother without any warning, "Does this mean you're fucking?"

Raven burned from his shoulders to his scalp, but his response, as always, was measured.

"Susan, it's much nicer when you try to be considerate."

"You're fucking? I know all about fucking. Arthur doesn't know much." The last comment was clearly aimed at Gillian, although Susan did not look in her direction.

"I don't think they give degrees in that subject," Gillian answered quietly. Arthur had advised her beforehand not to allow his sister to bulldoze or terrify her, and this one response seemed enough to quell Susan. In Arthur's rearview, Gillian, as usual, appeared entirely unruffled.

When his father died, Arthur had moved back into Harvey Raven's apartment. It was comfortable in a way. Arthur had lived for years in an efficiency in a high-style building near the Street of Dreams, where even a glance down to the sidewalk in the evenings was sometimes enough to leave him defeated by the world of fashion and allure he would never join. But there had been an element of surrender in his return to the dour environment his father had always wanted him to escape. Yet there was little choice. Susan was badly shaken by their father's death, and her counselors confirmed that the apartment held great significance for her. This was the only home in which Susan Raven had been healthy. For her, the apartment represented the otherwise elusive reality of mental stability. Abandoning the place would close a door forever.

Arthur pointed Gillian to an old metal kitchen step stool, while his sister and he pursued their usual routine. The kitchen, with its white enamel cabinets, was narrow but they worked well side by side. Susan made mashed potatoes, her specialty. She worked the potatoes over as if she was putting down a subversive force, frowning and staring into the pot. Her only commerce with Gillian involved smoking Gillian's cigarettes, rather than her own.

The entrée, beef stew, came from a large plastic container that Arthur had removed from the freezer in the morning. Now he dumped the contents into a large pot and added various fresh ingredients. There was probably enough here to feed twelve. When dinner was over, the substantial leftovers would be refrozen. By Arthur's calculations, there had to be a few cubes of beef in there that had been thawed every week since the early '90s. It was an appalling health hazard. But this was the way their frugal father had done it—waste not, want not—and his sister would not abide any other procedure.

Susan set the table for three, her first overt acknowledgment of Gillian's presence. Arthur dished out portions from the pot. Susan then picked up her plate and settled in the living room in front of the TV.

"What did I do?" whispered Gillian.

"That's part of the drill."

"You don't eat together?"

Arthur shook his head. "Her show is on. It's the only thing she can watch without getting zooey."

"Which is?"

"You ready? *Star Trek*."

Arthur held his fingers to his lips to caution Gillian against laughter, and she had to stuff half her fist into her mouth to keep silent. Apparently finding it a safer subject, Gillian then asked about Rommy's case. She had not heard about Harlow's ruling and seemed pleased for Arthur's sake by the news.

"What's your next step now, Arthur?"

"I can't think of anything. I've filed every motion, issued every subpoena that makes any sense. There are absolutely no jail records left to show who was or wasn't in the House of Corrections on the night of the murders. Jackson Aires won't let anyone talk to Erno's nephew, and Muriel's not about to give him immunity, and the judge can't force her. As of June 29th, the limited discovery period closes. I think I should just run out the clock. After Harlow's findings, it's really on Muriel to try to do something to undermine Erno's credibility before we go back to the Court of Appeals for a ruling on whether the case can proceed."

Arthur's biggest challenge was likely to come from Reverend Blythe. As expected, dealings with the Reverend were entirely a one-way street. After their first meeting, the Reverend no longer deigned to call Arthur directly. Instead, he had an aide who phoned every day for a detailed briefing, information Arthur was obliged to share because Rommy, who had been thrilled by Blythe's visits to Rudyard, had requested that Arthur do so. There seemed to be no countervailing courtesies. Although Blythe now referred to himself as Rommy's spiritual counselor, and claimed Arthur and he were a team, the Reverend ignored Arthur's efforts to moderate Blythe's rhetoric or even to gain advance warning of when the next blast would issue.

"I'm scared to death," said Arthur, "that with all this stuff about 'racist oppressors' he'll infuriate the Court of Appeals."

"But they have to let you go on, wouldn't you think? Erno can't be disregarded, not without a full hearing. Isn't that what Harlow was saying?"

That was how Arthur saw it, but he had failed many times in his career to guess correctly about what judges would do.

When the show was over, Susan rejoined them for dessert. She loved pastry. Then the dishes were washed and everything was shelved. Before Arthur left the apartment, he opened the freezer and replaced the container of stew.

IN THE DIM STAIRWELL of the three-flat, Gillian followed while Arthur led his sister down. These old tenements were as solid as destroyers, but the maintenance here had been neglected. On the treads, the carpeting in several places was worn to the backing, and amoeboid forms spotted the walls where the plaster had rejected the paint.

There were few occasions when she got out, besides work and uncomfortable visits with her sisters, so Gillian had actually found herself looking forward to this evening, and she had not been disappointed. It had pleased her enormously, much as it had on the first occasion, to watch Arthur's adroitness with his sister and his persistent, loving manner.

As they drove back, Susan gave him a precise recounting of the *Star Trek* episode. Like everyone else in the joint, Gillian had watched her share of TV, and she asked a couple of well-versed questions about Kirk and Spock and Scotty, to which Susan responded with eagerness. When they arrived at the Franz Center, Gillian got out of the car to say good night and to take Susan's place in the front seat. And there on the curb, with the year's longest light still in the sky, Gillian briefly met the other Susan Raven. Her hand came up somewhat awkwardly and she pumped Gillian's arm too hard. But she made unwavering eye contact, and Gillian could feel herself recognized in an entirely different way.

"It's very nice to see you again," said Susan. "I'm glad Arthur has such a nice friend."

Arthur walked Susan in. Gillian lingered just outside the Center's front door to have a cigarette. She found herself strangely moved. When Arthur reappeared, Gillian, who never cried, had to push away tears. Arthur noticed at once, and as they were on the way back to Duffy's, Gillian explained that she had finally seen Susan as she was capable of being, almost as if a pair of eyes had stared at her out of a forest. Arthur mulled her remark for several blocks.

"The truth," he said then, "is that for me,

that person, the woman who just spoke to you—she's always there, you know, the shadow of the girl I grew up with."

"She was in good health as a child?"

"That's how it usually is with schizophrenics. It just happens. She was fourteen. And I don't think you'd ever have guessed. I mean, she was eccentric. She collected soldiers and staged battles. That was unusual for a girl. She kept rocks from the riverbank, and was compulsive about figuring out how old each one was. She couldn't sleep until she had them in chronological order. But we all thought she was brilliant. Well, she is. And then one day, she was naked in the corner of her room and wouldn't come out. She'd smeared her shit all over herself. She said my mother's mother had come back from the dead to tell her my parents were talking about her in code.

"That scene," said Arthur sighing, "that scene is in my head like a movie poster under lights. You know, framed next to the doorway of the theater? It's there every time I walk in to see Susan. Because it was one of those instants when you realize that everything about your life from top to bottom is now different."

"It must have been devastating."

"That's the word. For my parents, at least. I mean, as soon as they heard the word 'schizophrenic' they knew they were doomed. And they were right. My mother was out the door in two years. I was nine when Susan got sick, and I didn't know what to think. I mean, the truth, the ugly truth, is that I can actually remember being happy."

"Happy?"

"She was so bright. She was so beautiful. Susan was the starring attraction. The Great Susan. That's what I'd always called her in my head. And suddenly she'd been swept aside. I cringe, remembering it. Not just the childishness. But because I was so wrong. The dumbest, funniest, saddest part is that I still idolize her. Maybe I almost feel obliged to, so that somebody on earth really knows how tragic it is. The Great Susan," said Arthur again.

"Yes," said Gillian. Arthur brought the sedan to the curb in front of Duffy's. She looked toward the squat bungalow, but she was not quite ready to give up the conversation. "I had a brother like that," she said. "Whom I idolized."

"Did you?"

"Yes. Carl. He was my favorite. Carl was four years older. Oh," she said, in a sudden rush of feeling, "he was gorgeous. And wild. I adored him."

"Where is he now?"

"Dead. He died on a motorcycle. He lived out his fate in eighteen years." She cleared her throat and declared, "He was the first man I ever slept with."

Somehow, after a moment, she found the resolve to turn to Arthur. He stared, but it was a dense, thoughtful look. She could see him laboring to comprehend what this meant to her. Here, as so often before, she was startled to discover what a grown-up Arthur Raven had become.

She found she had lit a cigarette, without even thinking that she was defiling the perfect environment in Arthur's fancy car.

"I've shocked you," she said.

He took some time before he answered, "Of course."

"Yes," said Gillian. She closed her purse and went to toss out the cigarette, then drew it back to savor one last puff. "Of course, it's shocking. I've never really known what to make of it, so, frankly, I don't think of it at all. Because I wanted it to happen. It was more confusing afterwards—over the years. But at the time, I was pleased."

To a fourteen-year-old it had been momentous but without any sinister aspect. As a judge, she routinely sentenced men—fathers, stepfathers—for the sexual abuse of children and deemed it unpardonable. But her own experience resided in a category beyond the social expectations of the law. She had been willing and seductive. And she loved Carl far too much to burden him with blame, even in memory. They had always been one another's favorites. From an early age they shared a certain purchase on things, usually expressed in telling glances. He was her pal while she warred with their parents. So many other young women craved his attention and his beauty. One night, Carl came home staggering. He cuddled her. She clung. Nature provided the momentum. The next morning, he said, 'I'm more fucked up than I think I am.' 'I liked it,' she told him. There were two more occasions. She listened for his arrival, and went to him. *She* went. After that, he began to lock the door to his room, and angrily rebuked her when she dared to ask why.

'Sometimes it comes to me, what I've done, and I want to pull the ears off my head so I can't hear that. This is insane,' he said. 'Insane.' She'd succeeded in repelling him. That was the most painful part. They'd barely spoken in the months before his death.

"I wanted to die after he died. I thought about killing myself. I'd make up plots. Schemes. Ways to do it. I'd have discussions with friends. Hanging. Fire. Drowning. I wanted to jump under a train—I'd already read *Anna Karenina*. And then for a while I actually burned myself with cigarettes. In places other people couldn't see. But it passed. I stopped acting like that. I stopped thinking like that, or about why I'd felt that way in the first place. People do bizarre things when they're growing up. We all do. We survive them. But there was nothing about the experience that ever squared for me with the word 'abuse.'" She looked down to find herself about to put fire to another cigarette. The left hand holding her lighter was steady, but in the other, the cigarette was teetering between her fingers as if there were a strong wind.

"I've never told anyone that story, Arthur,"

she said. "No one." She had sat through dozens of hours of confessions in various groups, and had shared everything with Duffy. Or thought she had. She found the courage to look again at Arthur, who was studying her.

"You don't have a clue what you're doing, do you?" he asked.

So he had figured that out as well.

"No," she said.

Leaning against the car door, he used the wheel to pull himself forward. His face ended up inches from hers, and he spoke quietly.

"When you grow up with somebody as frantic as my father," he said to her, "you spend a lot of time figuring out what there is in the world that's really worth being scared of." He reached across her to open the passenger door, but his eyes never left hers.

"And I'm not scared of you," he said.

23

Paging Dr. Kevorkian

IT WAS PAST 5:30 by the time Larry phoned Muriel and agreed they should set out separately for the airport. Morley and Larry made good time back into the city going against traffic, but on a stretch of road called "the Connector," they came to a dead stop. The radio said a truck had spun out not far from Turner Field. At 6:15 Larry's cell rang. It was Muriel in her taxi. She'd started out half an hour ahead of them, but at this point was only a couple of miles closer to Hartsfield.

"We're toast," she said. By now, as usual, she had explored all options and executed a plan. The Delta 8:10 was booked solid, with eighteen people outranking them on the standby list; a switch to another airline was impossible because their tickets were government rate. Instead, Muriel had reserved seats on an early-morning flight and had taken two rooms at an airport hotel.

When Larry arrived there, fifty minutes later, Muriel was in the lobby with her bags, running the P.A.'s Office by phone from a thousand miles away. A gang murder case was deteriorating in standard fashion— every witness, including the ones who'd been locked in by testifying before the grand jury, now claimed to have misidentified the defendant. Judge Harrison, who thought developments in the rules of criminal procedure had ceased when he left the P.A.'s Office forty years ago, was being impossible, and by the time Muriel dropped her cell phone back in her briefcase, she'd authorized a mandamus petition, to ask the state appellate court to set Harrison straight.

"Every day a new clown in the circus," she said. She'd registered and handed Larry his key, but neither of them had had lunch, and they agreed to go directly to the restaurant. Larry nearly sat up and begged when the waitress offered a drink. He ordered a boilermaker, but quaffed the beer first, downing almost all of it at once. He could feel his clothing adhering to his body and removed his light sport coat, tossing it over a chair at the table. They had to measure the discomfort index in this city in four digits. Not that he'd helped by sprinting after Collins. He told Muriel the story. She laughed heartily until he reached the part where Collins had said his uncle was telling the God's truth and that Collins himself asked Jesus to forgive him every night for what they had done to Gandolph.

"Ouch," said Muriel. "That's not good. Was he smoking you?"

"Probably. He was pretty cagey. Said flat out he'd never talk against Erno. And wouldn't admit to anything." There was bread on the table and Larry buttered his second piece. "To tell you the truth, he does a pretty good impression of a grownup. Says he's born-again. There's a cross the size of Cleveland on the wall of his office and he gave me a real mouthful of that Holy Roller bullshit."

Muriel fingered her wineglass and frowned.

"Don't dis God, Larry."

He looked at her.

"He's there," she said. "Something. He, She, It. But it's there. I actually look forward to church. It's the most complete I feel all week."

She wasn't telling him anything he didn't know. Not about the big picture.

"Catholicism ruined religion for me," Larry said. "The pastor in our parish is wonderful. We have him to dinner. The boys love him. I could talk to the guy all day. But I can't go through the door to the church. I do my praying in the garden. That's the only time I feel like I have the right to ask."

He smiled hesitantly and she smiled back in the same fashion, but he was unsettled by the thought that Muriel had undergone a transformation. Some of the stuff that had come out of her mouth lately, about God or babies, made him wonder if she'd had a brain transplant at some point in the last ten years. It was funny what happened to people after forty, when they realized that our place here on earth was leased, not owned. There seemed a peril, one he could not name, in finding Muriel had grown softer in ways.

Rather than face her, Larry surveyed the dining room. It was half empty, done improbably in a tropical theme, with palm fronds, and bamboo railings and furniture. Everybody in here was tired. You could see it. Who could call a clean bed and a room of your own a hardship? Yet it seemed hard, being removed from home and set down in places you'd never been. There was something unsound in losing connection to your own piece of earth, he thought. Somehow, everything in life took him back to the garden.

He decided to look for a pay phone. He'd just about burned up his free long-distance minutes on his cell and the Force refused to reimburse any overage. He needed to leave messages at home and at the Hall about getting stuck down here. Walking toward the lobby, he was still thinking of Muriel. He'd had a thought to ask if Talmadge went to church with her, which would have violated the promise he'd made on the plane. He knew enough now, anyway. Like everybody else's, Muriel's life was, at best, complex. But he could not quite quell a grim satisfaction. Muriel believed that God made order in the universe. In his hardest moments, Larry thought it was revenge.

"WE HAVE A PROBLEM," Muriel said when Larry returned. She'd thought it through carefully while he was gone. "The other shoe dropped this morning: Harlow buys Erno."

"Fuck," Larry said.

She explained the ruling, which Carol had read to her over the phone.

"Fuck," Larry said again. "The other judges—they don't have to go along with that, do they?"

"The Court of Appeals? In theory, no. But they didn't see the guy testify. Harlow did. They won't have much choice about accepting his views unless we can come up with something new that makes Erno a liar. And this stuff with Collins today only cuts the other way. Once I tell Arthur, he's going to whine and lie on the floor and renew his motion to force me to grant Collins immunity."

"And?"

"The motion's still a loser. Immunity is strictly a prosecutorial decision. But he gets the information in front of the appellate court that way."

"You don't have to tell Arthur diddly. I promised Collins I wouldn't write any of it down. As far as Arthur is concerned—or anyone else for that matter—the conversation never happened."

"That means we won't use it against Collins. We still have to tell Arthur."

"Why?"

The thought was confusing. She reasoned out loud. Legally, strictly speaking, the obligation to disclose favorable evidence pertained only to trial. And since Collins wouldn't testify, his statements to Larry were inadmissible hearsay.

"So?" Larry asked. "What's the problem?"

"Well, hell, Larry. It's not smart, for one thing. Collins is going to call Jackson. If it comes out that we didn't disclose this, we'll look terrible."

"Collins's version to Aires is, 'I didn't tell the cop diddly.' He's not going to let Jackson flame him for opening his mouth. And besides, as far as he's concerned, he *didn't* say anything. Why make life complicated?"

"Damn, Larry, what if Collins is telling the truth? What if his uncle and he did frame Rommy, and he does get on his knees before Jesus every night asking for forgiveness?"

"No chance."

"*No* chance? None? You mean, you haven't had just one second where you thought maybe there was this eensy-teensy possibility that Erno's telling the truth?"

He passed a heavy hand through the air to wave off the demon of the ridiculous.

"The little asshole confessed, Muriel. He confessed right in front of you."

"Larry, the guy's out of his depth in a puddle."

"What the hell does that mean?"

Blessedly, the waitress arrived with dinner. She put the plates down and made sweet chitchat. She was from rural Georgia and had an accent out of *Gone With the Wind*. By the time she'd left to bring one more round of drinks, Larry had chewed through half his steak and still wouldn't look at Muriel. She knew she could wait to have this out with him, but there was an order—'hierarchy' was actually the word—to be maintained. Cops always hated it when the attorneys made the decisions. To the lawyers, the job was all words—the words they spoke in court, or wrote in briefs, or read in police reports. But for the coppers, it was life. They did their jobs with a gun on their hips and sweat dripping down to their shorts from beneath their bulletproof vests. The witnesses who appeared neatened up in the courtroom to answer the prosecutors' questions had been pulled out of rank shooting galleries by officers who didn't know if they should worry more about a bullet or HIV. The police lived in a rough world and they played rough if they had to. For a prosecutor, giving in, even to somebody as good as Larry, only encouraged recalcitrance.

"I want you to promise me that this isn't going to be Hitler's bunker," she said.

"Meaning?"

"Keep an open mind. Just a little. I mean, maybe, Larry, just maybe, we made a mistake. Shit happens. It's not a perfect system. We're not perfect people."

He did not take it well.

"We didn't make any fucking mistakes."

"I'm not attacking you, Larry. In this line of work, we're expected to be faultless. That's what the standard is, really. Beyond a reasonable doubt. Legal certainty. But even our best work and best judgment isn't always perfect. I mean, it's possible."

"It's not possible." Despite the flesh that had accumulated on him, the veining was becoming visible in his square neck. "He's the right guy. He knew two of the victims. He had motive on both of them. He confessed. He knew what the murder weapon was before we did, and he had Luisa's cameo in his pocket. He's right, and I'm not letting you act like the Virgin Mary. You'll fuck yourself doing that, and you'll fuck me, too."

"Larry, I don't care what kind of noise Arthur makes, or the judge, for that matter. You think I'd take a walk on a triple murder? You think I'd turn my back on John Leonidis or those two girls? You look at me and tell me you believe that about me."

He picked up the scotch as soon as the waitress delivered it and took down half. The liquor was not helping him. He was clearly having trouble reeling himself in. Beneath it all, he was an angry guy. She'd always known that.

"I don't want to hear any more of this shit about making mistakes,"he said.

"I'm not saying it's a mistake. I just want to be able to say I actually discharged a professional obligation to consider the prospect."

"Look, I worked this case. On my own. The whole Force hit the pause button once the headlines faded. I'm the one who kept pressing. I made this case. And I made it with you. And for you, if you want to know the truth. So don't say it's any frigging mistake."

"For *me*?"

Fury throbbed through him. It enlarged his eyes—all of him really.

"Don't pretend like you don't get it, god-damn it. It's one thing, Muriel, isn't it? This case. You becoming P.A. You deciding to be great. You deciding to marry Talmadge. You deciding to march down the path of history. You deciding not to take me. So don't tell me it's a fucking mistake. It's too late for any fucking mistakes. I've had my piss-poor little life, and you've gone ramping up to star-dom. Don't pretend like you don't know what the game is, because you made all the fucking rules." With that, he hurled his green cloth napkin down on his plate, and stalked off fast enough to bowl someone over had anybody gotten in his way. The small duffel he'd carried from home bounced on his shoulder as if it were as insubstantial as a scarf.

In his wake, she felt her Adam's apple bobbing about. Something huge had hap-pened. At first, she thought she was shocked by the force of his outburst. But after a sec-ond she realized the true news was that even a decade later, Larry's wounds remained ten-der. She thought he was one person very much as he chose to present himself—too self-sufficient to be vulnerable to any lasting injury. That was more or less the way she tried to think of herself.

One of her friends liked to say that in junior high school you learned everything there was to know about the way love starts and ends. The vast region in between, the dark jungle of sustained relationships, was penetrated only in adulthood. But the nuclear flash when love began and concluded was the same, no matter what stage of life. And what they would have said about Larry's outrage in the junior-high girls' room was probably true: it meant he still cared. Assaying all of this, she felt herself in some danger.

He'd left his sport coat slung over the chair. She looked at it a moment, then picked it up and went into the bar, thinking he'd escaped there. There was no sign of him. Upstairs, she knocked lightly on the door to his room.

"Larry, open up. I have your coat."

He already had his shirt unbuttoned over the mound of his belly, and he held a dwarf bottle of Dewar's from the minibar. Half of it was gone. He took the coat from her and threw it behind him to the bed without ever quite mustering the courage to look her way.

"Larry, how about if we get un-pissed off? We have a long way to go on this case."

"You're not pissed off. I'm the one who's pissed off." He glanced down at the little bottle, screwed the cap on, and tossed it several feet into the trash can, which rocked from the impact. "And now I'm less pissed off than embarrassed."

"Maybe we should talk."

"For what?"

"Don't make me stand here, Larry." She had bags in both hands, her swollen briefcase in one and the small overnight pouch in the other. He considered her situation and motioned her in, turning from her. The bald spot on his crown had grown bright pink from the liquor.

"Muriel, I don't even know where that came from."

"Hell, Larry."

"No, I won't say I didn't mean it. But the thing that bothered me was at the end. What I said about myself. I don't think my life is anything to complain about. It's good. Better than good. It's just that I'm like everybody else, you know. Nobody ever gets what they want when it comes to love."

The statement—the exactness of it—struck her dumb momentarily, because she knew he had expressed her deepest conviction, one that she seldom had the wherewithal to say to herself. She was drawn back for a second to that howitzer shell he'd lobbed at her on the plane: the notion that she'd chased the same improbable dream in both her marriages. The idea had been with her all day, like a bad meal whose taste kept returning. She'd think it through on Sunday. Because love, most often, was what she was praying for in those precious moments in church, believing and not believing. Now she pondered love's quest, the way it led us to persistent unhappiness and blithe moments when, however chimerically, love seemed to have been found. Everything else in life—professional attainment, art, and ideas—was just the feathers and hide on the foraging animal of love.

"This meant a lot to me," he said. He circled a finger between them. "Afterwards, I had Kevorkian on speed-dial for a while. That's all. I just, you know, react."

Men like Larry, like Talmadge, did every-thing possible to avoid appearing fragile. But they were all fragile, and the moments when that was revealed were an unending crisis. It was never going away. That's what he was telling her.

"I don't want you to tell Arthur," he said then. "About Collins."

"Larry."

"You said yourself it's not legal that you have to tell him. I don't want to be charitable just so he has these bullshit opportunities to throw up smoke."

Even after all of this, she was disinclined to actually say yes. She took a seat in a desk chair near the doorway while she deliber-ated. He grew frustrated watching her.

"Christ," he said. "Just do me a fucking favor, will you? Will you?" He'd reignited, heard himself, and flared out in a matter of seconds. He fell to the bed several feet from her, exhausted by himself. Next door, the ice machine thumped a full load of cubes into its belly.

Sooner or later, she'd inform Arthur, but that could wait until Larry settled down. He felt too defeated at her hands to absorb an-other blow now.

"Well, this is a moment of auld lang syne, isn't it?" she said, at last. "You and me and a hotel room and an argument?"

"The arguments never meant anything, Muriel."

"Really? You mean I was just wasting my breath?"

"It was all foreplay."

She lacked the daring to answer that.

"You just liked sex to be a form of rivalry," he said.

"Thank you, Dr. Ruth."

"It worked, Muriel. It always worked. Don't tell me you don't remember." He'd found the stamina to look at her one more time. For him, she realized, the story of what had happened between them was inscribed like law on tablets, often revisited, fully parsed and understood. Denial of any element was an affront.

"My Alzheimer's is only early stage, Larry. I remember."

With that acknowledgment, the past, its passion and pleasure, lay before them, like a corpse at a wake. Only this body was not quite dead. The longing that had always consumed them was suddenly present. She could feel Larry, intent as he measured her response. With his persistent directness about Talmadge, she knew what he wanted to ask, but even Larry recognized that boundary as unapproachable. Nor was there any point in comparisons—a marriage wasn't a fling, the world knew that. She was person one zillion who enjoyed sex more before marriage than after, although she honestly would never have guessed. Going to bed with someone had never seemed challenging. Important. Fun. But not difficult. She had always assumed Talmadge and she would find a rhythm. But they hadn't. She never thought she was someone who could live without it, but whether it was exhaustion or age, it was less and less a preoccupation. When she woke to yearning, as she did a few times each month, it came as a surprise.

And she was surprised now.

"I remember, Larry," she said again softly. She glanced up, thinking only to acknowledge him, but her desire was insistent enough that she could feel it beaconed from her. It was less than an invitation. Yet he had to sense that if he moved toward her, she'd find it hard to say no. But she could not go first. She'd made so many choices that Larry regarded as against him. There would be something vaguely imperial were she the one. Instead, she was left feeling like some breathless coquette, shy and powerless, as he pondered, a sensation she'd lived her life to avoid. She listened for movement, so she could rise to him. But his bitterness probably constrained him. The moment prolonged itself. And then the possibility of some rash grasping after all that former glory slipped beyond them, departing with the same slyness with which it had arrived.

"I'm beat," he said.

"Yeah, sure," she answered. From the threshold, she said she'd see him in the lobby at 6:30. Then she walked along the hall, an endless arcade of closed doors and low light, where she would eventually find the solitary room that was hers for the night. She carried her bags with her, wondering as she peered at every number, how hard it would be to go forward from here with the rest of her life.

24

JUNE 25–28, 2001

The Deposition
of Genevieve Carriere

IN THE MAIL, which always seemed to contain
bad news on Monday mornings, Arthur
found a form notice from Muriel Wynn.
Three days from now, on Thursday, the state
proposed to take the deposition of a woman
named Genevieve Carriere at the offices of
the lawyers she had hired, Sandy and Marta
Stern.

"So who's the mystery guest?" asked
Arthur when he succeeded after several attempts to get Muriel on the line. On the few
occasions over the years when Arthur had
dealt with Muriel, they had engaged in the
good-natured badinage appropriate to former colleagues. But the adversity of the
current proceedings had left Muriel's manner with him no better than crisp. Arthur,

who suffered from the loss of anyone's affections, had prepared himself for more of the same, but he found Muriel in good cheer. He suspected immediately she felt she'd renewed some advantage.

"Arthur," she answered, "let me say two words to you: Erno Erdai." Muriel, like many prosecutors in Arthur's experience, lived by a simple watchword in dealing with defense lawyers: don't get angry, get even.

"I had to do that, Muriel."

"Because you didn't want to give us a fair chance to investigate."

"Because I didn't want you guys to black-jack Erno down at Rudyard. Or string things out until he was dead or incompetent. He's telling the truth and you know it, Muriel."

"Hardly. Your guy confessed, Arthur."

"My guy has an IQ of 73. He knows other people are smarter than he is. He's accustomed to not understanding things and accepting what he's told. And don't think Larry didn't provide some incentives. Most of the time when a grown man craps his trousers, it's because something's scared him to death—not because he has a guilty conscience. You don't live in Shangri-la, Muriel, and neither do I."

The reference to Shangri-la, which had been such a zinger from Erno in court, was too much of a dig. Muriel's voice took on more heat.

"Arthur, I was there. There wasn't a mark on your guy. And he looked me in the eye and said he'd been treated fine."

"Because he was too bewildered to say anything else. Rommy has no history of violence. Erno's shot two other people, not even counting these murders. Who does the collar fit, Muriel?"

Oddly, Arthur felt he had the upper hand in this argument. He had more points. His only problem was that Rommy had never explained his confession in terms that made any sense. He did not really claim the statements were coerced, nor had any of his earlier lawyers, with whom Arthur still had had only minimal communication.

As usual, when she was falling behind, Muriel cut the conversation short and said simply, "Thursday." Arthur tried his luck next with Mrs. Carriere's lawyers. Sandy, always courtly, took a moment to praise Arthur's work in this case.

"I'm following your progress in the press, Arthur. Most notable." Stern, the dignified dean of the criminal defense bar in Kindle County, understood the value of his compliments. Having dispensed them, he transferred the call to his daughter Marta, with whom he'd practiced for nearly a decade now. She was representing Mrs. Carriere.

Arthur had still been a deputy P.A. when Marta had started here. In those days, she offered a studied contrast to her father, scrappy even when it was unnecessary, socially awkward, and less than tidy in her appearance. But she was devilishly bright and people said Sandy'd had a moderating influence on her over the years. Usually, criminal defense lawyers were collaborative. They had a common enemy in the state and a joint cause in limiting intrusions on their clients' rights. But over the phone, Marta seemed stiff, probably due to her skirmishes with Arthur years ago. She would disclose virtually nothing, beyond the fact that Genevieve was a close friend and co-worker of Luisa Remardi's.

"Genevieve has directed us not to give previews to either side," said Marta. "She wants no part of this. She has to interrupt the family vacation to come down here for the dep, as it is."

"Is she going to hurt me?"

Marta deliberated. The protocol among defenders required at least fair warning.

"If Muriel sticks to her announced agenda, there will be wounds, but nothing fatal. But make sure you walk in Muriel's footprints on cross. Don't try to break new ground."

After the call, Arthur pondered the value of this advice. The Sterns both played straight, but if their client was a reluctant witness, it was very much in her interest to discourage prolonged questioning.

On Thursday, a little before 2 p.m., Arthur walked over to the Morgan Towers, the city's tallest building. Sandy Stern was an immigrant, but his office was furnished as if someone in the family had been around to fight the Revolution. In the reception area where Arthur was required to wait, there were Chippendale pieces, decorated with china figures and sterling silver implements. Eventually Muriel arrived her standard ten minutes late, with Larry in tow. Marta then led them back to an interior conference room. Mrs. Carriere sat tensely beside an oval walnut

table with a glass top. She was dressed formally, in a dark suit with a collarless jacket,
and looked very much the physician's wife, a
bit plump, rather pretty, with soupspoon
eyes. Her hair, white decades early, lent her a
forthright air. Muriel greeted Mrs. Carriere, but
received a bare hello in return.

The court reporter, who'd set up his steno
machine beside the witness, asked Mrs.
Carriere to raise her right hand and applied
the oath. To start, Muriel's questioning went
no further than Arthur had anticipated based
on Pamela's usually thorough research. Mrs.
Carriere was at home now, after working for
years for Trans-National Air as a ticket
agent. Her husband, Matthew, was an in-
ternist in the suburbs in Greenwood County,
and they had four kids. Genevieve answered
with pained exactness. Marta had schooled
her well. Her client considered the questions
and responded as briefly as possible. She
was going to get an A+ in Witness 101.

When Muriel finally mentioned Erno,
Genevieve acknowledged knowing him as
the TN Security Supervisor at DuSable Field.

"Did Luisa Remardi ever discuss Mr. Erdai
with you?" asked Muriel.

Arthur objected immediately that the

question called for hearsay. Muriel and he fenced for a moment, making arguments for the record, but in a deposition under the federal procedure, a judge would only rule later. For the time being, Mrs. Carriere was required to answer, and Marta reinforced that with a slight nod toward her client. As the years had slid by, Marta had grown somewhat stout, but she also had cleaned up her act. She'd assumed a coiffed look, and wore a wedding ring, too, Arthur noticed. The parade went on. Everybody but him.

"Yes," said Genevieve.

"Did she ever discuss the nature of her relationship with Erno Erdai?"

Genevieve said she did not understand the question.

"Did she ever express negative sentiments about Mr. Erdai?"

"Yes."

"And were there occasions when she made these expressions and appeared to be in a highly excited or emotional state?"

"I suppose you could say that."

The rule excluding hearsay had an exception allowing so-called excited utterances to be admitted, on the theory that when people were overwrought, they were unlikely to speak calculated untruths. The exception, like many rules of evidence, had been around for centuries and took no account of contemporary learning about the soundness of what people said or observed under stress, but with that foundation, Arthur knew Genevieve Carriere's testimony, whatever it was, would be received in court.

"Mrs. Carriere," said Muriel, "I would like you to think back to the occasion when Ms. Remardi was most excited and spoke to you about Erno Erdai. Can you remember that time?"

"I remember a time. I don't know if it was when she was most upset, but she was upset."

"All right. When did this conversation occur?"

"About six weeks before Luisa was killed."

"Where were you?"

"Probably at the ticket counter at DuSable Field. We shared a drawer. Our shifts over-lapped. Things were usually very quiet then and we'd count out the drawer and spend a lot of time gabbing."

"And do you know of your own independent knowledge what had taken place to upset Ms. Remardi?"

"If you mean did I see what had happened, the answer is no."

"Did Luisa describe the event?"

Arthur asked for a continuing hearsay objection. He could tell that Muriel realized he was just attempting to break her flow, because she did not even look in his direction as she called on Mrs. Carriere to answer.

"Luisa said she'd been searched for drugs. A pat-down search."

"Did she explain what was upsetting about the search?"

"She didn't need to explain. It's obviously upsetting to come to work and get frisked. But she was especially angry with the way they went about it. She put it in pretty crude terms."

"What exactly did she say?"

Genevieve darted a resentful look at Muriel and permitted herself a sigh.

"She said they searched her through her clothing, but it was pretty thorough—she made some remark to the effect that she'd had sex with men who hadn't touched her in all those places."

The court reporter, whose job description required him to remain as uncommunicative as statuary, broke code and laughed out loud.

Around the table, the lawyers smiled, but Mrs. Carriere did not relax her tense expression.

"And when after this search did she speak to you about it?"

"Within an hour. They'd done it right before I came on."

"And what did she say about Erno Erdai?"

"Verbatim, again?"

"Please."

"I try not to use those words. It was also very colorful. What they call in the paper 'barnyard epithets.'"

"Would it be fair to say that she expressed hatred for Mr. Erdai?"

"Very fair. She said he knew she had nothing to do with drugs and that he'd lied to get her searched."

Muriel appeared caught off guard. Up until now, there seemed to have been a reasonably good understanding between witness and questioner. Arthur took Marta at her word when she said she hadn't permitted Muriel to interview Mrs. Carriere again, but Marta and Muriel had obviously engaged in a certain amount of back-and-forth, aimed, from Marta's perspective, at getting her client out of here as quickly as possible.

Arthur saw Larry lean over and whisper to

Muriel. He was wearing an open-necked polo shirt and a khaki poplin sport coat that had wrinkled up like a used paper bag in the summer heat. The casual attire seemed characteristic of Larry and many other detectives, always eager to remain aloof from the formalities of legal proceedings. In spite of the court reporter, Larry had a small spiral-topped pad, in which he was scratching his own notes now and then.

"Did she say how she knew it was Erno Erdai who had lied to get her searched?" Muriel asked.

"No."

"She assumed that?"

Arthur objected to Mrs. Carriere testifying about Luisa's assumptions and Muriel retreated, withdrawing the question. Larry again held his hand to her ear, beneath the billowy black curls.

"Did she explain what she thought Mr. Erdai was trying to accomplish by having her searched?"

"No. She just said it."

Muriel's obsidian eyes remained stuck on the witness. Tiny as Muriel was, the force of concentration sometimes made her look like a puppet on a string.

"When she made these negative remarks about Mr. Erdai, was that the first time you'd heard her speak about him?"

"No."

"And in any of those earlier conversations, had she talked about Erno Erdai in any capacity other than his role as a fellow employee and head of security at DuSable Field?"

Genevieve once more took her time before saying no.

"And had she previously made remarks that indicated she disliked him?" Muriel asked.

"I don't remember her saying before the search that she actually disliked him."

Usually sternly poker-faced as an advocate, Muriel betrayed some disappointment.

"Did she indicate any positive feelings about him?"

"I don't recall anything close to that. No," said Genevieve.

"Is it fair to say that the overall tone of her commentary about Mr. Erdai prior to this occasion was negative?"

Arthur objected on form to the question. Instructed to answer by Muriel, Mrs. Carriere said, "That's probably fair."

Muriel looked down to her yellow pad, apparently ready for a new subject.

"Mrs. Carriere, you repeated a remark Ms. Remardi made to you referring to her love life."

Genevieve pouted, displaying a dimple on her chin. She clearly regretted the unforgiving nature of this process.

"Did Ms. Remardi often discuss her intimate life with you?"

"Often?"

"Did she tend to keep you posted on what was going on with men?"

Once more, Arthur said, "Hearsay." Muriel again said she expected to overcome the objection and asked the court reporter to read back the question.

"I probably listened to more than I should have," said Mrs. Carriere, showing the very first wisp of a smile. "I got married when I was nineteen."

"Did you ever see Ms. Remardi in the company of men?"

"Occasionally."

"Now, based on your close friendship with Luisa Remardi, your many conversations with her, and your observations, do you have an opinion about whether or not Luisa

Remardi had an intimate relationship with Erno Erdai?"

For the record, Arthur objected at length that this was not a proper subject for opinion testimony. When he was done, Muriel again requested an answer to her question.

Mrs. Carriere said, "I don't believe they had an intimate relationship. I knew Erno. It would have been unlike Luisa not to tell me if she was seeing somebody I knew."

Muriel nodded once, her thin mouth fixed by the effort to evince no sign of triumph. With that, she tendered the witness to Arthur.

He took a moment, wondering how much weight Harlow or the appeals court judges might put on Mrs. Carriere's testimony. Probably a good deal. Judges trusted people like Genevieve, one of those industrious, decent sorts who kept the world spinning straight. Overall, he agreed with Marta's assessment of his situation: he had been wounded but not fatally. Mrs. Carriere's opinions were not enough to counterweigh Judge Harlow's finding that Erno was credible. Arthur reminded himself to proceed delicately with the damage control.

He began by eliciting the obvious, asking her to acknowledge, as she readily did, that she had no means to know if Luisa told her everything about her personal life or kept some secrets. Mrs. Carriere remained prim, but appeared slightly more receptive to Arthur, probably because he was not the antagonist who'd forced her to come here. To his latest question, she responded, "I'm sure there were things she didn't tell me, because I sometimes disapproved."

The answer provided a cushion for Arthur to take a few chances in hopes of rehabilitating other aspects of Erno's account.

"And bearing in mind that there may have been things about Ms. Remardi's personal life you didn't know, were there times she indicated she was seeing more than one man?"

Genevieve pursed her mouth and looked downward in thought.

"I need to explain to give a fair answer," she said, and Arthur motioned her to go on. "After her divorce, Luisa didn't really have much use for men. At least not for relationships. Sometimes she wanted company. Sometimes she wanted something else. And when she was in the mood, frankly, she wasn't especially choosy. Or even discreet. And there could have been months in between. Or a day. She could see somebody once. Or several times. I don't know the right word. Pragmatic? I think I'd say that when it came to men, she could be pretty pragmatic. So yeah, now and then, I heard about more than one guy."

Arthur had merely been hoping to nudge Genevieve toward acknowledging that it was possible that Luisa pursued multiple interests. This was a small triumph. He considered whether to ask if she had ever heard about Ms. Remardi conducting encounters in the airport parking lot, but Mrs. Carriere's responses about Luisa's practical approach to amour gave him enough latitude to argue the point.

Instead, he turned last to Mrs. Carriere's opinion that Luisa and Erno had never been romantically involved, which was already somewhat undermined by Genevieve's concession that Luisa might have kept things to herself.

"You do know," he asked, "from what Ms. Remardi said, that there was bad blood between Erno Erdai and her?"

"Bad blood?"

"Let me rephrase. You knew that as of six weeks before her death, she was very angry with him?"

"Yes."

"And that she thought he'd used a pretext to have something very offensive and physically invasive done to her?"

"Yes."

"Which she related, by her remarks, to intimate acts?"

Genevieve actually smiled at Arthur, enjoying the lawyers' sleight of hand, before she said yes.

"And the fact, as you testified before, is that she never really told you what she thought had led Mr. Erdai to initiate that search?"

He could see instantly that he'd gone one step too far. Genevieve's eyes briefly fastened to his, as if in warning, and she rolled her lips back into her mouth.

"As I said, she didn't explain what she thought Erno was trying to accomplish."

Anxious over whatever he'd missed, Arthur chose to smile benignly, as if her reply was just what he'd hoped for. "Nothing further," he added. He didn't dare look at Muriel and wrote several lines on his pad. Were it he across the table, the nuances of Genevieve's response might well have escaped him. But this was Muriel, possessed of something extrasensory, a kind of unreasoning sonar. He was not at all surprised when she asked the court reporter to read back Arthur's last question.

"Did she tell you why Erno Erdai initiated the search?" said Muriel then.

"She didn't explain what she thought he was trying to achieve, no."

"Not my question. I'm not asking what end she thought he had in mind. Did she say anything to explain what led Mr. Erdai to do it?"

Genevieve waited, then said yes. Muriel turned to Larry. Arthur saw Larry flip up his palm: what the hell.

"And why was that?" asked Muriel.

Again Mrs. Carriere looked to her lap and sighed heavily.

"Because of something I had said to Erno the week before."

"*You* had said? Let's wind this back—"

Genevieve lifted her hand. On her wrist, a charm bracelet jingled and among the miniature figures swinging back and forth were four golden silhouettes, surely representing her kids.

"After Luisa was searched, she was angry at Erno. But she was also angry at me. Because I'd told Erno something and she thought that was why he'd had her frisked. That's the reason she told me about it in the first place. She was basically reading me out for opening my mouth."

"And what had you told Mr. Erdai?"

Genevieve again took her time.

"I was working the overnight, which I usually alternated with Luisa, but for some reason she worked the early morning shift that day. Anyway, a man had come in looking for Luisa."

"A man? Did he give you his name?"

"No. He didn't give his name."

"Can you describe him?"

"In what sense?"

"What did he look like to you? What was his race?"

"He looked darker. Probably black, but I wouldn't say that for certain. Maybe Hispanic."

"Age?"

"Couldn't tell. Not old, not young."

"Build?"

"On the thin side."

"All right. This is what you told Erno Erdai the week before Luisa Remardi was searched: a man had come in."

"Right."

"And did you have a conversation with that man?"

"Right. And that's what I told Erno about."

"And what did the man say?"

"This gentleman asked me where Luisa was and he told me to tell her that he had seen the Pharaoh."

"'The Pharaoh'? Like in Egypt?"

"That's how it sounded to me."

Plainly perplexed, Muriel again studied Mrs. Carriere.

"And did the man say anything else other than he'd seen the Pharaoh?"

"The man said he'd seen Pharaoh and Luisa couldn't do that to him."

"And who was Pharaoh?"

"I didn't know."

Arthur saw Muriel tip her head. She'd heard something.

"Do you know *now* who Pharaoh was?"

"All I know is what Luisa told me."

"When was that conversation?"

"The next day. After that man came in."

"And tell us what she said and what you said about Pharaoh."

"I told her that this man had come in and what he said about seeing the Pharaoh and that I had told Erno. And she got upset with me. For telling Erno. And so one thing led to another. She told me who Pharaoh was."

"And what did she tell you?"

Mrs. Carriere now looked back at Muriel with the same intensity Muriel had directed toward her. Then Genevieve covered her mouth with her hand and started shaking her head.

"I'm not going to say," she declared, her voice warbling a bit, despite her emphatic tone. "All I know is what she said. Which my lawyer says can't be used in court. Which is why I don't understand why I have to go through this."

"Off the record," said Marta. She waved Arthur and Muriel across the corridor to her office. It was furnished like a gentleman's library in a bygone era, all leather, with deep sofas and matched sets of books with spines imprinted in gold aligned on the long shelves. Arthur could smell Stern's cigars from next door. One of the side tables held an array of family photos of Marta and her husband, who appeared Hispanic, and their two children. There were also several photographs of her parents in earlier years. Especially in today's outfit, a double-breasted pantsuit, Marta, to Arthur's eye, was a dead ringer for Stern, decades ago.

"Hypothetically," said Marta, "let's imagine that Ms. Remardi was defalcating certain property from TN." Marta was treading lightly. 'Defalcating' was fancy for 'stealing.'

"What kind of 'certain property'?" asked Muriel.

"Airline tickets."

"Airline tickets?"

Larry, who had followed them in, was the first to catch on. "She was fencing them through this Pharaoh, right?"

"Hypothetically. Now TN is ruthless in pursuing employee dishonesty. Zero tolerance. They got burned about ten years ago trying to sweep something under the rug with one of their higher-ups. One of the lawyers who was supposedly investigating a theft ended up running off with four million bucks."

"I remember," said Muriel.

"These days it's the gallows for everyone. Prosecution, if possible, and civil suits to recover what was stolen. No matter who or what. The Remardi kids are living on a TN pension."

"TN won't sue orphans."

"If they were your best friend's children, would you take that chance?" Marta opened her short hands toward Muriel. "You don't really need Luisa's activities to be part of the record, do you?"

"Right now, I'd say no," said Muriel. "But I don't want to keep chasing your client over hill and dale to get a straight answer."

Marta nodded several times, then turned to Arthur. He was startled and uncertain what to think. For the time being, he reminded Marta that this was a capital case. He said he'd let the issue go as long as he could, but he reserved the right to re-examine it, if on reflection he thought it could materially aid Rommy.

"Of course," said Marta.

Once they were done, Marta, Arthur, and Muriel returned to the conference room, and Marta called her client outside. When Genevieve resumed her seat beside the court reporter, she mouthed, "Thank you," toward both lawyers. She still appeared unsettled and had her purse in her lap and a hankie in one hand.

Muriel did not appear much pacified by Genevieve's gratitude. In fact, with time she seemed to have grown vexed. She bounced on her chair several times settling in. Arthur suspected Muriel felt Marta had shortchanged her in their conversations beforehand.

"Back on the record," Muriel said. "A man whose name you didn't know had come in looking for Luisa Remardi some time in May of 1991—is that the correct time frame?"

"It is."

"And this man said something about Pharaoh or the Pharaoh. You then told Erno Erdai what that man said and Luisa Remardi was angry you had done so and therefore explained to you who Pharaoh was and the nature of their relationship. That's the basic outline?"

"Correct."

"Did she tell you Pharaoh's last name?"

"No."

"Did she say whether that was a nickname?"

"No."

"Did she tell you where Pharaoh lived or worked?"

"I don't know anything else about him. Once Luisa told me what they were doing together, I didn't want to hear another word. Frankly, the only thing I was curious about was how they were getting away with it. I'd never heard of anything like that working in the long run. But I decided I didn't even care to know that."

"And this man who came in—did Luisa Remardi explain what his connection was to Pharaoh and her?"

"He'd introduced them."

"I see. And did he have any participation in the enterprise in which Luisa Remardi and Pharaoh were engaged?"

"Luisa said he'd wanted a share, but he didn't get it."

Muriel muttered "Mmm-hmm." She'd already figured as much. Arthur replayed it for himself. This third man had been the connect. He'd put Luisa in touch with Pharaoh to fence the tickets and was looking for a piece of the play, which he didn't receive.

"Now I want to be sure I have this right. You had no idea who Pharaoh was or what Ms. Remardi's relationship was with him until she explained that to you the day after this other man appeared? Right or wrong?"

"Completely right."

"And if you didn't understand the nature of Ms. Remardi's relationship with Pharaoh, why did you tell Erno Erdai what the man said?"

"Because Erno was the head of security." Marta, on the other side of her client, made a subtle movement and Genevieve lifted her chin to Muriel. "Because the man had made threats against Luisa."

"Specific threats? Specific actions?"

"Yes."

"And what action did he threaten?"

Genevieve's eyes wilted toward her hands, now covering her purse in her lap.

"He said he was going to kill her."

Arthur's vision jumped, as if a film had skipped frames. Muriel, never nonplussed, sat with her mouth open.

"Erno Erdai said that?"

"The man who had come in that night said it."

Growing agitated, Muriel re-arranged herself in her chair, shook her shoulders, straightened her neck. Then she stared down Genevieve, speaking to her stiffly.

"Now I'm going to ask a question, Mrs. Carriere, and I expect you to answer bearing in mind that the oath you took requires you to tell the whole truth. Do you understand?"

"Yes."

"Tell me everything that man who came in said to you."

"He asked for Luisa and I said she wasn't there. And he was upset. And he said something like, 'You tell her I just saw Pharaoh, and she can't do this to me, and when I find her, I'm going to kill her.' And naturally I was concerned for Luisa. Going off shift, I saw Erno and I thought Erno, as head of security, should know that. So I told him."

After the court reporter's machine had stopped clicking to record the answer, there was full silence. The momentousness of what he'd just heard stole in on Arthur. Luisa had been involved in dirty business with someone named Pharaoh, and a third man. And the third man had said he was going to kill her. There was a whole other circle to this case, a ring of crime and possible conspiracy, which had nothing to do with Rommy and not much to do with Erno either. And it was all good news for Romeo Gandolph. With multiplying suspects, no one could have the certainty required to put poor Rommy to death.

Muriel, too, clearly fathomed the damage she had sustained. Her small face was screwed up tight. Muriel could be mean.

"Now, this man said he was going to kill Luisa Remardi about two months before she was murdered, is that right?"

"Yes."

"And after Ms. Remardi was murdered, Detective Starczek, who's sitting right here, came out and questioned you about this case. Twice, as a matter of fact. Do you remember?"

"Yes."

"And you never told him, did you, that there was a man who had come into Du-Sable Field and threatened Luisa Remardi's life?"

"He didn't ask. And I didn't think it had anything to do with her murder. When I'd told Luisa about it, she'd laughed it off. She was sure he was just talking."

"Of course not," said Muriel, "why should you think it had anything to do with Luisa's murder? A man says he's going to kill her and she gets killed. What possible connection could there be?"

"I object to that," said Marta.

"*You* object?" asked Muriel. She pointed at Larry. "Go look in the hall," she said. "Maybe there are six or seven more people out there who want to say they killed the three of them."

"And I certainly object to that," said Marta.

"I need to adjourn," said Muriel. "I'm too angry to continue." Her head bounced around like a bobble toy's.

Always quick-tempered, Marta flared up at once. She and Muriel had agreed to a two-hour dep. Genevieve was not coming back. The women warred for a moment while Arthur looked on. As far as Marta was concerned the deposition was over.

"The hell it is," answered Muriel. Genevieve, she said, was far too consequential a witness to be dealt with summarily. Now that Muriel knew that, she wanted time to investigate before continuing.

Sitting there, Arthur struggled to think it through. The discovery period the Court of Appeals had authorized was over tomorrow. Muriel, clearly, was hoping to move to extend the deadline. And Arthur just as surely did not want her to succeed in doing that. With discovery closed, this new piece of information would guarantee that the Court of Appeals would allow Rommy's *habeas* to go forward. Indeed, Kenton Harlow, finally empowered to actually decide the case, might quickly grant Rommy a new trial on the basis of Erno's testimony and Genevieve's.

Arthur tried to play peacemaker, in hopes of bringing the deposition to a conclusion.

"What do you need to investigate?" he asked Muriel.

"Well, for one thing, I'd like some clue about this mystery man who comes in and threatens to kill Luisa."

"What can Mrs. Carriere possibly add? She's already given you a physical and said she didn't know the man's name."

The court reporter interrupted to ask if this was on the record. Arthur said yes and Muriel said no.

"Oh, for crying out loud," said Arthur. "On the record: Mrs. Carriere, is there anything you can tell us today that will help us identify this man who said he was going to kill Ms. Remardi?"

He thought he'd asked this as kindly as he could, but Genevieve fixed him with a bitter look.

"I'd rather stop now," she said. "I can't tell you how upsetting this is. It was all so crazy." Genevieve had never surrendered her handkerchief and she looked down to be certain it was at the ready.

"Perhaps you can just say yes or no to my question," said Arthur, "and we can be done."

What flashed very briefly from Genevieve toward Arthur was raw enough to be hatred. It seemed out of character, but in that look of loathing she'd found his enduring vulnerability, and Arthur flapped a hand against his side.

"Okay," he said. "I'll agree to adjourn."

The next voice seemed to come from nowhere.

"I think she should answer that question right now." It was Larry.

They all turned to him. The court reporter's hands were poised over the long keys of the steno machine, uncertain if he should take down an interruption from a non-attorney. Muriel in the meantime was staring at Larry with sufficient wrath that Arthur was surprised she had not simply belted him.

"Make her answer," Larry told Muriel. There was a moment between them, some test of faith, Arthur could see. Then Muriel relented.

"Okay," said Muriel. "Answer."

Genevieve instead faced Marta. Marta scooted her chair an inch or two closer to her client and covered Genevieve's hand with her own, waiting for her to compose herself.

"I think this is all pointless," said Genevieve. "None of this is going to help those girls. And with Erno now, no one's going to know anything for certain."

"Move to strike as nonresponsive," said Muriel. "Answer the question. Do you know anything that will help identify the man who said he would kill Luisa Remardi?"

"It's my question," said Arthur. "I'll withdraw it." He had no idea what he was doing, except instinctively pulling as hard as he could against Muriel.

"I'll re-pose it," said Muriel.

"It's not your turn," said Arthur. "And we just agreed to adjourn."

"Let's finish," said Muriel. Through the brief byplay, she had never removed her eyes from Genevieve, who seemed powerless to do anything other than stare back, notwithstanding a leakage of tears.

"You didn't ask if I knew him," she said to Muriel. "You asked if he gave his name. And he didn't. But I'd seen him before. Around the airport. And I know his name now." She turned then to Arthur, and in the utter gravity of Mrs. Carriere's large brown eyes, he suddenly comprehended the meaning of her warning glances and the depth of his foolishness.

"It was your client," she said to him. "Mr. Gandolph. He's the man who said he was going to kill Luisa."

PART THREE

DECISION

25

JUNE 29, 2001

He Did It

ARTHUR DID HIS BEST to escape from the Sterns' overdone offices alone, but Muriel and Larry arrived while he was still awaiting the elevator, and in neutered silence the three stood in front of the crafted brass doors. Muriel eventually said something about filing a motion to dismiss in the Court of Appeals, but Arthur did not have the stuff to respond, or even to listen. He let them go down ahead of him when the first car arrived.

A few minutes later, he reached the entry to the Towers, where a fan of steel and glass swelling overhead offered protection from a sudden summer downpour. Arthur peered out, then walked into the rain, traveling more than a block before he noticed he was getting wet. He ducked into the doorway of another Center City building and then, after a moment in which he once more fell into agitated reflection, started through the storm again. He had to get back to the office. He had to tell Pamela. It occurred to him, in time, that he was hungry and weary and needed to pee. Yet as he was pelted, all he could hold in mind was Mrs. Carriere's final answer. *Your client. Mr. Gandolph.* He chewed her words down to a vile, indigestible remnant, until he felt obliged to accept the obvious and find dry ground. Then in a few minutes, he was hurtling forward again, walking out of desperation, as if, in another location, her testimony might mean something else.

By now, Rommy existed in his mind solely as a woebegone innocent—and more important, he himself as the valiant champion of a just and miraculous cause. If Rommy was guilty, then Arthur's world was different and gloomier, a place he had grown convinced he was no longer required to inhabit. Life again would be only hard work and duty.

Eventually, he found himself in front of Morton's. Desperate by now, he stepped in, intending to look for the men's room, but once through the doors he thought of Gillian, inspired by a peripheral impression of her fox-colored hair. Approaching the cosmetics counter, he saw no sign of her. He was sure it had been an illusion when she suddenly reared up before him, after replacing stock in the drawers below.

"Arthur." Gillian stepped back with a long hand lying over her collar.

"He did it," said Arthur. "I thought you should know. Muriel will leak it to everybody. You'll hear soon. But he did it."

"Who did?"

"My client. Rommy. He's guilty."

Gillian emerged through a small hatchway in the counter. She took Arthur by the elbow, as she might a wandering child.

"What do you mean, 'He's guilty'?"

Arthur described the deposition. "I can't figure any of it out right now," he said. "I feel like my brain's been in the microwave or something. Where's the washroom?"

She called to a colleague that she was taking her break, then steered him along, offering to hold on to his briefcase. Down the escalator was a coffee bar where she would wait for him.

A few minutes later, hoping to calm himself, Arthur took stock in front of the mirror over the bathroom sinks. His hair had more or less washed off his head and, under the intense fluorescents, looked like an ink spill. His gray suit was soaked black across the shoulders. No wonder Gillian had jumped at the sight of him. He looked like a homeless person rolled out of a gutter.

Outside, he briefly phoned Pamela, assuring her that the news was every bit as bad as it sounded, then rode the escalator down to the small coffee bar Morton's had recently opened in the basement as yet another lure to keep customers in the store. The effort was working well today. Although lunch was long over, most of the small white tables were occupied by ladies waiting out the rainstorm, with their shopping bags beside their knees.

A few feet ahead, Gillian sat with her back to him, finishing a cigarette. If nothing else, the sight of her removed him somewhat from the shock of Mrs. Carriere. In spite of his growing chill, and his current confusion, Gillian, as a figure, continued to inspire in him both excitement and hunger. But he could not pretend she had not achieved some of what she intended with her revelations the last time he saw her. It was the vision of a demonized teenager, applying cigarettes to her flesh, which had haunted him. He could see her, very pale and thin, pushing the ember against the sensitive region inside her arm, and all along maintaining a solemn face despite the pain and the hideous pungency of her own smoking flesh.

Returning now, that image stopped Arthur in his tracks. He knew himself as a person of endless unsatisfied dreams. But overlaying the creature in perpetual adolescence was the man he had become in his thirties, neither a child nor a fool, someone who had begun to learn from his mistakes instead of repeating them to the point of infinity, someone who now could not only curb his yearnings but even leave them behind. In the last week and a half when he took a reprieve from work in the office to stare at the river, he had thought often of Gillian. Yes his heart swelled, yes he analyzed his conversations with her until they no longer remained intact in his memory, having grown jumbled with the sly interjections he imagined from himself thanks to the high-revving motor of his fantasies. But then his pulse slowed with a sense of the true risks facing him. He knew longing well, but he was less schooled in heartbreak.

His divorce had been devastating. But he had married Marjya largely because she would have him. She was very pretty. And certainly bright. And Arthur was unrelievedly horny. But he did not live one of the forty or so days they spent together feeling he understood the first thing about her. He could not get her to close the door to the john, or to take pleasure in most American food. Who could have told him how hard it was to explain yourself to someone who'd grown up without a television set, who had only a vague idea of who Richard Nixon was, let alone Farrah Fawcett or Rubik's Cube? Every instant was a surprise—especially the final one when she said she was leaving him for a countryman, a tile fitter no less.

How could she just abandon him, he asked, their life?

'Ziss?' she replied. 'Ziss is nossink.'

That had been bad. But Gillian, as someone he aspired to in such an exalted way, no matter how foolishly, posed a danger far beyond what Marjya had wrought. In this world, he had next to nothing. But there was his Self—his fragile soul. A person as smashed and compromised as Gillian, a person who had been so conquered by her devils she could succumb to drunkenness and criminality and incestuous love and God knows what else—someone like that was as unpredictable as Susan. He had told Gillian he was not frightened of her. That had been dashing—and foolhardy. Afterwards, he had realized it was not wholly true. In the late afternoons, when he turned from his desk and let his mind escape on the scales of orange light on the river, the thought of Gillian also brought a cool realization of the way love could become a catastrophe.

Standing still in the store basement, he thought it all through one more time. Then he continued ahead. He could only be himself, which meant pursuing the chance, no matter how slight, to be with someone he dreamed of, to vault the unconquerable distance between what lived only in his mind and what actually was. Like food and health and shelter, everyone, he believed, was entitled to that.

WHILE ARTHUR WAS GONE, Gillian sat at the little white table and went through several cigarettes. Recently, she had been holding to less than a pack a day, but by now it had become a virtual certainty that her encounters with Arthur would shake her. The disruptions often seemed worthwhile in their way, but she still needed to be fortified by nicotine. She'd quit smoking in law school, and started again only at Hazelden, where she was hospitalized while she kicked. At the NarcAnon meetings there, everyone seemed to have a cigarette between their fingers. She knew she'd traded one addiction for another, the new one nearly as lethal, and less fun, but such were the terms of a life to be lived one day at a time.

Turning around, she caught sight of Arthur wandering back, very much lost in himself. She had something important to say to him and did not even wait for him to sit down.

"You shouldn't give up, Arthur."

His mouth drooped open as he sank to a seat.

"I have no right to give you advice," she said. "But let me. You've done too much good work. If there's one undiscovered witness, then there may be others."

Initially, as she'd awaited Arthur, she had felt troubled for his sake. After visiting Arthur in his home, after meeting Susan, after listening to his adoring accounts of his father, she wished for the light of something wonderful to shine on Arthur, because, quite simply, he deserved it. Losing Gandolph's case would be an undeserved blow.

But what brought her face-to-face with the Gillian who was so frequently a shock to herself was her own fierce disappointment at Arthur's news. Everyone who had made a life in the criminal courts knew that defendants generally deserved their punishment. But as she'd sat smoking without interruption, the ash deepening in the little foil tray on the table, she had gradually—and calmly—recognized that she had wanted Rommy Gandolph to go free. She had wanted her judgment of him to be, like so many other judgments of that period, recognized as an error. And reversed. For today she finally understood: she equated a new life for Rommy Gandolph with her own renaissance. And she had depended on Arthur, that paragon of sincerity, as her knight errant. Because that was Arthur. Dependable. And virtuous. Perhaps what was most startling was that she was unprepared to let go. She felt no duty to explain her motives, but she remained determined to revive him.

"The problem," he said, "is I believed Genevieve. She really didn't want to say it."

"And you believed Erno, too. Do you think now that he was lying?" He did not appear to have considered that. "You need time, Arthur. To talk to your client. And Erno."

"Right."

"Don't give up." She reached forward and clasped both of his hands. She smiled this time and, a bit childishly, he seemed to reflect her encouragement. He nodded, then bundled his arms against his body. He was freezing to death, he said, and needed to get home to change. She had no trouble believing that; his hands had been like marble.

"Forgive me, Arthur, but looking at you, I wonder if you can keep your mind on the road. Am I being too much of a granny?"

"Probably not. I'll take a taxi."

"You'll be lucky to find one in the rain. Where's your car? I could drive. I've been practicing a bit with Duffy's station wagon. And I have my lunch and dinner hours coming."

Arthur appeared muddled. From a house phone, she called Ralph, her boss, who told her to take her time. He expected little trade in light of the storm.

"Come along, Arthur," she said. "Worrying

about your fine automobile in my hands will keep your mind off your troubles."

Arthur's monthly space was half a block down, which they reached through a series of basement arcades connecting the buildings. The lot was under one of the newer skyscrapers, and exited onto Lower River, a parkway that ran beneath River Drive above. Newcomers to the city could never make sense of the road, and Gillian, who hadn't been down here in a decade, was not much better off. Lower River had been designed to move trucks off the Center City streets, allowing them access to the loading docks of the big buildings. It worked well for that purpose, but the roadway was tortuous and the environment surreal. Sulfur lights glowed down here twenty-four hours a day, and over the years, the homeless had made this their chief refuge. The wilted cartons and soiled, spring-shot mattresses where they slept were piled into the recesses between the concrete buttresses supporting River Drive. Rain dribbled down between the seams in the street overhead, while grimy men in ragged clothes loitered between the roadside pillars, looking, at best, like creatures from *Les Misérables*, if not *The Gates of Hell*.

In the car, Arthur remained focused on today's catastrophe.

"Do you feel vindicated?" he asked.

"Not at all, Arthur," she said with some vehemence. "In no way."

"Really? After the beating you've taken in the papers, I thought you'd be bitter."

"In that case it was courageous of you to come and tell me this yourself. Frankly, I'd rather thought I'd heard the last from you, Arthur."

Gillian drove with the hesitance of the elderly, jiggling the wheel and braking too often, watching the shining pavement in the same fixed way she would a minefield. Nonetheless, when they coasted to a light, she permitted herself a sideward glance. In Arthur's present state of mind, it seemed to take him a while to understand she was alluding to what she'd told him about her brother in their last conversation.

"More the reverse," he said then. "I thought I might have offended *you* by what I said when you got out of the car."

"Oh, I'm sure you were right about that, Arthur. I probably was trying to adjust your high opinion of me."

"You arrange everything so nobody has a

chance with you. You know that, don't you?"

She became aware in a moment of how tightly she was gripping the steering wheel.

"I've heard that before," she told him. "That doesn't mean my warnings aren't to good effect, Arthur. It probably justifies them."

"Right," he said. "I've heard all your caveats. But I never imagined you were faultless, Gillian. Just appealing."

"Appealing? How so?"

She could feel him staring. They were getting close to his apartment and Arthur's final directions were issued in a bristling tone. Plainly, he was irritated with her for putting him on the spot. But he answered.

"I think you're very smart and very beautiful, the same thing everybody else has always thought, Gillian. You know what bells you set off, don't pretend you don't."

"You mean sexually appealing," she said. Being behind the wheel seemed to allow for bluntness. Or perhaps it was just her faultless instinct for keeping everyone at bay. But she thought she had a point.

"You sound like you resent that. It's a fact of life, isn't it?"

Arthur gestured to the old brick three-flat, and Gillian pulled the car to the curb with a sense of relief. She faced him now.

"But that's the root of it, isn't it? Sex?"

Pained, he screwed up his face. He was regretting everything. She could see it. This conversation. Anything else he had said that had exposed him to her uncivil tongue.

"Really," he said, "what would be so wrong if I said yes? You want to reduce it to the basics? Sure, I'd like to make love to you. Eventually. You're a very attractive woman. I'm a man. It's pneumatics and instinct. I mean, I don't think that's going to happen today—or tomorrow, or anytime in the near future. I'd like to know you. I'd like you to know me. I'd love you to know me and like me so much that you'd want that to happen. You can make fun of that, too, Gillian." He opened the car door, and she reached after him.

"I'm not making fun, Arthur. I have a point."

"About?"

"What was your word. 'A crush'? You're grasping after your own images. From eons ago. You don't see me as I am, Arthur."

"Maybe I see you more clearly than you see yourself."

"There's a great deal you don't know, Arthur." She looked down the street, over-hung by the stout arms of large old elms, hardy survivors in full leaf. Beneath them, the rain had dwindled to a few drops. The word 'heroin' was on her lips, but her motive for telling that story would be immediately suspect, taken, like her revelation about Carl, as yet another dramatic warning shot meant to hold Arthur at arm's length. "A great deal," she repeated. "And it frightens me."

"Because?"

"Because it's inevitable that you'll be dis-appointed. I'll feel like a villain and you'll be far more dashed than you imagine."

"Well then, that will be my problem," he said. He pushed the door wider. "Look, I'm sick of this conversation. I'm sick of you telling me what to want. You're entitled to say no. I've heard it before, and I haven't jumped off any bridges yet. So say no, once and for all, and let's get this over with. But stop acting like a tease."

"I don't want to say no," she answered. The words froze her heart. Arthur, too, looked taken aback. Gillian stared through the windshield, spotted with rain, suddenly bewildered and frightened, then, with nothing else to say, asked him if the car was okay as it was.

"Fine," he said. "Come on up. I'll give you a magazine and a cold drink while I change."

As his father probably had, Arthur kept the shades on the southern windows drawn in the summer, and today the dim apartment had an elderly smell, undusted, with cooking odors greased into the wallpaper and plaster. Like her, he seemed unsettled by the conversation they'd just had, and he traveled around nervously, turning up each of the window air conditioners. He asked what she wanted to drink and then immediately corrected himself.

"I mean, a soft drink. Only I don't know what's in the fridge." He started in that direction, but she said she was fine. "Right," he said. "I won't be a minute." He stared, then without another word disappeared into his bedroom and closed the door.

She stood alone in the living room several minutes. From the bedroom, she could hear drawers slamming as Arthur hastily shed his clothes. Eventually, she turned to the window and lifted the shade. In the sky, there was suddenly an inkling of sun. Arthur

Raven, she thought. Who could imagine? But even at that, a shiver of delight penetrated her. This was why it was worth getting up every day. Because life could still hatch surprises. She went then and rapped firmly on the center panel of the dark bedroom door.

"May I come in, Arthur?" she asked.

He cracked the door and peeked out. He asked her to repeat what she'd said and she did.

"Why?" he asked.

She looked at him.

"Oh, please," he said. "So you can prove to me it's not worth all the drama?"

He might have been right at that. She seemed embarked on one of those moments of numb action that had gotten her into so much trouble over the years. But she'd been right to contend that this relationship could never stand the light of day. A shuttered boudoir was the only place it could be conducted in earnest.

"Arthur, don't play hard to get. I doubt I'll have the courage to do this again." She inched her way over the threshold and kissed him. It was dry and cold and unimpressive, even for a first effort. But it served to make the point. When he stood back, he was wearing only his wet socks.

"How should this go, Arthur?"

He looked at her bleakly. "Slowly," he said.

He kissed her now, not much better than the first time, and took her hand and led her to the bed. He drew the shades fully, darkening the room. He spoke to her without daring to look at her.

"You take off your clothes. And then let's sit next to each other. Just sit here."

She undressed with her back to him. She folded her clothes and left them on a chair and sat again, then felt the bed sag with his weight. He was close enough that she felt his thick thigh brushing her flank. She glanced down, almost against her will, and saw his organ already pointing between his thighs. She knew in Arthur both tenderness and greed. She could not guess which would prevail. Probably, if she drew a picture, she'd expect him to maul her. But she'd committed herself to this. It was a leap into darkness.

Nothing happened at first. It was still afternoon and the daylight seemed to soften the sounds from outside. With the end of the rain, bugs were sawing away in the trees and a bus snored off blocks away.

After a few minutes, she felt his fingertips on her thigh. He touched her slowly. He touched her knee. He lightly touched her back and her shoulders. He touched her neck. As he'd promised, he moved slowly. By the time he touched her breasts, her nipples had peaked. He kissed her then—her shoulders, her breasts. He kissed her mouth briefly and then worked his way downward. He parted her knees and with time brought his mouth against her there. After circling forever, he dove farther inside.

For a moment then, she opened her eyes to the sight below of Arthur Raven's shiny scalp. Several of his dwindling hairs were standing up straight as a rooster's comb, and she had to choke back the fatal impulse to laugh. She hung there an instant, coldly conscious, lecturing herself although there were no particular words, but wanting the right thing, endeavoring only to feel, and sinking slowly toward the well of sensation. A few times she rose back up, but she escaped more willingly on each occasion, until, by the time he was inside her, she had finally joined herself to the pleasure. This was life, she thought then. These sensations, so long gone, were the river that fed that lost thing called life. She rode upward on the silvery current and could not even remember reaching out to him, but they were bound now, her head crushed to his shoulder, her legs locked behind him, as her body responded in equal reflection of his rhythm.

Afterwards, he opened the blinds to let some light into the room. She shielded her eyes, but felt the full weight of his vision as he stood nearby and examined her.

"You *are* very beautiful," he said.

"I'm one of those women, Arthur, who looks her best in clothing." She had spent many hours in self-assessment and knew what he saw. She was freckled, with long limbs and shallow breasts, and so pale that her shanks looked almost blue.

As for Arthur, he was not purely the man he appeared. He was drooping in the middle, but he had actually spent some of his lonely hours keeping fit. His round shape was more the result of a rib cage so bowed it resembled a helmet. He had thin hips and birdy little legs, and beautiful, strong arms. He was also the hairiest man she'd ever seen. Without his clothes, he somehow seemed spry and quick. In retraction, his male organ glimmered amid the forest like a bulb. It was like the rest of Arthur, thicker than some, but not long. He was beside the bed, studying her, and she reached out and then brought herself forward and put the whole thing in her mouth. It grew larger for a while.

"Not yet," he said.

But she was not ready to release him. She worked at it with a deliberate tenderness, the tenderness he had shown her, until he was fully erect again, then she ran his penis like a wand, across the ridges of her face, her eyes, her cheeks, her mouth, then took him in again. When he fell down beside her this time, he slept.

She found a coverlet at the foot of the bed and lay within it, staring at the old ceiling fixture, a frosted square of brain-dead '50s design, reviewing the sensations in her own mind. She had not realized he was awake when he spoke to her again, some time later.

"The Bible has it right."

"The Bible? Is that what you're thinking about, Arthur?"

"I am."

She closed her eyes. It would be terrible if this moment turned to homily or cant.

"I am. I'm thinking about that phrase. 'He knew her.'"

"It's from the Greek."

"Is it? It's right. Isn't it?"

"Do you know me, Arthur?"

"Something, yes. Something essential."

She considered the notion and dismissed it as preposterous. No one knew her. She didn't know herself.

"What do you know about me?" she asked.

"I know you've suffered your whole life, just like I have. I know that you're sick of going it alone. Is that right?"

"I have no idea," she said.

"You want the respect you're entitled to," he said. "You need that."

She sat up. The conversation was making her uncomfortable.

"Don't think." She kissed him. "Can you do this again?"

"I have great reserves," he answered. "A lifetime."

"I want to do this again."

When they were done, she went to Arthur's small bathroom. This time for her had been far better. Sensation rippled through her enormously whenever he moved. She had made sounds, cried out, and a spectacular wave of feeling had engulfed her at last, a quaking, serial orgasm that belonged on the Richter scale. She rocked there at the height of it, like a nest in the top of a tree, beyond breath or time, not wanting to let it go and letting go only because she knew she would pass out shortly if she didn't.

The echoes of pleasure had left such tremors in her legs that she was unsure how long she could stand. He was such a simple man, she thought, looking about. His car was from Beverly Hills, but his bathroom belonged in a tenement. The sink rode on chrome legs. Long ago, someone had fixed a frilled skirt over the toilet tank and a shag cover on the seat, and she sat on that, again remembering her pleasure. When she went back in memory this time, she began to weep. She was shocked—shocked by the emotion that ripped through her and the phrase that rose to her lips.

She howled. She threw both hands over her mouth, but she could not stop. In time, Arthur overheard her, knocked repeatedly, and finally forced his way in. Naked, still, she sat looking up at him.

"I wanted it so badly," she said to him, as

she had been saying to herself. She had no idea what 'it' was exactly, but surely not the creature act. The relief of momentary pleasure in a miserable world? Respect, as he'd said? Or merely connection, loving connection? The fury of this unnamed desire, which had lain obscured by debris inside her like some archaeological treasure, stunned her. Oh, how she had wanted it!

She sat there crying, crying for all the world, saying again and again that she wanted it so badly. Arthur knelt beside her on the cold tiles of the bathroom and held her, saying, "You have it now, you have it."

26

Smart

"OH MY GOD!" As soon as the brass elevator doors had met, reuniting the leafy Deco designs embossed there and leaving Arthur Raven safely behind, Muriel clapped her hand to her chest and sagged against Larry, planting her narrow shoulder on his arm. "When did you know?"

"Before Arthur." Larry shook his head in pity. He still liked Arthur, especially now that they'd kicked his fanny. Upstairs, outside the Sterns' offices, with the air between the three of them brittle as glass, Arthur looked as if he might faint, as if his heavy briefcase might drag him to the floor. "Talk about the poster child for the pale and clammy. I thought of dialing 911. Where does he go now?"

"Probably to Rudyard to read out his

client—or to County to do the same thing to Erno, assuming he's still alive. I heard he took a turn for the worse."

Larry made a sarcastic remark about Erno's well-being, then asked what he'd meant to originally, whether Arthur had really run out of options in court. Muriel shrugged. For the moment, she seemed far more interested in hearing how he'd figured out it was Rommy who'd threatened Luisa.

"I just kept asking myself, What's this lady's story?" Larry said. "Genevieve's good people. Usually a better-than-average person has got to have a decent reason to stiff the truth. The way I read her, she figures Luisa's dead, can't change that, let's do the best for the daughters. And that means keeping the lid on the real story—not just because TN may turn the dogs loose, but because it spreads fertilizer all over Mommy's grave. Once you say Rommy was the one threatening Luisa, you have to say why. The whole world hears about the tickets now, including Luisa's girls."

They emerged into the brighter lobby. Muriel was tanned to a summer glow, but Larry could see that she'd also been lit by victory. In her happy moments, when she was relaxed, Muriel was the funniest girl in the world. And she was happy now, especially with him.

"You're the man, Larry." She beamed up at him, revealing that little gap between her front teeth. He wished with all his might this declaration didn't excite him, as it did. Probably if Muriel and he had worked it out ten years ago, they'd be the Bickersons by now, like every other old couple. But you always wanted what you didn't get, and since his meltdown in Atlanta, he'd been coming to terms: he wasn't getting over Muriel, not in this lifetime.

His thoughts of her were always attached to the idea of destiny. She was in every fiber a person who believed there was a Plan, one she intended to be part of, and in her company he was inevitably under the same spell. What he had lost most, when he lost her, was the belief that great things were in store for him.

It was raining hard, but Muriel managed to flag a taxi. Larry had left his stuff in her office and jumped in beside her. On the way Muriel asked his opinion about who in the press to give this to. She still had time for the TV news. On her cell, she called Stanley Rosenberg at Channel 5. Then she phoned Dubinsky at the *Tribune*. "Stew? I have tomorrow's headline today. 'Witness: Gandolph Said He Would Kill July 4 Victim.'"

Larry felt less exuberant. Being around Muriel probably dampened his mood. But he'd shoved aside a lot of questions during the dep that were bothering him now. First off, he had to be dumber than a box of hair not to tumble to a ticket agent stealing tickets. Then he remembered what had misled him.

"You know," he said, as soon as Muriel was free, "I've gone over my notes of my conversation with Erno back in October '91 probably a hundred times. Two hundred. And when I asked him how Luisa was minting money, *he* brought up the subject of stolen tickets and said they hadn't had any problems for years."

"Maybe he didn't know what she was doing. The stuff Genevieve heard from Squirrel—I saw Pharaoh and I'm going to kill her—that might just sound to Erno like Luisa had been stepping out on him."

"On Rommy? And besides, why would

Erno have Luisa searched, if he didn't know about the tickets?"

Muriel was too high to worry, but he persisted.

"Okay, and here's another thing. I've got it in my notes that Erno told me we ought to subpoena Genevieve to the grand jury."

"Thinking she'd put it on Rommy?"

"Obviously. But why so coy? Why not say straight up Genevieve could tell me Squirrel had threatened to kill Luisa, instead of playing dumb?"

The rain was nearly solid when they left the taxi. Muriel held her briefcase over her head, her heels smacking up little spurts on the granite steps of the Kindle County Building. The structure was a century old, a red-brick block built in the same style as the gloomy factories of that era. Even in good weather, the interior light had the quality of old shellac. Muriel was royalty inside this building. The bailiffs at the metal detectors greeted her as 'Chief,' and passing through the lobby she was accosted every ten feet by somebody else. Two deputy P.A.'s, interviewing a nine-year-old in connection with the murder of another child, chased after her, seeking permission to cut a deal. She told them it was too soon, then moved on to happier tasks, greeting at least a dozen people by name. She was far more natural at this kind of politicking than he would have imagined ten years ago, looking genuinely eager to hear about grandma's progress after a hip replacement, or how the third-grader was doing in her new school. Only those who knew Muriel best might recognize it was a one-way street, that she seldom shared much about herself.

Larry went ahead to wait for her by the elevator bank, still puzzling about Erno.

"Try this," he said to Muriel, without any preamble, when they boarded the car alone. "Erno hears about Squirrel and Luisa from Genevieve. Squirrel's a thief, and, like Erno told me, tickets are the best things around there to steal, and Luisa's a ticket agent. So he has her searched on a pretext."

"Right."

"But he doesn't find the tickets. So he picks door number two: just some weird screwball with a crush who's talking trash. And instead, six weeks later, she gets offed. So now he can't raise his hand and say I know what this is about."

"Because?"

"Because he fucked up. Because he'd have to admit that he violated the union agreement and had searched her on a pretext. And never bothered informing the cops about Squirrel. Some good plaintiff's lawyer with orphans for clients will choke a fortune out of Erno and the airline, and his bosses will blame Erno for being asleep at the wheel.

"But then his handsome nephew gets cracked, and Erno thinks it over again, because he really wants to save Collins. I don't know which of them found out Squirrel had the cameo, if Collins came up with that or Erno had been gumshoeing around on his own and fed it to Collins, but either way, Erno deals it out to me in pieces to make sure he doesn't get any shit on his shoes. 'Go talk to Collins. And by the way, subpoena Genevieve.' It sort of fits, doesn't it?"

They had entered the vast outer office of the P.A. and the Chief Deputy. Muriel stopped at one of the secretarial stations to pick up messages and an armful of mail. In her office, she closed the door and had him play the whole thing back one more time.

"It was the truth," concluded Larry. "What Erno was telling us way back when. It was always the truth. He's just burned now because he helped us out and he's still dying in prison."

He watched her assess this, lips rumpled.

"Okay," she said. "Call for the heralds. And several witnesses."

"Because?"

"I'm going to say it." She reached the considerable distance up to his shoulder. "You were right. At least, close enough. You're right." Her dark eyes were lively as diamonds. "You're always right, Larry." There was a little hiccup there, before she finally lowered her hand. "You're right," she said again and threw the mail down on her desk. "Happy?"

Now that she asked, he found he wasn't completely.

"Something is bugging me about the fence. King Tut or whatever. The Pharaoh."

"What about him?" she asked.

"I don't know. But I want to be the first boy on my block to remind him of old times. If Pharaoh is a super-big pal of Squirrel's, he might even deny everything Genevieve gave us, especially if Arthur gets to him before I do and gives him a road map."

"So let's find him."

"I'm figuring 'The Pharaoh' for a gang handle, right?"

That had been Muriel's thought, too.

"I'll get with the guys in Gang Crimes," Larry said. "They've been helping me figure out the Gangster Outlaw angle on Erno."

Muriel lolled on the side of her desk, thinking it all over. She shook her head in wonder.

"Dude, you've been taking your smart pills."

"Yeah," he said, "if I'm so smart, how come I didn't think of wheels on luggage? I ask myself that whenever I walk through an airport."

Muriel laughed at that one. She'd worn a little jacket over a sleeveless dress and she removed the cover-up now. The P.A.'s Office seldom got below eighty in the summer, even with the air-conditioning on full throttle. Her shoulders were peeling. When she focused again on Larry, she had a far more sober look.

"No, you're smart, Larry," she said quietly and took another instant to herself. "You really rocked my world down in Atlanta."

They hadn't spoken of Atlanta—not on the plane back or in the days since—and Larry didn't want to talk about it now. He'd blame the booze, if he had to. He was relieved to find she had another moment in mind.

"That equal sign you put between Rod and Talmadge? That tune's been on replay for days."

"I was out of line."

"You were," she said. "You were definitely out of line. But what I've been wondering about is why would you even say that to me? You just sort of drop by and say, 'Sucks to be you.' What is that, Larry?"

"I'm not sure, Muriel. I guess I thought I was right."

"Well, what good does that do you? Or me, for that matter?"

He suddenly felt like squirming. "I'm sorry, Muriel. Honestly. I should have kept my mouth shut."

But that, clearly, was not the answer she wanted. She watched him at length, until her look had softened to a rare aspect for Muriel, something approaching sadness.

"I mean, Jesus, Larry," she said quietly, "really, when did you get so smart?"

"I just know you, Muriel. I don't know much. But I know you."

"I guess you do," she said. There was a

moment down in Atlanta when he thought she had it as bad as he did, and from the way she was eyeing him now, he was starting to get that feeling again. What would that mean? Nothing good, he decided. From a filing cabinet in the corner, he retrieved the things he'd left behind, his case file and, in a demonstration of appalling meteorological skills, his folding umbrella. It was the size of a baton and he displayed it to her.

"Not as smart as you think," he said.

She'd sat down at her desk to begin working, but shook her head resolutely to show she did not agree.

27

JUNE 29, 2001

The Enemy

"HE'S GOING TO EXPLAIN IT," Pamela told Arthur when he'd picked her up at 6:00 this morning for another odyssey to Rudyard. She had persuaded herself overnight, but Arthur suspected even Pamela did not completely believe it. After nine months in practice in the big city, she was already beginning to acquire a skeptical air. Opponents had lied to her. Judges had ruled unfairly. There had even been a few bitter remarks about men.

But this morning, he would not quarrel with anyone about what was possible. He drove—but his heart was airborne. Right now a beautiful russet-haired woman slept in his bed, a woman with slender shoulders and a network of golden freckles on her back. He, Arthur Raven, had exhausted himself making love to a woman he desired, a woman he had desired for so long that she was the image of desire. He spoke to Pamela about the case, but his mind, like a homing signal, came back to Gillian, and he had to struggle to keep laughter from frothing up out of his chest.

She was a convict, of course. His spirit frolicked along a mesa with deep gorges on either side. There was Rommy, shown to be guilty after months of desperate labor. And now and then he recalled the sick fog of disgrace that hovered over Gillian. At those instants, he remembered her warnings about how soon she would disappoint him. But then, almost against his nature, he allowed himself to be engulfed again by a syrupy joy.

At the institution, they waited as always. When Arthur phoned the office, his assistant read him the motion that Muriel had filed this morning with the Court of Appeals, asking it to bar further proceedings in Gandolph's case. She'd included transcripts of both depositions, Genevieve's and Erno's, and argued what Arthur would have in her place—the issue was not Erdai but Rommy. The state was under no obligation to establish whether Erno was a bitter freak taking grim pleasure in overturning one more ap- plecart before exiting the planet, or sincere, albeit deluded. The sole question for the court was whether a substantial basis ex- isted to believe that Rommy Gandolph had not had a fair opportunity previously to con- test the charges against him. Genevieve's testimony, obviously reluctant, had only in- creased the sum total of evidence of Gandolph's guilt. In that light, the litigation had gone on long enough. Applying to the Court of Appeals, rather than Harlow, Muriel might as well have labeled her paper 'Mo- tion to Prevent Further Rulings by Bleeding Heart Judge,' but the Court of Appeals was, probably, the proper venue, and its judges in any event would defend their jurisdiction in their ongoing battles with Kenton Harlow. Arthur and Pamela would have to begin framing a response shortly, a challenging task if Rommy did not have some answer to Genevieve.

As Rommy's case had gained notice, there had been two fairly obvious reactions from the staff in the penitentiary to Arthur and Pamela's frequent arrivals. Most of the correctional officers, who identified them- selves with law enforcement, greeted the lawyers coldly. The Warden, for example, had initially denied them a visit today, claiming the usual shortage of personnel, relenting only after Arthur had called the General Counsel for the Department of Corrections. Yet there were others in the prison hierarchy who were more sympathetic. To them, it was a long-accepted fact that a percentage of prisoners were not as bad as all that, and that there were even a few who were actually innocent. After daily contact with Rommy for a decade, several of the guards liked him and a few had even implied to Arthur that it was preposterous to think Rommy could ever have been a murderer. In the guardhouse today, Arthur caught a sidelong glance from a female lieutenant at the front desk who had been particularly warm for weeks now, and who apparently felt ill used after seeing the headlines in the last twenty-four hours. Being himself, Arthur felt a flush of shame that he'd misled her and so many others.

Rommy had to know why his lawyers had abruptly appeared. The inmates were inveterate TV watchers, and the prison grapevine, the chief vehicle for news of the world outside, moved at the speed of the

Internet. Yet Rommy, chained hand and foot, sauntered to his side of the glass in the attorney room, looking thin and lost, but virtually effervescent.

"Hey, hey, how you-all doin?" He asked Pamela, as he did every time, whether she'd brought her wedding gown. This was perhaps their tenth visit, and it still remained unclear to both of them whether Rommy's proposals were in earnest. "So how you-all been?" he asked. To Rommy, it was a social call. In point of fact, he was growing accustomed to visitors. The Reverend Dr. Blythe and his minions were here often, events Arthur could trace because of the regularity with which Blythe's harsh rhetoric was echoed, in whatever mangled form, by his client.

"We've had a setback," Arthur said, then realized that the term was probably beyond Rommy, who had great difficulty with nuance. Rather than explain, Arthur simply asked him if he remembered Genevieve Carriere from the airport.

"Black, ain she?"

"White."

"Kind of plump?"

"Right."

"And she got this gold cross with a little sapphire she always wearin?"

Arthur recalled the jewel only now that Rommy mentioned it. There was no faulting a thief's eye. He found his throat thickening around the next question.

"Well, did you ever tell her you wanted to kill Luisa Remardi?"

"Is that what she sayin?"

"That's right."

Rommy narrowed his face to a walnut, concentrating as if this had not been the talk of the cellblock for hours.

"I don't think I done said that to her. Nnn-uhh." He continued to shake his head with growing confidence. When Arthur peeked at Pamela, who was holding the telephone handpiece between them, some of the light seemed restored to her long face. "No," said Rommy. "I think the onliest one I gone on to like that was the other dude. And ain no-body seed him in years."

"Like what?"

"You know. Killin and all that. Her. The lady."

"You did say that?"

"But I'm sayin, he gone and all, that other dude. He got hisself cracked, even before them po-lice come down on me. Must have been into somethin nasty. Dudes he kicked with, they was like, he ain never gone come out. But I ain seen him down here. He doin fed time, or he dead, how I figure."

"What dude are we talking about?"

"Dude what was getting them airline tickets from the lady."

Arthur looked down at his yellow pad. He had a habit of rubbing the few woolly patches left on his head, as if he couldn't wait to get it over with, and he caught himself doing this now. Pamela and he had talked to Rommy countless times and never heard a word about airline tickets. When Arthur started at the firm, Raymond Horgan had told him, 'Remember, not only is your client his own worst enemy, he is also yours.'

"Are you talking about Pharaoh?" asked Arthur.

Rommy actually smiled. "Tha's him. Tha's what he was callin hisself. Couldn't hardly 'member his name."

Pamela inquired if Rommy had any memory of Pharaoh's last name.

"Might be I knowed another name, but all I recollect is Pharaoh." He spelled it out in four letters: F, a, r, o. Pamela smiled fleetingly.

"And how did you meet him?" Arthur asked.

"I ain too sure 'bout that. I knowed him awhile. I'm thinkin could be he used to hook me up. But I ain seed him in a long time. Then I run across't him in a club. I was doin some bidness, and how you like that, there he is, didn't even 'member his name, but he knowed me. We got to kickin. He had hisself a whole new scene. How you call it?" Squirrel asked himself.

"Stealing," said Arthur. At his side, Pamela recoiled, delivering a stark look, but he didn't really care. This was getting worse by the minute. As for his client, Rommy had learned long ago to humor rather than confront his antagonists. He chuckled amiably at his lawyer.

"No, I knowed that word," he said. "He had somethin goin where he was tellin me he could unload hot airline tickets and never get cracked or nothin. Pushin them through some company. So he had in mind if maybe I knowed somebody might get some tickets for him, be good for us both. Tha's how the lady got into it."

"Luisa? Remind us how you knew Luisa," said Arthur. From the corner of his eyes, he issued a warning look to Pamela. He didn't want her trying to dig Rommy out from under any of his earlier lies.

"She been takin some stuff off me, actually."

"Stuff? You mean stolen merchandise?"

"Stole?" countered Rommy. "I didn't never aks no man his bidness. If I could make a dollar, tha's all I wanted to know."

"But Luisa bought from you?"

"Wasn't nothin really. They was one them dispatch guys over at T&L, with the trucks? Him and me put some stuff on the street. She took a radio, I 'member. That's how I knowed her to start. She was always kind of a talky one. Middle of the night, they wasn't a whole lot for her to be doin. She be rappin to the walls if it wasn't for me. The other, what'd you say her name—"

"Genevieve?"

"She just liked to sit with her book, if they wasn't no planes. I ain never talked with her much. She probably don't even know my name, truth be told. Must be she sayin she know me cause that po-lice got her like he done with me. Ain that right?" Rommy peered over a hand to see how this defense, undoubtedly assembled for him last night by prison mates, would go down. Arthur suggested he continue.

"Well, tha's all. I aksed that other lady, Lisa, one night, said I knowed somebody might want to buy some extra tickets. She wasn't too interested to start, but I kept aksin—Pharaoh, he said this here was real money—and finally she say she gone meet up with this dude just to be done with it. Was over there by Gus's, and I's kinda walkin by the window, cause ol Gus was there and I couldn't go in. She seem to be shakin her head mostly, but Pharaoh, he musta tole her somethin good cause no more'n a week later, she gimme a nice handful of green money, mine for doin the hookup and all.

"Then I didn't hear no more of it. So one day, I's on them streets and yo, man, there's that Pharaoh and it falls out, man, he and this lady, Lisa, they been doin somethin together every month or two. And I ain gettin no more. Pharaoh, he like, I thought for sure she be kickin down to you, she sure as hell gettin some on her end to do that. So I told him I's gonna kill her next I see her, holdin out on me like that. That ain right, not a-tall. And she knowed it, too, even though she wudn't admit it. We scream and holler some, but in the end she give me that necklace thing to shut me up."

"The cameo?"

"'Zactly. She gimme that to hold on to, cause she been afraid I's carryin on so round there at the airport, badmouthin with one person and another, she gone lose her job or somethin. Said that necklace was the most precious thing to her with her babies' pictures inside, and once I had that I's gone know she gettin me the money. Only she didn't never get round to it."

"So you killed her," said Arthur.

Rommy sat straight back. He frowned in a manner that seemed, against all Arthur's inner warnings, entirely spontaneous.

"You thinkin that now, too? You gone over with them po-lice?"

"You didn't answer me, Rommy. I asked you if you killed Luisa."

"No, hell no. I ain the kind to kill nobody. I's just woofin a little, cause she made me look so bad with my man Pharaoh and all."

Rommy tried all the inept little tricks he'd affected throughout his messed-up life to enhance his credibility. He gave a small crippled smile and waved a thin hand, but eventually, as Arthur continued to study him, Rommy reverted to his fearful, skittery look. Still scrutinizing his client so intently that he might have been a code, Arthur thought suddenly of Gillian—not so much her plea to cling to hope but rather the sweetness of loving her. He felt somehow that protecting the Rommys of the world from the harshness that befell them was a piece of that. Those people were his, because, save for his father, he might well have been Rommy. Susan was Rommy. The planet was full of creatures in need, who could not really fend, and the law was at its best when it ensured that they were treated with dignity. He needed all of that in his life—love and purpose. He did not know, now that he'd finally embraced that, if he would ever be able to let go.

So with the desperation with which he wanted love, he wanted to believe Rommy. But he could not. Rommy had a motive to kill Luisa. He had said he would do it. And then, when he had been caught with her cameo in his pocket, he'd admitted he had done it. It could not have all been a coincidence.

While Arthur deliberated, Pamela was

watching him, as if she needed his permission to hope herself. He moved his chin back and forth very slightly to let her know where he stood. Her look in response was deadened but resigned. It was she who then put the right question to their client.

"Why didn't you tell us this, Rommy? Any of it? We've talked with you about this case I don't know how many times."

"You didn't never aks. I tole all them lawyers what aksed."

There was always a point with Rommy when belief in his utter guilelessness evaporated, or more properly, where it was revealed as yet another mask. He may have had an IQ south of 75, but he knew how to be deceitful. From the start, he had realized the impact the truth about Luisa would have on Arthur and Pamela and their enthusiasm for his case. He knew that because he had seen what happened before, when he had told his earlier lawyers about fencing tickets with Luisa, getting shortchanged, and vowing to kill her. At the start, Arthur had decided not to pierce Rommy's privilege with any of his former attorneys, bearing in mind the motto he had repeated to Pamela the day they first met Rommy—new lawyer, new story. But there was no longer any mystery about why Rommy's trial counsel had used an insanity defense or why their successors had never challenged Rommy's guilt. Given his prior education, Rommy had no trouble reading what was on his present lawyers' faces.

"I ain kill't nobody," he repeated. "I ain the kind." Then even he seemed to acknowledge the pointlessness of his protests. His shoulders lost shape and he looked away. "That don't mean they ain gone kill me though, do it?"

Arthur would do his duty and fight. He would remind the appellate court of Erno's confession and the tardiness of Genevieve's testimony about Rommy's threat. But there was nothing to substantiate Erno, while Genevieve's version was consistent with all the known facts. Its sincerity was bolstered by her reluctance. Worst of all, as Arthur now knew, what she'd said was true.

"No," said Arthur. "It doesn't mean that."

"Yeah," said Rommy, "I knowed that, cause I already started in havin the dream again last night."

"What dream?" asked Pamela.

"How they comin to git me. How it's time.

When I was first in Condemned, I's havin that dream all the time. Wake up, you sweatin so, you smell bad to your own self, I swear. Sometime I think they ain gonna have to bother killin me. All us Yellows, we always talkin 'bout it. You hear some dude cryin in the night, man, you know he done had the dream. It ain right a-tall to do that to a man, make him hear all that. They let me outta here," said Rommy, "I ain never gone be right."

Neither Arthur nor Pamela could find a response to that.

"You know, man, I been here when they come for a guy. Couple days before, they take you down there to the death house. Move you and all, I guess, when you still got some hope, so you don start in strugglin or nothin. Man, the last guy they done, Rufus Tryon, he was next cell to me, man. He wudn't gone let them take him. Say he gone get somebody 'fore he go. They wump him good. Even so, they say he done it again at the end. Had that last meal and throwed it all up on hisself—probably had some broken bones when they tied him in, but it don't matter none then, do it? You think it's better to get drug in or just walk, let them do what they gone do?"

Pamela was nearly as red as a stoplight. She finally scraped out some word of consolation and told their client that the best thing was not to have to go in there at all. Rommy, who knew a joke when he heard it, offered his jack-o'-lantern smile.

"Yeah, tha's better all right, but still and all, you got to think on it. Gets on your mind, too. How'm I gone let them do me? Most of the time, I's thinking, walk in there with your head up. I ain done nothin anybody ought to be killin me for. I stole some stuff, but you can't get death for that, right? But that-all's what I'm gone get anyway."

Past the point of professional dignity, Pamela had surrendered to promises she could not keep.

"No, you aren't."

"Yeah, I'm use to it. I mean, that got to be some time, don't you think, knowin someone gone kill you? Thinkin to youself and all, I go walk down that hall and somebody gone kill me, this here the last walk, this the last stuff I'm gone see and I cain't do nothin about it. That got to be some time. Man, I look down that way, in my head and all, I start to shake so bad." Rommy hunched up his shoulders and, in the sight of his lawyers, dwelled with that terror. "Man, you doin all you doin, but I'm still here. Ain nothing changed for me."

Rommy's anger was usually a shadow even to himself, but he suddenly marshaled much of it, due undoubtedly to the influence of the good Reverend Dr. Blythe. But at least Rommy found the rare strength there to bring his sepia eyes directly to Arthur's through the glass.

"I'm innocent, man," he said then, "I ain kill't nobody."

28

Secrets of the Pharaoh

EVENING IN THE OFFICE. At her vast desk, Muriel moved through the papers which had awaited her all day. On the rare nights when she and Talmadge were both home, she would bundle the draft indictments, the mail, and the memos into her case, and after dinner read everything over in bed, occasionally seeking her husband's advice while the TV blared, the sheepdog and the cat competed for space on the covers, and Talmadge, loud at the best of times, held forth in a body-shaking timbre as he talked overseas, still unpersuaded that he did not have to shout across the ocean.

But she preferred the solitary stillness of the office at six. When she was done tonight, like most nights, she would put in an appearance at a fund-raiser for a pol or a cause, banking a little more capital for her own campaign. Muriel would remember her precise destination only as she departed, when she picked up the file her assistant had left outside her door.

For the moment, she was intent on a series of responses to a memorandum she'd circulated late last week, proposing a pilot diversion program for first-time narcotics offenders. The Chief Judge had signed off with timid commentary, intended to garner no blame if anything went wrong. Naturally, the General Counsel of the Police Force was opposed—the police wanted everybody in jail. Ned's one-word note read, "Timing?" He wouldn't put more in writing, but he was concerned about the political ramifications of allowing dope peddlers—albeit small-timers—back on the street in an election year. Yet Muriel would brave it. Counseling and job training were far cheaper than prison and trial, and she'd defang the right by talking up the tax savings; at the same time this initiative would help forestall Blythe and his camp followers in the minority communities. More important, it was the right thing to do. Kids with the guile and energy to sell drugs could still find a place in the legitimate world, if you got them started.

"I'm sick of using the criminal justice system to clean up other people's messes," she wrote back to Ned. 'The other people' she had in mind were the schools, the social service network, the economic institutions, but Ned didn't need a lecture. Nonetheless, she recognized the voice resounding through her note—her father's. Tom Wynn was gone more than twelve years, but she heard herself uttering his populist wisdom frequently these days, and with more pleasure than she would have imagined a decade ago. Courtroom dramatics, much as she relished them, were already receding into her past—in fact, Erno Erdai might be the last man she ever cross-examined. She wanted to affect more than one life at a time. And the brute truth of prosecution was that you rarely made anybody's existence much better. You stopped the bleeding. You prevented more pain. But you didn't walk out of the building at night expecting to see any trees you'd planted.

Her inside line rang. Her first thought was Talmadge, but the Caller I.D. showed Larry's cell phone.

"You're working late," she said.

"No, you are. I'm at home. But I just thought of something. And I had a guess I'd find you there. I'm calling to tell on myself."

"Have you been naughty, Larry?"

"I've been a moron. Was it me you were stroking the other day about being so smart?"

"To the best of my recollection."

"Maybe you should ask for a recount," Larry said now.

Muriel wondered if this conversation was picking up where they'd left off. She'd never regarded herself as introspective by any measure. All her life, she'd been so bound up in being in the world, in doing, that she was liable to lose track of herself, like the fact that she was starving or needed the bathroom. Yet in the weeks since she'd been to Atlanta, she seemed to be spending a lot of time with her fingers on her own pulse. And one of the main questions that leaped out of the underbrush in her mind several times each day was exactly what was going on with Larry and her. It wasn't breaking news when Larry had informed her on the way to Atlanta that she'd settled for less in her marriage. Reflective or not, she'd understood that much. What she'd missed was the repetitive nature of her mistakes.

She had married idols, knowing all along she'd been rubbing her toes on clay feet at night. It would require some time, maybe a century or two, for her to sort out what that meant about her.

For the present, Larry was the puzzle. She was glad she'd put him on the spot the other day after Genevieve's dep, trying to get him to say why he'd been so determined to wise her up to herself. Was he wreaking vengeance or offering an alternative? It was obvious Larry had no clue, which was just as well, because she wasn't sure either possibility would have made her particularly happy.

As he went on now, she realized he had not called for a personal discussion.

"I actually went to visit with Rocky Madhafi at Gang Crimes this a.m.," he said, "and I'm there telling him how I've got to find some gangbanger called the Pharaoh and all the sudden I see the light. Remember you told me to dig up the guy Erno shot at Ike's four years ago?"

"Sure."

"Well, do you remember his name?"

Eventually, she said, "Cole."

"What about his first name?"

She was blank.

"F, a, r, o," said Larry.

She took a second to get it, and her initial reaction was skeptical. For some reason, she'd assumed 'Faro' was pronounced like 'Fargo.'

"Well, there's a good way to find out if it's the same guy," Larry said. "I mean, maybe there is. That's what I just thought of."

For the hearing in front of Harlow, Larry and she had assembled a transfer case full of documents, which was now in the bay window behind Muriel's desk. Among the records was a photocopy of the address book the evidence tech had found in Luisa's purse at Paradise a decade ago. Originally, Muriel was planning to cross Erdai on the fact that his name wasn't in there, but she decided to forgo it, since Arthur would just argue that a woman having an affair wouldn't be calling her married lover at home. Muriel pulled the phone down to the carpet beside her and talked to Larry as she thumbed through the papers until she'd found the copy.

"No 'Faro Cole,'" Muriel announced.

The sound of his cell spit on the line. "Check under F?" Larry asked finally.

She hadn't. 'Faro' was written in pen, in Luisa's precise hand, which looked as if it had been inscribed against a ruler. 'Cole' had been added in pencil some time later.

"Fuck," Larry said.

"Time-out," Muriel said. She rewound and tried to go through it on her own. "Erno shot Luisa's fence six years later? Is that a coincidence? Or do we know there's a connection between Erdai and him?"

"When Erno was arrested at Ike's," Larry said, "right after the shooting, Erno claimed Cole went off because Erdai had investigated him way back when for some kind of ticket fraud. Had to be referring to the scam Faro had run with Luisa and Squirrel, right?"

Larry had been thinking about this all day and was way ahead of her. She asked how he got that.

"Because we figured out last week that Erdai must have pieced together what the three of them were up to. That's why he had Luisa searched. And Genevieve said she had mentioned Faro's name to Erno. He must have found him."

"And why is Faro pissed enough at Erdai six years later to come after him with a gun?"

"I don't know, not exactly, but in the five-sheets on the shooting, the coppers all said that Faro was screaming about how Erdai owed him for messing up his life. He must have put Faro out of business somehow. That would be like Erno, right? Whether Luisa was dead or not, he was still the sheriff in that town. It's the same as I figured the other day. Erdai wanted the bad guys to get theirs. He just couldn't let on that he could have saved Luisa's life."

"So is this good news or bad news?"

"Christ," said Larry, "it's gotta be good. It's gotta be great. Remember how Erno jumped out of the witness chair when you asked him about the shooting? Didn't want to go near it. Five gets you ten, that's because he knew Faro could tell you what a load of crap Erdai was peddling on the stand. I say this boy Faro is going to give you the movie version of the coming attractions we heard from Genevieve last week. It'll be *Squirrel the Asshole Murderer* in Technicolor."

She thought it over, but Larry was making sense.

"The only hitch," he said, "is I spent a good week pissing for shit and giggles looking for this Faro. Near as I can tell, he flew up his own behind." From what he'd found, Larry said, Faro Cole seemed to have appeared on the local scene in 1990, when he'd applied for a driver's license. He had an address and a phone, but was gone a year later, then returned in 1996 at another apartment. Once he was released from the hospital in 1997, following the shooting, he skipped again.

Larry had made dozens of calls and had canvassed both prior addresses with Dan Lipranzer, but had added little to what they already knew, except that Faro was six three, 220 pounds, and born in 1965. Any paperwork, like credit reports or employment history which the phone company or his landlords had gathered, was destroyed long ago, and the state archived only the written data from his driver's license. Faro Cole had no arrest record here—or elsewhere, according to the FBI. That was unusual for a fence, but Larry checked several precincts, and no one knew Faro's name. In desperation, Larry had even called a little birdie he had at Social Security who whispered in his ear now and then about whether payroll taxes had been paid on a number anywhere in the country. These days, Faro Cole appeared to be jobless or dead or using another name.

"A guy who came into a bar waving a gun around," Larry said, "I'd have figured they'd put some charges on him, but I guess with Faro bleeding out on Ike's floor, nobody was thinking much about that. Undertaker looked like a better bet than the paramedics. Anyway, there's no mug shot or prints. The only thing I find from the case is Faro's gun and the shirt they stripped off him in surgery—still inventoried in evidence, actually. I thought if I send the pistol over to Mo Dickerman, it's possible he can pick up a print on it. Maybe with that, we find Faro under another name."

Dickerman was the Chief Fingerprint Examiner and as good as anyone in the country. Muriel liked that idea.

"And if you want to pop for it out of the P.A.'s budget," Larry said, "we can do DNA on the blood on the shirt, too. See if he's in CODIS." CODIS stood for Combined DNA Index System, but that was a $5,000 long-shot. Larry, however, wanted to pull out all the stops, and she didn't fight him.

"Happy?" she asked, as she had last week. Once again Larry hesitated.

"I'm still missing something," he said.

"Maybe you miss me, Larry." She found that line hilarious, but she didn't linger on the phone to see if he, too, was laughing.

29

JULY 2001

Together

THEY WERE TOGETHER whenever they were not at work. For Gillian, who had defied the inclination to cling even in junior high, the experience was otherworldly. Arthur stayed in the office until she was done at the store, then picked her up for dinner at eight or nine. Usually she'd shopped at the gourmet counter at Morton's and was waiting with a heavy shopping bag when Arthur's round sedan cruised to the curb. At his apartment, they made love and ate and made love again. Most nights she slept there and returned to her place at Duffy's for a few hours once Arthur left for work.

Consuming physical passion had never really been part of any of her prior relationships. Now Arthur and the stimulation of sex remained at the periphery of her mind throughout the day. Often some stray association she could not even name sent a pleasing throb through her breasts and pelvis. Arthur and she seemed stuck in the sweet valley of sensation. The strong stalk that grew from Arthur was like some secret self. Real life commenced here. This was the moist cellar of being, the dark mysterious foundation rooms. If she—or Arthur—had previously made the descent they might have an idea how to rise up from time to time, but now they seemed melted together at the core of pleasure.

"I'm an addict," she said one night, and was immediately struck dumb by her carefree remark. There were a thousand thoughts she was unwilling to explore.

Their languor was reinforced by Gillian's reluctance to carry their affair beyond Arthur's bedroom. It seemed impossible to her that their relationship could survive once they began to mix with others, once they inserted themselves in the context of history and expectations and endured judgment and gossip. Like some enchantment, what existed between them would perish in the light of day.

Arthur, on the other hand, would have

been just as happy to take out front-page advertisements announcing his dedication to her, and he was frequently frustrated by her unwillingness to venture out together, even to visit the homes of his high-school and college friends who he insisted would be discreet and accepting. Instead, the only consistent company they kept was with Arthur's sister, Susan. Every Tuesday, they drove to the Franz Center for Susan's injection and the subsequent trip to the apartment. On the way back, Arthur narrated the events of his day, pretending Susan was keeping track. At the lights, she would glance to the backseat, almost as if she were checking that Gillian was still there.

In the apartment, the agenda was always identical to their first evening together. Gillian remained largely an outsider as Arthur and Susan cooked, then Susan retreated with her plate to the television set. She spoke to Gillian infrequently. But when she did, the salvaged Susan, the coherent personality which collected inside her, the asteroid in a belt of space dust and gravel, was in charge. She never confronted Gillian with her madness.

One night Arthur had to reset a circuit breaker in the basement. Seeking another cigarette, Susan approached Gillian on her kitchen stool. She now trusted Gillian to trigger the lighter for her, and she took in the first breath as if she hoped to reduce the entire cigarette to ash with a single drag.

"I don't understand you," Susan said. Shielded by the bluish veil she'd released between them, Susan darted her pretty green eyes toward Gillian.

"You don't?"

"I keep changing my mind. Are you a Compliant or a Normal?"

Gillian was taken aback, not by what Susan was suggesting, but because on her own, Susan had adopted the same coinage Gillian had applied at Alderson to the travelers on the trains that clattered past the prison boundary. They were Normals to Gillian not due to any inherent superiority, but because they were free of the stigma of confinement. That, undoubtedly, was how Susan regarded the so-called sane.

"I'm trying to be a Normal," Gillian said. "Sometimes it feels as if I am. Especially when I'm with Arthur. But I'm still not sure."

There was no more to the conversation,

but a few nights later, Arthur called out to Gillian in excitement. She found him in the apartment's second bedroom, where the only light was the cool glow from his office laptop, which he lugged home every evening.

"Susan sent you an e-mail!"

Gillian approached the screen with caution. As she read, she sank slowly to Arthur's knee.

> *Arthur give this to Gillian.*
> *DON'T READ IT. It's not for you.*

Hi, Gillian.
Please do not get too excited about this. I have been working on this e-mail for three days now and Valerie has given me some help. Usually, I cannot put down more than a sentence or two. There are only so many moments in the day when I'm able to hold on to words long enough to write them, especially when they are about me. Either I can't remember the term for the feeling, or the feeling disappears when I recall the word. Most of the time, my mind is fragments. Normals don't seem to un-

derstand that, but for me the usual state in my head is images jumping up and disappearing like the flames over a burning log.

But I am having good days and I had some things I could never tell you face-to-face. Conversation is so hard for me. I cannot handle everything at once. Just the look in someone's eyes can be distracting. Let alone smiling or joking. Questions. A new saying is enough to send me off for several minutes, wherever it leads. It is better for me like this.

What did I mean to say?

I like you. I think you know that. You don't look down on me. You have been to some bad places—I can feel that. But the more I see you, the more I realize we are not the same, even though I wish we were. I'd really like to think I can make it back the way you have. I want you to know how hard I try. I think to Normals it appears as if I just want to succumb. But it takes a lot of strength to hold my own. I am afraid whenever I see a radio, or hear one. I go down the street all the time saying Don't listen, Don't listen. And the sight of people on the bus with headphones may be my undoing. I hear only the voices I don't want to whenever I see those pads over somebody's ears.

Even as I am typing these words, I can literally feel the electricity coming out of the keyboard, and there is no way to turn off the certainty that someone like the Great Oz is out there at the heart of the Net, waiting to take me over. All my strength goes into resisting. I'm like those people in movies I remember from childhood, where there is a ship-wreck and huge waves, and the survivors are paddling desperately in the water holding on to a life ring or a piece of floating junk, so they don't go down.

I can see you are trying every day, too. Keep trying. Keep trying. It would be harder for me if I ever saw someone like you give up. You make Arthur happy. It is easier for me when he is happy. I don't have to feel I've ruined his life. Please do your best to keep him happy. Not just for me. For him. He deserves to be happy. It would be horrible if you weren't with him. It is better with three.

Your friend,
Susan

Gillian was devastated. It was like receiving a letter from someone held for ransom, someone you knew would never be freed. When she allowed Arthur to read the screen, he, predictably, wept. The messages he got were seldom more than ten or twenty words, produced in the isolated moments of coherence that fell upon Susan briefly every day, like a magic spell. But he was not envious so much as moved by his sister's concern for him—and also, to Gillian's eye, suddenly frightened.

"What is she worried about?" Arthur asked. Gillian refused to answer. But she felt a pall encroaching. Even someone as perpetually hopeful as Arthur had to consider a peril that was obvious to a madwoman.

That night, when they made love there

was an absence—still tender but more an-
chored here on earth. Afterwards, as Gillian
reached to the bedside table for a cigarette,
Arthur asked the question neither of them
had ever ventured aloud.

"What do you think will happen with us?"

At the inception, she'd made her predic-
tions, and much as she would have it
otherwise, her view had not changed.

"I think in time, you'll move on, Arthur.
Perhaps build on what you've learned about
yourself with me and find someone your
own age. Marry. Have babies. Have your
life." She was startled to find how fully she'd
envisioned the outcome. Arthur, naturally,
was taken aback and pulled himself up on
an elbow to glower.

"Don't pretend you don't understand,
Arthur. This would have been far better for
you at another stage."

"What stage is that?"

"If you were twenty-five or fifty-five the
difference in our ages might matter less. But
you should have children, Arthur. Don't you
want children? Most people do."

"Don't you?"

"It's too late, Arthur." That was the ultimate calamity of the penitentiary: it had

taken the last of her childbearing years. But that thought was down there in the valley with the broken bodies of a million regrets.

"Why is it too late?" he demanded. "Are we talking about biology? The world is full of children who need someone to love them." In her presence these days, Arthur was often impetuous, even inspired. Was there any difference greater among human beings than between the abject fatalist who had been run down by living, and those determined to shape their lives to the contours of a large idea? And she was his idea. Oh, she willed herself to reject that, to cross her wrists before her face and forbid his exhilaration in her company, as her father forbade blaspheming. But it was far too wonderful, far too much of what she had assumed she would never have again. He did not see her yet. And when she came chillingly into focus, he would be gone. But she was determined to savor the moment. She took him into a lingering embrace, before she resumed the slow march to the truth.

"Don't you see, Arthur, you're already trying to find a way to have with me everything you want in your life. This is an adventure for you, this entire period. But when it ends, you won't be able to abandon what you've always imagined for yourself."

"Are you saying you'd never want to be a parent?"

It was inconceivable. Her own survival still required her full attention.

"It would be an enormous change, Arthur."

"But that's the point of life, isn't it? Changing? To be happier, more perfect? Look how much you've changed. You believe you've changed for the better, don't you?"

She had never thought of it that way.

"I really don't know," she said. "I like to believe I have. I like to believe I wouldn't make the same mess of my life. But I'm not certain."

"I am. You're sober."

"Yes."

"And you've had no trouble doing that."

She felt a superstitious reluctance to agree. But Arthur was correct. Formally, she adhered to the mantra of one day at a time. Yet except for her most dismal moments of panic, she had not felt even a remote yearning. Clarity, in fact, seemed much more her quest. The completeness of her release from addictive hungers was troubling at times, because it seemed at such odds with the reports of other persons who battled dependencies. One night she'd asked Duffy if she was fooling herself. He'd taken his time looking at her. 'No, Gil,' he finally said, 'I think you already accomplished everything you meant to.'

She repeated Duffy's answer to Arthur now, but he was too intent on his own point to linger over the meaning of the remark.

"So you're free, then," Arthur said.

No. That was the word. She was different. But not free.

"Have you changed, Arthur?"

"Are you kidding? This is the happiest I've ever been. It's not close."

"Truly, Arthur, wouldn't you be happier with someone your age?"

"No. Never. I mean, I'm an old-fashioned guy. I like things that are against all odds. Love as destiny. I still watch '30s movies and cry."

"I'm not that old, Arthur."

He poked her but continued. "I'm happy," he insisted. "Nothing could make this better, Gillian. I'd like to break into song."

She groaned at the thought. Challenged,

Arthur, round and short, stood up naked in the center of the bed and crooned.

I dreamed of someone like you.
You seem too marvelous for
it to be true.

The second line was like a stake through her heart. But he continued. Typical of Arthur's ability to surprise, he had a fine voice, and he had clearly spent hours listening to schmaltzy show tunes. At peak volume, he sang every line, every chorus, until Gillian, for the first time in years, had lost herself in laughter.

30

JULY 24, 2001

Bad for Me

FOR ERNO ERDAI, the deathwatch had begun. Even as a state prisoner, Erno had been granted the benefit of many of the latest high-tech treatments over at the University Hospital, not only surgical procedures but alpha interferon and experimental forms of chemotherapy. But an ancient enemy had caught him at a low point. In the midst of a new round of chemo, Erno had contracted pneumonia, and despite enormous intravenous doses of antibiotics, his lungs, already compromised by the cancer, did not seem healthy enough to recover. The doctors with whom Pamela and Arthur had spoken were increasingly pessimistic.

Erno was again in the jail ward in County Hospital. Effectively, Arthur needed the consent of both the Superintendent of the

House of Corrections and Erno's family before he could see him, and one party or the
other had been holding him off for weeks.
Finally, Arthur had threatened to go to Judge
Harlow. Harlow would not order Erno to
speak, but he would forbid any obstruction
by those who either were doing Muriel's bid-
ding or thought they had her interests at
heart. Arthur had twice won delays for filing
a response to Muriel's motion in the Court of
Appeals to terminate Rommy's *habeas* by
claiming that further time was needed for investigation, which basically meant seeing
Erno. The court had given him a final deadline of Friday this week, which had added to
the urgency of getting to Erdai.

After more than an hour in the ward
vestibule, Arthur was admitted at last. He
was searched cursorily and escorted back
along the linoleum corridors, where the light
of the schoolhouse fixtures spread gener-
ously before him.

The deputy assigned to Erno explained
that the family was agitated because their
visit had been interrupted to make way for
Arthur. Drawing close to the room, he saw
two women in the hallway. One was shorter
than the other and somewhat dowdier. She

proved to be Mrs. Erdai. Her nose was red and a balled-up Kleenex grew from her fist. The other, wearing a straight skirt perhaps too short for a woman of her age, was Erno's sister, Ilona, the mother of Collins, the man whom Erno had started out to save. She was tall and sturdy, with long hands and light hair losing color, overall a better-looking version of Erno—the same thin face, and a hardness that crept through it. With little said, the two women made clear that they resented everything about Arthur, his intrusion and, worse, the humiliation he'd wrought for Erno, which would survive for them long after his passing, even as it went for naught. Ilona, who had her brother's piercing light eyes, delivered a haunting, magisterial look of reproof. Arthur promised to be only a moment.

On the phone, the nurse had said Erno was feverish but usually lucid. His condition was complicated by the fact that his cancer had reached his bones and was causing great pain. At this point, the principal problem in his care was balancing the opiates against a respiratory system on the verge of collapse.

When Arthur entered, Erno was asleep

and looked very much a man about to die. He'd lost more weight since his court appearance. The new round of chemo had killed off about half his hair, leaving little weedy patches here and there. Several IV's ran into his arms, and his nosepiece had now been replaced by a plastic oxygen mask that clouded with each shallow breath. Erno was also experiencing some kind of liver involvement. His skin was virtually the same color as a legal pad. Another yellow man, Arthur thought.

Pulling up a chair, he waited for Erno to awaken. In his mind, Arthur had tried out a hundred scenarios in the hopes that Erno would redeem his credibility, but Arthur hadn't seen yet how both Genevieve and Erno could be telling the truth. Muriel, who had called Arthur yesterday to remind him that she would oppose any further extensions in the time to respond to her motion, had a new theory about Erno's motive for lying.

'He's against the death penalty now,' she said. 'He fingered Rommy for execution and now he's gone through this big Catholic revival and won't die in mortal sin, so he's trying to prevent it the only way he can.' It was not very persuasive, but Arthur regarded it as an improvement over Muriel's earlier approach in that it didn't make Erno out to be a monster. In fact, as he sat here, Arthur felt quite a bit of tenderness toward Erdai. He could not fathom why at first, but as the minutes passed with the nurses' voices and the bells and beeps resounding from the hall, he realized that Erno looked a good deal like Harvey Raven had in his final days. The thought of his father and the valor of his supposedly ordinary existence as always filled Arthur with sentiment, but the chasm seemed less deep now that Gillian was in his life.

Returning to the present, he realized that Erno was staring at him through the horizontal bars of the bed rail. Arthur had been asked to wear a paper face mask and he pulled it down so Erdai could recognize him. Erno's disappointment was plain.

"Hoped you were. My nephew," Erno said. His voice had been whittled to a husk and he had no breath. Nonetheless, Erno smiled faintly at the recollection of Collins. "Coming tonight," he said. "Good boy. Turned out fine. Hard time. But fine. Beautiful kids." Erno closed his eyes, content with that thought.

Arthur gave him a second, then asked if Erno had heard about Genevieve. He nodded. Suddenly, after waiting weeks for this conversation, Arthur could not figure out the next question.

"Well, shit," he finally said, "is it true?"

"Course," whispered Erno. "Why I. Blamed Squirrel."

"Because you knew he'd threatened to kill Luisa?"

"Right." Every effort at communication seemed to require a tautening of Erno's whole body, but he appeared to be tracking well. Erno was saying he'd pinned Luisa's murder on Squirrel in the first place because he'd known about the threat. Erno had killed Luisa for his own reasons, but Squirrel had made himself a scapegoat in advance.

"Told Larry. Subpoena Genevieve." Erno wiggled his chin side to side, chagrined by Larry's stupidity. "Should have figured this out. Ten years ago."

"The tickets, you mean?"

"Not tickets. Not good for me."

"Because you were head of security?"

Erno nodded and tossed his hand around. It was an involved story, apparently, but

Arthur was close enough for the purposes of a man without breath to explain.

"Genevieve." He coughed weakly, swallowed, and closed his eyes to contend with pain that had arisen from somewhere. When he recovered, he seemed to have lost his place.

"Genevieve," said Arthur.

"Didn't think she knew. About tickets."

"Why?"

"Wouldn't have told me about Squirrel. Bad for her friend." Bad because of the peril to Luisa of getting caught for pilfering tickets. Thinking it over, Arthur realized Erno had been close to correct. Genevieve hadn't known about the ticket scam when she reported Rommy's threat. She learned of it only afterwards when Luisa had upbraided her for involving Erdai.

"Right," said Arthur. "So what was Larry supposed to figure out?"

"Luisa. Squirrel. Threat." Erno wove his fingers and tied all ten together. "The rest—" He whittled his face in the air again, to indicate it wouldn't matter. The most likely conclusion, if Genevieve had reported only Rommy's threat to Larry, was that crazy

Squirrel had been disappointed in love. It would do fine for a motive.

"Christ, Erno. Why didn't you tell me this before?"

"Complicated." Erno waited out some kind of spasm. "Bad for Squirrel." He was right about that, too. A story that started with Squirrel threatening to kill Luisa would never have gotten much further. Yet even accepting the good intentions, Arthur could feel his heart falling, for it was clear how conniving Erno had been with the truth.

In pain or reverie, Erno's eyes were still. The full measure of his illness showed there—a web of veins, sallow streaks, a glassy thickening. His lashes were gone and the lids looked inflamed.

"Me too," he said suddenly.

"You too what?" asked Arthur. "It would have been bad for you, too?"

Erno reached up in time to catch a cough, but nodded as he shook.

"Why?" Arthur asked. "Why would it be bad for you?"

"Tickets," said Erno. "Stole tickets, too."

"*You* did?"

Erno nodded again.

"Hell, why would you do that, Erno?"

He gave his hand a disgusted little toss and looked toward the ceiling.

"Stupid," he said. "Needed money. Family problems. Was two years before."

"Before Luisa was doing it?"

"Right. Stopped. But afraid."

"You were afraid?"

"Catch her, catch me." Erno stopped to breathe. "Why I went to restaurant. Stop her. Fought. Gus came with gun." Erno closed his eyes. The rest did not bear repeating.

"So there was never an affair?"

Erno smiled thinly at the notion.

"Jesus Christ," said Arthur. His voice was too loud, but he was suddenly desperate. He had the feeling that often overcame him when things went disastrously wrong, that he was deeply at fault, and that as a consequence he would have liked nothing more than to escape his own skin, shirk it, even peel it off if that was necessary. "Jesus, Erno. Why didn't you *say* this?"

"Pension," he said. "Twenty-three years. For my wife now. Better this way. All around."

Better for Rommy, better for him—that's what Erno meant. Except that like every lie, it could disintegrate along the fault lines of the truth. Arthur calculated. His first instinct was to summon a court reporter, someone who could get this down. But he played out the steps. Muriel's contention that Erno had shaped his tale to his own purposes would be proven. In fact, Erno had perjured himself wantonly before Judge Harlow. In the eyes of the law, therefore, he would be entirely unworthy of belief. And that was before you added in the fact that he was a thief, who'd cheated the employer that had trusted him for more than twenty years.

"Is that all of it, Erno?"

Erdai summoned himself to a decisive nod.

"What about this guy, the Pharaoh?" Arthur asked. "Can we find him?"

"Nobody. Cheap hustler. Gone for years."

"Did he have anything to do with the murders?"

Erno made a little expectorant sound which was the best he could do for a laugh at the thought of yet another suspect. He slowly turned his face back and forth, a gesture he'd apparently repeated often. A bare spot had been worn by the pillow through the frazzle of hair at the rear of his head.

"Me. Just me." He reached between the

slats of the bed rail and took Arthur's hand with fingers hot from fever. "Your guy. Nothing. Not there. Completely innocent." Erno went through the same brief paroxysm, the cough and then the rising and passing of pain. But he had not forgotten where he was. "Completely." Although it required huge effort, Erno rolled himself in Arthur's direction so that he could bring his face closer. The shade of his eyes seemed to have grown more intense, but that was probably just the contrast to his jaundiced complexion. "Larry won't believe me," he whispered. "Too proud."

"Probably."

"I killed all them." The effort of this declaration and the accompanying movement had exhausted him. He fell to his back, still clinging to Arthur's hand. He stared then so fixedly at the ceiling that Arthur was afraid Erno had passed right in front of him, but he felt some stirring yet in Erno's palm. "Think about it," said Erno. "All the time. All I see. All I see. Wanted it different. At the end."

As the conversation had progressed, Arthur could feel a vacuum forming inside him. The world Erno had portrayed—Luisa in the parking lot, the lovers' quarrel that followed—scenes Arthur had visualized as if he'd seen them on film, had been wiped away. Once he left the hospital, what would abide would be the fact, cold as stone, that Erno was a liar, one whose motives were perhaps no better than the grandiose pleasures that came from drawing everyone in. The last version crashed and shattered? Glue together another. Yet here in Erno's presence, Arthur could not doubt him. Perhaps that was simply a credit to Erno's skills as a con. But against all reason, he believed Erdai, just as surely as he'd taken him as a fake before Erno had opened his eyes.

A very long moment passed.

"Always knew this," Erno said then.

"Knew what?"

Erno gathered himself again to roll to the bed rail, and Arthur reached out to help. Erno's shoulder was only bone.

"Me," Erno said and grimaced.

"You?"

"Bad," he said. "Bad life. Why?"

Arthur thought the question was philosophical or religious, but Erno had meant it as a rhetorical query to which he had the answer.

"Always knew," he said. "Too hard."

"What?"

Erno's eyes, rimmed red and bald of lashes, lingered.

"Too hard," he said, "to be good."

31

AUGUST 2, 2001

The Court Rules

"WE WON." Tommy Molto, with his face of vanilla pudding, grabbed Muriel's arm as she left Ned Halsey's office following the morning meeting. The Court of Appeals had issued its opinion: Gandolph's *habeas* had been dismissed and the stay on his execution lifted. "We won," said Tommy again.

Tommy was a strange case. He rarely saw the forest, but he was the guy you wanted if you had to chop down a tree. A decade ago, when Squirrel had been tried, Tommy was the kahuna and Muriel the underling taking lessons. He had never griped as the years passed, as she equaled him in office standing and finally was named Chief Deputy, a job Molto had always coveted. Tommy was Tommy—humorless, dogged, and utterly dedicated to victims, to the police, to the county, and to the fact that the world was better without the company of the people he pursued and convicted. Muriel wrapped him in a huge hug.

"Never a doubt," said Tommy. He departed with a laugh, promising her a copy of the opinion as soon as Carol returned from the courthouse.

Ned by now was visiting with State Senator Malvoin, so she left him a note. On the other side of the large public area that separated Halsey's office from hers, Muriel checked her messages—four reporters had called already—then shut her door. Behind her big desk in the bay window, she closed her eyes, surprised by the magnitude of her relief. In a job like this one, you rode the big waves. There were plenty of good times when you got to shore, and lots of thrills along the way, but you always knew that if you went under for the count, the last thing you'd think as the waves smashed you down to the eternal depths would be, I was a fool, a fool, how could I have risked everything? It wasn't just the election that had been on the line in Rommy Gandolph's case. It was being written off as someone whose career, in the end, had been built on a false foundation.

But the experience—the up and down—
had been worthwhile. For once in her life,
she was actually clear on something: she
wanted to be Kindle County's next Prosecuting Attorney. Losing her grip on the prize
had allowed her to realize how much it
meant to her—both the pride and the consequence that would come with the job. But
she was also certain that if the Gandolph
case had cratered somehow, if her judgment
was publicly scorned and the Reverend
Blythes of the world roadblocked her path to
the adjoining office, she would have remained intact. She didn't believe in a God
who was up there giving hand signals or
pushing around pieces. But if she wasn't
P.A., it might have been for the best. She'd
woken twice in the last several months
thinking of Divinity School. In daylight, the
notion had seemed laughable at first, but
she'd begun to linger with it as a serious alternative. Perhaps she could do more of
what mattered from a pulpit.

With a knock, Carol Keeney, a frail blonde
with a persistent redness at the tip of her
nose, brought in the opinion. Muriel glanced
through it, largely for Carol's sake. Muriel
never had had much concern about the ar-

cane reasoning that emanated from appellate courts. The conflicts in the law that interested her were writ large—guilt or innocence, the rights of individuals against the rights of the community, the proper uses of power. The scrimshaw involved in etching decisions into words was largely decorative in her mind.

"Good job," Muriel told her. Carol had drafted the winning papers, pulling an all-nighter after Genevieve's deposition. Yet they both knew that Carol's failure to suss out what Arthur had been up to when he'd moved to depose Erno would be fatal to Carol's chances to become a trial prosecutor. In this job, Muriel handed out a lot of bad news, not just to defense lawyers and their clients, but within the office, where only a few deputies got the cases and court assignments, the titles and salary increases they desired. With the spoils around here so few, bruising battles were fought among contending egos over three square feet of office space. And Muriel, with Solomonic coolness, decided who won. Carol, who did not have the instincts for trial work, had lost.

"The natives are restless," said Yolanda, one of Muriel's assistants, looking in as

Carol emerged from the office. Yolanda was waving several more phone messages from reporters. Muriel called Dontel Bennett, the office's media spokesman, who congratulated her.

"Tell the pressroom I'll be receiving their abject apologies at noon," Muriel responded.

He laughed and asked whom she wanted beside her on the podium. Molto and Carol on one side, she said. Harold Greer was now the Chief of Police and deserved to be there for many reasons.

"Starczek?" asked Dontel.

"Absolutely," said Muriel. "I'll call him myself."

Before getting off the phone, Dontel said, "No gloating now, girl. Just remember. Skepticism is part of the press's job description."

"You think that comes before or after selling advertising?"

She called several numbers before she found Larry at the desk he rarely occupied at North End Area Two.

"Congratulations, Detective. The Court of Appeals thinks you got the right man."

"No shit."

She read him the better parts of the opinion. He laughed like a greedy child at the end of every line.

"It's time for Meet the Press," she told him then. "Can you pretty yourself up by noon-time?"

"I'll have to see if my plastic surgeon can fit me in. So does this mean I can cancel my cable to Interpol asking for information on Faro?"

"Apparently." The investigation that had been renewed by Erno's testimony was over. For another year or so, the case would probably schlep on with Arthur or some other cause lawyer rolling out barricades to execution. But Larry's job was done, his commerce with her concluded.

When Muriel put down the phone, it struck her with a clarity that had not emerged before that she had absolutely no intention of letting him go.

THE CHIEF CLERK of the Court of Appeals called at 9 a.m. to notify Arthur that they would release the decision in the *Petition of Gandolph ex. Rel. Warden of Rudyard Penitentiary* in an hour. When Arthur reached Pamela with the news, she volunteered to retrieve the written opinion so that Arthur would have time to gather himself before dealing with reporters. She stopped in his office on her way out to the courthouse.

"We're going to lose," he told her.

Before she'd met Rommy Gandolph, Pamela Towns probably would have argued the point. Today, the spirit faded from her long face and she answered simply, "I know." Twenty minutes later, she reached Arthur from the Federal Building. He could hear the despondence even as she said hello.

"We're dead," Pamela said, on her cell phone. "Well, he's dead literally. We're just dead legally." She read Arthur the decisive portions of the opinion.

"'In connection with his effort to file a second *habeas corpus* petition, Mr. Gandolph was granted a brief period to adduce evidence of actual innocence that could not have been discovered at an earlier date. Although Mr. Gandolph's court-appointed counsel—' That means us," said Pamela, as if Arthur, after thirteen years of practicing law, might not know. "'Although Mr. Gandolph's court-appointed counsel has scoured out a new and material witness to

Gandolph's innocence, the testimony of Erno Erdai is uncorroborated by forensic evidence of any kind—' Funny they don't care about forensic corroboration when it comes to the case against Rommy."

"Go on," Arthur told her.

"'In addition, Mr. Erdai is a convicted felon with a perceptible motive to punish the same law-enforcement authorities who punished him, and also admits having made statements ten years ago that fully contradict his present version of events. It is also noteworthy that another witness against Mr. Gandolph has been uncovered by the state, Genevieve Carriere, who has related a highly incriminating statement by petitioner Gandolph, and pointed up important new evidence of Mr. Gandolph's motive to kill one of the victims. Unlike petitioner's new witness, Ms. Carriere's account is consistent with other evidence of record. We are aware that a respected District Court judge—'

"I'm surprised they didn't put 'respected' in quotation marks," interjected Pamela, referring to the appellate judges' distaste for Harlow. Arthur made no effort to conceal his impatience this time when he told her again to go on.

"Right," said Pamela "'. . . a respected District Court judge made limited credibility findings concerning Mr. Erdai, but that took place before Ms. Carriere's testimony was known, clearly lessening the significance of those findings.

"'Mr. Gandolph has waited nearly a decade to make any claim of innocence. Although that obviously casts doubt on the verity of this new contention, under the law it is more important that petitioner had the opportunity to raise this claim and bypassed it at trial, as well as in subsequent collateral attacks. A *habeas corpus* petition, particularly a repetitive request, is limited solely to remedying a violation of a defendant's constitutional rights so grievous as to amount to a miscarriage of justice. There is no basis to believe that Mr. Gandolph will satisfy that standard. We agree with the state that the direct evidence of Mr. Gandolph's guilt, on which the trier of fact long ago relied, has gone unquestioned; indeed the quantum of evidence against petitioner has only increased through the process to date. Accordingly, we conclude that there is no basis in law to allow the filing of a second *habeas corpus* petition. To whatever

extent our prior order, allowing a brief discovery period, might be construed as
permitting that filing, we conclude such
permission would have been improvidently
granted. The appointment of counsel to assist Mr. Gandolph in this process is, as a
result, terminated, with the thanks of the
Court. Our prior stay is hereby dissolved
and no longer bars the Superior Court of
Kindle County from setting a date certain
for execution.'"

After he hung up, Arthur faced the river,
feeling very much as if he were drowning in
its dark waters. Execution. His mind ran to
the consequences for Rommy, but his heart
was submerged in sorrow for himself. The
media would not pick up the drift, but he detected the court's message. They thought
he'd ginned up Erno's story, or at least had
not been appropriately skeptical. As appointed counsel, his assignment was to
conduct himself with a moderation they appeared to feel he'd abandoned. And he
realized that was true. It was not news to
Arthur Raven these days that he was a person of passion. What Rommy had helped
him discover was that those passions had a
place in the law. The light had gone forth,

and now by court order, it would be shuttered again.

LARRY HATED JOURNALISM. There were several reporters whom he found good company, but he could never buy into their enterprise. They barely saw the flames, never felt the heat, and still tried to tell everybody else about the fire. Which was why he took such pleasure watching Muriel duke it out with them today.

The P.A.'s pressroom had been carved out of the former grand jury chamber. The rear wall had been painted in the electric blue favored as a backdrop, and a raised podium had been erected, with the county emblem emblazoned just below the mike in plastic, rather than brass, so there was no distracting gleam from the rack of high-wattage studio lights installed overhead. Beneath their intense whiteness, Muriel was calm and pleasant, but commanding. She introduced everyone on either side of her, mentioned Larry specially, then serenely praised the judgment of the U.S. Court of Appeals and hailed the laborious but accurate workings of the legal process. She said, as she had for months now, that it was time to proceed with Mr. Gandolph's execution. Several of the reporters wanted her to comment again on Erno's story and she simply referred them to the court's opinion. Gandolph, not Erno, was the issue. Squirrel had been proven guilty and the court had said unequivocally the proceedings had been fair. Three faceless judges several blocks away had now become tireless advocates on Muriel's behalf.

As soon as the lights were off, Larry loosened his tie. The Chief shook his hand, and then Larry kidded around for a second with Molto and Carol. Muriel was waiting to walk out with him and together they crossed the marble entryway of the County Building, which was teeming in the lunch hour. Surrounded by the crowd, it seemed somewhat harmless when she took his arm.

"You did a great job on this case, Larry. I'm sorry it's given us such heartburn this summer, but this is it."

He asked her what would happen next and she described the various legal hand grenades that Arthur or his successor could lob. All, she promised, would be duds.

"Is Arthur really gone from this case?" Larry asked.

"That's up to Arthur. The court is clearly giving him a way out."

"I say Arthur is the Energizer Bunny. He won't quit."

"Maybe not."

"So," he said. He faced her, with emotion swelling as they came to a standstill amid the throng comprised of lawyers and citizens with business here, as well as denizens of the building coming or going from lunch. "I guess this is so long."

She laughed pleasantly. "Hardly, Larry."

"No?"

"You're going to have to fight to get out of my life again, bub. Give me a call. We should have a drink to celebrate. Seriously." She reached up and hugged him. A master of the outward look of things, like most good courtroom lawyers, Muriel managed the gesture with a certain sterile composure. To the stream of passersby it could not have appeared to be more than the appropriately fond farewell of respected colleagues. But there was more in the instant her body lingered against his. "I expect that call," she said as she let go. She walked off, and then waved cutely over her shoulder, the first and only moment that someone watching might have called her a flirt. He'd been getting the message for a while now, but this was the first moment he'd been dead certain he wasn't mistaken.

Dazzled, he passed between the long Doric columns that fronted the County Building. On instinct, he reached for his shades, then saw the dim sky. The air, in fact, held the heavy scent of rain.

Once before, he'd thought this case was pretty much over, although he'd not taken much joy in it at the time. He'd just finished sitting next to Muriel for two weeks, during Squirrel's trial and sentencing in early '92. Muriel and he were kaput by then and she was getting ready to marry Talmadge. Larry had gone into the weeks of trial preparation with a boy-meets-girl movie once more showing in his head, in which just rubbing elbows with him would restore Muriel to her senses. When that hadn't happened, he'd been so far down he wasn't sure who it was the jury said was going to die.

Goofing or flirting, Muriel had passed a re-mark a few weeks ago that he missed her, and if she'd stayed on the line he probably would have said something dumb like, 'I do.' But he didn't want to go through any of it again—it was like volunteering to take a forty-story fall. It was just ironic, was all. From start to finish, the two things had been synonymous: the end of Rommy and the end with Muriel.

From the sidewalk, he looked back at the solid red-brick block of the County Building and saw the words chiseled in the limestone over the columns. *Veritas. Justitia. Ministerium*. If his parochial-school Latin was any good, that was something like truth, justice, service. He felt prickling across his body. Those were still the right words, still what he was about, still what had kept him going on this case, despite the personal crap and Rommy's revolving defenses. But somehow, standing here, he was certain of only one thing.

He still wasn't happy.

GILLIAN DID NOT HEAR of the ruling until midafternoon. She was at the Center City store and Argentina Rojas, who came in for the late shift at the counter, told her what she'd learned on her car radio. It was the first time Argentina had indicated any awareness of Gillian's prior life and she'd clearly broken her own taboo in the expectation she was bringing welcome news, after what had been printed about Gillian in the days following Erdai's testimony. Gillian did her best to thank Argentina, then went as soon as she could to the employees' lounge to phone Arthur.

"Alive," he answered, when she asked how he was. "Sort of." He described the decision. "I didn't expect to get slammed."

"Why don't I take you out to dinner, Arthur?" She had not calculated this in advance, but her desire to console him was intense and she knew how badly he'd wanted them to escape the apartment. Even trampled by disappointment, he was clearly pleased by the prospect. She said she would meet him at the Matchbook, a Center City standby where Arthur could get the steak and potato that remained his preferred fare. When she arrived at eight, he was already slumped at the table, a visible wreck.

"Have a drink," she told him. When they were together, he refused alcohol for her sake, but if there was ever a man in need of a brisk scotch, it appeared to be Arthur.

He had brought her a copy of the opinion, but he did not allow her to read much of it before he let loose his misery. He'd told her several times they would lose, but the reality of it was more than he could bear. How could the judges have done this?

"Arthur, I learned something on the bench. Lawyers see one another in far more accepting terms than they see judges. How many times have you forgiven another attorney—Muriel, for example—saying she's just doing her job? But when it comes to judges, lawyers express outrage. Judges, too, are merely doing their jobs. Doing their best. Someone has to decide and so *you* decide. You decide even though you're secretly convinced that several of the people whom you pass on the street on the way to work might do better on particular questions. You decide. At first you're terrified that you're going to make a mistake. Eventually you know you often will, that it's expected, that there would be no need for courts of review if judges were infallible. So you decide. Humbly. Humanly. You do your job. They've decided, Arthur. But that doesn't mean they're right."

"That's comforting. Because it's essentially the last word." Legally, there was more skirmishing left. But as far as Arthur was concerned, only writing on the wall of Rommy's cell would have foretold a more certain doom. "And I can't believe they had the gall to fire me," he added.

"With thanks, Arthur."

"Halfhearted would probably overstate their enthusiasm. And it was so slimy. They just don't want anybody who has the re- sources to devote to the issues to be handling the case."

"Arthur, they were trying to relieve you and your partners of the burden. Nothing pre- vents you from representing Rommy directly on a *pro bono* basis. He can retain you, rather than the court."

"Right. That's just what my partners want. Me in a pissing match with the Court of Appeals."

Accepting the fact that no words would comfort him, she fell to a familiar gloom. She was certain that what existed between Arthur and her was fragile. There were a thousand reasons—but now she saw one more. A beaten Arthur would not be able to maintain this relationship. In his misery, he would see less in himself and soon, in con- sequence, far less in her.

In the few hours she spent back home at

Duffy's house each day, Gillian frequently asked herself the question that Arthur had not yet dared to pose. Did she love him? He was, without doubt, the lover of her life. But love? She was startled how quick she had been to conclude that the answer was yes. With him there was something renewing, eternal, essential. She wanted to be with Arthur. And it was with terrible sadness that she had realized again and again that in the long term she would not be. She had wondered for weeks if she would be willing to struggle when the inevitable unraveling began, or simply accept her fate. But no, she would not stand still to be mowed down again. Arthur at his best made better of her. She needed for both their sakes to provide some resilience.

"Arthur, may I ask you a question?"

"Yes, I still want to make love to you tonight."

She reached across the table and slapped his hand. But she was encouraged that his libido had outlasted his disappointment.

"No, Arthur. Is the court right?"

"Legally?"

"Is your client innocent, Arthur? Truly, what do you think?"

Arthur's scotch had arrived now, and he cast a heavy-hearted look toward the glass, but did not touch it.

"What do you think, Gil?"

It was an apt riposte—although she hadn't anticipated it. She had not tested herself with that question in weeks. In the interval, the reasons to disbelieve Erno, whom she'd suspected from the start, had multiplied. And yet for her the facts of the case remained a swamp—the records suggesting Gandolph might have been in jail, Erdai's account, Luisa's thefts, the question of whether Gandolph had violence in his character. Today, despite her effort to apply cold reason, there were doubts, reasonable ones, and thus, on the current evidence she could send Rommy Gandolph neither to death nor even to the penitentiary. By whatever means, Arthur had persuaded her of that much, although she would hesitate to vouch for Gandolph's innocence, or to criticize her decision of ten years ago, given the proof she saw at the time.

"But I'm of no account now, Arthur," she said, after explaining her views. "What's your opinion?"

"I believe Genevieve. Even Erno admitted

that she'd told him that Rommy had threatened to kill Luisa. And every time I go over it, I see that Erno was lying about something else. But I still *need* to believe Rommy's innocent. And so I do." He wrung his head in misery at the absurdity of what he had said.

"Then you have to go forward. Don't you? As an attorney? Could you really face yourself if you deserted an innocent client at this stage? Do what you can, Arthur. At least try," she said.

"Try what? I need facts. New facts."

Whenever Arthur spoke of the case, as he did constantly, she listened with interest but confined her commentary to encouragement. Yet she'd made her own calculations and there seemed no point tonight in keeping them to herself.

"You know I hesitate to make suggestions," she began.

He waved off her apologies, inviting her to continue.

"You haven't told Muriel that Erno was also stealing tickets, have you?" she asked.

"God, no," said Arthur. "It only makes Erno look worse. What of it?"

"Well, Erno said that was why he confronted Luisa at Paradise—because he was afraid her activities might lead to discovery of his own. Correct?"

"So?"

"But Erno had had Luisa searched and found nothing. So why did he remain so certain of what she was up to? And if he wasn't having an affair with her, then what brought him out at midnight on a holiday weekend to confront her?"

"That's what I meant about Erno," Arthur said. "I can't even fight my way through his lies anymore."

"Well, perhaps I'm fresher on this, Arthur. But thinking it over, I suspect Erno was watching Luisa—on his own, because he couldn't tell his underlings about his suspicions, for fear it would reveal something about his own thefts. And with his eye on her, he must have caught her in the process of stealing."

"Makes sense. He said he went to Paradise to stop her."

"But why didn't Erno stop her at the airport?"

"He probably wanted to see who she was delivering the tickets to. That's the usual routine in a surveillance, isn't it?"

"Which brings you back to her buyer. Pharaoh?"

"Pharaoh. What about him?"

"Well, he must have been there, Arthur. At Paradise. At some point."

She could see Arthur, almost against his will, revive. His posture improved and his face brightened, but after a second he once more shook his head.

"We can't find him. Rommy said Pharaoh took a major conviction, but Pamela matched the name against court records and we got nothing. Even Erno said he's vanished."

"I know, but one thing caught my attention. Genevieve said she couldn't figure out how Luisa and Pharaoh were able to get away with this. Is that right?"

"That's what she said."

"So Pharaoh had a far more sophisticated means of disposing of the tickets than peddling them on a street corner."

"Rommy said he was pushing them through some company." Arthur took a second to follow her. "What are you thinking? A corporate travel department?"

"Something along those lines."

Together they began to plot possible approaches, and Arthur became more himself, enlivened with hope of the improbable. Then, quite abruptly, bleakness settled in again and his small, soft eyes suddenly stuck on her.

"What?" she asked, thinking there was some new flaw in their reasoning.

Instead, he reached out for her hand.

"You were so good at this," he said.

32

Obvious

SHORTLY AFTER FRIDAY midnight, Erno Erdai died. Arthur received the news when Stew Dubinsky called him at home early Saturday morning for a comment. Arthur expressed condolences and then, recalling his duties as an advocate, praised Erno as a man who'd found the courage to set right past wrongs in life's final moments. Rarely had Arthur uttered words with less sense of whether they were true.

Nonetheless, his role as Rommy's representative required him to attend the funeral mass for Erno on Tuesday morning at St. Mary's Cathedral. Summer, this year especially, was a slow news time, and Erno's death occupied center stage in the local press, notwithstanding Genevieve's revelations and the Court of Appeals' opinion.

Given that, it was no surprise that the Reverend Dr. Carnelian Blythe had somehow been engaged to eulogize Erno. The Archdiocese had also rallied to Erno, and Monsignor Wojcik, the rector at St. Mary's, officiated. But the star was Blythe, who was magnetic in the preacher's role that had first brought him to prominence nearly forty years ago.

Reverend Blythe was a genius in many ways. Most white people in Kindle County had laughed at Blythe at some point, amused by his excessive rhetoric and his twenty-four seven state of rage. Arthur was no exception. Yet he also remained mindful of Blythe's many achievements, not only the legendary feats, like walking with Dr. King and forcing desegregation of the county's schools, but less celebrated accomplishments, such as a free breakfast program for poor children and several redevelopment projects that had changed the faces of neighborhoods. Perhaps what Arthur admired most was the voice of hope and identity Blythe had long provided to his community. Arthur could still remember at the age of eleven and twelve tuning in the Reverend Blythe's Sunday broadcasts to listen to him lead a congregation of thousands in intoning,

I AM
A Man.
I AM
Somebody.

As Carnelian Blythe's voice rocked from his depths, young Arthur felt every bit as inspired as the members of the Reverend's flock.

But Blythe's aptitude for engaging the press might have been his most unrivaled skill. If Blythe was there, so were the cameras—he was good for fifteen seconds on the evening news any time he opened his mouth. Arthur could hardly object. The Reverend had kept Rommy's story on the front page, when the media would almost certainly have lost interest were his cause championed by anyone else. Yet Arthur still felt his client would be better served if he kept his distance from Blythe's fulminating.

After the final hymn, Blythe followed Monsignor Wojcik and the family from the Cathedral, bowing his bald head as Erno's casket, bearing a spray of white flowers and the Stars and Stripes, was delivered to the hearse. The photographers, never with any sense of propriety, crowded in. Collins, the nephew whom Arthur recognized from his mug shot, was the first of the six pall-bearers. In his suit and tie, he appeared every bit the solid citizen he was said to have become. He lifted a gray glove to his eyes as the box disappeared into the vehicle, then went to comfort his aunt and his mother, both dressed in stark black. Together, the three moved toward the limousine that would follow Erno's remains to the cemetery.

As soon as the family was on its way, Blythe began repeating much of his eulogy verbatim for the cameras that surrounded him on the Cathedral steps. Arthur snuck away, stopped by the lone reporter who recognized him, Mira Amir from the West Bank *Bugle*, who beat Stew Dubinsky to almost any story of note. In response to her questions, Arthur assured her that Gandolph would be filing a motion for reconsideration of the Court of Appeals order dismissing the *habeas*. Arthur prophesied success, but had little to say when Mira pressed him for the specific grounds he would raise.

Returning to his office, he was glum, discouraged about Gandolph's case and, inevitably, morose with the feelings for his father that had arisen from the occasion. On his desk, Pamela had left a stack of documents at least eight inches high and an explanatory note. For the last two days, following up on Gillian's suggestion, Pamela had been attempting to identify anyone in the travel industry in Kindle County who had been referred to as Pharaoh, or by any name that might have sounded anything like that. She'd had no luck after spending much of yesterday on the phone, and at Arthur's suggestion, had journeyed today to the Department of Registration to examine the rolls of travel agents in the state.

The records she'd assembled were carefully grouped: the rosters of corporate travel departments, the membership of a local travel industry trade association, and microfiche copies of the registration forms of four travel agents. Here, unlike most states, travel agents were licensed by law, a process that required an Associate's Degree, a passing grade on a statewide exam, and proof of good moral character, which, generally speaking, meant no history of felonies or of stealing clients' money. According to a vivid account in her handwritten note, Pamela, in order to identify travel agents licensed in 1991, had had to return to the predigital era in the Department basement, where the mold count had nearly been enough to choke her and the microfilm reader had left her with a brutal headache.

Arthur picked up the gray copies of the registration forms she'd printed out. Ferd O'Fallon ('Ferd O?' Pamela's paste-on note read). Pia Ferro. Nick Pharos.

Faro Cole.

It took him only a second to place the name and he ran up the stairs to Pamela's office. She was on the phone and he jumped around, waving his hands until he had forced her to get off.

"That's the guy Erno shot!"

To be certain, he made Pamela dig the police reports from the shooting out of the file drawers in the corridor. Once she had, they sat in her spare office, a narrow space in beige laminate, where every flat surface had been surrendered to irregular piles of cases and statutes and draft briefs. In a corner, she'd added a Shaker rocker, adorned by a bold red blanket bearing the stitched image of the University of Wisconsin badger. She used the chair as a resting place for her coat and stray volumes she hadn't gotten around to returning to the firm law library and Arthur cleared it off, laying the blanket over the metal heat registers with the tender reverence Pamela thought it was due. He sat and Pamela rested her feet on a desk drawer. Together, as they'd done for hundreds of hours before, they noodled. It was Faro, not Pharaoh. A travel agent. It seemed so obvious now. Pamela, in fact, was chagrined with herself.

"Rommy said it was F, a, r, o," she said, "and I laughed at him."

"If your worst mistake as a lawyer is not taking spelling lessons from Rommy Gandolph, your career's going to turn out okay," Arthur told her. There was a more important question than trying to figure how they'd been so dumb. "Where do we find him?" Arthur asked.

Sick of dusty basements, Pamela urged paying one of the Internet search companies that had compiled a database of public records in all fifty states. His partners had begun to question the expenses mounting in a losing cause, but Arthur was even more impatient than Pamela for answers. What came back, however, after Faro Cole's name was entered and various detailed searches were ordered hardly seemed worth the $150 they had spent. There was a sketchy credit report showing little more than an address from 1990 and the data, last updated in 1996, that had appeared on Faro's driver's license. As for the myriad additional records QuikTrak supposedly canvassed, there was not a further hit in the fifty states. Faro was no longer licensed as a travel agent here, or in the other thirteen jurisdictions which certified agents. Faro Cole had never been to court—never sued, never bankrupt, never divorced, never convicted. He had never taken a mortgage or owned real estate; he had never been married. In fact, if QuikTrak was correct, he had not even been born, nor had he died, anywhere in America.

"How is that possible?" Pamela asked after they'd submitted the last search for birth information.

Arthur watched the screen. As before, once you saw the answer, it seemed obvious.

"It's an alias," Arthur said. "Faro Cole is an alias. We're looking for somebody else." And with that, one more thing was obvious, too.

They were nowhere.

ON WEDNESDAY, Larry was off, as he had been most days since the court's decision, burning the comp time he'd accumulated chasing around nights on the Gandolph case. He and his guys were finishing a new house near the top of Fort Hill and today Larry's taper hadn't shown. He had to don the face mask himself and sand drywall all day, dirty, tedious work in which the fine plaster dust seemed to penetrate even his pores.

Around noon, he felt his pager vibrating. The number went back to McGrath Hall. Police brass. If he'd been doing something worthwhile, he'd have ignored it, but today he took the break. At the other end, the secretary answered, "Deputy Chief Amos's office." Wilma Amos, Larry's long-ago partner on the Task Force that investigated the Fourth of July Massacre, was now Deputy Chief for Personnel. As far as Larry was concerned, Wilma and the job deserved each other, but she had maintained a rooting interest in the Gandolph case and had called a couple of times after Erno surfaced to get the inside stuff. Larry thought she might have been delivering an attaboy on the Court of Appeals decision, but when she came on the line, she said she had some news that might interest him.

"My sister Rose works at the Department of Registration," Wilma said. "A little girl came in there yesterday who said she was a lawyer in Art Raven's firm. Looking for information about travel agents in 1991."

"Nineteen ninety-one means Gandolph, right?"

"That's why I'm on the phone, Larry."

"And does your sister know what Arthur's associate got?"

"Rose helped her print out the registration forms. Made copies. I was going to send them over, but they said you're off, so I thought you'd appreciate the page."

"I do, Wilma."

She was ready to read him the names on the forms. Larry got a pencil from Paco, his chief carpenter, but he stopped writing once she mentioned Faro Cole.

"Crap," said Larry. He explained who Faro was.

"What does it mean that he's a travel agent?" she asked.

"It means I missed something," Larry answered.

Agitated, he went back to work. At first he thought he was upset because he'd fanned on something as obvious as Faro being a travel agent. But there was more to it. With nothing else to preoccupy him, he kept thinking it all through as he bossed the sandpaper over the seams. By the end of the afternoon he was stuck on an idea he didn't especially like.

Around four, Paco and his two guys knocked off, and Larry decided to walk the three or four blocks down to Ike's, the cop hangout where Erno had plugged Faro Cole. Maybe if Ike's wasn't nearby, he wouldn't have bothered. But there were worse ideas than having a cold one on a hot day and putting his mind at ease.

Larry did his best to clean up, but a floury dusting of plaster remained in his hair and on his overalls as he headed down the hill. The area was yuppying-up in a hurry. A lot of the locals were arriving home early to make the most of the daylight, and the men and women with briefcases looked like they'd been to the golf course, not the office. Larry's college degree was in business. Now and then, over the years, when he'd thought about the money he might have earned, one of his comforts was that he didn't have to half garrote himself every morning with a necktie. What a world. You just couldn't count on anything.

Ike's was no more than a bare-bones tavern. No ferns or hardwood here. It was a long dim room with poor acoustics and the distinct yeasty odor of spilled beer. There was an old mirrored bar of cherry, booths along the wall upholstered in red plastic, and picnic benches in the center of the floor. Ike Minoque, the owner, was an ex-cop who'd gotten shot in the head and gone on disability in the early '60s. Guys from Six began to hang out to help him out. Now Ike's was a destination for anyone on the job in Kindle County. There were two groups who arrived here during the week—cops, and ladies who liked them. When Larry came on in 1975, one of the old guys had said to him, 'You get two things with this job you don't get with most others—a gun. And girls. My advice is the same both ways. Keep it in the holster.' Larry hadn't listened. He'd shot two guys, albeit with justification. On the other score, he had no excuses at all.

The Code said nobody ever talked about what went down at Ike's—the tales told or who you left with. And as a result, you learned stuff here they couldn't teach in the Academy. Guys lied a lot—they covered themselves with false glory. But there were plenty of boozy confessions, too: when you hadn't covered your partner, when you got so scared your body failed you. You could cry about fucking up, and laugh about the world of bean brains who were out there just waiting for the police to find them.

When Larry entered, several voices rang out. He shook hands, taking crap and giving it, and worked his way back to the bar, where Ike was drawing drafts. The two projection TVs in the barroom were showing reruns of *Cops*.

As several other men and women had done already, Ike congratulated Larry on the outcome of the Gandolph case. This thing with Erno had bothered a lot of people—it always did when anybody who called himself part of the brotherhood went bad.

"Yeah," said Larry, "I didn't shed any tears when Erno took off on the highway for hell." The morning paper was on the bar next to him. Below the fold, there was a photo of Collins and the others rolling Erno's casket into the hearse. It had taken all Larry's self-control not to go down to St. Mary's yesterday with a sign reading 'Good Riddance.'

"Son of a buck was not my cup of tea, either," Ike said. "Something about the way he missed the job. You know, like mom kept him home when the other boys went out to play. I thought he had the wrong idea about things. Easy to say now. But," said Ike with a smile, "Erno wasn't all bad. Bought a hell of a lot of beer in here."

Ike resembled an elderly beatnik. His hair was gone on the top, but the snowy sides overflowed his collar, and he wore a goatee. He had a long apron, which might not have been washed in a month, and the eye that he'd lost when he was shot was a pure milky white and moved now and then for reasons of its own.

"Were you around the night he plugged that guy?" Larry asked him.

"Around? Yeah. But I was doing the same as I'm doing now. I didn't see nothing until I smelled the gunpowder. Isn't that a pisser?"

asked Ike. "That .38 probably shook plaster off the walls, but the first thing I remember is the smell." Ike looked into the barroom. "Gage over there was standing not three feet from the both of them. He seen it all."

Once he got a beer, Larry drifted over that way. Mike Gage worked Property Crimes in Area Six. His picture was in the dictionary next to the term 'good cop.' He was one of those blacks with a permanent part in his hair that looked like it had been applied with a chisel. He was a quiet type, church on Sunday, six kids. Larry had a theory that the quiet guys did the best on the job. Larry himself, especially when he was younger, was just too damned excitable. Mike was even. A lot of policemen tended to run bitter. In general, the job seldom turned out to be the adventure you hoped for. Even your kids got old enough to realize you weren't the legend you wanted to be in your own mind. It was paperwork and boredom, getting passed over in favor of the connected, and making far less money than half the creeps you snagged. And by the time you got hip, you had too little going to move on to anything else. But Mike was like Larry, excited to see the shield when he picked it up every morning. Gage still thought it was a great deal, helping people be good rather than bad.

Mike was with a bunch of other guys from Six, but made room on the bench beside him. One guy with Gage, Mal Rodrigues, extended his fist across the picnic table, and Larry gave it a knock, ballplayer style, celebrating last week's victory again. It was noisy in here—Creed was pounding out of the speakers—and in order to be heard Larry had to get close enough to Mike to cuddle. They talked about the case for a minute, what a strange guy Erno had proven to be.

"Ike says you were right there when Erno popped that character—Faro Cole?"

"Larry, I'm on the job long as you, and truth be told, that's as close as I've come to a bullet." Mike smiled at his beer. "The fool Erno shot—Faro?—he'd been wailing like some Iraqi woman, and Erno got the pistol out of his hand and pushed him outside, then all the sudden they were back in here and bang. Not three feet from me." Mike pointed toward the side door where he'd been sitting.

Larry asked one of the questions that had been bugging him for a while: Why was a complaint never lodged against Faro for threatening Erno?

"We all figured Faro for past tense. And Erno didn't want charges anyway. Once we took the gun, Erno started in bawling over the body."

"I thought Erno was saying self-defense."

"He was. But he kept telling us leave the guy alone."

"Not too logical."

"You're Homicide, you tell me, but I didn't think shooters were where you went for logic."

Larry took a second. Better sense told him to stop now, but at the age of fifty-four he still hadn't figured out how to heed the voice of caution.

"Here's the thing, Mike. Today, I'm starting to have bad dreams. I need comfort on one thing. You think you could make this guy? Faro?"

"Four years, Larry. Maybe Mal could. He had Faro's head in his lap for fifteen minutes while we were waiting for the mercy wagon."

"Lemme buy both of you a beer at the bar."

Ike had put today's *Trib* away and it took him a second to find it.

"This bird," said Larry, displaying the front page to Gage and Rodrigues, "this one. Just check me out that he doesn't look like the guy Erno shot."

Rodrigues peered up before Mike Gage but there was the same thing in both faces. Larry had been pointing to Collins in the photograph of Erno's funeral.

"Christ," Larry said. But the columns kept adding up, just as they had all day. Faro was a travel agent and so was Collins. Size, age, race all matched. Like Collins, Faro had been represented by Jackson Aires. 'Faro Cole' sort of looked like 'Collins Farwell,' turned inside out, s.o.p. with aliases, so the doofus using it would have a clue, when he was on the spot, about what he had been calling himself. And it wouldn't be unusual for a bad boy just out of the joint, as Collins was in 1997, to be toting phony i.d., to make sure he didn't give the coppers—and his parole officers—a head start if he got jammed up on something. But what bothered Larry the most was what had struck him while he was sanding: Collins's story about how Jesus had entered his life with a bullet through the back.

Rodrigues tried to console him. "You

don't need to trust a four-year-old eyeball, even if it's cops."

Larry went outside to use his cell phone. The high clouds were darkening and resembled an angry stallion rearing up. Storm tonight, probably. Then he rejoined the present and fell under its weight.

This fucking case.

33

AUGUST 8, 2001

At Sea

"YOU GOT TIME to leave the office?"

Muriel had grabbed her own phone after-hours. Not even bothering with a name or hello, Larry sounded cozy and familiar. She'd been waiting days for his call, and she was immediately dashed when he added, "Some guys down here you ought to talk to." She could not quite dampen a faint echo of embarrassment in her voice when she finally asked where the hell he was. It sounded like a tavern.

"Do we have a problem?" she said.

"Can of worms. No," said Larry. "Snakes. Rattlesnakes. Cottonmouth."

They had a problem.

"And, if you don't mind," Larry added, "bring the old file on Collins we put together when we went to see him in the jail." He told her where it was in the current materials stored in her office.

Pushing through the old oak door at Ike's a half hour later, Muriel could detect a current in the room. Generally speaking, there were two schools of thought about her in the Kindle County Unified Police Force: some liked her, some hated her guts. The ones in the second camp kept it to themselves when they were on the job, but off duty they owed her no such courtesy. They remembered the cases she'd nixed, the hard lines she'd drawn and sometimes enforced on police practices. Their world was far too macho to comfortably endure discipline—or ambition—from a woman. She could grant them that she was often hardheaded, even abrasive, but in her heart of hearts, she knew that the main issue for the guys staring at her came down to plumbing.

Larry was back at the bar. He was in overalls and looked like he'd been rolled in flour. His clothing and hair were pale with dust.

"Let me guess. You're going to be a sugar doughnut for Halloween."

He didn't seem to get the joke until he glanced at the beveled mirror over the bar and even then wasn't very amused. He explained that he'd been sanding all day, but he clearly had other things on his mind besides his appearance.

"Wassup?" she asked.

He told her, slowly, piece by piece. She got right next to him when he'd finished, so she didn't shout.

"You're telling me Erno Erdai shot his own nephew?"

"I'm saying it's possible. Did you bring that file?"

Larry waved Mike Gage over first to look at Collins's mug shot from 1991. Mike just gave him a look. Rodrigues said, "I take it 'Definitely' is not the answer you're looking for."

"Tell it like it is."

"The eyes, man." Rodrigues tapped the color photograph. "Almost orange. Village of the Damned or something."

"Right," Larry said.

"Let's get out of here," Muriel told him. This wasn't the place for a discussion. Even the cops who liked her were uncertain allies, many of them more loyal to the reporters who kept them on their call list than they'd be to her. Outside, she offered Larry a ride up the hill. He hesitated at the door, reluctant to bring his dust into her sedan. She'd owned the Civic since 1990, and it hadn't been tidy even when it was new.

"Larry," she said, "there is nothing this upholstery hasn't seen," and barely caught herself from laughing when she lit on a distant memory. He gave her directions as they drove.

"So, okay," she said. "Explain."

"I don't think it makes any difference."

"That's step two," said Muriel. "We have to know what the hell was happening first. Am I reading this right? If my mother wants to reconcile with her sister, she ought to try shooting her in the back?"

Larry laughed for the first time tonight. "Three thousand comedians unemployed, and you're making jokes."

"Seriously," she said. "Isn't that the sequence? Erno and Collins got all lovey-dovey after that."

"Fuck," said Larry, "I don't have a clue. And I don't care. Erno's family is as messed up as the next guy's. So what? It's TMI, as far as I'm concerned." Too much information. An acronym for the times, if ever there was one.

Larry was pointing up a long driveway. The house was a Victorian, which he had once described as his specialty. San Francisco colors had been applied on all the trim, bright contrasting shades to bring out the feathering and diamonds scored on the presswood exterior. Muriel leaned over the wheel to see it all through the windshield.

"Jeez Louise, Larry. What a beauty."

"Isn't it? This one especially, sometimes I'm walking around inside and it bothers me that I couldn't afford anything like it for myself when the boys were young. But that's the story, right? You never get what you want when you need it." He seemed to hear himself only after he'd spoken. She could see him tense up and avoid looking her way. To save him, she asked for a quick tour.

He started with the garden. The light was weakening and the bugs were on the attack, but Larry was undeterred, stepping carefully between the recently bedded plants. The legacy of color and glory he was leaving behind for whoever would buy the house was full-grown in his head and he took quite some time explaining how the various perennials—everything from crocuses to peonies to hydrangeas—would rise up and expand year by year. It was nearly dark when he quit, and that was only because she finally mentioned getting eaten alive.

Inside, he was more cursory. In order to contain the plague of dust, sheets of plastic hung over the doorways to the rooms being sanded. The challenge of a place like this, Larry said, was knowing which details to preserve in the name of character and which had to be sacrificed for the sake of the marketplace. Lighting was an example. When they were built, these rooms were dim as an outhouse, illuminated at night by gas sconces. Today's homeowners were innate energy hogs. Over time, Larry said, he had learned strong overhead light and lots of switches were prized by buyers.

It was neat to see Larry in his other life. He amused her as he always did, but she'd had no trouble imagining Larry as an entrepreneur. Even his tenderness in the garden was something she'd gradually taken account of. The guy she knew in law school liked to pretend that the only use for the word 'sensitive' was on a condom wrapper. But there was somebody else there—she'd always known that—and she admired Larry for letting him out.

"Does the plumbing work yet?" she

asked. Larry showed her where she was going. There was a little quarter-window across from the sink, and amid the lights below, Muriel could more or less pick out the neighborhood where she'd grown up a fourth of a mile from Fort Hill, a bungalow belt set amid rail yards and truck depots. Even today, it remained a land of endless parking lots, harshly illuminated to prevent theft, half-mile stretches where truck trailers or new Fords or rail containers waited beside the right-of-way to be loaded on trains. It was a good place. People worked hard, were kind and decent, and wanted better for their kids. But as was always the case with working people, they also felt the harshness of raw happenstance that kept them from counting as much as the folks who bossed them around. Not her, she'd vowed. Not her.

She held no illusions now. It would have maddened her if she'd lived a life isolated from power. But looking down the hill, she still revered the best of the place, the centeredness, the sense that you lived your life and tried to move half a step ahead, do more good than bad, and love somebody. The desire to reconnect with all that was part of what inspired the hour she spent in church each week where her heart almost flew from her body straight to God. Those babies she'd never had were there in church, unmet strangers, like the lover you figured was waiting for you somewhere in the world when you were thirteen. The future. The life of her spirit. In prayer, she still reached toward them as lovingly as she had for years in dreams. With the tingle that arose from Larry's presence in the quiet house she had a sudden sense of the wholeness that might have been possible in the love of a man.

He was waiting for her in an add-on family room at the back of the house. Originally, it had been done cheaply, and Larry said he'd tried to dress it up with nice carpeting. Almost to rebuff the strength of what she'd just been feeling, she returned to business.

"Larry, it's time to throw all this stuff about Erno and Collins on the table. I'm going to write Arthur a letter tomorrow."

He asked what she knew he would: "Why?"

"Because they're clearly desperate to find Faro. And it's a capital case, Larry, and I shouldn't hide stuff when I know it's material to them."

"Material?"

"Larry, I'm clueless about exactly what all this means and so are you. But bottom line, Collins was stealing tickets with Luisa, right? Don't you think that has something to do with why he knew enough to dime out Gandolph?"

"Muriel, sure as you're standing here, Arthur'll be in court trying to open everything up again. You know that. He'll be screaming about giving Collins immunity."

"That's his job, Larry. That doesn't mean he gets his way. The Court of Appeals will never force me to grant immunity. But I want to lay it all out for Arthur—Collins being Faro, and the shooting. And what Collins told you in Atlanta, too. I should have disclosed that a while ago, but I can act like it just dawned on me."

Larry stood still with his eyes closed, simmering a little in the stupidity of the law.

"We don't even know 100 percent that Collins is Faro," he finally said.

"Come on, Larry."

"Seriously. Let me get back to Dickerman, see if he gets a fingerprint off the gun. Then maybe we'll know it's Collins for sure."

"Call Dickerman. Tell him it's back on and

we need fast answers. But I can't wait to tell Arthur. The longer we hesitate, the louder he'll moan about me withholding favorable evidence. Arthur has a few more days to file one last motion for reconsideration in the Court of Appeals, and I want to be able to say we got him this information in a timely way, as soon as we saw any relationship to the events surrounding the murders. That way he gets a clean final shot and the Court then can tell him they've considered everything, and it's over."

"Christ, Muriel."

"It's just the last hurdle, Larry."

"Oh," he said, "how many times do we have to win this fucking case? Sometimes I want to go down to Rudyard and shoot Rommy myself, just to put an end to all of this crap."

"Maybe that's our fault. Maybe something's keeping us from putting an end to it." She, of course, knew what 'something' was and so did he, but that, apparently, was part of the crap he wanted over and done with. Stepping closer, she lifted her hand to his shoulder. "Larry, trust me on this. It'll come out okay."

That was just proving his point, though.

The Point. The case never was about the victim, or the defendant, or even what happened. Not really. For the cop and the lawyer and the judge you could never keep it from being about you. And in this case, them. Averted from her, Larry was taut in frustration.

"Really, Larry," she said. "If you didn't want to do anything about this, why go down to Ike's? Why bother calling me?"

He cast his gaze down, but finally reached up and clapped the back of her hand as a mode of assent. Even contact so brief swept her into the tide between them. She peered up at him with a brimming look, one that recognized damage and time. Then she squeezed his shoulder again and, with whatever reluctance, let go. She giggled an instant later when she saw her hand.

"What?" Larry asked.

She lifted her palm toward him, whitened all the way across by a layer of plaster dust.

"You left your mark, Larry."

"Did I?"

"Pillar of salt," she said.

His blue eyes shifted for a second, as he went after the reference.

"What was it that gal did wrong?"

"Looked backwards," Muriel answered with a wrinkled smile.

"Yeah."

Much as she'd promised herself in Atlanta not to be the first across the boundary line, she knew she wasn't going to stop. It didn't matter if it was auld lang syne or stardust or libido—she wanted Larry. Whatever bell he'd sounded had never been rung by anyone else. A decade ago, she hadn't seen it, but their relationship was, in large part, an altar to her, an appreciation of her power. It was unique in that way. Larry knew the strongest in her and, unlike Rod or Talmadge, didn't cherish it for his own use. He just wanted peace on their own terms, a full-blooded companionship, hard-nosed but not hardhearted, two for the world. She had forsaken an enormous opportunity years ago, and knowing that, she needed to be sure there was no chance today. She held up her palm.

"Is this God's way of telling me to keep my hands to myself, Larry?"

"I don't know about that, Muriel. I don't get much direct communication."

"But that's how you want it, right? Bygones as bygones?"

He took a long time.

"I don't know what I want, Muriel, to tell you the truth. I know one thing. I don't care to go back on the suicide watch."

"So where does that put you? You're saying no?"

He smiled faintly. "Guys aren't supposed to say no."

"It's just a word, Larry." She looked again at her palm. The pale dust clung on the high points, leaving the creases distinct. The loveline and the lifeline that the fortune-tellers read were marked as clearly as rivers on a map. Then she reached up and found the very spot on his shoulder where a vague positive image of her hand had been left behind.

THE THOUGHT that he could resist passed through Larry's mind as nothing more than an abstraction. The essence of Muriel was having her way. And as always, she had the jump on him. Why call her, she'd asked, if he wanted her to do nothing? He'd brought her here. And now she was making it as easy as possible. Little and fearless, she rose to her toes and placed one hand on his shoulder, bringing the other tenderly to his cheek, drawing him near.

After that, it had the desperation and speed of a caged bird hoping to fly. All that useless beating of wings, the smashing about. In the heat, there was a salty taste to her flesh, a smell, eventually, of blood that he was slow to identify. His heart pounded along in frightened spurts and it was, as a result, far briefer than he might have liked. And unexpectedly messy. She was just at the start or end of her period and had been urgent about having him inside her, as if she suspected he might think again.

She had ended up on top and clung to him afterwards as though he were a rock. The feeling of her resting there was far more satisfying than anything else. He searched her form with both hands and felt a desperate pang at how near it had remained in memory, the defined knobs in her spine, the ribs prominent as the black piano keys, the ripe turn of her behind, which he had always found the most becoming part of her anatomy. In the time since they'd split, he had wept only once, when his grandfather, the immigrant wheelwright, had died near the age of one hundred. Larry had been overwhelmed by how much harder life would have been for the old man's twenty-three children and grandchildren were it not for the blessing of his bravery in making the journey here. The example of a heroism that spread itself over so many lives bolstered Larry against any tearful mourning for his own sake now. But the safest harbor was humor.

"How am I going to explain to my guys why we have to clean a brand-new rug?"

"Go ahead," she said, "complain." Her small face perked up in front of him. At her collar, she'd worn a pin that, in their haste, had remained fastened, so that her dress, otherwise unbuttoned, flowed around her like a cloak. Her shoulders were sheathed with the filmy black polka-dot fabric, while her bare arms were crossed now under his throat.

"Are you sorry about this?" she asked.

"I don't know yet. I may be."

"Don't be."

"You're tougher than I am, Muriel."

"Not anymore."

"Yes, you are. At least, you know how to keep moving forward. When it comes to you, Muriel, I guess I can't."

"Larry. Don't you think I've missed you?"

"Consciously?"

"Come on, Larry."

"I mean it. You don't let yourself look back and see stuff. It's only hitting you now."

"What's that?"

"You should have married me."

Her blackish eyes were still; her small nose, decorated with tiny summer freckles, flared as she inhaled. They stared at one another, their faces only inches apart, until he could feel the strength of his conviction begin to wear her down. He could see then that she knew it already. But how do you walk back through the door at home, once you've said that out loud? And even so, he sensed the vaguest acknowledgment, a gesture with her eyes, before she again laid her head down on his chest.

"You *were* married, Larry. You are."

"And just a cop," he answered.

He'd never had the gumption to swing this hard at her, not at close quarters. And she never would have taken it. He could feel her laboring to come to the new day.

"And just a cop," she said finally.

He could not really see her, but merely with his hand on her skin he could feel the pulse of emotion. She felt fragile, narrow and small, briefly returned to the truth of nature, and Larry, large as he was, surrounded her. Lying on the pale rug, he rocked her for quite some time, as if they were aboard a ship, tossed back and forth on the swells of the terrible sea of life.

34

AUGUST 9, 2001

Former Acquaintance

AT 8:00, Gillian waited for Arthur at a table at the Matchbook, sipping bubble water. He was almost certainly with Pamela. Their motion for reconsideration was due in the Court of Appeals soon.

In the last week, with the exception of their Tuesday night dinner with Susan, Gillian and Arthur had been out every night—a play, the symphony, three movies. Arthur was a man set free. Leaving the apartment relieved Arthur of his anxieties about Gandolph's case in which neither of them had found much new encouragement. When he was walking with her down the street, Arthur even exhibited a trace of macho swagger. Whatever. There was very little about Arthur she did not find endearing.

Across the room, Gillian felt a glance light

on her. This was not an unaccustomed phe-
nomenon—she was, after all, the notorious
Gillian Sullivan—but when she peered that
way a dark pretty woman, a few years
younger than she, ventured the faintest
smile. Not a lawyer. Gillian knew that at
once. From the woman's tony looks—she
was wearing a silk, funnel-necked top they
sold in the store for more than $300—Gillian
might have thought she was a customer, but
Gillian sensed that the memory under re-
trieval had far more dust on it than that.
Then it returned in increments. Tina. Gillian
did her best not to recoil, but it was only the
fact that Arthur was probably on his way
that allowed her to disregard an immediate
impulse to flee.

They had never dealt in last names. This
woman was solely Tina, poor little rich girl in
a high-rise on the West Bank, who supported her habit by selling. The maid
actually answered the door when Gillian
came by to score. She had entered a unique
society—junkies of the professional class.
The manners were better and the danger
less, but this milieu was nearly as porous as
the street. People sank out of sight or into
the depths, and Tina was gone abruptly. She

had been busted. Terrified that she herself would be named, or had already been detected by a police surveillance of Tina, Gillian vowed to quit. But the drug now had first claim on everything inside her body. Like dealers in every trade, Tina had never introduced her to an alternative source. There was an actor from a local theater whom Gillian had seen going in and out several times. But it was too insane to call him. Thirty-six hours after her last fix, she donned a scarf and walked due west from the courthouse into the North End and copped on a street corner. In the event of arrest, she planned to say she was doing research for a sentencing, or on potential changes in the administration of drug cases. She had the good sense to approach another woman, a working girl in a leopard micro skirt and matching boots. 'You see Leon,' the girl told her, but looked Gillian over, shaking her head all the time, as she teetered between pity and reproof.

So, Tina. They stared at each other across a distance of forty feet, trying to make sense of the crazy turns of life and the burdens of the past, then Gillian broke eye contact first, pained almost to the point of laughter by the wisdom of her reluctance to be seen in public.

Arthur arrived then and immediately asked what was wrong. She was about to answer him frankly but she could see a significant smile drain from his face at the sight of her. Not tonight, she thought. She would not darken his mood or distract him tonight. Or any other night, for that matter. She had come to the brink of telling him too many times and then retreated. She was keeping her secret.

"You look as if something good has happened," she told him.

"Good? It may be good. It's majorly confusing. They found Faro."

"You're kidding!"

"That's not the half of it. Muriel wrote me a letter."

"May I see?" She had her hand out even before Arthur had fully removed the envelope from his pocket. It was on the letterhead of Muriel D. Wynn, Chief Deputy, Kindle County Prosecuting Attorney's Office. The reference line noted *People v. Gandolph* and the old criminal court case number. Even at this late stage, Muriel was reluctant to acknowledge she was stuck in the alien terrain of federal court.

Dear Mr. Raven:
Over the last two months, this office, in the course of its continuing investigation of this matter, has encountered a variety of information concerning Collins Farwell. As you know, Mr. Farwell has refused to offer testimony on the grounds of the Fifth Amendment. Furthermore, the information received appears to have no immediate relevance to your client. Nevertheless, in the interest of full disclosure, we wish to advise you of the following . . .

Eight bulleted items trailed down the page. Muriel had crafted the letter to be largely opaque, not to Arthur, who'd see through the obscurities, but to the Court of Appeals, to whom she knew the document would soon be displayed. But imbedded in the details of various records concerning Faro Cole, most of which Arthur had shown Gillian earlier in the week, were two matters of note: a summary of statements that Collins Farwell, Erno's nephew, had made in June while being served with a subpoena in Atlanta. And an acknowledgment that two police officers had recently identified photographs of Collins as Faro's.

"My Lord!" cried Gillian at that sentence. Her heart was racing. After a moment, she was struck by her own reactions, the fact she had no pretense of distance any longer. She asked Arthur what he was thinking.

"I'm not sure that what's going on in my head is called thinking," he said. "Pamela and I were just bouncing off the walls. I'll tell you one thing though: I won't be joining Muriel's campaign committee. A lot of this was pretty underhanded." Arthur suspected that Muriel or Larry had shadowed Pamela on her visit to the Department of Registration. And he was angry about the failure to reveal Collins's statements in Atlanta. "I'd already made a motion to give Collins immunity. In her response, Muriel claimed there was no evidence that Collins had anything favorable to say for Rommy."

Yet his chief disappointment seemed to be with Erno, who had told Arthur that Faro was a cheap hustler who had disappeared long ago.

"We'll never touch bottom with the lies Erno told," Arthur said. "It's like quicksand. We just keep sinking."

"I wonder," said Gillian. Erno was where her thoughts had gone, too, and had lingered. "Erno said he was out to protect Collins when he first involved Larry back in 1991. I wonder if he hasn't been protecting him all along."

"By shooting him in the back? Some protective uncle. I think I'd rather have a gift certificate."

Gillian laughed. He was right. But not completely.

"Even there, though, at Ike's, Erno chose not to acknowledge that Faro was his nephew. Have you wondered why?"

"I can guess. Collins walked into Ike's holding a gun. Felon in possession of a firearm is a two-year minimum mandatory."

"So Erno did protect his nephew," said Gillian.

Arthur shifted a shoulder, granting she might have some kind of point.

"I just wonder, Arthur, if at the end of it all, Erno didn't maintain his own consistency with you. Your instinct was that Erno always told you the truth about one thing."

"Which is?"

"That Rommy is innocent."

"Oh," said Arthur. "That."

"So let's assume he had two dominating motives: exculpating Rommy. And protecting Collins."

Arthur picked up Muriel's envelope and tapped it against his hand as he pondered. Soon, he was nodding.

"That would explain why Erno never mentioned the tickets before Genevieve's dep," Arthur said. "He was protecting Collins, rather than his pension. If the airline found out Collins had been stealing tickets with Luisa and Rommy, even if it was back in the Stone Age, they'd probably bounce him as a travel agent—and sue his ass, too."

"Possible. But I was actually thinking it could be more than that. Rommy was angry with Luisa for shortchanging him. Is it possible Collins was angry with her, too? For jeopardizing their scheme? Or perhaps he'd been shortchanged as well. Remember, we decided Faro was probably at Paradise that night."

Arthur stared at her. The sophisticated dinner clamor of the restaurant rose up around them, low strings, clinking stemware, pleasant chatter.

"You think Collins is the killer?"

"I don't know, Arthur. We're trading ideas. But clearly Erno wanted to free Rommy, without disclosing what Collins had been up to."

Arthur digested it, then said, "Our next move has to be to renew my motion to immunize Collins. Right?"

"You certainly want to hear from him."

"What do you think the chances are that the Court of Appeals will grant a motion to reconsider so we can pursue Collins's testimony?"

"Not outstanding. It looks like an eleventh-hour delay. And they'll want to adhere to their prior conclusions about the case, no less than other human beings."

Arthur nodded, frowning. He had the same opinion.

"You want a friendlier forum, if you can find one, Arthur. Someone who was inclined to believe Erno in the first place, I'd say."

"Harlow?"

"Why not?"

"He has no jurisdiction for one thing. The case is in the Court of Appeals."

But she had ideas about that, too. Like Muriel, Gillian's career had been made exclusively in the state courts. Her knowledge of federal law and procedure had been nil when she entered Alderson, but after years of helping other prisoners craft futile petitions for relief in the federal system, she had acquired considerable expertise.

Arthur reached down for his briefcase to make notes. Together, they began to sketch out a motion. Each came up with phrases and Arthur read the sentences back. He moved the candle on the tabletop next to his pad. In the wan light, she watched him, eager, happy with her and with himself. The focus of her concern was as much Arthur as Gandolph, but she shared his excitement in finding some hope for Rommy in the law. The power of the law, whose drab reality was nothing more than words on the page, struck her then, not simply its determining role in the life of other citizens, but in hers. The law had been her career, the site of her triumphs and of her downfall, and now, through Arthur, a source of recovery. Its words, long forcibly unspoken, remained the language of her adult being. Even as Arthur and she gently debated what to write next, she was unsure whether to accept that recognition with exhilaration or misery.

35

AUGUST 10, 2001

The God of Fingerprints

MIDDAY ON FRIDAY, Larry received a message from Maurice Dickerman, Chief Fingerprint Examiner and Head of the Kindle County Unified Police Force Crime Lab, requesting that Larry visit his office in McGrath Hall. After studying the slip, Larry rolled it into a ball the size of a pea and tossed it. Once he saw Dickerman, there would be no choice about calling Muriel, which Larry had avoided for the last two days. This morning, she'd left him a voice mail about Arthur's latest filing in the Court of Appeals, in which she'd sounded chipper and cute, clearly happy to have the excuse to track him down. He'd promptly pushed delete.

In the old days, he'd run from her after every encounter, but that was because he wouldn't say to himself that he was a complete case for this woman, that the air smelled cleaner and brisker when she was around, that he needed someone to go with him stride for stride. Now he was hiding because he was unsure about how much of that he wanted to say today.

And while he avoided Muriel, he avoided his wife as well. He had thought this stuff was done in his life—smelling his clothes before he put them in the hamper to ensure Nancy wouldn't catch the scent of another woman's powder or cologne. Ten years ago, he'd been so blown out and defeated when Muriel called it quits that he couldn't fake it with Nancy. One evening after he'd collapsed in a recliner, several beers to the wind, Nancy had stood over the chair.

'Ripped again? Let me guess. One of your chickie-poos dumped you?'

He felt too weak to lie, but she was astonished by the truth.

'Am I supposed to feel *sorry* for you?'

'You asked.'

'And I should cut you some slack?'

But she did, because she was Nancy and too nice not to. They tacitly agreed that they'd get back to the lawyer with whom they'd been discussing a bloodless division of property when Larry was in a better frame of mind. Six months later, they still meant to do it. Even after two years, Larry figured each of them was just waiting for something better to come along. Nancy, however, held certain trumps. She was never going to leave his boys. And as time went on, his gratitude to her for that and for a character worthy of canonization approached the boundless. There was no longer much point in other women—they did not measure up to Muriel, and, more important, he owed Nancy that much respect, after she'd passed on the opportunity to throw his ass out. Sometimes when Larry considered the prevailing amity between his wife and him, he wondered if this was simply how marriage was supposed to be, calm and respectful. But no. No. There had to be a melody line that grabbed you, not just harmony and chorus.

That conclusion brought him back to Muriel. No good was going to come of this, he thought. That was something his mother liked to say and she'd say it now. If he'd slept two hours total since Wednesday, that was a lot. The inside of his stomach felt as if it had been sandpapered, and in the mirror, his eyes looked like craters. And even he could not see there any clue about what he really wanted. All he knew for certain as he arrived at Dickerman's door was that his life had gotten beyond him.

An angular New Yorker, Maurice Dickerman was generally referred to by cops and prosecutors and even most of the defense bar simply as the Fingerprint God. Mo was a regular lecturer at universities and law-enforcement conferences around the country, a distinguished researcher who'd authored the leading texts on prints. Given his renown, on any given day he was more likely to be offering expert testimony in Alaska or New Delhi than supervising the Crime Lab, but on a police force where scandal was not infrequent—two separate crime rings of cops had been busted in the last year, one for selling dope, one for robbing jewelers—Mo was a precious asset, a unique source of credibility and distinction. In the mid-1990s, his threat to leave had finally choked the money out of the county to buy an automated fingerprint identification system, an innovation other departments of comparable size had possessed years before.

In 1991, when Gus Leonidis, Paul Judson,

and Luisa Remardi had been murdered, an unknown fingerprint generally could not be identified without isolating a specific suspect. Unless a perp had left behind all the fingerprints that appeared on his ten-card— the inked impression of each finger taken when a suspect was booked—there was no way to tell which finger a partial came from, and thus no way to match the unknown print against the vast catalog of fingerprints maintained by the Force locally and the FBI nationwide. Computer imaging changed that. AFIS, automated fingerprint identification systems, allowed the machine to compare an impression against the stored pictures of every known print in the county. AFIS had made it possible, for example, for Muriel to determine overnight that none of the prints left at Paradise in July 1991 were Erno's.

The major drawback of AFIS was time. Even with computers getting faster every month, each print submission tied up a machine for roughly an hour. In a case like Gandolph's, where seven or eight hundred latents had been lifted at the restaurant, there was no practical way to attempt to identify all of them, given the other demands on the Force. But if Mo developed a print on the gun Faro Cole had brandished at Ike's, it would be only a matter of minutes to match it against the county's database, which necessarily included prints from a multiple arrestee like Collins Farwell.

Mo had just returned from two and a half weeks in Paris, teaching fingerprint developments to the *gendarmes*, an absence that had kept him from responding to Larry's original request to examine Faro's gun. Now, he insisted on showing off the Parisian snapshots stored on his p.c. Mo was a hard guy to interrupt. He wasn't called the Fingerprint God only out of reverence. He spoke in complete thoughts and usually insisted on finishing them, and as he clicked his mouse, he told Larry a lot more than he'd ever wanted to know about the sculptures in the Tuileries and the antique district in the sixth arrondissement. In a hard chair on the other side of Mo's desk, Larry awaited the chance to ask if Mo had found anything on the weapon. When he finally put the question, Mo slowly turned from the computer and lumped his tongue into his cheek.

"Do I take it, Larry, that this is on the Gandolph case? The one I've been reading about in the papers?"

Given the Byzantine alliances in the Hall, Larry had not identified the case in the paperwork and so Mo's prescience caught him up short. There was an ethereal element to Dickerman. McGrath Hall was a good place to appear not to notice stuff, and Mo's consciousness was believed to be confined to only two subjects, fingerprints, naturally, and baseball, about which he also seemed to know everything, ranging from the seasonal totals for Home Run Baker to the present statistical likelihood of the Trappers scoring three runs in the bottom of the ninth, odds that always approached zero.

"That's a pretty good guess, Mo."

"I wouldn't really call it a guess, Larry." From the other side of his desk, where the crumpled paper bag from his lunch still rested, Mo treated Larry to an extended look.

"What are you telling me, Mo?"

"Well, let me just show you what I did. You can draw your own conclusions."

With that, from a metal file drawer behind him, Mo removed the pistol and the carbons of several forms that had accompanied the gun from Evidence. It had been resealed in the heavy plastic, now brittle and brown along the creases, in which it had been stored since Erno shot Faro in 1997. Larry hadn't seen the weapon until now. It was a revolver, a .38 by the looks of it. Given procedures established to combat the notorious propensity of firearms and narcotics to disappear from the police Evidence Room, Larry, in the absence of a court order, would have had better luck getting a look at the Crown Jewels, and he'd simply requisitioned the pistol to Fingerprints once he'd determined it had never been released. When a prosecution was complete, the legal owner of a firearm utilized in a crime could apply for return. Evidence would check with ATF and examine the indexes of stolen firearms. If the gun was clean, the owner could have it. But Faro Cole had never bothered, which hadn't surprised Larry, given Faro's disappearance after the shooting.

In his tedious fashion, Mo now explained how hard it was to lift fingerprints long after a suspect's last contact with the object. Because prints were generally left by an oily residue emitted with perspiration, they tended to evaporate over the years. Larry knew all of that, which was why, in the days when he was looking hard for Faro, he had requested that the Fingerprint God himself conduct the examination. Notwithstanding the lectures, it had been a good thought, because Mo appeared to have had some luck.

"In this case, the only latent that developed with standard techniques was right here." Mo pushed his black glasses up on his nose and pointed with an eraser tip, through the plastic, at a couple of spots on the barrel, then showed Larry the digital photos on his computer monitor. "They're very, very partial. AFIS kicked out about half a dozen ten-cards. After visual examination, I'd say they appear to be from the right middle finger and thumb of this guy. But I wouldn't call it a courtroom-quality opinion. A good defense lawyer would have me looking like a barking seal for making on such scant impressions."

He laid down the ten-card. It was a six-by-nine file card, filled with the familiar black reliefs of fingerprints, four each in two rows for the fingers, two larger blocks for the thumbs, and then, at the bottom, a simultaneous impression of five fingers on each hand. To ensure the reliability of the identification, a face-on photo of the finger-prints' donor was laminated to the upper left-hand corner of the card. The handsome young man, looking entirely vacant in the light of the flash, was Collins. Larry's better senses had told him this was coming, but apparently he'd held out hope, because a sigh forced itself from him. Life would have been easier.

"Seems he was holding the gun by the muzzle," said Mo.

"That's what the reports said," Larry told him. "But I still need to be 100 percent it's this guy." Larry tapped the ten-card. With something less than absolute certainty, Arthur would have a harder time making any use of the evidence.

"I understand. And I wanted to confirm my opinion. I did a second-tier examination. Down here on the butt, I noticed something. What does that look like to you?" He was indicating a filament of color, almost the same shade as the ochre handle of the gun.

"Blood?"

"I'd say this man has a chance to be a homicide detective. There's usually blood at a shooting. And blood is an interesting medium for prints. It dries quickly. And the impression is often more permanent than a finger-oil print. But when you're identifying prints in blood, the chemicals the techs routinely dust with, which adhere to sweat residues, don't work. Here the latent is literally etched in the blood, and often so faintly it's not visible. You don't see any bloody prints on that gun, do you?"

He didn't.

"A decade ago," said Mo, "that would have been the end of the line. Today, we take an infrared digital photograph that highlights the blood and screens out the underlying medium, in this case, the brown handle. Then I filtered that photo further for any striated imagery. And when I did, there were four blood-prints present—three partials and a very clear thumbprint. Two partials and the thumb turned up on the gun handle. And one partial was on the trigger."

Mo slid his chair back so that Larry could see the pictures on the large monitor. Larry nodded dutifully, but he was impatient.

"Did you run those through AFIS?"

"Naturally," said Mo.

Dickerman reached into his file folder and laid two ten-cards on the desk in front of Larry. One was close to twenty-five years old, taken upon Erno Erdai's entry into the Police Academy, the other from his arrest for shooting the man whom Larry now knew for certain was Collins.

"That's how come you realized it was the Gandolph case," Larry said.

Mo nodded.

"See," said Larry, "Erno took the gun off the guy who was holding it by the muzzle—let's assume it's Collins—and shot him. That's what Erdai was doing time for. And that's why his print's on the trigger."

"That information could have been helpful," said Mo dryly. "Not having it at the time, I went over the weapon once more, still hoping to confirm the identification of Mr. Farwell. As an afterthought, really, I did what I should have done in the first place and checked the cylinder for ammo. I was delighted to learn that Evidence had sent over a loaded piece—and that I'd been dumb enough to work on the trigger without checking to find out."

"Sorry," said Larry, "but that sort of figures. Erno's lawyer had said he would plead by the time they got him to the station. So I guess nobody bothered processing the weapon after that."

"I guess," said Mo, shaking his head at the legendary stupidity of everyone, including himself. "My wife thinks I have a nice desk job. Do you think anybody would have figured it was suicide?"

"Not during baseball season, Mo."

Mo made a mouth and nodded. He hadn't thought of that.

"How many rounds were there?" Larry asked.

"Just one. But there were also four casings in the other chambers with firing-pin markings."

Mo was saying the weapon had been fired four times. The reports were uniform that Erno had shot Collins only once. With Mo's permission, Larry reached out for the bag and pressed down on the plastic to get a better view of the gun. It was a five-shot revolver, definitely a .38.

"Any rate," said Mo, "once my heart started beating again, it turned out to be a worthwhile expedition. Very clear prints on every casing. Those chambers, I guess, kept things moist." Mo clicked to display new photos, then pointed to the bullets and the four casings in a separate plastic envelope inside the bag with the gun.

"And did you get a hit on the prints in the database?"

"Yep. Man was arrested in 1955 when he was twenty-two for Mob Action." Mob Action usually meant a bar fight, charges that were almost always dismissed. Mo laid that card down, too. After ten years, Larry had to work to place the face, particularly because the man in the picture was far younger than the guy Larry knew. But it came. The fellow with the hangdog look in the black-and-white mug shot was Gus Leonidis.

For just an instant, Larry was pleased with himself for remembering. Then a sensation of radical alarm fired through his limbs as he took in the meaning.

McGrath Hall had been built as a World War I Armory. The Force had occupied the building since 1921, and as the jokes went, several of the clerks had been here since then. It was a gloomy timeless tomb. In recognition of his status, Mo had an office with a northern exposure. The large double-hung windows overlooked the crumbling Kewahnee neighborhood nearby, buffered by a patchy lawn, an iron fence, and several trees. Larry could see a fast-food wrapper tumbling along in the wind like a frisky boy and he watched until it rose out of the frame. This case, he thought. Man, this case.

Larry bent again toward the weapon. It was a Smith & Wesson—Gus's gun, no doubt of that. And Gus's gun had Erno's print on the trigger, and one unfired round in the cylinder. Another slug had been removed from Collins Farwell in surgery. That left three bullets unaccounted for. Larry told himself, No, then No, then followed the train of thought to the end of the line.

"You think this is the murder weapon on my case, Mo?"

"I think Ballistics can tell you for sure. And I suspect the DNA deacons can say whose blood was on Erdai's hand. I need to send this gun back to the Evidence Room for purposes of the chain. But I'm going to make damn sure somebody comes over here and signs for it. I just wanted to give you a heads-up."

Mo handed over an envelope containing his report. Larry put it in his jacket pocket, but his mind was stumbling along. All Larry had to go on right now was the same witchy instinct that so often guided him. But the cool, deliberate homing mechanism of instinct said the blood on Erno's hand was not

Collins's. Now that he had time to think, Larry realized that the reports from the shooting at Ike's all said at least a dozen cops had jumped on Erno right after he shot. The gun had been wrested from him before Erno approached his bleeding nephew. So the blood on the handle of Gus Leonidis's gun came from somebody else. Like a slow grinding mill, Larry turned through the possibilities, fighting mostly himself. Luisa Remardi had been shot point-blank. And if Erno's fingerprint was etched on the trigger in Luisa's blood, that meant Erno was the shooter on July 4, 1991.

Erno was the shooter. This was the murder weapon. And somehow Collins had that gun in his hand six years later. Collins's prints were there, too. The only guy whose fingerprints weren't on it was Squirrel. And he had confessed.

"So Erno and/or Collins did this together with Squirrel," Larry said. "Squirrel didn't rat them out, and Erno returned the favor once he knew he was dying."

Mo shook his long face. "All I can tell you, Larry, is whose fingerprints are there."

Larry knew that. He was just explaining it to himself. Squirrel had confessed. Squirrel had known about this very gun. Squirrel had Luisa's cameo in his pocket. And Squirrel had told Genevieve he was going to kill Luisa. Nothing had changed. Not so far as Squirrel was concerned.

What in the hell was up with Collins?

When Arthur got hold of this, it was going to be mayhem. The case that wouldn't end was going to rev up again to 7500 rpm's. As Larry stood, Mo pointed toward his sport coat where Larry had placed the report.

"I'll let you be the messenger in Center City."

"Eternal gratitude," he said. He looked at Mo and added, "Fuck."

Outside, in front of the Hall, there were splintered park benches where the civilian personnel often ate their sandwiches in the summer months. The squirrels, accustomed to feasting on crumbs, came out of hiding and jumped around Larry as soon as he sat down to think.

There wasn't even a word for what he was. 'Upset'? But he always learned things at these moments of revelation. And what he was learning here was that he wasn't really surprised about Erno. He'd always factored in the possibility that Erdai was messing around in proximity to the truth. Erno was the shooter. He repeated it to himself several more times. The consequence shook him, but not the fact.

What bothered him more, as the minutes wore on in a day of wearying humidity, was Muriel. He was going to have to see her now. For real. He sat on the bench enduring everything he'd been going through for the last two days, the same congested feelings, his pulse skipping at the thought of being in the same room with her. And in this moment of revelation something else was clear: Muriel was never going to leave Talmadge. She was never going to sever herself from Talmadge's influence with an election sixteen months away. No matter what, she hadn't changed that much. And even forgetting the election, she'd invite scandal by admitting she was sleeping with a witness in an ongoing—and controversial—case. The hard-boned, clear-eyed part of Muriel that had always drawn Larry to her meant, in the end, that she'd never give up her entire career for his sake. What was left for the two of them was skunking around, more hotel rooms, begging for time. And Nancy, since she was a woman, the kind who paid attention, would know. What he was really butchering himself about was the life he'd made without Muriel. The fact that he was even considering chucking it in order to reach for something ungraspable filled him with bitterness, as if his heart was pumping battery acid.

He could feel the report in his breast pocket. He wasn't ready for any of this. Not for Muriel. Or to read in the press about some new fucking breakthrough in a murder case that was solved a decade ago. He was ready for Rommy Gandolph to be gone and for his own life to be at peace.

Or was he? These chances didn't come around very often—to recover what had been lost and was still regretted. To reverse the mistakes of a stupid and more ignorant self. Could he just let that opportunity go? He sat there dizzy with doubt, ready to cry out for no purpose at all. Then he tore the report into several pieces and dropped it in the trash. The squirrels rushed over, but for them, like others, there was only disappointment.

36

AUGUST 17, 2001

Lincoln Land

IN JUDGE KENTON HARLOW'S COURTROOM, there was no longer any expectation of drama. The vast gallery of onlookers was gone and the press contingent had dwindled to the standard retinue—Stew Dubinsky, Mira Amir, and a local news-service reporter, fresh from J school, who, even to Arthur's eyes, needed to learn how to dress. With the media, Arthur had downplayed the allegations of the motions he'd filed. Whatever hopes he had with Harlow would not be enhanced if the judge felt Muriel had already been punished in the papers for her lapses.

Arthur had not slept well. He was at a loss about exactly where Rommy's case was headed. With Muriel's letter about Collins, he might prop the coffin lid open for some time to come, and he even had flights of fantasy that Collins could somehow establish Rommy's innocence. Yet lately, for whatever reason, Arthur had become concerned for his future. Sooner or later, this was all going to end. As Gillian had put it weeks ago, life would be life again, not an adventure. Never without a long-range plan, he suddenly could see nothing clearly. And that uncertainty had reached his dreams, turning them turbulent. Near five, he had crept into the kitchen, to the eastern window, to watch the fiery disc of the sun burn its place into the sky. It's going to be okay, he told himself. He believed it, but never more so than twenty minutes later when Gillian in a thin white robe found him, drew her chair beside his, and, without a word between them, held his hand while the sun regally threw off its rosy disguise and in blinding beauty ascended.

With Carol Keeney, and a determined step, Muriel arrived in the courtroom. She was dressed in a sleek pantsuit, looking, as always, like a lean cat ready for a fight. She deposited her files on one of the counsel tables, then strolled across the courtroom and plopped down beside Arthur on the front bench where he, and several other lawyers

here on motions, awaited the commence-
ment of court.

"So," she said. "How big is that top hat of
yours? Any more rabbits left in there?"

"I'm hoping this one is enough."

"This is really clever, Arthur. I grant you
that."

Arthur had eked one more extension from
the Court of Appeals, this time for his motion
to reconsider the order terminating Rommy's
case, so he could investigate the matters
about Collins that Muriel had disclosed in her
letter. The next move, plotted with Gillian,
was far more unorthodox. Under Rule 11 of
the Federal Rules of Civil Procedure, Arthur
had asked Judge Harlow to sanction the Kindle County Prosecuting Attorney's Office for
failing to disclose what Collins had told Larry
in Atlanta. Essentially, Arthur claimed that
Muriel's response months ago to Arthur's
motion to grant Collins immunity had been
functionally false. As punishment, he wanted
Judge Harlow to order Muriel to immunize
Collins and allow Arthur to take his deposition. In theory, Judge Harlow no longer had
power over this case. Yet the original judge
was in the best position to determine if he
had been lied to and so such questions were

referred first to him. And the law would defer to the sanctions he imposed if he found a party had acted in bad faith.

"The Court of Appeals will see right through this, Arthur. Smart as this is, it's hopeless in the long run."

"I don't think it's hopeless, Muriel. I think Judge Harlow may feel you were hiding material information."

"I wasn't hiding anything, Arthur. It was Erno who was hiding—and lying."

"He was protecting his nephew."

"By shooting him? Besides, I don't think there's a motive exception for perjury. Erno's word is worthless, Arthur. It always was."

"Especially if you won't disclose anything that backs him up."

"Nothing backs him up, Arthur."

"How about Collins saying he prays every night for God to forgive him for what Erno and he did to Rommy? How could you possibly sit on that in good conscience?"

"It's b.s., Arthur, Collins getting his uncle's back on the cheap, blowing smoke up Larry's behind without the risk of perjury. And you got the information, Arthur, as soon as it appeared remotely relevant to anything."

"What else is there, Muriel, that you've decided isn't remotely relevant?"

"Arthur, I told you and the judge in my response that you have everything conceivably favorable to your client."

"Except Collins's testimony. You really think the courts are going to let you keep Collins in the closet while you execute Rommy?"

"Collins is a sideshow, Arthur. There's nothing that connects him to these murders. You've been very good at creating sideshows. That's your job. I give you credit. I'll tell you another sideshow that interests me."

"What's that?"

"A little birdie says he sees a lot of Gillian Sullivan around your office over there. And holding hands at the Matchbook. What's that about? Inquiring minds want to know." With the question, Muriel bestowed a lurid little smile.

That one set him back several steps, just as Muriel had intended. As Gillian had long predicted, Arthur was not entirely comfortable with the malicious sniggering that the wildfire news about their relationship seemed to have been evoking these days.

"What has that got to do with anything, Muriel?"

"I don't know, Arthur. It's unusual, don't you think?"

"There's no conflict, Muriel. You said on the record months ago that Gillian has no role in these proceedings."

"Sounding a little sensitive, Art. I always liked Gillian. Everybody deserves a second chance."

Muriel didn't care much for Gillian at all, according to Gillian. Both had tended to resent the frequent comparisons that had been made for years around the P.A.'s Office. And Muriel didn't believe in second chances. She was a prosecutor whose credo was punishment for all mistakes—except, of course, her own. Yet she'd accomplished what she wanted to. Arthur was eager to end the conversation. Muriel could see that and stood again.

Several weeks ago Arthur had taken the precaution of advising Rommy in writing that Gillian and he had become "close personal friends." But Muriel's point was not about propriety so much as vulnerability. She'd crossed the courtroom to warn him. If he went in for mudslinging, with high-profile assaults on her professionalism because she'd concealed the information about Collins, she had dirt on him of her own to hurl back.

He'd never been perfectly suited for this profession, Arthur realized. In spite of all the years in the trenches and everything he knew about Muriel, his first hope when she sat down beside him was that she'd come to pass time because she liked him.

"All rise." Harlow strode briskly up to the bench, various papers in his arms. He called and disposed of the few other cases scheduled to precede theirs. When he reached *Gandolph ex. Rel. Warden of Rudyard*, the judge smiled down at Arthur and Muriel as they assembled at the podium.

"I thought I'd seen the last of you folks. Welcome back." He called on Muriel first to respond to Arthur's motions. She was vehement.

"First," said Muriel, "the Court of Appeals has said that there's not a case pending. Second, Mr. Raven is no longer Gandolph's lawyer. Third, the limited discovery period that the court authorized concluded more than a month ago. And fourth, there were no misrepresentations of any kind in any statement we have ever made to Your Honor."

Harlow smiled, still amused by Muriel's style. Barely five feet and one hundred pounds, she hit like a heavyweight. In his tall chair, the judge pushed back to contemplate, combing his hand through his long white hair.

"With all deference to my friends out there who are the eyes and ears of the public," he said, "I think there are some things best addressed back in chambers. Why don't the lawyers join me there?"

The judge ushered them through his outer office into Lincoln Land, as the judge's chambers were often called outside his presence. There were at least fifty portraits and figures of Lincoln at all stages of his life on the walls and shelves, including the Brady photographs. Documents bearing Lincoln's signature were displayed around the room. The judge even had a collection of proof pennies in a case.

Harlow's law clerks, a white man and a black woman, had followed him from the courtroom, yellow pads in their hands. As the judge approached his desk and hung up his robe on a rack next to it, he was laughing.

"Folks," he said, "I have seen lawsuits for forty-some years, and I want to tell you, this one I'll remember. It reminds me of those college football games where everybody is scoring in overtime. If you go get a beer, you can't even tell who's ahead." He stretched a long hand toward the walnut conference table at the side of the room, where Arthur and Muriel and Carol Keeney and the clerks took seats.

The formalities of the courtroom obliged the judge to listen first to the lawyers, but in his inner sanctum, Harlow was far less hesitant to speak his mind. Without a court reporter, he tended to proceed by edict.

"I don't like hiding from the press, not on a case that's received this much attention, but at this stage we all need to be candid so we can move along."

There was a call then from the courtroom. Pamela had arrived, following an appearance in state court. The judge told his courtroom security officers to bring her back.

"Okay, now let's not kid around about these motions," said Harlow, once Pamela, too, was at the long table. "First, Ms. Wynn, you don't know me very well, and I don't know you very well, but I think, speaking privately, both of us will agree that you should have corrected your filings with this court after your detective spoke to Mr. Farwell."

"I wish I had, Your Honor."

"Fine. And Mr. Raven, we both know that if Ms. Wynn were really trying to do you dirt, she wouldn't have disclosed any of this."

"Granted, Judge Harlow. But she waited until after the Court of Appeals ruled. Now my client has to try to undo a virtual *fait accompli*."

"Timing, that's the best of your gripe, Arthur. Right?"

He turned his hand in the air evincing no better than half-hearted agreement.

"I'm not dismissing the point, Arthur. We all know the forum can make a difference. Frankly, Ms. Wynn, if I'd heard that Mr. Erdai's nephew asked God every night to forgive him for what they did to Gandolph, I'd have been pretty damn eager to hear what Collins Farwell had to say."

"With all respect, Your Honor," said Muriel, "our office never grants immunity at the request of defendants or civil litigants, or even courts, who want to gain access to testimony. If the legislature thought those persons should have the power to bestow immunity, it would have given it to them. And it hasn't. We wouldn't immunize Mr. Farwell, then or now."

The judge squinted at Muriel for a second.

"I don't think counting the missiles in our arsenals is the right approach here, Ms. Wynn. Each of us has various powers. You have the power not to grant immunity. And I have the power to enter certain findings you might not like. And Mr. Raven has the power to make sure they're heard far and wide. Rather than power, I'd prefer to talk about what's fair. It's obvious to all of us that Collins Farwell knows something about the circumstances that gave rise to this crime, which he didn't disclose a decade ago. Mr. Raven says we should know everything we can before we execute his client, and that strikes me as a pretty good point. Now, given what Genevieve Carriere told you about the way Mr. Gandolph was carrying on back in July of 1991, none of us is going to be very surprised if it turns out that Mr. Raven is sorry he asked to interrogate Mr. Farwell. But he'll have some peace of mind as his client and he face what's coming next. As will you. And I.

So I'd rather we all take a day or two to re-flect on what's fair, rather than our powers, since that may well just be the pathway to sorrow for all of us."

Beneath his overgrown eyebrows, shot with white, the judge again peered at Muriel. She said nothing, but clearly took the toll of what she was up against. The bottom line was exactly what Arthur had said to her in the courtroom. Kenton Harlow was not going to allow Rommy Gandolph to be exe-cuted without hearing Collins's story. The fact that Farwell's testimony might inciden-tally show up the Court of Appeals for putting an early close to the case was, with-out doubt, no small incentive to Harlow. But he was giving Muriel few options. With the press looking on eagerly, she could mag-nanimously immunize Collins, extolling her dedication to the truth, or she could fence with a far shorter stick against a federal judge who might send her off on her election campaign officially branded a liar.

"Why don't we all think about it?" said Harlow. He summoned his minute clerk and dictated a brief order, stating that Arthur's motion was entered and continued, and then sent them on their way. Muriel hurried

off, her face compressed by cold indignation. As soon as she was gone, Pamela
could not resist throwing an arm around
Arthur and giving him a robust squeeze,
further emphasized by another of her glimmering smiles.

"This was brilliant," she said. Arthur for
the moment was her hero.

He declined any credit and sent her back
to the office to draft a brief status report on
today's proceedings for the Court of Appeals.

37

They Know

WHEN MURIEL RETURNED to the office, she paged Larry, requesting he get here on the double; she also called the Detective Commander to be certain her message wasn't ignored. Immunity for Collins was the P.A.'s decision, but the case detective was entitled to be consulted. And it went without saying that it was past time for Larry to show his face. Angry and frustrated by Harlow, she had no more patience for Larry's juvenile antics.

But by the time he arrived an hour later, she had cooled. He appeared haggard, and she felt more or less as she had the last several days. In the past, Larry had often run away from her. She'd hoped both of them were different now, but they'd gotten to the crunch and no, apparently not. The whole thing—the misperceptions and the complications—left her feeling sad and, at moments, humiliated. But she'd departed from church on Sunday ready to believe it might be for the best that things between Larry and her were not going to work out.

At the moment Ned Halsey, the bantam P.A., with his bowlegs and white hair, was holding forth. Ned was famously affable, but he was exercised now. Halsey motioned Larry to close the door, then continued addressing Muriel, who was at her large desk set against the bay window.

"Kenny Harlow was an asshole when I went to law school with him forty-five years ago," said Ned. "He became an even bigger asshole when they gave him a robe. And at this stage, he's such a gigantic asshole that he deserves his own solar system. So if you're asking me will he actually behave like an asshole, the answer is yes."

"I still don't think the Court of Appeals will let him stuff an immunity down our throats, Ned," Muriel answered. As had been true throughout her life, the pathway from anger led to resolve. Stand up. Fight back. Those were her father's mottos in dealing with arrogant powers.

"He'll eat the flesh right off your bones before then, Muriel," said Ned. "'Judge Says Chief Deputy Lied.' Never mind yourself and the permanent damage he'll do to you. Do you care to see the office endure that? I know I don't."

"What?" asked Larry.

She explained in a few strokes what had gone on in court. Larry responded with pique.

"Christ, Ned, you can't give immunity. God knows what Collins is going to say. This far from events, he can basically make it up as he goes. We'll never be done with this case."

"Larry," said the P.A., "we can talk all we want about office policy. It still looks like we're hiding the truth. The guy as good as told you that he helped frame Gandolph."

"What if he was involved with the murders?" Larry asked.

Even Muriel wouldn't buy that one.

"Larry, there's no evidence tying Collins to the murders. No forensics, no statements. Besides, how can the state argue that somebody else might have been involved in the murders when we're trying to execute Gandolph for committing them? Christ, we make that argument, we oughta just build a pine box and jump in."

Ned, being Ned, patted Larry's shoulder reassuringly on his way out. From the door, he pointed at his Chief Deputy.

"It's your case, Muriel. I support you either way. But my vote is to try to cut a deal with Arthur. Offer the immunity in exchange for an end to all further appeals, if it turns out Collins doesn't help them."

She didn't think Arthur would bite on that.

"Good," replied Ned. "At least you'll have some political coverage if you decide to go *mano a mano* with Kenny."

Ned was a good man and wise. She liked his solution. Larry and she watched the P.A. close the door behind himself.

"So," Muriel said. "Was it something I said or something I did? No cards. No calls. No flowers?" A moment ago, she expected to say nothing at all, and even beginning to speak, she had thought she could manage to sound carefree. But the acid virtually sizzled. She placed both hands on her desk and took a deep breath. "Don't worry, Larry. That's not why I called."

"I didn't think so."

"I just wanted to hear you out about Collins."

"You can't give him immunity, Muriel. Dickerman finally got back to me on that gun."

"When was that?"

"Last week?"

"Last week! Hell, Larry, doesn't it say somewhere in the police manual that the prosecutor gets to know the evidence in the case? I filed a response with the judge on Tuesday saying we'd turned over everything we had concerning Collins. When were you figuring on telling me?"

"As soon as I knew what to say about the rest of it."

"'The rest of it.' Is that a personal reference?"

"I think that's what you'd call it."

Here, in the office, they had the advantage of a cooler, more abstracted tone. Across the desk from him, she folded her arms and asked if he thought what had happened between them last week had been a mistake.

"If I knew what I thought, one way or the other, Muriel, I'd have come around and told you. That's the truth. What do you think?"

She swam through the murk of her feelings for a moment, then lowered her voice.

"I thought it was wonderful to be with you. I was sky-high for a couple of days. Until I realized I wasn't going to hear from you. What's that about?"

"I can't take a lot more of this," he said.

She asked what 'this' was.

"Fucking around," he answered. "Me and you. Either we're going to go for it or forget it. I'm too old to live in between."

"I don't want to be in between, Larry. I want you in my life."

"As?"

"As someone I'm connected to. Intensely connected to."

"Part time? Full time?"

"Jeez Louise, Larry. I'm talking about a need, not a battle plan."

"I'm not sneaking around again, Muriel. Either we're in or we're out."

"What's 'in' and what's 'out'?"

"I'm talking about you leaving Talmadge, me leaving Nancy. I'm talking about saying once and for all we made a mistake, a big mistake, way back when, and that we'll try to rescue what's left to be saved."

"Wow," Muriel said. She touched her chest where her heart was now hammering. "Wow." Her thinking had not gone much further than the next opportunity for romance, which until a few seconds ago she'd accepted was likely to be never.

"I'm serious."

"I can tell."

"And I'm not 100 percent sure I want that. But I'm more certain that when I put it to you like this, there won't be anything for me to reckon on."

"Tellin it like it is, Lar."

"I'm trying to."

He was angry, as he was so often, already smarting from the rejection he'd presumed. As for her, she'd left him last week troubled, of course, sad about many things, and brittle with guilt. But in spite of that, percolating to the surface was an airy happiness. She was free of something. For all the danger and stupidity and selfishness of what she had done, she felt herself reaching outward. In the face of his subsequent silence, she was saddest about losing that.

"I'm glad you said this," she said. "I mean it." She spoke calmly, but within, panic still prevailed. So many things were suddenly piled precariously on top of one another. Her marriage. Her job. Her future. Who she was. Shit.

Was love worth not having the life you wanted? That plainly, the question zoomed at her out of the back of her mind. Was love—real, tumultuous love at the advanced age of forty-four—enough to make up for all the other things she aspired to? The poems and the storybooks declared that the only answer was yes. But she wasn't certain what grown-ups said. At least this grown-up.

"I need to think about this, Larry. Think hard." She could see it was the first remark she'd made that pleased him.

"Yeah," he said. "Think hard." He looked at her a little longer. "But you probably won't be talking to me."

"And why is that?"

His anger was abruptly behind him. He collapsed in the oak chair at the corner of her desk.

"Because," he answered, "I still haven't told you what Mo said about that gun."

LARRY HAD SPENT MOST DAYS in the past twenty-plus years chasing around the most dangerous so-called humans in this city. He'd pursued them down dim gangways and around dark corners, even led the charge in full-body armor years ago when they pinched Kan-El, leader of the Night Saints, who was holed up with a cache of weapons he'd somehow bought from the Libyan army. Larry was always exhilarated on those occasions, dancing along on his nerve endings, a feeling reprised from game time when he played high-school ball. He never felt the dread, or the sick gastric backup in the rear of his throat he was experiencing now. The person in the world who scared him most, he realized, was seated across the room. It was suddenly inconceivable why he hadn't told her about the gun last week. The truth, near as he could figure, was he'd just been sick of letting Muriel make all the rules.

As he spoke, she shrank back and grew hard and cool as a stone.

"And what did you do with Dickerman's report?" she asked when he'd finished.

"Let's say I lost it."

"Let's say." She rested her forehead against her hands.

"It doesn't matter, Muriel. Squirrel did it. You know he did it. If he did it with Erno and Collins, he still did it."

"That's a theory, Larry. That's your theory. Maybe it's our theory. But their theory is that

Erno did this alone. And their theory is maybe just an eensy-teensy little bit more persuasive when you add in that his fingerprints are in blood on the trigger of the murder weapon."

"Maybe the murder weapon."

"I have a hundred dollars it is, Larry. Have you got a hundred it isn't? How about ten?" She burned him with her stare. "How about fifty cents?"

"Okay, Muriel."

"Jesus," she said, and sat winding her head. "What the *hell* were you thinking, Larry?"

"My bad," he answered.

"Don't give me any crap, Larry. I want that revolver to Ballistics this afternoon. And to Serology the minute they're done with it. And get ATF to do the trace on the serial number."

"Yes, ma'am."

"You're lucky the way this fell out. If Arthur had discovered this, you'd have ended up in Rudyard as an inmate. Do you understand that?"

"Spare me the melodrama, Muriel."

"I'm not kidding."

"Fuck that stuff, Muriel. I'm telling you now. It's a few days late. The prosecutor never knows everything. You don't want to know everything."

"Meaning what?"

"Come on, Muriel. You know how this works. You don't go to the butcher and ask for his sausage recipe. It's sausage and you know it's sausage. There's nothing in it that'll kill you."

"What else don't I know, Larry?"

"Forget it."

"No *más*, Larry. We're not gonna play Trust Me after this."

"Is this truth or dare?"

"Call it what you want."

It was a contest all right, as he'd always known, and he was going to lose.

"Fine. Do you think that cameo was really in Squirrel's pocket?"

He shut her up with that. Even Muriel the Ferocious showed a reflex of fear.

"I did."

"Well, it was."

"Fuck you," she said in relief.

"But it wasn't there the day I arrested him. It was there the night before and some light-fingered copper took it home. I just sort of replaced it. That's what I'm talking about. Don't tell me you're shocked."

She wasn't. He could see that.

"Larry, hiding fingerprints on the murder weapon isn't the same thing as tightening up the case. You know that." She faced the forward panel of the bay window behind her. "What a mess," she said.

Larry watched her knocking a thumbnail on that gap between her front teeth as she thought it through. In a second he could see her good sense, like a life jacket, beginning to bring her back to the surface.

"I'm going to give Collins immunity," she said then.

"What?"

"If Arthur gets what he wants, he won't ask why. Maybe, if we're lucky, Jackson will let us hear Collins's story in private first."

"You can't give him immunity. The guy was running around with the murder weapon."

"I have no choice, Larry. You gave me no choice. I can't fight this. I can't say Collins may be the murderer and proceed to execute Gandolph. It's one or the other. Hell, Larry, with Erno's fingerprints on that trigger, we're back to square one. And Collins may be the best chance we have. Harlow is right. Collins could put Rommy in once and for all."

"No," Larry said. It was a general protest. He was furious about everything. "It's the election, right? You'd decided to give Collins immunity anyway. Ned already had you turned around. I'm just the excuse. You don't want to fade the heat with Harlow."

"Oh, fuck you, Larry!" She picked a pencil off her desk and threw it at the window. "Goddamn it, don't you understand this? The election is the least of it. There's still the law. There are rules. And fairness. Christ, Larry, it's ten years later and listening to you right now, I wonder myself about what actually happened. Do you get that?" Leaning across her desk, she looked like she was ready to come over and throttle him.

"Oh, I get it." He went to the door. He said, "I'm just a cop."

IN THE EARLY-SUMMER EVENING, Gillian stood at the curb in front of Morton's downtown store, awaiting Arthur. The late office workers were largely dispersed and traffic had eased. A few feet away, two weary women sat slumped beside their large shopping bags inside a glass bus shelter.

By now, Gillian could mark the duration of her relationship with Arthur by the light, which was fading earlier these days. The sun, which they'd seen rise this morning, was now diving into the river, its hot glow spread like a hawk's tail across the light clouds on the horizon. In the shifting winds, there was the faintest omen of fall. Although she'd been told repeatedly that it was the sign of a depressive character, she'd never fully abandoned the inclination to treat natural phenomena—the onset of darkness, or the dwindling of summer—with superstitious concern. Life was good. It would not last.

Arthur was late, but it was clear once the sedan arrived, he was excited.

"Another Muriel-gram," he said as Gillian slid in. He'd brought her copies of two short motions the P.A.'s Office had filed this afternoon in both the U.S. District Court and the Circuit Court of Appeals. Acknowledging receipt of "new and material information concerning the nature and circumstance of the crime," Muriel asked that all proceedings be stayed for fourteen days to enable the state to investigate.

"What in the world?" Gillian asked. "Did you call her?"

"Naturally. I demanded the new information and she wouldn't budge an inch. We fenced around for a while, but we finally agreed that if I give her the two weeks, she'll acquiesce in a motion to set aside the Court of Appeals' order and reopen the case. Essentially, she's taking the points off the scoreboard."

"My God!" Although Arthur was driving, she slid closer to embrace him. "But what could this be? Is she going to immunize Collins?"

"I can't believe that she'd concede in advance that he's credible enough to merit reopening the case. If she doesn't like what Collins says, she'll just call him a liar. It has to be more than that. It's got to be big."

For months now, Arthur had cleaved to an improbable vision of Muriel suddenly seeing the light about Rommy. Gillian held Muriel in much lower esteem, but Arthur refused to view anyone he had worked beside years ago in anything but a kindly light. In any event, she shared his suspicion that there had been a dramatic development.

"So you've had a wonderful day," she said.

"Okay," he answered.

"Some negative development?"

"Nothing on the case. And not really negative. Muriel passed a comment about us. They know."

"I see. And how did that make you feel?"

He shrugged. "Uncomfortable?"

Gillian's harpy of a mother would have uttered a withering I told you so. All of Gillian's cultivated reserve was a means to recycle and restrain that voice which she would never really get out of her head. But poor Arthur always wanted people to like him. Being belittled and mocked for his choice of companion was affecting him, much as she'd always known it would. At 6 a.m., she'd found him lost in thought, staring out at the sunrise.

"Are you trying not to say you warned me?" he asked her.

"Am I so plain?"

"We're going to make it," he said.

She smiled and reached over for his hand.

"Seriously," he said. "What I was thinking this morning was that we should run away."

"Oh, really?"

"I mean it. Just pack up and find another spot. Start from scratch. Both of us. I've made some calls, Gil. There are states where a few years from now, assuming everything stays stable, you'd have a good chance if you applied for readmission."

"To the *bar*?"

He dared to look at her, nodding stoically before returning to the traffic. The notion was breathtaking. She had never even considered that she might be eligible to return from exile.

"And your practice, Arthur?"

"So what?"

"After all those years to make partner?"

"That's all about fear of rejection. I wanted to make it because I wouldn't have been able to stand myself if I didn't. Besides, if this is what I think it is with Rommy, I'm going to be rich. If we clear him, Rommy's going to have an amazing civil suit. I can leave the firm and take his case. He'll get millions. And I'll get my share. I've thought about it."

"Apparently."

"No, not like it sounds. I've just never been really good in private practice. I'm a worker bee. I'm not smooth enough to attract big clients. I just want to find a good case and work like hell on it. Preferably something I believe in."

Years ago, from a distance, Gillian had thought of Arthur as middle-aged from birth. But that was a function of his looks and the fatalistic air he'd acquired from his father. With Rommy's case, he had come to terms with himself as someone who was happiest striving toward ideals, even if they were un- attainable.

"And what of your sister?" asked Gillian.

This, too, ran true to form. In his face, the workings of Arthur's internal life were now as clear to her as if they were being broadcast on a screen, and she watched as his heart was pierced by reality and buzzed back to earth inside his chest.

"Maybe we stay in the Middle West. I couldn't go too far, anyway, if I was handling Rommy's civil case, because I'd have to be able to get back here a couple of times a week. How about I tell my mother she's on? She's been AWOL for thirty years. I've been the parent, she's been the child. What if I just say to her, Time to grow up?"

Gillian smiled, while Arthur actually seemed to reflect on the prospect. She'd never had Arthur's unbounded capacity to surrender to improbable hopes, which was one more reason she'd found refuge in drugs. But she loved watching him fly free. And now and then, recently, she'd found herself airborne with him. It endured no longer than one of those unstable isotopes created in a reactor whose existence was mostly in theory, but she laughed in the dark and closed her eyes and for that fragment of time believed with Arthur in a perfect future.

38

AUGUST 22, 2001

Another Story

JACKSON AIRES took no small pleasure in being a pain in the ass. Initially, he agreed that Collins could be interviewed before his testimony, so long as the meeting took place in Atlanta and the P.A.'s Office paid Jackson's plane fare down there. Then it turned out that Collins had returned to town to deal with Erno's estate. But, Jackson said, his client had now decided that he would speak only after having first been sworn to God to tell the truth. Muriel had the option of reconvening a grand jury to continue investigating the Fourth of July Massacre, because there was no statute of limitations on murder, and she preferred that to a deposition. That way she could examine Collins without Arthur looking over her shoulder or leaking the parts of the testimony he liked, and she'd also avoid violating her office's policy against granting immunity in a civil case. Even Jackson favored the grand jury, since by law, Collins's testimony would remain secret.

On August 22, Collins arrived in the anteroom outside the grand jury chamber. He was in the same dark, stylish suit he'd worn to his uncle's funeral. In his hand was a Bible, encircled by a chain of wooden beads holding a large cross. The book had been thumbed so often it had softened up like a paperback. Along with Aires, Collins's big blond-haired wife was beside him.

Muriel presented the form immunity order, which Jackson read word for word, as if he hadn't seen it dozens of times before, then Muriel opened the door to the grand jury room. Jackson tried to enter with them, knowing full well that his presence was prohibited. Only the witness, the prosecutor, the court reporter, and the grand jurors were allowed inside.

"Got to be present," said Aires. "No choice about that."

After another half hour of negotiation, they agreed Collins would be sworn and his testimony then suspended. A recorded interview would take place at Jackson's law office this afternoon, with the tape supplied to the grand jury later. Muriel was just as happy to get out of the courthouse, where a reporter might get wind of something.

Jackson had several offices, one in Center City and another in Kewahnee, but his principal place of business was in the North End, not far from DuSable Field. Like Gus Leonidis, Jackson had refused to give up on the neighborhood where he had come of age. His office was in a one-story strip mall, which Jackson owned. The anchor tenant on the corner was one of the national pharmacy-convenience chains that he'd cajoled into renting years ago. On the other end of the strip, Jackson's suites branched off beyond the glass vestibule.

Muriel had driven separately from Larry and Tommy Molto. The week had brought intense heat, gusts from the south, and a sun that was a scourge. Tempted to wait outside for the other two, Muriel, after a few minutes, retreated indoors for the air-conditioning.

Eventually, they were all assembled in Aires's large inner office. Given Jackson's vanity, Muriel would have expected that he, like so many others, would have treated his walls as a monument to himself, but most of what surrounded him were photographs of his family—three children, all lawyers in other cities, and, if Muriel's count was accurate, nine grandchildren. His wife had been gone a few years now. Looking at the office, hearing the bustle beyond where Jackson employed two other attorneys, Muriel wondered whether he would tell you that America was a great country, or that he shouldn't have had to scrap so hard for what he deserved. Both were true.

"Muriel, you sit here." In an act of unexpected gallantry, Jackson was offering her the large chair behind his desk. The furniture throughout the room was square and functional, Danish modern in the hands of an office discount store. In the meantime, Aires took an armchair at the front corner beside his client. Like a chorus, Collins's wife and Larry and Molto all found seats behind them. Jackson, being Jackson, took out his own small tape recorder and laid it on the desk next to the one Muriel had already placed there.

As soon as both recorders were rolling and tested, Collins looked to Aires and asked, "Can I talk now?"

"Let the lady ask you a question, why

don't you?" said Jackson. "This isn't drama class. You don't give a soliloquy."

"There's only one thing worth saying," Collins answered.

"Which is?" asked Muriel.

"My uncle Erno killed those folks and Gandolph was no part of it."

She asked how Collins was so sure. He looked to Aires, who lifted the back of his hand to him.

"Well, you started in, you can't hardly stop now," Jackson said.

Collins closed his remarkable umber eyes momentarily, then said, "Because, may Jesus forgive me, I was there to see him do it."

Aires's chair was too tall for Muriel. Her high heels hung off her feet and she had to kick a couple of times at the carpeting so she could turn to get a better look at Collins. His hair had receded a bit, and he'd thickened, but Collins remained one of God's unearthly beauties. His face was fixed as if he were attempting to show courage in the face of the truth.

"I don't ever want to tell this story again," Collins said. "That's why I need Anne-Marie to hear it now, so it can be said and done with. My Lord and Savior, He knows I was born in sin, but it is a sad thing to think about the kind of man I been without Him."

When Muriel glanced at Larry, he was slumped in his chair next to the air-conditioning register. In the intense heat, he'd removed today's sport coat, folding it carefully on his knee while he studiously observed his own foot tapping the carpet. They were just at the beginning, but she could tell that Larry had already heard too much about Jesus. Over the years, he'd listened to a lot of it, naturally, dudes who'd sliced gang signs into somebody's abdomen and then came to God about thirty seconds before their sentencings. That stuff never bothered Muriel, though. God could sort it out. That was why She was God. Muriel's job was assigning responsibility here on earth.

Muriel backtracked for a minute, spoke the date and time, explained the nature of the proceeding, and asked everyone in the room to speak up briefly so the tape bore a specimen of each voice.

"Let's start with your name," said Muriel to Collins. After he gave it, she asked him for any aliases he had used as an adult. He rattled off at least half a dozen.

"What about Faro Cole? Have you used that?"

"True."

"As an alias?"

"More a new life," he said, and smiled to himself in apparent chagrin. "I'm like a lot of folks," Collins said. "I kept on trying to have a new life until I finally got one." He looked over at his lawyer then. "Can I tell this how I want to?" Aires pointed to Muriel. "I got this in my head a certain way," said Collins to her. "You-all can ask what you like, but first off I'd like to tell it how I know it."

He would anyway. Muriel knew that much. Collins could frame it however he wanted to—as a sinner repenting, as one of the earth's wounded and ill used. At the end of the day, she'd stuff it back into the rigid little boxes of the law. She told him to suit himself.

Collins took a moment to smooth his jacket. He'd worn a white shirt and a smart tie. He still kept himself neat.

"End of the day," he said then, "this is really just a story about my uncle and me. Not that there aren't a lot of other folks who should have mattered. But they didn't. That's the first thing you-all have to see.

"Me and Uncle Erno walked a long road. May never have been on the face of the earth two men who hated each other more than we did sometimes. I think it was because we were the best the other had. I was all he had that might be like a child, and he was near as I had to any kind of father, and it wasn't either one of us who thought he'd got a specially good deal. Here I am, black to everybody who sees me, and this long-nosed hunky, what he really wanted is for me to carry on just like him, and how was I ever gonna do that?"

Collins looked down to the cross and the Bible in his lap.

"I couldn'ta been more than thirteen, fourteen years old, I was done with all them in the old neighborhood. I was black whether they were gonna say so or not, and I was the baddest brother that ever would be. Only it was like I said—Uncle Erno, he was never gonna leave hold of me. I was on those streets, doin the dumb stuff I did, selling crack cocaine mostly and smokin it too, and my uncle, he'd make like he was the police—he loved to do that—come pull me out of those hellholes and tell me I was wasting my life. Was my life, I'd tell him, and just go right back to it. Course, soon as the po-lice had me, I'd call Erno and he'd help me out and tell me never again.

"First adult conviction was in '87. Erno got me in the Honor Farm. And when I came out, you know, I really meant to do good. If you mind yourself, they wipe the slate clean for you. Erno and my ma sent me to Hungary, get away from the influences, and I took my own self to Africa. When I came home, I asked my uncle for help getting into the travel business.

"In 1988, that was the happiest Erno ever was with me. I did all that stuff he was forever telling me I had to do. I went to school, and I studied, and I passed my travel agent's exam and got a job at Time To Travel, and made the scene at work every morning. I walked past the brothers on the street I'd kicked with like I didn't know them. And man, it was hard. It was hard. Erno, you know, he and my mom, they were always tellin me how bad they had it in Hungary— they ate squirrels and sparrows they caught in the parks, all of that—but I was workin and workin and I didn't have money. Twenty-some years old and back to livin with my ma? When I moved up to agent, I was on straight commission at Time To Travel, and there wasn't one of those big corporate accounts wanted to do business with any young black man. And I finally said to him, 'Uncle Erno, I can't make it, man, I tried and tried, but this just isn't gonna work out.'"

Collins glanced up to see how he was being received. Molto took advantage of the interval to stand to check that their tape recorder on Aires's desk was running. Jackson, naturally, did the same thing.

"Erno could see I was headed for backsliding and he was pretty much desperate. At one point, he had some idea that he'd shift airline business to me. One crazy notion after another. And that's how the ticket stuff started. First off, he pretended like these were just tickets that had gotten lost somehow. How stupid was that? I figured the go-down on that real soon."

Larry cleared his throat. "Mind if I ask a few things?" He did not really sound friendly. Caught in the spell of his story, it was an instant before Collins looked up.

"Starczek," said Collins then.

Larry's first question was simple. Where did the tickets come from?

"Back then," said Collins, "tickets were

just startin to come out of a computer. The printers never worked—jammed, wrote on the wrong lines. Half the time, agents still issued tickets by hand and then ran them through that validating machine with their die. If you made a mistake writing up a ticket, you voided it and put the number on an error report. These tickets Erno gave me, they were blank validated hand tickets, listed on the error report so nobody was lookin for them."

"The airlines keep telling me," said Larry, "that sooner or later somebody flying on those tickets would get caught."

"Probably so," said Collins. "But wasn't anyone that ever flew on those tickets. I turned those tickets in to cover the cost of other tickets."

Muriel glanced to Larry to see if she'd missed something, but he, too, appeared confused.

"Suppose I had a customer," said Collins, "who paid in cash for a trip to New York. I'd take a ticket that Erno got me, and write it up as a New York ticket for an earlier date. Validation made it look like it had been issued by hand at the TN ticket counter. Then I'd turn Erno's ticket in to cover the cost of my customer's ticket—as if it was an even exchange. I'd put my customer's cash in my pocket, instead of turning it over to Time To Travel. Rather than a little-bitty piece of a commission, I got the whole price of the ticket. And my share of commission, too. Airline accounting matched the flight coupon against a validated ticket and never looked any further."

"Smart," said Muriel.

"Wasn't me," Collins told her. "Erno was the one who figured it out. He'd seen every ticket scam. Guess he finally got one in his head that would work. Probably took it as a kind of challenge. That's how Erno was."

"Right," said Larry. "That's what I'm wondering about—Erno. Why didn't he just do what a semi-normal person would do and *give* you money?"

Collins tipped his head back and forth as he weighed out an answer.

"Erno, you know, he was one strange kitty cat."

"No shit," said Larry. Collins's narrow mouth turned down. He didn't care for either the language or the idea of somebody else dissing Erno's memory. Muriel delivered a look. It was probably the first eye contact she'd had with Larry since he walked in. Given the tenor of their parting last week, she might have expected defiance, but he responded with a mild nod.

"First off, Erno was cheap," said his nephew. "That's the truth. Once he had hold of a dollar, he didn't care too much to let it go. And, you know, he could get grouchy about how the airline should have treated him better on one thing or another. And heck, man, that outlaw life, it can be real excitin, ask somebody who knows. Erno always pined over all he missed out on when he got tossed from the Academy. But you know, when I hold those babies of mine, I'm always tellin them, 'There's nothin I wouldn't do for you.' And I've thought on it, and I think that's pretty much what Erno was saying to me: You try to make something of yourself, there's nothing I won't do to help."

Collins bent forward to see if Starczek was satisfied. Larry made an equivocal face: Go figure with crooks. Collins went back to his story.

"Even so, I guess I felt like I was still on Erno's string. Went overseas on vacation and scored in Amsterdam and just fell in with the drugs again. When I got taken down this time, Erno quit on me. Put his own self on the line and this was how I repaid him. That was the speech. I was in medium security in Jensenville and he didn't come visit once.

"I didn't really see how bad off I was until I got out in 1990. I only knew two things, really—slangin dope and travel agenting. Black and white, in my mind, if the truth be told. And I couldn't do either. One more narcotics conviction, I was Triple X and gone for life. And I'd lost my travel license when I got convicted in '89. Should have just moved, but young folks, you know how it is, figured I'd beat the system. Called myself Faro Cole, faked the degree information, and sat the license exam all over again."

"Ah," said Muriel. Collins responded with a rueful little smile.

"Got a job at Mensa Travel, strictly commission, and it was the same as before, tryin hard and no money. Well, that thing with the hand tickets had worked okay the first time. Just had to find somebody who could scratch them off the books the right way. Now, I couldn't go over there to TN myself— Erno would have run me out—but I was hangin in the wrong place one night and in comes Gandolph, tryin like always to unload something somebody or another stole. I knew who he was. I'd worked out at the airport right after high school for a couple of months. He used to buy weed off me. By then, he couldn't begin to reckon my name, but I figured, since he always knew if something had come loose of its owner, he might know a ticket agent out at DuSable who'd like to work something. Promised him if it cooked, we'd look after him. That's how I got hooked up with Luisa.

"She didn't want any part of it at first. How I convinced her finally was when I told her Erno had done the same thing. That had some traction with her. She wasn't gonna be Erno's fool or anybody else's."

Muriel asked when this was.

"Oh, we must have started in January of '91. That's when they all got killed, right, '91? I'd say January, then. And it went along fine till I ran into Gandolph in that same place, Lamplight, and it turned out she wasn't givin him anything from her end. Might be she didn't really get it that she was supposed to cover him. Man, I know I told her, but she hadn't done it, and he went all over the airport runnin his mouth, till she finally give him her cameo, just to shut him up while she tried to get together what she owed him."

"You're saying Luisa basically pawned the cameo to him?" asked Muriel.

"Exactly," said Collins. "Said it was like a family heirloom. Course it was too late, cause with Squirrel mouthin off, Erno had fallen to this now and he was trippin. Soon as he heard my name, he knew darn well what was goin down and he got up in my face. He wasn't gonna have me stealin right under his nose, in his shop, specially not as he was the one who taught me how to do it. He told me to quit, or he'd stop it, and next I heard, he'd had Luisa searched for some phony reason—"

"Drugs," offered Larry.

"Exactly," said Collins. "Drugs. Said she had drugs on her. Maybe Erno thought since she was mixed up with me, that we were doin that, too. But she wasn't anybody to treat that way. After that, man, it was on. She wanted money anyway for Gandolph, so she could get her cameo back.

"Early July, she give me the word. Said she'd been real careful, but she had some tickets stashed. She wasn't worried any about Erno, either. Said she'd hide those tickets so wasn't anyone would find them, not to worry. Fourth of July, nobody around, she figured that was the time.

"So come to July 3rd, actually July 4th, past midnight, we had a meet at Paradise. She wasn't in the door two seconds when Erno runs in behind her. He'd been watching her error reports, sneaking around, following her. 'You had it now, lady,' he says to her. 'I gave you a chance.' Looks at me and says, 'You get the hell out of here. And as for you,' he says to Luisa, 'you hand me those tickets you got stuffed in your underwear and write out a resignation right now, or I'm calling the cops.'

"Luisa, man—she was tough. She didn't take it from nobody. 'F you,' she says. 'You ain callin no po-lice. You call the po-lice on me, I'll tell them you did the same thing.'"

Lifting a hand, Collins shifted. The sun was straight in his eyes. Jackson stood to rearrange the blinds. Either recovering his place, or responding to the memory of what he was describing, Collins was still for a second.

"See there, when she said that to him, that was what you'd have to call the turning point. Cause Erno, it didn't even enter his mind that I'd have let on about him. He just figured I'd turned on Luisa. But he would never think I'd tell that kind of secret. Not to somebody who wasn't family.

"Erno—he had a temper. Get all red, eyes like saucers. And you could see right then, he was ready to kill somebody. For real. Only it wasn't Luisa he meant to fade. It was me. If he'd had a gun in his hand, he'd have shot me dead for sure. But he didn't. Not yet. He just started busting on both of us; screamin and what not, and Gus came over and told him to get his butt out of there, and Erno wasn't hearin it. That didn't go on too long before Gus came back with his pistol.

"After that, it was pretty much like my uncle said in court. Erno told Gus he wouldn't shoot anybody, and Luisa grabbed that pistol out of Gus's hand, and Erno went after it. I don't think it was as much of an accident as Erno made out that he shot her. To me, it looked like he had that gun full out of her hand. But it was all so dang fast. Bang! That sound, man, it was like it was still shaking the restaurant five minutes later. And there's Luisa, looking down at this hole right through the center of her, and *smoke*, smoke floating up, like it was coming off a cigarette. For a second, none of us knew what to do except stand there and look at her, it was so peculiar.

"Finally, Gus snapped out of it and went for the phone. Erno told him to stop and Gus didn't stop and Erno put him down, like he was shootin a horse."

"And you?" asked Larry of Collins.

"Me?"

"What were you doing?"

"Man, I'd heard all kind of woofin and carryin on, but truth is, I hadn't never seen somebody killed. It was terrible. Truly terrible. All I was thinkin at first was, Now, how am I gonna get him to take this back? It was so crazy, I couldn't make myself believe it was gonna last. Like things just had to snap back to normal. Then it comes to you, that isn't gonna happen.

"After Erno shot Gus I bust out crying and my uncle, man, started in hollerin. 'Whose fault is this, anyway, Collins? Whose fault?' Right then, I figured I was next, and I even started lookin out the windows, tellin myself there were two shots now, somebody had to hear and call the police. But it was the Fourth of July, nobody's thinking nothin 'cept firecrackers.

"Then Erno saw the last one. Hiding. Poor dude, he was under a table. Erno pointed the gun and marched him down to the freezer. Then I heard the shot. Didn't sound like the first two, for some reason. Something worse about it. For Erno, too. After he came up and looked at me, all that anger, that was done. He just sat there wasted and told me what to do. We were gonna make it look like a robbery. 'Get this.' 'Wipe that.' I did it all."

"Was he threatening you?" Muriel asked.

"He still had the gun, if that's what you mean. But from the look of him, I wasn't thinkin anymore he was intending to shoot me. Truth of it is that it probably didn't ever occur to him that I wasn't gonna do what he said, cause it didn't ever occur to me either. It was just family," said Collins. He stopped and took a heavy breath over that thought.

"And it was you who dragged the bodies downstairs?" Larry asked.

"Right. Cryin the whole time, too." Collins chucked his face in Larry's direction. "You thinkin about those footprints?"

"That I am." Forensics had matched Paul Judson's shoes with the footprints trailing through the bloody drag patterns left by the bodies.

"When I come up the last time, Erno saw that my slip-ons were soaked through with blood. He said, 'You can't go out on the street in those. Go downstairs and see which of them dead men got shoes that might fit you.' That was the first time it even came to me to say no to him. 'I ain putting my foot in no dead man's shoe.' Can you imagine? We actually carried on about that for a while. But I finally did like he said, same as the rest of it."

Collins pointed at Larry. "You go check those shoes that came off the third one, the businessman. Nice pearl-gray pump, I-talian. Faccione, the brand, I think. Too big for him, too. I couldn't ever believe nobody noticed those shoes. What businessman goes round in a pearl-gray pump?"

Muriel could see something moving behind Larry's hard expression: the shoes were clicking. It seemed to be hitting home with him that Collins was probably telling a large chunk of the truth. She hadn't had much doubt of that for some time now.

"We were ready to leave outta there, already at the front door, when Erno snaps his fingers. 'Hold this,' he says. He had everything, wallets and jewelry, bank deposit, the gun, all of it wrapped up in one of Gus's aprons. He sort of tiptoed down the stairs and when he comes back up, he's got a johnny in his hand."

"A condom, you mean?" Muriel asked.

"Exactly. Used, too. After everything else—" Collins just shook his head several times. "Anyway, Erno says, 'Stuffed those tickets up her behind. Couldn't have found them with a miner's light, if I hadn't seen the edge of this here.' She had maybe fifteen tickets rolled tight in that rubber."

Collins for the first time looked back to Anne-Marie. Behind him, his wife had sat with her mouth compressed against the heel of her palm, appearing, to Muriel's eye, as if she was doing her best not to react. But when Collins turned to her, she responded at once. She reached out and the two sat holding hands for a second.

"You okay?" Aires asked his client.

Collins wanted water. They took a break. Everyone needed a minute. Muriel searched out Larry's eye, but he looked funky and wrapped up in himself. Out in the hallway, waiting for the john, Muriel asked Tommy Molto what he thought. Molto picked with a fingernail at spots of tomato sauce on his shirt and tie, and said he didn't know what to think. Muriel wasn't sure either.

When they returned, Anne-Marie had slid her chair beside Collins's and was holding his free hand. The other was still gripping his Bible. After a minute or two of fiddling with the tape recorders to be sure they were running, Muriel gave the date and time, then asked Collins what happened when they left Paradise.

"I followed Erno back to his house, and sat with him in his car. He'd been through some changes that night. We both had. At Paradise, he'd been outta-his-mind angry, then all blown away and subdued. Now he was just flat-out scared, trying to think out every angle not to get caught. He had one lecture after another for me. Make sure and mention to some folks how him and me went out for a pop last night. Don't ever get myself inebriated and start braggin about all this to my homes or some lady I was after. The big thing on his mind, though, was how to get rid of that apron full of stuff in his trunk—the gun, the wallets, the jewelry, it was all in there. It was past three by now and both of us were just too messed up and worn out to deal. I didn't want to have no more to do with any of this. And Erno was flat paranoid. All he could see was how we were bound to get caught, if we went to toss the apron in the river, or built a big fire and burned it all, or buried it in the Public Forest. There'd be light by five. But there was a toolshed in his backyard with a dirt floor—if we dug there, no way anybody was gonna see us. And so we each shoveled till we were halfway to China and threw that apron in there. He said he was gonna come up with a better plan when he calmed down, but I knew the both of us would be happy never to look at any of that again. Then he walked me to my car and right there on the street reached up and hugged me. That hadn't happened since I was ten, and in the middle of all that craziness, maybe the craziest thing of all was how good that felt. Murdered three folks and hugged *me*. I drove off cryin like a child.

"After that night, there just wasn't a way for me to be right with myself. I was done bein Faro for a while, case the po-lice figured out anything 'bout the tickets. It wasn't a week, and I was back in to dopin. Erno tried hard to stop me, but with time to think, I wasn't havin any more of him. One day I'm at Lamplight and there's Gandolph. This has to be two months after all this mess. And with twenty dudes around, he reaches into his pocket, and wrapped in this ratty piece of tissue, there's Luisa's cameo. I knew it straight out. I'd seen it on her neck.

"'Faro,' he says to me—that's all he knew to call me—'Faro, man what-all'm I gone do with this thing now? Ain worth nothin to nobody else.'

"I'm like, 'Word up, nigger, you gone put yourself under. You best get rid of that. Police be sayin you the one who busted a cap in her.'

"He's like, 'How they do that, when I ain done nothin? I'm in mind to find her kin. They pay good for this here, now that she dead. They owe me, cause of how she held out on me.'

"I'm like, 'Do what you have to, brother, but maybe you oughta hold up with that till somebody else is under the weight for dropping her down six. And I don't want to never hear nothin over them tickets.'

"He says, 'Ain no chance of that.'

"Uncle Erno, man, he just was trippin when I told him. He was lookin around for Gandolph after that, gonna roust him and get that piece off him before he made trouble for himself and the both of us, but Erno didn't ever find him, I guess. Wasn't quite winter yet, so Gandolph wasn't hangin at the airport."

Muriel made a sound. Winter. As carefully as Erdai had papered over Collins's role, he'd missed that detail when he'd invented his own encounter with Gandolph and the cameo, and she'd nailed him on the witness stand. It was the first instant she was certain he was lying.

"Pretty soon, I had trouble enough on my own," Collins said. "Second of October I got set up on a big buy-bust. Videotape and everything. Cops knew they had me bad, even when they were shovin me in the cruiser. 'Third time for you, boy. Take a good look out the window, cause you ain never gonna see the street again for the rest of your life.' They were cold. But I had to give them something. I would have started in talking on the way to the station, if I didn't figure those Gangster Outlaws I was kickin down to would kill me first night in the jail.

"Anyway, couple hours back inside, and I'd gotten it in my head that this was all Uncle Erno's fault. If he didn't go and shoot those people, I wouldn't be jammed up like this. And if I stooled on my uncle, wouldn't be any gangbangers to kill me for doing that. Erno though, he was a smart one. Knew damn well what I was fixin to do. He was the first visit I got.

"He's like, 'You told them anything?' I was pretending I didn't understand, but he wouldn't let me get away with that. 'Oh, don't bullshit a bullshitter. I know what you're thinking. And I'm not gonna tell you not to do it for my sake. But I will say that for yours. You tell them the truth, they'll put you right in the middle of it. Whose shoes are on that dead man? Who was stealing tickets with that girl? You're facing life for the dope. They offer fifty, sixty years for murder, you gotta take it. That's not what you want, is it?' Course not. And I'd rather not blame my uncle, specially when I was lookin at him. And he was right anyhow. Erno knew how the cops worked.

"Said he had a better idea. Put all of the blame on that poor lame Gandolph. He'd been runnin his mouth 'forehand how he was gonna kill Luisa anyway. Sort of made himself suspect number one. Just had to lead the po-lice the right way. I wasn't sure

Squirrel'd be silly enough to keep that cameo around after I warned him, but Erno said not to worry, he had all that stuff still buried under his toolshed at home, worse came to worst, he'd figure some way to put a piece of that in Gandolph's hand, say they discovered some stash of his at the airport. Never had to, of course, because that poor hook was still holdin on to the cameo when you-all found him. Still gonna get himself the money he was owed. Dude that soft, once an idea gets into his head, you can't get it out." Collins shook his face in grim wonder.

"Only thing is, I couldn't ever believe anybody would look at that skinny little Squirrel and figure him for a killer. 'Dog'll do it to any bitch he finds,' Erno told me, 'once he smells heat.' My uncle knew the po-lice."

Muriel glanced over to see how Larry had taken that observation, but he was zoned again, staring through the blinds at the parking lot. The truth, as far as Muriel could see, was that Erno had figured things pretty well. His biggest risk was that when Squirrel was arrested, he would start talking about the tickets in order to explain the cameo. But apparently even Gandolph realized that story put him in too deep. Threatening Luisa was way too close to killing her. And even if Squirrel had coughed all of that up, Erno and Collins both knew the police would have a hard time finding Faro.

"That's why you said at the jail in '91 that you'd never testify, right?" she asked Collins. "When you told us about the cameo?"

"Right," said Collins. "Couldn't do that. Rommy would have recognized me as Faro straightaway. No way to keep the whole tale from comin out then. But it worked. I got my ten, and Uncle Erno, he just drove on by like it was an accident on the highway.

"My uncle was good to me all the time I was inside, come visit, packages, whatnot, lecturing me to make the most of this chance when I got out. That came late '96. Old Faro, nobody had tumbled to that, so I was Faro again, ready to go back into travel agenting, but the truth is I wasn't on the street forty-eight hours 'fore I had a pipe in my hand. Everything the same. I was strung out, Erno wouldn't even speak my name. Only thing, I was afraid to start in slanging again. I knew it was life for sure if I got busted with quantity. Couldn't give up my uncle on the murders this time, cause I'd put

Gandolph inside already and there'd be no-body to believe a different tale.

"One night I was hurtin bad. Needed to cop and didn't even have those moths in my pocket they show in cartoons. And it come to me that Erno had said all that stuff that we took out of Paradise that night was still under his toolshed. I went over there with a shovel and started in diggin till I found that apron. Cloth was full of holes, but everything was inside. All I had in mind to do was sell some of it—the watches and rings—so I could buy a couple bottles, but I saw that gun in there and it come in my head that if I had that, I could shake big money out of my uncle. Might be that his fingerprints were still on the gun, so he'd have no choice, gonna have to give what he owed me. I was back to that. How he owed me. Owed me and owed me.

"My aunt came home and said he was down at Ike's. I run in there holdin that gun by the barrel, so I didn't wipe off any prints Erno'd left on the handle. I was screamin about how he messed me up and owed me. I wasn't thinkin too good, naturally enough. Half the folks in that place were po-lice and armed, and they all had their gats out and pointed straight at me ten seconds after I said my first word.

"'Gimme that thing,' Erno says and takes the pistol straight out of my hand, pushed me outside, trying to talk sense, how I was gonna get killed carryin on like this, and couldn't put those killings on him now that I put them on Gandolph. I said, 'Hell, that gun probably got your fingerprints all over it.' 'What of it?' he says. 'Twenty cops just saw me take it out of your hand.' He was right, too, probably, but it was the same old doo-doo so far as I was concerned, him right and white, and me black and back. 'Yeah,' I say, 'I got the rest of where that come from back at your house and a hole under your shed where it been, and you ain walkin from what you done this time, I'm goin back in there, tell everybody you know what a murderin coward you been.'

"Erno, like I said, he didn't care for surprises. Not at all. I was sashayin back inside, and he was screamin out to me, Don't do it, don't do it. If I'd been in a better frame of mind, I surely would have remembered Gus. But I didn't. Anyway, last I recall was goin through the door. Don't even remember the bang. Just the light. I saw Jesus' face that night. I truly did. I heard His voice. I was layin on that floor dyin, I think, but wherever I was, I knew I was all right now.

"And I have been. I went down to Atlanta not long after I was out of the hospital. Been there since. Had my life and finally done right.

"Now, course, it was all turned around. Erno was inside and I was outside. I was the one goin to visit and tellin him how Jesus could be lookin out for him, too. Might be he heard me, I was never sure. But somethin come to him once he knew he was sick. Couldn't just die with all those sins on him. I went to see him not long after New Year's, when he got the word about how bad the cancer was. I was tryin to offer comfort and he just looks at me in the middle of stuff, and says, 'They're gonna execute that poor moron pretty soon.' I knew what he meant. Wasn't the first time we'd talked about it. 'We can't let them do that,' says Erno.

"'Do what you have to,' I told him.

"'No,' he says, 'I ain gonna have shot you through the back to save your life and mine just to put you in the middle of all this now. It's still the same as I said—the po-lice will never believe you weren't in on the shooting.

I'll tell what needs to be told. Not too sure I can get anybody to listen. But I'm gonna try. You just keep your mouth shut. Call Lawyer Aires. Fifth Amendment all the way.'" Collins looked up from his lap and his light eyes found Muriel's again with the same directness as when he'd started.

"That's what happened," he told her.

IT WAS ONE OF THOSE DAYS when it was just going to get hotter until the sun set. Even at 4 p.m., as she stood with Molto and Larry in the parking lot outside Aires's office, she could feel the blacktop softening under her feet. She'd left her sunglasses in her car and she squinted at both men. Facing the tyrannical sun, you didn't have to wonder why people had worshiped it.

"So?" she asked.

Each was mopey.

"I need to think about it," said Molto. "I want to go over the case file. Give me twenty-four. Let's all have a conference on Friday."

Larry and Molto made at once for their cars to escape the heat. Muriel walked to Larry's Concorde before he left. She could feel a touch of the air-conditioned cool inside when he let down the window.

"We never had that talk," she told him.

"No, we didn't." He had put on his Oakleys and she couldn't see his eyes, which was probably just as well. "Any point?"

"I have some things to say."

He shrugged. "I'll be at that house tomorrow night," he said, "putting together a punch list for my crew. Stop by for a beer if you like."

"There or square," she said.

He pulled out without looking back at her.

She opened her car and was still outside, letting the heat escape, when Jackson toddled from the glass doors toward his Cadillac, his briefcase under his arm. He was in a hurry.

"Got a date?" Muriel asked.

Spry and lively, Jackson nonetheless showed an additional spark when he answered, "As a matter of fact. Taking a fine lady to the Symphony in the Park." He'd been a widower for two or three years now.

Muriel asked how Collins was doing. He was in his wife's arms when they'd left.

"He's in there prayin, like he oughta be doin. Take him some time, but he'll be all right. That was the God's truth you just heard, Muriel. I hope you're smart enough to know that."

"If God wants the job, Jackson, I won't even bother trying. But otherwise I'm going to have to figure this out on my own."

"Don't you play with me, Muriel. There wasn't a word that young man spoke that didn't ring true. I'm not even gonna worry about you thinkin otherwise." To start his car and lower the windows, Jackson leaned over the column. After touching the wheel, he cursed the heat and took a second to lick his thumb, but that didn't stop him from waving a finger at Muriel when he turned her way again.

"One thing you should know, Muriel. I been representing that young man since he was a juvenile. Bad a hoodlum as all the rest, but Erno, may he rest in peace, he kept up sayin, 'He's all right, he's all right, he's gonna be okay.' Never can tell, Muriel, which of them will come around. You folks don't even care to try these days. Lock 'em up as long as you can, as many as you can, even kill 'em if they give you a chance."

"Did I just hear you use the word 'hoodlum,' Jackson?"

"Hoodlum or not, you can't ever give up on a human being," Jackson said. "You know why? Because there is just no point in that. Can't be any reason to what we're doing here, if we're gonna give up on people."

If you made Jackson Aires the P.A. tomorrow, he'd condemn half his clients faster than he swatted flies. But he never saw a side he wouldn't take, as long as it put him opposite a prosecutor.

"Enjoy your evening, Jackson."

"I certainly intend to." He allowed himself a wicked laugh, then he sat stiffly on the Cadillac's red leather front seat with his feet still in the parking lot, using his hands to drag his legs beneath the wheel. Apparently, his back was giving him trouble, but whatever his infirmities, Jackson was not too old for love. Nobody was. He revved the engine enthusiastically. With Larry's recent departure, Muriel again was dragged down in an undertow of regret. A few days ago she'd been wondering if she might be willing to trade everything for love. The bizarre ironies of the way this case was working out suddenly pierced her. Somehow it had ended up winner take all. Jackson and Arthur were going to walk their clients and have love to boot. Muriel would get nothing.

"Have you heard the latest on this case?" she asked Jackson before he could close his window.

"What's that?"

"Arthur Raven and Gillian Sullivan. In the chapel of love."

"No," said Jackson. He emitted the same high cackle he had a second before. "How long is that goin on?"

Muriel shrugged.

"Doesn't that beat everything?" Jackson asked. "Arthur Raven and the Junkie Judge."

"The who?"

"Oh, that's just what I called her. The Junkie Judge. Gillian the Junkie Judge. I had several clients who swore they saw her coppin out on the street when she was still on the bench."

"Crack?"

"Heroin. So they said."

"Are you sure, Jackson?"

"They were just street riffraff, but there were plenty of them. Probably be happy to tell you the same thing today if you had any need to hear it. Put them in an angry frame of mind when they had to come up before her, I'll tell you that. Even a thug, Muriel, knows what's fair."

She couldn't tell if she was more astounded or amused. She laughed as she contemplated the whole notion.

"A junkie," said Muriel.

"That's what she was. But she isn't today. Today she's in the chapel of love." Jackson put his car in gear, but he smiled at her with great satisfaction. "See," he said, "it's just like I said."

"What's that?"

"There's just no point to ever give up on a human being."

39

AUGUST 23, 2001

First

FIRST, THEY FUCKED. He'd heard her say 'talk' in Aires's parking lot, but he knew what was coming. She wasn't through the door thirty seconds before they were together, and he couldn't say who had moved first. There was no logic to resisting. Nothing was going to get any better or worse.

But they were less shocked by themselves and thus more at ease. They went to the center, to that timeless essential place where pleasure becomes our whole purpose on earth. At the end, there was an instant when they were changing positions, her hand was on him, and his hand was in her, they had each other's button, and as her eyes briefly opened she gave him a grin of perfect celestial delight.

Afterwards, they lay on the same rug that

still hadn't been cleaned, naked and silent for quite some time.

"Wow," said Muriel finally. "Home run. Grand slam."

He repeated her words, then went off to the kitchen to get a beer for each of them. When he returned, he took a seat on a stepladder one of the painters had been using.

"So," he said, "I take it this is *au revoir*."

"You think that's what I came here to say?"

"Isn't it?"

"Not exactly."

"Okay, so tell me."

Nude, she sat up with her hands behind her. He wondered exactly where her tits had gone. She hadn't had much to start with, but now it was just beans on a plate. Not that he had anything to talk about, with a stomach that got in the way of his hard-on. Life, when you faced it, was cruel.

"Larry, I've done a lot of thinking. I want things that run smack into each other."

"Such as?"

"Am I running for P.A.?"

"You're running. What's next on the checklist?"

She gave him a look. "Do you think it would be as crystal clear if it was your life?"

"It is my life."

"Larry, how can you make love to me like that, then hate me so much ten minutes later?"

"Because I'm not going to make love like that to you again. Right?"

"What if you ease up a little, and come sit beside me, and do something stupid like hold my hand, and talk to me as if we're two people who care a lot for each other, instead of the Palestinians and the Israelis?"

They weren't hand-holding types. He and Muriel never had found a middle ground. Either they were fully joined or completely apart. But he settled next to her on the rug and she circled her arm over his biceps.

"You're right, Larry, I'd like to make this campaign. But I'm not sure that the windup on this case is going to permit that. Either way, though, I'm not walking out on Talmadge today—for the right reasons and the wrong ones, too. I can't win without him— that's the brutal truth. But, Larry, he also deserves better than that from me. I need to look him in the eye and tell him this marriage hasn't gone very well. I've never done that."

"And you think that'll fix things?"

"Look, I married Talmadge on dubious premises. And I don't mean because I'm ambitious and he's ambitious—the truth is, that's the one part that's worked and always will. I'm talking about the way I see myself and see him. You're the one who read me that headline. But I'm going to work that through with my husband, not with you. Wherever that leads. Which, best guess, is probably out the door."

She was asking him to stand by, he realized suddenly. She was telling him they might still have a chance.

"And so what am I supposed to do? See if I can remember the words to 'You Keep Me Hangin' On'? I told you I can't live in between."

"I heard that. And I'm not proposing a life of secret passion. For both our sakes, this better stop. I'm just letting you know what I'm thinking. But I haven't paid my subscription to the psychic hotline. Who knows what happens? You said ten years ago you were getting out of your marriage, and you've still got the same address."

"Different situation."

"You get the point."

He did. He looked straight down at the rug. His dick, which had always gotten him in so much trouble, was bunched up like a baby. But that wasn't the part that hurt. He was desperate to stay angry, because it would keep the rest of it at bay. In the meantime, her grip tightened on his arm.

"But look—I have to say one more thing. What happened with this case—Gandolph? What was disclosed and what wasn't? A lot of that's my fault. I see that now. You told me you weren't like me and I didn't listen. There's a reason people say not to shit where you eat and not to fuck where you work. And I did it anyway. Because I had to know what it was like to be outside my marriage. I wanted to see how it felt."

"And how was it?"

She looked at him a long time.

"Pretty damn good," she said. She stayed there one more second. "But it was stupid and selfish, too. And unprofessional. So if there's blame to pass out on this case, let it land on me. Whatever the impact on my plans."

He liked that. He liked a lot of what she'd said in the last few minutes. It was honest.

Usually, Muriel could be savage about everyone but herself.

"By the way," she said, "speaking of the case, you ready for today's humor?"

"I could use some right now."

She told him what Aires had said about Gillian copping on the street.

"No way," said Larry.

"I scoped it out a little today. Called Gloria Mingham at DEA. Technically speaking, none of this stuff about Gillian is grand jury, but Gloria still didn't like talking about it. She just sort of hummed to me."

"You mean actually hummed, or a figure of speech?"

"Actually hummed, as a matter of fact."

"What was the tune?"

"'Toot, Toot, Tootsie! Goo'bye.'"

Larry had a great laugh when he got it. "Gillian tooted? Smoked H?"

"Apparently."

"Makes sense. Can't get a needle into an iceberg, right?"

"Gloria said they had allegations, but nothing they could really nail down. The witnesses were all dopers."

"God, these people are hypocrites," Larry said.

"The feds?"

"Arthur."

"Maybe Gillian never told him."

"Great. Is this something else we have to disclose to him?"

"I don't think so." Muriel laughed. "I think a court would find that Arthur had ample opportunity to plunge into that body of information." She offered a naughty smile, then abruptly took hold of her chin. He could see her mind had gone elsewhere.

"New idea?" he asked.

"Maybe. Something to consider for this case. Let me think it through."

"And where *is* this case going? What's the view from the top today?"

She took a second, then asked what he'd thought about Collins's interview.

"Memorable performance," Larry said. "Just like his uncle's. Must run in the blood."

"Do you think he was there? At Paradise?"

"Collins? I know he was there."

"You do?"

"I got Judson's shoes out of Evidence. Collins was right about the brand. And I beat up on the DNA guys all day. They already had a profile on Collins from Faro's bloody shirt, and they found plenty of sweat residue inside the shoes. You know, they'd like six years to be definitive, but bottom line, sweat DNA doesn't match the blood on the shoes, but it has the same alleles as the shirt. They're Collins's shoes—not that the DNA guys could have told you that in '91."

She took a slug of her beer while she thought it through.

"That change anything for you?" he asked.

"Nada."

I.e., she already believed Collins had been at the scene.

"Well, I'll tell you something I don't believe," he said. "I don't buy the innocent-bystander shit. No kidding Erno told Collins the police would think he was involved in the murders. You telling me you drag around dead bodies when you had nothing to do with the killings?"

"It's a strange story," allowed Muriel. "But family stuff is strange. The only way you know about Collins moving the bodies is because he told you—the same reason you know about the shoes."

"So you don't think he was in on it?"

"Only Erno's prints are on the trigger and the handle, and they're in Luisa's blood, Larry, right?"

"Her type anyway. I didn't pound the DNA guys on Luisa—you can imagine the backtalk I was getting already and the serology was pretty conclusive." The blood on the gun was all B negative. Only 2 percent of the population were B negatives and Luisa Remardi had been one of them. Judson, Gus, Collins were all type Os. Larry had held out some faint hope that Erno was B neg, but the jail hospital said no. To Larry, though, Erno being the shooter wasn't the whole story.

"My big one is still the same," he told her. "I don't buy that Rommy had nothing to do with it. Maybe Erno and Squirrel confronted Luisa and Collins together. But Collins is just finishing the job his uncle started, taking Rommy out, because he dummied up for them."

"You really see Rommy as a stand-up guy, Larry? He couldn't even stand up for himself. Besides, there's just no evidence to back that."

Larry had an idea, however. He had half a dozen cadets on standby for tomorrow. He wanted a search warrant that would allow them to dig under Erno's toolshed in hopes of finding everything taken from the victims at Paradise on the night of the murders.

Collins said Erno had recently flirted with having the apron dug up to confirm his testimony, but had realized Collins's prints were likely to be found on several items. Larry suspected that Erno was also hiding Squirrel's prints or DNA.

"You'll have the warrant by 10 a.m., and I'll be rooting for you, Larry, believe me. But if we don't find some speck that ties to Squirrel, it's going to be one more biggie on their side. All the forensics back Erno and Collins now. If that stuff is there like Collins said and only his prints and Erno's are on it, we'll be toast. It's a new trial, Larry."

"A new trial?"

"We can fool around for a year and a half in front of Harlow, when the Court of Appeals sends the case back, but long story short, if you look at all of it—the testimony, the prints, the DNA, the records suggesting Squirrel was in the can at the time of the murders—" She paused over the magnitude of what she was saying. "Gandolph's *habeas* gets granted."

She might have been right on the law, but he could also see she didn't want the bad news bleeding out, making headlines day after day for her election opponent.

"And that's not the bad part," she said.

"What's the bad part?"

"We can't try this case again."

"Because of Collins?"

"Collins has told two different stories, blaming and saving the same guy. He's a dope peddler and a fraud by his own account, and gets impeached with three felony convictions. He can praise Jesus all he likes. A jury will still hold its nose when he gets on the stand. My problem is how we get the cameo into evidence."

"How about the same way we did last time? I testify."

"No chance, Larry. A lot of weird stuff happens in a courtroom. I'm not going to say I haven't had a chuckle or two listening to my own witnesses, but I've never put somebody on the stand knowing he was going to commit perjury. And I'm not going to start now."

"Perjury?"

"That's what they call it, Larry, when you make up stuff under oath." She was looking straight at him, and not as she had a moment ago. This was Muriel the Fearless.

"Would you prosecute, Muriel?"

She looked herself over, still without a stitch on, and said, "I think I'd have to disqualify myself."

"Seriously," he said, "would you call that a crime?"

"I think it's wrong, Larry. Really wrong. And I'm not going to let you testify you found that cameo in Squirrel's pocket when you didn't."

As long as he'd known her, he'd never been certain how firmly Muriel stood on principle. She meant what she said. But she'd never fully remove self-interest from her calculations. If she let him fib, he'd always have something on her.

He thought through the alternatives. With Arthur's agreement, they had given the cameo back to Luisa's daughters in June, so there was no way to print it now to prove it had been in Squirrel's hands.

"What if I admit I lied before?" he asked.

"That's moral turpitude on the job, Larry. They fire your ass. And you'll have to hold a farewell party for your pension. And you still wouldn't have a chain of evidence putting the cameo in Squirrel's pocket unless the copper who stole it gets up there to admit that, which won't happen unless he doesn't like his pension either. We'd be screwed anyway."

"How so?"

"You'd be admitting you lied to get a conviction, right?"

"To convict a multiple murderer."

"Then who's to say you wouldn't do it again? You're the only witness to a lot of what went on between Rommy and you at the station house in October '91. Next time around, Arthur's going to say that confession was coerced somehow. All we'll have is a perjuring police officer to say no."

"We lose the confession?"

"Good chance. And the cameo. And ruin you. I mean, worst-case here, Larry, if we admit you lied about the cameo, and someody figures out you shit-canned Dickerman's report, the U.S. Attorney's Office will probably prosecute you for obstruction of justice."

"The feds?"

"We're in federal court, Larry."

"Shit." They indicted cops for sport over there, part of the never-ending conflict between federal and state law enforcement.

"We can't try this case again, Larry."

He hated this stuff, the law—and Muriel when she was its mouthpiece. He squeezed his arms around his knees and asked whether they could make a deal with Gandolph for a long prison term.

"That's the best option," she said. "But what was it you called Arthur? Crusader Rabbit? Crusader thinks he has an innocent client. Crusader's probably going to hang tough and take him to trial."

"What happens then?"

She didn't answer. Larry, suddenly on all fours, gripped her arm.

"I don't want to hear about time served, Muriel, or anything like that. I don't want to have to look at this guy on the street. I'd rather take my chances in court, lose my pension, obstruction, whatever. This is me to you, Muriel. I mean it. Promise me you'll stand in there."

"Larry."

"Promise me, damn it. What's the name of the Greek guy pushing the rock up the hill and never getting to the top? Sisyphus? I'm not Sisyphus. That was a curse, Muriel. They did that to that guy as a curse. And that's what you'd be doing to me."

"I'm trying to save you, Larry."

"Is that what you call it?" he asked as he grabbed his clothes.

But he'd suddenly lost her attention. She was far off again. It took him a second to realize that she thought she'd found the way to do that.

40

AUGUST 24, 2001

Heroin

THE RECEPTIONISTS at O'Grady, Steinberg, Marconi and Horgan recognized Gillian by now. She walked in with a wave and moved through the pale halls of the law firm, receiving the tepid smiles of those who either didn't know her or knew her too well. As she'd predicted, Arthur had not made a choice of companion popular among his partners. Rather than respond, Gillian kept her eye on a new serpentine-chain ankle bracelet she had bought this morning. During her lifetime, her feelings about this fashion accessory had varied. Her mother had told her ankle bracelets were trashy, which meant Gillian insisted on wearing one throughout her teens, and had eschewed it thereafter as juvenile. But in the late summer, when even she had acquired some

746   SCOTT TUROW

semblance of a tan and could go without hose, the thin chain had a promising sensuality against her bare skin. Slender evidence of something. It reminded her for indeterminate reasons of Arthur. She rapped on the doorsill of his office and craned her head about the metal frame.

"Dinnertime?" she asked.

In his chair, his back was to her and his face lowered. She thought he must have been reading, but when he revolved she could see he'd been crying. Arthur had been as good as his word. He wept all the time. She felt no alarm whatsoever until he spoke a single word.

"Heroin?" he asked her.

He said it several more times, but she never found her voice to reply.

"This morning," he said, "Muriel made an emergency motion before Harlow to reopen discovery and depose you."

"Me?"

"You. The motion said you appear to have information favorable to the defense. It was so ridiculous and low, I refused to upset you by mentioning it. I came through the courtroom door firing hot ammo. 'Cheap.' 'Theatrical.' 'Unethical.' 'Scummy.' Words

I'd never used in public about another lawyer. The idea of trying to make this case personal! And finally, when I was done carrying on, Muriel asked the judge for ten minutes and handed me six affidavits, all from people who sold you heroin or saw you buying it. Even so, I wasn't going to take the word of smack whores. But I met two of them this afternoon, Gillian, face-to-face. Both had kicked. One's a drug counselor. I mean, they weren't happy to say it. They didn't have a beef with you—one of them had showed up in your courtroom years ago and you gave her probation, and she had a damned good idea why. I mean, they were just telling the truth. Telling *me* the truth about *you*. Can you imagine how that felt? I mean, Jesus fucking Christ, Gillian, heroin?"

There was probably no word for this exactly. She'd taken a seat in a tweed armchair, but she hadn't any idea how she'd made her way there. She felt as if she was on an elevator that had dropped dozens of stories and then slammed to a halt. She'd descended at high velocity and had been flattened. For a trifling instant, she'd felt an impulse to deny what he'd said, which made her despair even more over herself.

"Arthur," she said. "It makes everything so much worse, Arthur."

"It certainly does."

"For me. It makes everything so much more disgraceful. And I'd had all I could bear, Arthur. You know that. You understand that much."

"Gillian, I mean, this was the first thing I asked you. You told me you were sober at the time of Rommy's trial."

"I answered your question. I told you I hadn't been drinking to excess. I was a witness, Arthur, an educated one. I answered the question."

"And then? Some time in the last four months, you didn't think—I mean, don't you realize what a fucking problem this is legally?"

"Legally?"

"For Rommy. Legally. He was tried before a heroin addict."

"He's not the first defendant whose trial judge was impaired. The case was appealed, Arthur. Twice. There have been endless postconviction proceedings. No court has ever found anything near reversible errors."

"And what about the Constitution?"

She couldn't follow the reference. "The Constitution?"

"The Constitution, Gillian, promises every defendant a fair trial. Do you think that means a trial before a judge who's committing a felony on a daily basis? Not only a judge whose thinking is bound to be disturbed, but who's out on the street and, therefore, has a powerful motive not to antagonize the prosecutors and the police?"

Ah. She sat back. She had not thought of this part at all. She'd given the whole subject brief contemplation the first day she met Arthur for coffee, reasoned a bit with Duffy, and stowed it away. The only justice that had concerned her was her own. But had she reflected with just an instant of discipline, she could have recognized the implications for Gandolph, exactly as Arthur laid them out. She was as guilty as Arthur found her.

"Muriel's already called to ask what I'm going to do," he said.

"And?"

"And I told her I'm going to move to amend my complaint for *habeas corpus* to allege that your addiction violated Rommy's right to a fair trial."

"You're going to put me on the witness stand?"

"If I have to."

She was about to suggest he was being histrionic, or impulsive. How could he interrogate the woman he was sleeping with? But that answer, too, was plain. She really was not as fleet with all of this as she had once been, she thought sadly. Obviously, she was no longer the woman he was sleeping with.

"My God, Gillian. I can't even bear the idea. You in doorways, copping from hookers—and then going back to sit in judgment of other human beings? I can't imagine this. And you? Who in God's name are you?"

Yes, well. She'd known that sooner or later he'd have the good sense to ask that question.

"Do you expect to prevail, Arthur, with this new tack?" She was afraid it might sound as if she was asking for mercy. Then she realized she probably was.

"You mean, would I do this just to get even with you, Gillian? No. No. Pamela's started the research. A new trial is dead-bang. But my position is that retrial is barred under the double jeopardy clause. The state failed to meet the fundamental responsibility of providing a competent forum. Muriel seemed willing to listen on that point."

For a second, Gillian imagined how Muriel was taking this. Even in defeat, she'd have the last laugh. That was a rare success in litigation. To be able to break your opponent's heart.

"Let me understand," said Gillian. "I'm the scapegoat. A triple murderer is going to walk away because I was addicted to heroin. That's how it's going to be explained in the press?"

Arthur chose not to answer, but only because there was no point in denying it. She had been a wretch in the eyes of this community, and a disappointment. But now she would advance to the category of monster. Arthur, she realized, saw her that way already. Across the small distance between them, his red-eyed stare was terrifyingly objective.

"It's my fault, Gillian. You warned me. You told me just what you've done to the men in your life. You even gave me an entire case history. And I jumped in anyway."

Despite her complete muddle, she felt a new source of pain, as if muscle had severed from bone near her heart. It was certain now that Arthur and she were done. He had never before spoken to her cruelly.

She blundered out of the office, down the pale halls, to the elevator. Reaching the street, she stopped on the pavement. 'Heroin.' She heard the word from him endlessly. 'Heroin.' How could she ever have done this to herself? She truly needed to remember, and thus, for the first time in years, she experienced a clear sensation of the potent oblivion of the drug.

41

AUGUST 27, 2001

The Midway

UNDER THE LONG GREEN HANDS of the oaks and elms on the Midway, Muriel and Larry walked in search of a bench. Each had a sub bundled in wax paper tucked under an arm, and the bright red cup of a soft drink in hand. This narrow pleasance, miles long, had been leveled and planted not long after the Civil War, an urban garden amid a road where horses clip-clopped in front of carriages. Now four lanes of traffic, two on the east, two on the west, whizzed by, discouraging any effort to speak until they were side by side in front of a bench of splintering crossbeams on a cement base.

"Here?" asked Muriel.

"Whatever." He remained grumpy about taking this stroll.

"I was just thinking about us, Larry, and I

realized that all our time together has been in confined spaces. You know? You keep talking to me about gardens but we've always been within walls. Courtroom. Office. Hotel room."

A huge bus motored by at that point, roaring as it accelerated and spilling poisonous smells from its exhaust.

"Very rural," said Larry. "Why did I have the feeling as I was walking, Muriel, that I was on a death march?"

She could not quite muster a smile. She'd unwrapped her lunch but put it down. Somehow the next sentence required two hands.

"I've decided to dismiss our case against Rommy Gandolph," she said. It was not really a difficult analysis. Larry's treasure hunt under Erno's shed had yielded six more items with Erdai's prints, or Collins's, and not a bit of evidence against Squirrel. But she still dreaded speaking the words.

Larry had bitten off a large section of his sandwich and continued to chew, but he was otherwise rigid. His tie, dragged down six inches from his collar, rode up and stayed parallel to the ground for quite some time on the wind.

"You're the first person I've told," Muriel said. "After Ned, I mean."

He swallowed, then said, "I'm out here so nobody can hear me screaming. Right?"

She hadn't thought of that. But, as always, instinct had probably led her this way for a reason.

"You have to be kidding, Muriel. You're in a perfect position. You said Arthur wouldn't deal, but now he has no choice if he doesn't want to butcher his girlfriend in court."

After all this time, she still hadn't internalized the differences in their worlds. Larry was one of the smartest people she knew. He read books. He could think abstractly. But to him the law was only tactics. He'd never bothered to fool himself, as lawyers did, into accepting its lines of trivial consistency. He saw only a big picture where the practitioners thought up logical reasons for doing whatever they wanted to.

"I doubt he would do that," said Muriel. "He'd be selling out his client to save Gillian."

"It's worth a try."

"It's unethical for both of us, Larry. Him— and me to propose it."

"Who are you talking to, Muriel?"

"Larry, I'm no better than anybody else, I

get caught up, but I do try. I believe that stuff about how you can't enforce the rules if you won't live by them. Besides," she said and felt her heart shiver, "I don't really believe Squirrel is guilty anymore."

Even before she spoke, she knew what she was saying, but the effect of watching him shrink from her remained heartbreaking. His spine, his face became hard as concrete. He was the one man on earth who'd loved her in the way she would have chosen and he was going to be her enemy.

"He confessed," said Larry quietly. That was the essence of it. In the end, she could say Larry fooled her. But Larry, a detective for more than twenty years now, would have to say he'd fooled himself. It might have been either a failure of integrity or a lapse in competence. Or a little of both. Yet at this stage, it would be even worse for him to attribute his mistake to his passion to please her.

The other day she had thought he was being melodramatic when he said she couldn't do this to him. But with a frequency unmatched by anyone else, Larry often beat her to the finish line, and he'd done it then. To accept her judgment, he would have to ruin himself in his own eyes. No one's devotion went that far.

"Larry, the way it's going down, it will all be on Gillian. No Dickerman. Or Collins. No doubts about the investigation. Off the record, our story is that we couldn't risk a double jeopardy ruling when it might mean opening the prison door for everyone who appeared before Gillian over the years. If we have to fight that fight, we can't do it in a capital case, where the procedural law is so exacting."

As she explained, Larry's blue eyes never left her. Finally, he got up and walked several feet to a mesh waste bin and slammed the sandwich down in it. Then he recrossed the ragged parkway where the grass had failed, leaving circles of mud between the bent grass and dandelions.

"You know you're full of shit, don't you?" he said. "Laying this on Gillian—that protects you a hell of a lot more than me."

"I understand it helps both of us."

"Once you cut Rommy loose, the first thing Arthur does is file a big civil suit—all this stuff about Dickerman and Collins, that will come out in discovery."

"There won't be discovery, Larry. They

wouldn't take the chance of letting Squirrel be deposed—he could say anything. That case will settle quick and dirty."

"Right after the primary."

In his imagination, she no longer retained any dimension. She calculated and did not feel. But she nodded in response. She was who she was. And it wasn't always pretty. She wondered if it was worth telling him how large her ache for him would be. There were going to be horrible nights. But she would stay busy. The worst times would probably be years from now.

Yesterday, she had prayed fervently in church. She had thanked God for her blessings. A meaningful life. Talmadge's grandchild. No one got everything. She did not have love, but that was probably because she wanted it less than some other people. Still, she felt dizzy again as she came to her feet. She wanted terribly at this instant to crawl against him. But loneliness was what she had chosen. Larry was hunched forward with his mouth against the heel of his palm, clearly colored by rage. When he thought about her, she knew, it was always going to be as the woman who had ruined his life.

"I have to go see John Leonidis," she said. "I told him I'd meet him at Paradise."

"Back to the scene of the crime," said Larry.

"Right."

"Don't ask me to cover you on this. With him. Or the Force. I won't, Muriel. I'm going to tell the truth about you to anyone who asks."

Her enemy. His truth. She looked at him one last time and then turned to flag down a taxi.

She cried quietly for half the trip to the restaurant. Then in the last few miles, she began to think about what she would say to John. She was going to tell him everything, all the details. He was not the kind to blab and if he did, so be it. Instead, she tried to imagine something to console him. John Leonidis had waited a decade for a death to make up for the crime against his father. Even if she could convince him that Erno alone had killed his father, which she herself accepted as a certainty—even then, John would be roiled and miserable at the thought that Erdai had left life on his own terms. At the end of the day, after a decade of trying murder cases and communing with the victims' families, Muriel was convinced that most of the survivors in some remote segment of their consciousness—the primeval part that was scared of the dark and loud noises—assumed that when the right person died, the one who deserved to be removed from the planet, when that occurred their lost loved one would come back to life. That was the pathetic logic of revenge, learned in the playpen, and of the sacrificial altar, where we attempted to trade life for life.

She'd seen three executions now, as a supervisor. At the first, the father of the victim, a mother of two who'd been shot down at a Stop-N-Go gas mart, came away embittered, angry that what had been held out as a balm had only made him feel worse. But the two later families claimed that they'd gotten something from it—an end point, a sense of an awful equilibrium being restored to the world, the peace of mind that at least no one else would suffer again from this dead bastard as they had. But hurting as she did at the moment, she could not really remember why inflicting more harm would make life on earth better for anyone.

Muriel pulled aside the heavy glass door

at Paradise, with a clear recollection of how she had felt in the raw summer heat when she had entered with Larry a decade ago, the cool air suddenly embracing her bare legs, which were still tingling from her activities with Larry an hour before. That was gone. He was gone. She faced that again. Perhaps it was the thought of Larry, and his dedication to what she now took as a fiction, but her mind passed briefly to Rommy Gandolph. In a dreamlike moment, she saw Squirrel as if in a cartoon, beneath a pale light in a dripping dungeon. Her inclination was to laugh, but somehow the light she envisioned, like a small porch lamp, was actually the first point of radiance of her increasing pain. It would take decades, the rest of her life, to contend with what they had done to him and the reasons why.

As always, John received her warmly. He hugged her, then took her back to the office which had once been his father's. Gus's photographs remained in the same spots on the walls.

"This isn't good news, is it?" he asked. He'd seen the papers over the weekend about Gillian. Aires's phrase, "the Junkie Judge," had proved a headline writer's fave.

"I don't know, John. I don't know what to call it."

As he listened to her, he bit again and again at his thumbnail, to the point that Muriel feared she would see blood. She could barely prevent herself from trying to stop him. Yet she had no place telling him how to face all of this. He was, as ever, loyal. The conclusiveness of the fingerprint and blood evidence was plain to him, and he was more willing than she expected to accept her judgment that Gandolph had no role in the killings. Whether she deserved it or not, John, like so many others, had faith in her as a lawyer. The only consolation he wanted was what she had anticipated.

"Would you have gone for death on this guy? On Erdai? If he told and all, but he got the miracle cure and didn't die?"

"We'd have tried, John."

"You wouldn't have gotten it?"

"Probably not."

"Because he's white?"

Even now, her steady impulse was to say no. Jurors judged the gravity of these crimes by the value of the lives lost. In that calculus, like so many others, race and social status became indistinguishable. They would have cared mightily that Erno's victims were hard-working family people. But the counterweight was their assessment of the killer, and there color in itself mattered little.

"In the end, juries only give death to people they think are dangerous and completely worthless. It would make a difference that Erno did one good thing," she said to John. "He wouldn't let an innocent man die in his place. Maybe two. He cared about his nephew." Flesh of my flesh. Blood of my blood. It might also have proved significant that Muriel understood his passion.

"What sense is that?" asked John. "Honestly. Does any of this make sense? Everybody's just as dead. My father and Luisa and Judson. That guy Erno was a shit from what you're telling me. A murderer. A liar. A liar under oath. A thief. He was scum. Twice as bad as anybody ever thought Gandolph was. And he'd have lived?"

There was no arguing with that. Erno was as bent as they came.

"That's how it is in death cases, John. It's so extreme—the crime, the stakes, everybody's feelings. You try to make rules and somehow none of them stick, or even make sense."

She had brought a transcript of Collins's interview. John turned a few pages, then handed it back.

"It's done," he said and with those words sighed enormously. "At least we'll have that. It's done."

At the door, she apologized to him again for her own role in making this so prolonged, so torturous, but he would hear none of it.

"Never for a second," he said with the same fierceness with which he'd decried the senselessness of the law, "is anybody going to tell me that you weren't doing your best. You and Larry. Tommy. All of you. Never."

He hugged her with the same energy he had when she came in, then went to find a bandage for his thumb.

Outside, she stopped to look back at the restaurant where ten years ago three persons had met a hideous death. Muriel would never see this simple, low building, its compound-brown bricks and large windows, without being scoured by some of the terror that Luisa and Paul and Gus had each experienced in their last moments. Standing here, she revisited once more the unbearable instant when each of them realized that this life that we all love beyond anything else was about to conclude at the whim of another human being, an ending where the sustaining forces of both reason and humanity proved worthless.

Inside, John had repeated something he often said—that to this day he still saw the blood on the floor. Yet John had not closed Paradise. The restaurant was Gus's monument, home to his spirit. A bright place on a dark night. A warm place on a cold day. Food for the hungry. Company for the lonely. Life abounding in a site where humans strived, like Gus, to be each other's friends.

She would return.

42

Release

THE CLOTHING in which Rommy Gandolph had been tried and in which he'd been committed to the prison system had been mislaid long ago. Perhaps they didn't bother saving the apparel of the Yellow Men. Just outside the town of Rudyard, Arthur and Pamela drove into the lot of a Kmart and bought three pairs of wash pants and a few shirts for Rommy. Then they continued their happy journey south.

By the time they reached Rudyard, there was already a significant encampment of news vans in the parking lot. The Reverend Dr. Blythe was conducting a press conference. As always, he was accompanied by a cast of thousands. Arthur never understood where all the people around Blythe came from—some were staffers at his church, a few provided security, but the affiliations of the rest were an absolute mystery. The cohort of at least thirty included a half brother of Rommy's whom Arthur had never known to exist until last week, when the papers began to speculate about a civil suit. Blythe's entire legion was ebullient, relishing both the occasion and the fact that by dint of numbers and press attention they had taken over a portion of the prison grounds.

Apparently Blythe had carried a portable stage—a tall pallet and a podium—in the trunk of the stretch limousine in which he had traveled and which was parked at a distance, out of sight of the cameras. Blythe had been good enough to call to congratulate Arthur after Muriel filed her motion to dismiss Rommy's case, but he'd heard nothing from the Reverend or his staff since. Naturally, though, Arthur was not surprised to see Blythe here. With his glimmering bald head and large white mustache, Blythe looked entirely avuncular until he started speaking. Approaching, Arthur heard him bemoaning the injustice of a system in which drug-addict judges sentenced innocent black men to die. He had a point,

Arthur figured, but it was funny how it looked from up close.

As some of the reporters surged toward Arthur, the Reverend invited him up to the podium. Blythe shook Arthur's hand robustly and patted his back and told him again he had done well. It was from Blythe, in their final conversation, that Arthur had heard that the state had taken a statement from Erno's nephew, and that Muriel was simply covering herself by blaming Gillian. Jackson Aires, who insisted on keeping the secret for his client's sake, had stowed Collins back in Atlanta and refused to confirm what Arthur suspected Jackson had privately shared with Blythe. Aires confined himself to a single detail. 'Your man didn't do it. Wasn't there. Rest of it doesn't matter anyway. Helluva job, Raven. Never thought you had much prospect as a defense lawyer, but I seem to have been wrong. Helluva job.'

The truth about Collins might yet emerge in the civil case, especially if the state was obstinate about settling. On the drive back to the city today, Arthur hoped to talk to Rommy about filing the lawsuit. Yesterday, Arthur had informed Ray Horgan that he expected to handle Rommy's civil case and leave the firm.

In the guardhouse, Arthur and Pamela handed over a pair of pants and a shirt to the lieutenant on duty, who wouldn't accept the clothing.

"The ones out there, Reverend Blight, they brought a suit. Five hundred bucks if it's a dollar, too." The lieutenant, who was white, glanced circumspectly in each direction, thinking better only now that he'd heard himself.

In a moment, Blythe arrived. Accompanying him was an impressive-looking man, tall and handsome, splendidly dressed, an African American whom Arthur recognized from somewhere. Not from town, Arthur knew that much. Another hero was all Arthur could recall, perhaps an athlete.

The lieutenant lifted his phone, and in a few minutes the Warden, Henry Marker, appeared. Also black, he warmed noticeably to Blythe and invited the entire party to accompany him. Inside the first gate, they turned in a direction Arthur and Pamela had not gone before and entered the separate orange-brick administration building. There were the same locks and guards, but here the purpose was to keep inmates out, not in.

On the second floor, Marker showed them into his office, large but spare. Before the Warden's desk, in a suit and tie, Romeo Gandolph sat slumped and fidgeting. He jumped up when the group entered, predictably puzzled about what he was supposed to do next. His hair had been shaped by someone and when he spread his hands in welcome, Arthur noticed that Rommy at last was free of manacles. Despite himself, Arthur, who had cried a great deal in the last week, began weeping again, and found Pamela in the same state. In the meantime, Blythe fell upon Rommy with a huge embrace.

The Warden had several papers for Rommy to sign. Arthur and Pamela reviewed them while Blythe took Rommy to the other side of the room. Arthur heard them praying, then some high-spirited conversation. After Rommy scrawled his name on the documents, they were all ready to go. Marker walked them to the front gate. The buzzer sounded, and the Warden, like a butler, stood aside to open the door. As he did so, Blythe wiggled past Arthur and Pamela and was beside Rommy as the daylight fell upon him.

The camera people as always were lawless, shouting and jostling. Blythe held Rommy's elbow and steered him to the podium in the parking lot. He invited Arthur and Pamela up, giving them places in the second row behind Rommy and himself. Pamela had prepared a brief statement for Rommy, which he held in his hand, but Blythe took it from him and handed over a different sheet. Rommy started to read, then looked around helplessly. The half brother, now at his side, pronounced a few of the words. It occurred to Arthur for the first time to wonder how many rehearsals had been required before Rommy read the videotaped confession prepared for him a decade ago. For a moment, as he stood there, not knowing what to expect, the utter monstrousness of what had happened to Rommy Gandolph stormed over Arthur—that and the supreme satisfaction of knowing that Pamela and he had commanded the power of the law for Rommy's benefit, that the law had made right what it first had made wrong. No matter how fuddled he became at the end of his days, Arthur, at this instant, believed he would remember he'd done this.

Gandolph by now had given up on the

statement. The stampede of reporters and technicians through the gravel parking lot had raised a haze of bitter dust and Rommy was blinking furiously and rubbing his eyes.

"I can't say much 'cept thanks to everybody here," said Rommy.

Reporters kept shouting the same questions—what did it feel like to be out, what were his plans. Rommy said he'd like a good steak. Blythe announced plans for a celebration at his church. The conference broke up.

As Gandolph jumped down from the riser, Arthur pushed forward to reach him. On the phone, they had agreed that Rommy would drive back up to Kindle County with them. Arthur had been scouting out job prospects for Rommy. And there was also the lawsuit to discuss. But Rommy held back when Arthur pointed him toward the rear lot.

"I was kinda goin with them-all," said Rommy. If he was aware that he was disappointing Arthur, he gave no sign. But his face was wrinkled by curiosity. "What ride you got?"

Arthur smiled a bit and gave the brand and the model. Rommy seemed to search the parking lot, but his eyes lit on the stretch.

"Naw, I'm gone ride with them," he said. His expression remained mobile and uncertain. Blythe's security people were holding several reporters at bay. "I want to thank you-all for what you done, I truly do." He offered his hand then. It was, Arthur realized, the first time he had ever touched Rommy Gandolph. His hand was oddly calloused and narrow enough to be a child's. Gandolph pawed around in front of Pamela, who leaned over to hug him.

"Tole you you should've hitched up with me," he said. "I'm gone get me a wife pretty as you, only black. I'm gone be rich now, too. Get me some stock." At that point the handsome man who had accompanied Blythe inside came to reclaim Rommy. In his company, Rommy Gandolph turned away and never looked back at either of his lawyers.

They were in Arthur's sedan on the way out of Rudyard when Pamela told Arthur who the man was—Miller Douglas, a noted civil rights lawyer from New York. No doubt now who was going to handle Rommy's civil case. Rommy would sign the retainer agreement in the limo—if he hadn't done it in the Warden's Office already. Arthur pulled his car to the graveled shoulder of the road to come to terms with the news.

"This is terrible," he said. Pamela, still young enough to be remote from the business side of law, shrugged, unsurprised.

"Don't you think he's got the right lawyer?" she asked. "Our firm doesn't even do civil rights cases."

Arthur, who had never much bothered with that consideration, continued to suffer the ironies. Rommy was free. Arthur was not. Horgan would probably laugh when he took Arthur back, but there would be costs for years to come. At least Ray had asked him to reconsider. 'Generally speaking, Arthur,' he'd said, 'you may find that there's a bit of a drought before your next innocent client. A decade or two.' Arthur took a second to ponder how he might package this for Ray, then gave up. As a disappointment, Rommy's choice of a new lawyer still took second place. Despite the maelstrom surrounding Rommy's release, the ceaseless phone calls from reporters, the exultation in the law firm, where Arthur now found he had many supporters, there was one misery, one low point where his spirit inevitably rolled to rest, as it did again now.

Gillian. My Gillian, my Gillian, he thought, and yet again began to cry. Muriel had done a masterful job of vilifying her. Two days into it, the *Tribune* had actually gotten hold of Gillian's FBI mug shot, taken when she was arrested in 1993, running it on the front page along with a report of several thousand words on Gillian's drug taking, gleaned from sources as diverse as drug agents, defense lawyers, and addicts on the street. The story of the Junkie Judge had even reached many of the national news outlets, especially the ones that usually traded in celebrity gossip. Only a few stories mentioned that Gillian was sober either when she had been sentenced or now.

As Rommy's lawyer, it would have been improper for Arthur to call Gillian to console her. And he was far too hurt to do that anyway. As he could best recall, she had not even apologized. Perhaps, he told himself, if she had made some effort to express her regret for so deceiving him, perhaps then there might have been some path through the incredible thicket of conflicting obligations to his client. For days, he reviewed his voice messages every half hour and even left the office at lunch on Monday to check his mail at home. Perhaps his rebukes had been too stern, especially the parting shot he'd immediately regretted about her 'case history.' Possibly, she was held back by the imperatives of the legal situation. Most likely, she had simply given up, now that her prophecies of doom had come true. Three nights ago, amid stormy dreams, he awoke with a cold fear that she had returned to drink. Then, in a minute, he remembered that drink was not the problem. By now his fantasies had turned gruesome, dim images of Gillian on rain-soaked streets disappearing in dark entryways doing God knows what.

When they reached the city, Arthur parked near the IBM Building, but he hesitated as Pamela and he were about to enter. It suddenly struck him that he was no longer Rommy Gandolph's lawyer. Despite his disappointment about the civil case and the disappearance of the fortune which, being his father's son, he'd never truly believed would come to him, he experienced in this instant a sensation of clean release. He'd shouldered an enormous burden, staggered under it at times, but carried it to the end, and for many reasons was entitled to be relieved.

In front of the revolving doors of the office building, Arthur kissed Pamela's cheek and told her she was a great lawyer. Then, in a state of dread and anticipation, he marched the four long blocks to Morton's. Gillian was not at the counter. Argentina, her colleague, leaned across the glass case, careful not to touch it and leave prints. She told Arthur quietly that Gillian had not been in all week, neither here nor the Nearing store.

"The reporters are goons," she whispered. "I think Gil quit."

"Quit?"

"That's what somebody said. They don't expect her back. Supposedly, she's leaving town."

As he walked back down Grand, with its magnificent shops and tall buildings, Arthur considered his options. He had absolutely no experience as a strategist in matters of the heart, and even now, he was too hurt to be certain what he wanted. But he was, after all, himself. Arthur Raven was a master of neither subtlety nor style. He knew only how to go forward at a steady pace.

At least one person in Duffy Muldawer's house was delighted to see him. Spying Arthur through the window of the side door,

Duffy lit up, even while he was fiddling with the chain.

"Arthur!" the old man cried out and threw one arm around him, as Arthur moved into the tiny entry. He didn't let go of Arthur's hand and clearly would have relished the chance to hear the details of the last week, engaging in the fraternal joy of defenders who had rare occasion to celebrate. But Arthur's eyes had already fallen on Gillian, who in response to Duffy's noise had appeared at the bottom of the stairs. Apparently, she'd been cleaning and was dressed in casual attire Arthur would have bet she did not even own, her thin pale legs emerging from a beaten pair of shorts. A T-shirt was rolled up at the sleeves. She was wearing rubber gloves and—a first in Arthur's experience with her—hadn't bothered with makeup. Behind her, he saw a suitcase.

"It's over," he said. "He's out."

Gillian said congratulations and stared up in the weak light of the short stairwell, then set a foot on the bottom step. Somewhere along, Duffy had had the good sense to disappear.

"May I hug you?" she asked.

When perhaps a full minute passed, they let go of one another and sat on the stairs. She held fast to his hand. Gillian, who never cried, had cried, and Arthur, ever tearful, had merely savored the intense pleasure of having her close to him again. Sitting, he discovered he had an astonishing erection. Gillian, too, felt desire, but at the core of his embrace she had experienced a sense of consolation pure enough to be brotherly. Neither of them had any idea what would happen now.

"Are you okay?" he asked at last.

She threw up her hands futilely. "Not stoned, if that's what you're worried about. Duffy's seen to that."

"You're leaving?"

"I have to, Arthur. Patti Chong, a woman I knew in law school, has agreed to hire me as a paralegal in her firm in Milwaukee. Do research. Perhaps, in time, if all goes well, as you suggested, I could reapply to the bar. But I have to get out of here." She shook her head. "Even *I* finally feel that I've taken enough, Arthur. I had to send Duffy to the store for me yesterday to pick up a prescription. That picture!" She wrenched her eyes closed at the thought. Taken when Gillian was at her lowest point, sleepless most nights and ravaged by despair, the photo in the paper made her a bleary hag. Her hair looked wild. And of course her eyes were dead.

"I'd have appreciated a call," he said. "It would have been terrible if I came around here eventually and just found out you were gone."

"I couldn't, Arthur. I couldn't ask you for sympathy when every lash I took benefited Rommy. Besides," she said, "I was much too ashamed. Too afraid of your reaction. And too confused. I can't stay here, Arthur, and I knew you'd never go."

"I can't leave," he said. "My sister."

"Of course," she answered.

He was glad he had said it, because in him something opened like a gate. What he had told her was not true. He could leave. The people at the Franz Center would help Susan cope. His mother might finally find a way to be useful. And if all else failed, he would move Susan up there. The firm even had an office in Milwaukee. That could work. It could all work. Even the two of them. The best and most impregnable part of him, which always hoped, was again in charge.

"I don't know why I do things, Arthur," she said to him. "I've been trying to understand myself for years—I think I'm getting better, but I have a long way to go. But I really believe I was trying to protect myself. It's been as bad as I thought it would be, too. You have to admit that."

"It would have been easier with someone standing by you, Gillian."

"It couldn't have been you, Arthur. That was part of the problem."

To him that sounded like an excuse and she could read that in his expression. But she was clear on this much.

"I know what it feels like to want to hurt someone, Arthur. I know that very well. I swear my purpose wasn't to cause you pain."

"I believe that."

"Do you?"

"I'm sure you were far more interested in hurting yourself."

"Now you sound like Duffy."

"I'm serious. You keep undermining yourself. It's really remarkable."

"Please, Arthur. I can't handle any more analysis of my character. It's not the kind of thing I want to take on alone. This has been very, very hard, Arthur, this period. There have been some white-knuckle evenings around here. I had forgotten what it felt like to yearn for intoxication."

Arthur considered that. Then he continued.

"I want to be with you, Gillian. Leave with you. Live with you. Love you. I want that. But you have to see how hard you've worked at destroying yourself. So you don't do that to us again. If you can promise that you see that and will wrestle with it for both our sakes—"

"Please, Arthur. I'm neither dumb nor blind. I know exactly what kind of bleak Quixotic quest I'm on, rising so I can fall. But it's hopeless, Arthur."

"Not hopeless," he said. "Not at all. I can give you what you need."

"Which is?" She yearned to be skeptical, but because he was Arthur she believed him at once.

"Me. I'm your man. I can say something to you, which I don't think you've really heard before." He took both her hands. "Now, look at me and listen. Listen."

He watched her elegant slender face turn to him fully, the blond lashes and perfect intelligent eyes.

He said, "I forgive you."

She watched him for quite some time. Then she said, "Please say it again."

"I forgive you," said Arthur, as he held her hands. "I forgive you, I forgive you, I forgive you." He said it several more times after that.

Note

AS USUAL, I've gotten by with a little help from my friends. Technical advice from Colleen Berk and Joe Tomaino about airline ticketing, from Jeremy Margolis about firearms, from Jay Reich about Hungarian, and from Drs. Michael Kaufman and Carl Boyar about postmortem pathology was critical. I also had the benefit of comments from several discerning readers, Annette and Rachel, first, as always, and then from Jennifer Arra, Debby and Mark Barry, Leigh Bienen, Ellie Lucas, Jim McManus, Howard Rigsby, and the amazing Mary Zimmerman. I am hugely indebted to each of them. Jon Galassi and Gail Hochman remain the moon and stars of my literary life—and Laurie Brown will be special to me forever. My assistants, Kathy Conway, Margaret Figueroa, and Ellie Lucas, were indispensable. To all: thanks, guys.